D1110115

DATE DUE

OCT 26 2013		
NOV 0 9 2013		
AUG 1 9 2014		
SEP 0 6 2014		
SEP 0 2014		

The Heart Whisperer

Also by Ella Griffin

Postcards from the Heart

The Heart Whisperer

ELLA GRIFFIN

First published in Great Britain in 2013 by Orion Books,
an imprint of The Orion Publishing Group Ltd
Orion House, 5 Upper Saint Martin's Lane
London WC2H 9EA

An Hachette UK Company

1 3 5 7 9 10 8 6 4 2

A CIP catalogue record for this book
is available from the British Library.

ISBN (Hardback) 978 1 4091 2241 8
ISBN (Trade Paperback) 978 1 4091 2242 5
ISBN (Ebook) 978 1 4091 2243 2

Typeset at The Spartan Press Ltd,
Lymington, Hants

Printed and bound in Great Britain
by Clays Ltd, St Ives plc

The Orion Publishing Group's policy is to use papers
that are natural, renewable and recyclable products and
made from wood grown in sustainable forests. The logging
and manufacturing processes are expected to conform to
the environmental regulations of the country of origin.

www.orionbooks.co.uk

For Matt and Eileen.
I still think of you both every single day.

'Sometimes your head is shouting so loudly,
you can't hear what your heart is whispering.'

Anon

Prologue

The woman looked out at Claire from a long-forgotten sunny afternoon. Her hair was the burnished copper of an expensive saucepan. She wore a man's blue and white striped shirt with the sleeves rolled up and a white cheesecloth skirt. The hem was tucked up into the waistband to reveal her long pale legs. Her feet were bare. She was using an upturned tennis racket as a cricket bat, bending over it, grinning up through the curtain of her hair, waiting for the ball.

Claire looked a lot like the woman in the photograph. They both had the same almost translucent Irish skin. The same cinnamon-coloured hair. The same wide, dark green eyes. The same fair eyebrows and eyelashes. But the woman was a fraction taller and half a stone lighter. Her hair was straight and silky, not a tangle of curls. She didn't have a small gap between her top front teeth or a blur of freckles across her nose and cheekbones. And there were other differences too – ones that a camera couldn't capture. Claire's life was going nowhere but the woman had everything to live for. And though they were both thirty-three, Maura would never make it to thirty-four. And that was Claire's fault.

Part One

1

Mossy, Claire's ancient Citroën 2CV, shuddered, backfired twice, then shot past a cyclist on the Ranelagh Road. Ray saw his outraged face in the wing mirror before it disappeared in a cartoon puff of blue exhaust fumes. Claire gripped the steering wheel. 'Are you sure you didn't have plans?'

'Sure I'm sure.' Till an hour ago, Ray had plans that included Liza, the blonde yoga teacher who was still asleep when Claire had finally given up texting him and climbed up the fire escape to tap on his window.

'It's an emergency,' he had said, hurrying Liza back into her clothes. 'My best friend. Death in the family.' Which was true, though the death had happened twenty-seven years ago.

Mossy shot past a coach that was pulling away from a bus-stop. Ray's foot pumped an imaginary brake pedal and something caught under his heel. It was a broken windscreen wiper, the rubber frayed, the spindly metal arm gritty with rust.

He picked up the other one. 'BTW, these are supposed to be on the outside of the car.'

'FYI, they were, until some gouger pulled them off last week. Why is Mossy such a magnet for delinquents?'

Ray didn't know where to begin. The heat was activating his tequila hangover and Mossy's BO, a gut-churning blend of petrol fumes and vegetative matter from the sagging soft top. He tried to roll down his window but the handle was stuck so he switched to breathing through his mouth.

Claire turned around and stared at him as if they were sitting on a sofa and not belted into a rusting metal death-trap hurtling through suburban Dublin. 'You're panting.'

'I'm fine,' he croaked.

'Oh God,' Claire looked back at the road and bit her lip. 'I wish Nick wasn't going to be there. I could handle this if it was just me and Dad.'

Her hair had that obstreperous look it always got when she was upset. Her narrow shoulders were hunched up so far they were practically touching her ears. Ray was glad he was here and not on the road with his mobile turning into a fiery little brick in his hand while he tried to talk her down off the ceiling. Birthdays were hard for Claire but he'd get her through this. No matter where he was, he always did.

They swung off the Milltown Road, clipping a kerb, and he watched the familiar, neat rows of the semi-d's slip past. Hawthorn Crescent, Hawthorn Close, Hawthorn Lane. Nothing had changed.

There was the low wall by the bus-stop where he used to wait for Claire after school, and the narrow laneway that led across a football field to the railway tracks where they used to smoke. And there was Lennon's corner shop where Ray had once been caught by Beaky Lennon sneaking a tin of beans he'd taken from his mother's cupboard on to a shelf. Reverse shoplifting. Jesus, he hadn't thought of that for years.

A couple of bikes were flung on the grass beneath the chestnut tree on the green in front of the row of shops, and two figures were starfished on the grass where he and Claire used to lie on hot summer days when there was nothing to do.

Nostalgia, sharp as a fish-hook, caught in his throat. Nearly twenty years had flashed past. How had that happened?

He flipped the sun visor down and peered into the speckled mirror. There were two faint lines running from the side of his nose to the corners of his mouth but he looked pretty good for someone who'd only had four hours' sleep.

Claire pulled over and switched the engine off and they sat listening to a dog barking and the distant whine of a lawnmower. The sound of the suburbs, Ray thought. He looked across the road and there was his old house. He half expected to see his father's Corolla in the drive but his folks had moved to Malaga fifteen years ago.

'You could have warned me that there were Dora the Explorer curtains in my bedroom window.' He glanced at Claire. Not even a smile. 'You want me to come in with you?'

She shook her head and opened the door but stayed where she was, zipping her small gold locket back and forth on its chain and staring into her lap.

'I've got a new one for you!' Ray drummed on the dashboard with the broken wipers and sang the chorus of 'Addicted to Love', changing the words to 'you're a duck with a glove'.

'Ha, ha,' Claire said very quietly.

'That's got to be worth three "ha"s.'

'Ha!' she whispered.

Claire closed the front door and let the atmosphere of the house settle round her. The trailing ivy on the porch had swallowed up all the June sunshine and the narrow hall was murky. She always felt sorry for the house – it had been cheated of the life it should have had. Years of sadness and silence seemed to have soaked into the peeling paint and the faded carpets. Almost nothing had been changed since her mother had opened this door for the last time.

Her dad was standing at the kitchen window. Claire had given him plenty of new shirts over the years but today he was wearing the old blue one with frayed cuffs. His long, thinning grey hair was caught under the collar. There was a tiny piece of tissue stuck to his chin. He must have cut himself shaving.

'Dad!' He didn't move. 'Dad!'

'Sorry. I was listening to something on the radio.' He pulled an earphone out of his ear. He smiled and his grey eyes met hers for a moment and then dipped away and she felt a low ache under her ribs. The spreading bruise of guilt. 'Do you want some tea?' He held up his cup. 'I just made some.'

'Nick will be waiting, we should go.' She took his mug. It was full but stone cold. 'I've got Ray with me.'

'Ray,' he said vaguely, as if he was having trouble placing him. Sometimes Claire worried that her dad was losing his memory, then she reminded herself that he'd been like this for most of her life. There, but not really *there*.

He went over to the sink and gathered up a bunch of lilac that was on the draining board. He always brought her mother flowers, even after all this time. 'I don't suppose Nicholas would like it if I brought Dog,' he said. There was a sudden scrabbling of claws on the lino and a huge, shaggy grey head appeared from under the table. Claire backed away to the door. Dog had moved in twelve years ago, two weeks after she had moved out. Some kids had tied him to a shopping trolley with a bent coat hanger and he'd been crashing around the supermarket car park damaging the cars and scaring the customers. Her dad had untied him and they'd been inseparable ever since.

Dog looked as if he should be gnawing a huge bone in front of a baronial fireplace instead of lurking in a small suburban kitchen. He yawned and stretched and Claire inched a little farther out into the hall, but he didn't even bother to look at her. Dog had stopped trying to win her over years ago. Instead he ambled over to her dad and tucked his head under his arm for a cuddle and Claire wondered, again, why her dad was able to show more affection to a hairy lurcher than he was to his children.

Kelly stood a little way off beneath a stand of trees to give the Dillons space. They were queuing at the end of a long row of upright headstones like people waiting in a bank teller's line.

Nick was at the front, the peonies she'd picked from their garden a blaze of crimson against his white shirt. His dad was standing a few feet behind him holding a bunch of wilting lilac. Then there was Nick's sister Claire, tugging at her tangle of red hair, shifting from foot to foot in her too-short grey dress and her too-high strappy sandals. Claire hadn't brought flowers. She'd brought the guy who was hanging round the gate of the cemetery dressed from head to foot in black.

'This is Ray,' she'd said in the awkward moment when they'd met outside and Kelly had thought, 'No way!' Her old college room mate, Haru, used to have a screen saver of Ray Devine. 'Smoke Covered Horses' had, as they said, been big in Japan. They'd broken up a few years back but he was still rocking the bad boy look with the Aviators and the carefully messed-up black hair. When she was at high school, he was exactly the kind of guy she'd daydreamed about but she'd grown out of that pretty fast.

Kelly had gotten pretty good at guessing what kind of places people lived in and she was willing to bet her last dollar that his had black sheets and Helmut Newton nudes and framed pictures of himself in the bathroom.

She looked at her husband with his close-cut sandy hair and his broad, solid back and her heart did a little flip of relief and gratitude. There was nothing boyish about Nick. He was all man.

Nick put the peonies down by the headstone, relieved to be free of them. There was something mawkish about bringing flowers when he could hardly bear to be here at all. He turned away and walked over to where Kelly was waiting. Just looking at her in her light linen dress with her long, dark hair loose was like having a long, cool drink of water. 'Hi,' he said.

'Hi.' She slid her sunglasses down so he could see her eyes.

'Wherever she is,' she whispered, 'I know your mom is really proud of you.' The flinch was almost invisible, but she caught it. 'Are you okay?'

'I just need a couple of minutes of us-time before lunch.'

'Sure.' She took his arm. Nick was edgy about seeing his family and Kelly got that. Her parents reminded her of parts of herself she'd rather forget. She had moved to New York to get away from her past. And then crossed an ocean, just to be sure.

Claire watched them hurry along the path to the gate, the perfect stranger who used to be her brother and his perfect wife. She had thought, when Nick first moved back to Dublin, that he was coming home, but this was only the second time she'd seen him in nearly a year. She didn't blame him. He couldn't help it. She looked back down at the grave. It wasn't just her mother who was buried beneath the rectangle of granite chippings, it was all of them, the family they would have been if she were still here.

Her dad unwrapped the stems of wilting lilac and put them down on the gravel. 'Well . . .' He turned, talking to the air just behind her shoulder, saying what he said every year. 'I'm just going to see if I can find Phil Lynott's marker.'

There was a blank in Claire's mind where the funeral should have been. The first time she could remember coming to the graveyard was on her seventh birthday. She remembered sitting on the bottom step of the stairs and holding her feet up, one by one, so Nick could tie the buckles of her red sandals, the ones with the daisy pattern punched into the toe.

He had told her that they were going to visit their mum so she had thought that they were going to heaven because that was where everyone said that her mother had gone.

She had stood just here, holding Nick's hand, looking around at the strange stones that stuck up out of the ground and the heaps of wet clay and the faded plastic flowers under dusty plastic domes. She had been expecting angels with harps and white clouds. Why was everything so dirty? When was her mum going to appear so they could all go home?

She bent down now and touched the silver inscription on the slim, white marble headstone.

Maura Dillon (née McHugh)
Died 1st June 1983
Aged 33.
Beloved wife of Tom and mother of Claire and Nicholas.
'Tread carefully, for you tread on my dreams.'

She rearranged the flowers, fanning the stems out so that they covered the gravel. What had her mum's dreams been? What did you dream about when you had everything to live for?

Nick took a moment before he opened the door. He had lost it there for a minute in the graveyard but he felt calmer after the drive back with Kelly. He grounded himself with an affirmation. 'Nothing can harm me when I am guided by my higher self.'

'Nicholas.' The old man shuffled past without looking at him and disappeared into the living room. The distant roar of a crowd at a football stadium drifted out into the hall from the TV.

'Little boys' room?' Devine bounded past him and up the stairs.

Probably to snort a line of coke, Nick thought. What was his sister doing still hanging around with that lowlife? He watched Claire locking her decrepit old car and wobbling up the short driveway in her ridiculous shoes.

'Look,' he said, trying to sound pleasant, 'I don't want to cause conflict but it's really not OK to invite a stranger into my house without asking.'

Claire flushed. They would be at her dad's house if Nick hadn't insisted on having lunch here, and Ray was practically family. 'I'll check with you next time.' Nick closed the door and she followed him down the hall to the kitchen.

The walls and the open shelves were painted French greys and greens. A pretty chandelier hung over a table and some carefully mismatched antique chairs. There was a bottle of white wine chilling in a silver bucket on the table. She was dying for a drink but she needed to pace herself.

Kelly was in the garden putting up a parasol and Claire was relieved when Nick went out help her. There were a dozen photographs mounted in white frames on the wall. Nick and Kelly in a rowing boat, in a forest, in a hammock, on bicycles, in ski gear. She scanned them until she found the one she was looking for – a black and white shot taken on the steps of the City Clerk's Office in New York. Claire had never seen a picture of their wedding. There was Kelly in a short, elegant white dress. Nick in a dark suit grinning. It made her tearful to see him look that happy but it made her happy too.

Shit! Ray thought, looking at the hunch of Claire's shoulders. She was on a downward spiral. He pulled the wine bottle out of the ice bucket and held it like a microphone. 'And they call it . . .' he sang, '. . . yuppy luh-uh-uh-uve.'

'Shh!' She pointed at the garden. 'They'll hear you.' He handed her the wine and she took a quick gulp. 'What's that on your face?'

'Nothing.' He rubbed it in. It was a blob of Dr Sebagh's Serum. He'd had a little rummage in the antique cabinet in the bathroom. Kelly had great skin. He peered at a photograph of her in a pair of hiking shorts. She had great everything. Old Nick hadn't done too badly for himself. 'I caught Miss America checking me out in the graveyard.'

'Don't,' Claire jabbed him in the ribs with her elbow, 'even think about flirting with her.'

Ray put his hands up. 'I'll behave, I promise.'

Kelly was trying to be nice, Claire could see that, but she thought that lunch would never end. Drinking in the sunshine always gave her a headache and just looking at her sister-in-law made her feel exhausted. Kelly was three years younger than she was but she made Claire feel like a scruffy teenager. She was so perfect, so polished, so completely unruffled by her dad's mono-syllabic answers and Ray's little in-jokes and the fact that Nick seemed irritated by everything.

She sat there in her linen dress sipping soda water, chatting about books and films and exhibitions as if they were normal people, as if this was just an ordinary Sunday lunch. What had Nick told her, Claire wondered, about the accident? When they were growing up, he couldn't talk about their mother at all.

'You've hardly touched your salmon, Tom,' Kelly said now. 'Can I fix you something else?'

'No, I'm fine, thank you.' Her dad stood up. 'I might just go inside for a while.' He went back into the house and, after a moment, the sound of the TV drifted out into the garden again.

'Tom Dillon. A man of few words.' Ray put down his napkin. 'And most of them are "I'm fine".'

'Poor Dad,' Claire said quietly, and Nick felt a hard knot of frustration gather in his stomach. The old man wasn't some tragic figure nursing a broken heart, he was a fraud.

'Honey,' Kelly leaned over and laced her fingers through his, 'you haven't told Claire your news! Nick's going to be doing a regular spot as a Couples Coach on the OO *in the Afternoon* show. He's designed a relationship fitness programme. Isn't that fantastic?'

'Way to go!' Ray smirked. 'Love the radio show.' He some-times listened to Nick's agony uncle slot on Fish FM just so he could wind Claire up about it. He'd text her messages saying things like 'love is a verb, not a noun' and 'you've got to be friends to be lovers'.

Claire kicked him under the table. 'That's fantastic news. I probably won't see it because I'll be at work.'

Ray kicked her back. 'I can record it for you.'

'Sounds like you're busy, Claire?' A tiny diamond on a fine chain sparkled on Kelly's collarbone. 'What have you been up to?'

'Um,' Claire's hand went to her locket; she pressed the small gold disc between her finger and her thumb, 'nothing really.'

Ray refilled her glass. 'That's not true. You did that short film and that corporate video thing and you had a couple of days on *Forensic* last month.'

'But it wasn't really acting.' Claire flushed. Extra work didn't require an audition or up-to-date head shots or an explanation for a three-year gap in an acting résumé. You were a face in the crowd of football fans in a freezing stadium, cheering an empty pitch, or a customer in a restaurant picking at the same cold plate of food over and over while the real actors got their lines right. 'I was just a blur in the background.'

'I'm sure you're just being modest.'

'Modesty is Claire's middle name.' Ray leaned over and patted Claire's hand. She laughed and swatted him away.

Nick stood up and began to collect the plates. Maura was Claire's middle name, and if he had to look at Ray Devine's smug face for one more minute he thought he might punch it. Ray was the one who'd encouraged Claire to go to drama school instead of doing medicine or teaching, and now she was in her thirties, broke, with no career prospects, living like a student, and she seemed to think it was a big joke. He dropped a pile of forks into the salad bowl with a clatter.

'Do you want a hand?' Kelly asked him softly.

He shook his head. 'I'm fine.' Christ, he thought, he sounded just like the old man. The kitchen was cool after the heat of the garden. He stood at the sink Seven-Eleven breathing, trying to slow his heart rate. He couldn't remember the last time he'd felt this overwhelmed.

After a minute, Claire came inside with the serving dishes. She put them down on the draining board. She had taken off her shoes under the table; her toenails were painted purple and chipped. 'Did I say something to upset you?'

'I just don't think there's anything funny about the fact that your career is going down the pan.'

'Neither do I.' She turned away and began to scrape salad leaves into the bin. 'But it's tough out there. There's a recession. Budgets are being slashed.'

Claire had always been a terrible liar. He looked at her now. Barefoot, she only just came up to his shoulder. She seemed almost childlike, but she wasn't a kid any more. She was thirty-three. 'I just think that maybe it's time to name the elephant.'

'What?' She was washing her hands. She smiled at him over her shoulder.

'The huge issue that you're pretending doesn't exist.'

'Which is?'

What was he doing? He had spent the first half of his life trying to fix Claire. He was supposed to be done with all that. But apparently he wasn't. 'That you don't have what it takes for a cut-throat world like acting.' Claire's smile faded. 'I'm sure you have talent, but you don't have the . . .' He searched for the word. '. . . resilience.' *The ability to recover from setback and cope with rejection.* Claire had always been too soft. Too quick to give up and give in. She was doing it now.

'I didn't come in here for a coaching session. I came in to say I was sorry . . .'

'Are we all supposed to just stand here and watch you throwing your life away? What's wrong with you, Claire?'

She flinched as if he'd slapped her.

He tried to sound professional, as if she was a client instead of his sister. 'Look, it's not rocket science. If what you do isn't working, change it. If you can't change it, do something else. Don't let your fear keep you stuck. Do one thing that scares you every day.'

'Can she do the one thing that scares you,' Ray Devine was standing in the doorway, glaring at him, 'instead?'

*

'Damn!' Kelly said, after everyone was gone. 'I totally forgot!' She went over to the fridge and brought out a glass stand with a cake on it. 'I made this for Claire.'

It was perfect, like everything she put her hand to. White-iced and tied with a red satin ribbon. There was a black icing stiletto with a red sole standing on the top.

Nick had a flashback to walking down to Lennon's shop to buy Claire a cake after they got back from the graveyard that first year. He didn't remember what kind of cake he'd bought. He just knew that none of them had eaten it.

Kelly put the cake back in the fridge. 'Honey, you look stressed. Why don't we go upstairs and Two-Listen?'

Nick shook his head. He was too burned out to talk. Whenever he was around Claire and the old man, all the years of therapy disappeared. He regressed to being a teenager, trying to fix everything again and failing. 'Can we just Hug Until Close?'

'Sure.'

He took her in his arms and they stood in the middle of the kitchen holding on to one another for a long time and Nick forced himself to focus on the moment. The way their breathing slowly synchronised. The weight of her hair on his bare arm, the warmth of her body through his shirt. She was his family now, this beautiful woman, not the messed-up girl and the monosyllabic old man. That was all that mattered.

'Jesus,' Ray said. 'Is it not enough that your brother is the King of Psychobabble? Does he have to win the prize for World's Biggest Shit too?'

'It's not his fault.' Claire was jiggling the key in the lock of the door in the laneway.

Claire's capacity to live with broken things astonished Ray. Her taps dripped. Her water pipes howled. She had no letter 'P' on the keyboard of her laptop. Once, Mossy had lost reverse for two months and she'd just driven around Dublin, parking on corners.

'Let me do that.' Ray took the key and gave the door a sharp kick. A flake of faded green paint chipped off but the door swung open. He followed Claire through the tiny, nettle-choked garden and down the steps to the door of her basement flat. 'Your place or mine?'

Claire shook her head. 'I've had it with today.' They went inside and she kicked off her shoes and switched on the fairy lights that were looped above the old-fashioned kitchen presses.

'Come on. One mojito? Or a manhattan or margarita.' They were supposed to be working their way through the A to Z of cocktails but they'd been stuck on 'M' for months.

Claire sank down on to a folding IKEA chair, put her elbows on the table and rubbed her eyes with her fingers. 'I'm supposed to go to an open casting first thing tomorrow.'

'For what?'

She took a baggy sweatshirt off the back of the chair and pulled it on over her head. 'That new costume drama, *The Spaniard*,' she said from underneath it. Her head reappeared, her hair springing out like corkscrews. 'I think Lorcan sent me the email by mistake.'

Ray leaned against the draining board and folded his arms. If Claire was really going to start going back to auditions, this was not a good time to do it. 'Are you sure you're able for a cattle-call?' he said carefully.

She tugged the sweatshirt down over her knees and hugged them. 'I'm not sure of anything,' she said.

'Tell you what, skip the casting, let's do Muckanagheder-dauhaulia. I'll make a mix-tape.' Claire loved road trips and Ray had a thing about visiting randomly named Irish villages. Thermonfeckin, Emo, Bastardstown, Camp.

Claire tugged the sweatshirt sleeves down over her knuckles. 'I don't know.'

'It means "a piggery between two briny places". And I'm not leaving you here on your own unless you say "yes".' He began to sing, loudly. 'I've been to paradise, but I've never been to Meath.' Muckanaghederdauhaulia was in Galway but that didn't scan.

'OK!' Claire put her hands over her ears.

'Hey.' He went over and put his hands on her shoulders and gave her a squeeze. 'It's over for another year.'

Claire waited till the door that connected her flat to Ray's apartment had closed. She listened to him bounding up the stairs, then, when she was sure he wasn't going to come back down again, she got up, opened a bottle of wine and found a glass, then went up the three shallow steps and along the narrow hall to her bedroom.

It was still bright outside. She could see a tiny triangle of blue sky tinged with pink at the top of her window but the raised front garden blocked out most of the light. She turned on her bedside lamp and knelt on the floor. She opened the bottom drawer of the mahogany dressing table, took the lid off the box that was inside and spread them all out on the rug by her bed – all the things she had taken from her dad's room over the years. Things she knew he'd wouldn't miss.

The empty Consulate packet. The round wooden hairbrush with a few coppery hairs still caught in the bristles. The glass Opium bottle with the gold and orange lid that still had an oily trickle of perfume in the bottom. The single Aran mitten with the scorch mark on the palm. The cream lace dress with the slippery lining. The stethoscope with the worn green rubber tubing. The tube of Coty 'Schiaparelli Pink' lipstick. The photographs in their fat little stack, held together with a thick plastic band.

Claire didn't look at photographs much any more, they couldn't be trusted, not even the one in the silver frame she kept on her bedside table. She didn't really remember the day they'd played cricket in the garden but for years, she thought she had. Photographs superimposed themselves over the fragile impressions of her own memories.

The tiny flecks of yellow in her mum's dark green eyes. The way she smelled of Opium and Juicy Fruit chewing gum and menthol cigarettes. The static crackle when she brushed her hair. The contradiction between the serious, preoccupied doctor and the light-hearted, mischievous mother who sometimes came out to play. Who teased and tickled and double-dared. Who sculpted Claire's soapy hair into Mohicans and devil-horns at bath time and scooped her into her lap and sang 'Clair de Lune' and 'Oh Claire', making up entire verses when she didn't remember the words. Who would suddenly decide, on a sunny afternoon, to close up her surgery and pick Claire up from Montessori and take her on magical mystery drives.

Nothing compared to that feeling of having her mum, who was

usually so busy and important, all to herself. Claire was the navigator and she was allowed to say which way they went. 'Left or right?' her mum would say at the end of the street, laughing. 'Quick, make up your mind!' And Claire would be so excited that she almost felt sick.

Where did they go on those drives? All she had were hazy fragments. A shop where her mum tried on clothes behind a curtain while she sat on a blue velvet stool pressing her fingertips against the brass buttons. The grey ribbon of a country road. A restaurant with a huge gilt-framed mirror where she had a whole banana split to herself. She could still feel the weight of the heavy silver spoon in her hand, see the beads of condensation on the frosted glass dish.

Claire poured another glass of wine and slipped her hand into the Aran mitten. She didn't remember where the other one had gone or how this one had gotten the scorch mark but she had never forgotten the night her mum had come into her bedroom with her red coat over her nightdress and carried her downstairs wrapped in her duvet. The back door was already open and the air outside was a feathery blur of white. There were footprints leading out to a blanket spread out on the glistening lawn. She could still remember the surprise and the heart-stopping beauty of the garden. It must have been the first time she'd seen snow.

They had snuggled together on the blanket, one mitten each, their knees drawn up to their chins, their faces turned up to the whirl of slowly falling snow, catching flakes on their tongues.

It must have been cold but all Claire remembered was the sound of their laughter in the quiet garden. The thrill of being awake in the middle of the night. The feeling that whenever she was with her mum, something wonderful was going to happen.

Another, darker memory came to the surface of her mind and she pushed it down again. A sunny afternoon, six months later on her seventh birthday. Her mum sitting in a garden chair, wearing a yellow summer dress, looking at her over her sunglasses. 'What is wrong with you, Claire?'

She was still asking herself the same question, twenty-seven years later. She picked up the hairbrush and looked at the coppery hairs caught in the bristles. Each one of them held a DNA blueprint of her mum, a complete map of who she had been. All Claire had was a dozen memories, but they told her all she needed to know. There was nothing wrong with her mum. She had been perfect.

At seventeen, when Claire was hanging out on the riverbank with Ray, smoking and playing sweary Scrabble, her mum had been in medical school. In her twenties, when Claire was waiting for the big break that never happened and having her heart broken, she had been getting married and getting pregnant and setting up her own GP practice. At thirty-three, she had everything to live for, but hadn't had a proper acting job or a relationship for three years. She was barely scraping by.

The stethoscope was still looped around her neck. She kicked off her shoes and climbed onto the bed, slipped the little metal buds into her ears, slid the cold disc down under the neck of the sweatshirt, beneath her dress, and listened to the stubborn hammer of her heart. She was still here and her mother was gone. It wasn't fair.

When Claire woke up it was getting light again. Her leg was fizzing with pins and needles and her mouth tasted sour and vinegary. She took off the stethoscope, put everything carefully back into the box and closed the drawer and went to the bathroom. Ray must have been down in the night. There was a metal hanger with an FCUK gift voucher pinned to it hanging on the door handle and, beneath it, a tube of salt and vinegar Pringles with a jaunty pink birthday candle pushed into the lid.

She brushed her teeth and took off her make-up. She undressed and put on an old Smoke Covered Horses T-shirt that was hanging on the back of the door. She looked at her reflection in the mirror in the half-light from the hall, but it was her mother's face she saw. The tears she'd been holding back all yesterday came, but they weren't soft tears of sadness or of self-pity, they were tears of shame. Nick was right. How was she supposed to stand at the grave a year from now, knowing that she'd just wasted another year?

It was too late to try to be like her mother. That door had closed a long time ago. But she had to do something. She would give herself twelve months to try to salvage something from the mess she had managed to make of her life. She had made promises like this before but this time she meant it. She blew her nose and went back into her bedroom and set the clock.

'Do one thing that scares you every day,' Nick had said. She could start by going to the open casting. It was three years since she'd been to an audition and, right now, she couldn't think of anything more terrifying.

2

'Hi, I'm Claire Dillon, I'm with the Lorcan Norton Agency.' She paused, turned to the right, paused, turned to the left, turned back and smiled brightly at two shadowy figures sitting on a sofa in the darkness beyond the spotlight.

'You've just drifted off your mark there.' Sam, the casting director, was perched on a tall stool by the camera. He looked bored. At least fifty girls had already been in and out of the room since Claire had arrived three hours ago.

'Sorry!' Claire said, stepping back up to the line of masking tape on the floor.

'Can you tell us a bit about yourself?'

'I graduated from the Dublin Academy of Dramatic Arts in 2000. I toured with Broken Bell's production of *Three Sisters* that was runner-up in the Westport Theatre Festival in 2001. I won the "Erin" Best Newcomer for Valerie in *The Weir* in 2003 . . .'

She could hear the 'tippity-tap' of someone texting from the sofa. Her faked confidence was leaking out of her like air from a punctured balloon. It had all happened so long ago. Maggie in *Dancing at Lughnasa*. Theresa in *Scenes from the Big Picture*. She tried to sound more enthusiastic. 'Then I joined Red Rows and—'

'Really?' Sam looked up. 'Was Declan Brady artistic director then?'

A flush crept up past the collar of Claire's white audition shirt. She could feel a clammy patch at the small of her back where it was sticking to her skin. She hugged the pages she'd been given to her chest. 'Yes.'

'How long were you there?'

'Three years.'

Claire's acting life had fallen, neatly, into three-year time slots. Three years at drama school. Three years slogging around the country doing regional theatre. Three years of giving it what her friend Eilish called 'socks'. Doing every audition. Trying not to take it personally when she didn't get the job. Trying not to feel threatened when waves of new hopefuls were let loose every summer. Trying to schmooze even though she was terrible at it. Trying to believe that she was still going to get a break.

Then three years with Red Rows Theatre Company feeling as if she'd finally found her feet. Falling for Declan Brady. Sweet, serious, talented Declan, who was five years older than she was. Who had joined all her freckles with a biro the first time they slept together and asked her to move in with him after a month. Who had told her that she was the Irish Isabelle Huppert and cast her as Stella in *Streetcar* and May in *Fool for Love* and Sister Woman in *Cat on a Hot Tin Roof*. And then had an affair behind her back.

Claire should have been used to rejection. All those years of auditions should have toughened her but they hadn't. She had cut herself off from the acting world. Avoided her old friends, stopped calling her agent, passed on auditions. She had spent the last three years hiding out in Ray's basement licking her wounds.

Sam was talking to her. She forced herself to concentrate. 'Sorry?'

'I was just asking about TV and film.'

She gabbled her way through her credits. Nurse Bernie, in three episodes of a short-lived sitcom called *Wards and All*. Walk-on parts on *Fair City* and *The Tudors*. A teacher in one episode of *Life Lessons*.

'That was in, what, 2007? Any more recent TV work?'

'No.'

'*Recent* theatre work?'

She was throwing it away. She could feel it. 'Not really.' She couldn't tell him about the extra work. That was the lowest rung of the acting ladder, a fraction of an inch above jumping out on Japanese tourists on the Haunted Prison Tour or dancing around Samantha Mumba in panto.

'Do you have a recent headshot?'

'The thing is . . .' She heard the desperation in her voice. 'I've been out of the picture for a while and I'm just kind of getting back in again.'

'Well,' Sam looked embarrassed, 'I'm sure you will. That's it for today. Thanks for coming in.'

Claire tried to keep the disappointment out of her face. She had prepared the dialogue she'd been given, but now they weren't going to ask her to read. 'Thank you!'

'Is that your hair?' a woman's voice said from the sofa at the back of the room.

Claire was already at the door. 'Sorry?' She had spent an hour this morning blow-drying her hair straight but it had started to frizz up before she left the house.

'Hang on a second,' Sam left his stool and she hesitated, her hand on the door handle, while he whispered to the woman on the sofa. After a minute, he came back. 'Would you mind reading something for us?'

Claire forced herself to let go of the handle and walk back into the spotlight. He pulled two pages from a thick script. 'I know you haven't had a chance to prepare but it's only a couple of lines. We'd already cast but the actor's just broken her wrist. It's the shepherdess. I'll read Lady Kathryn.'

Claire nodded.

'Tell me what you saw, girl!' Sam shouted in a scary falsetto.

'I saw a Spanish galleon.' Claire stumbled over the line. 'Out beyond Hare Island.'

'Have you breathed a word of this to my husband, the Earl?'

'No, milady,' Claire said.

'If you do, I will see to it that your family will suffer!'

'I won't. I swear.' Claire turned the page. There was no more dialogue, just a short line of direction.

'*As the terrified SHEPHERDESS watches LADY KATHRYN gallop away, she begins to cry.*'

'What was the competition like?' Eilish stirred her cappuccino and licked the foam off her spoon.

Claire stared out of the window of Butler's Café. Wicklow Street was splashy with sunshine but she shivered. 'Usual film audition crowd. It was like a Barbie Doll convention. They were all about twenty with acres of hair extensions and fake tan. I felt like an ancient crone.'

Eilish let out a horribly convincing cackle.

'Ancient-er.' Claire sighed.

Eilish cackled again and the man at the next table looked worried. 'Don't mind us,' Eilish said. 'We're thesbians.'

Eilish was the only acting friend Claire could bear to see after she had broken up with Declan. Eilish had dropped off the acting radar five years ago, after her husband, Steve, had left her. She'd been too busy bringing up her daughter Holly to take on six performances and a matinee every week.

'I still can't believe you went to an audition,' she said now. 'Details! Gories! Tell me everything.' Claire filled her in on her promise and about blowing Ray off and messing up the audition and having to go back and read with Sam.

'You did that crying thing?' Eilish gazed at her over the rim of her coffee mug. 'It's so weird and freaky when you do that! Were they impressed?'

Claire remembered the awkward silence in the room as tears trickled down her face. 'I think they were mortified.'

Eilish put her mug down and put her hands over her face. 'Don't talk to me about mortified! Not after this morning.' She had come straight from an extra job.

Claire put down her cup. 'How did it go?'

Eilish dropped her dark head down on to the table and held up her hand. 'Picture this!' she said. 'A corporate video for a chemical company that makes toilet cleaner. To show how fun cleaning toilets can be, some sadist came up with the idea of a flash mob – sorry, a "flush-mob" – of cleaning ladies. So I've spent the morning in a crimplene housecoat and curlers and saggy Norah Batty tights, dancing up and down Dawson Street.'

Claire almost choked on her tea. 'You're making this up for *Eyelash and Eclair*.' Whenever they were stuck on the extra bus for hours on end, they passed the time inventing a sitcom about two failed actresses.

'Would I make up a song,' Eilish sat up and looked at Claire from beneath her black fringe, 'to the tune of "Flash Dance" that went: "What a feeling! Now I'm cleaning!" It was up there with the time we had to wear those really tight bacteria body stockings and attack the giant tooth in that ad for denture cleaner.' She groaned. 'You're right, Claire. You have to get out of this extra hell and I'll be right after you. When Holly goes off to uni next year, I'll start going back to auditions too.' She toasted Claire with her empty mug. 'I'm proud of you!'

'For doing the worst audition ever?'

'For finally coming out of the three-year tailspin you've been in since Declan.' Eilish's blue eyes were serious. 'I'm glad you want to get your life back on track. But don't do it for your mum, Claire. Wherever she is, she doesn't need that. Trust me, I'm a mother, all that mushy malarkey about unconditional love is true. Do it for you.'

The battered black leather sofa in the No Name bar reminded Ray of a jacket he'd bought on the King's Road the day Tarantula had signed Smoke Covered Horses. He'd thrown it into the crowd in the Ruby Room in Tokyo in 2008. He could still remember the scrum of girls who had fought one another to get hold of it. He missed it. The intoxicating thrill of holding a crowd in his hand. Being the one still point in a room gone wild. People who thought cocaine was addictive had never tried fame. Ray still got the double-takes and the second glances, though it was happening less and less, and on the days when nobody recognised him at all, he just reminded himself to enjoy the anonymity because it wasn't going to last. He was going to get it all back and this time it would be on his terms.

He opened his laptop. He'd been hanging around the apartment all day trying to crack a brief for an advertising jingle. He'd thought maybe a change of scenery would help. The jingle thing was just a way of passing the time until Chip Connolly swallowed his pride and they could reform the Horses but it kept Ray out of trouble, for a few hours a day anyway. It wasn't like he needed to work. Between the royalties from 'Asia Sky' and the fee he was paid by the airline that used it in their ads, he was set up for life.

After he'd moved back to Dublin, a UK jingle company had tracked him down. Sounds Familiar specialised in ad soundtracks for obscure foreign brands. Tracks that sounded like well-known songs, but not enough for an original artist to sue. Ray, it turned out, was very good at them. He'd come up with 'Crumbelievable!' for a Canadian stuffing and 'You Tape my Breath Away' for a Kenyan dental floss. He scanned the brief for King's Cooking Oil, a Tasmanian brand. They wanted something 'anthemic and emotive'. Didn't everyone? He opened a lyrics database and started a search. 'Big boys don't fry?' No. 'It's my party and I'll fry if I want to?' That had possibilities.

'Hey! It's Ray, isn't it?' A dark-haired girl at the next table was smiling at him. Sounds Familiar were expecting ideas in the morning but she had a mouth like Penelope Cruz and he wasn't going to argue with that. 'You have no idea how much I love you!' She shook her head. 'I mean, your music.'

'This is a bit unfair.' He closed his laptop. 'You know my name but I don't know yours.'

She picked up her drink and moved on to the sofa beside him. 'I'm Cara, actually.'

'Cara actually' didn't leave Ray's apartment till half three in the morning. After she'd gone, Ray showered, made a pot of coffee and sat down at his desk then cracked the King's jingle in under an hour. It wasn't a *rip-off* of Westlife, it was a *homage* – 'Frying without Kings'.

Nick sat up as straight as he could on the overstuffed chair and stared at the winking red light on the huge camera that was trained on his face.

'I love new challenges,' he repeated to himself. 'I approach them with boldness and enthusiasm.' His stomach fluttered and then jolted down into his gut. He'd prepared his piece and run over it with Kelly a dozen times. He'd hoped he'd get a chance to talk it through with the hosts but they had only just appeared.

'Howya, Nick!' Oonagh Clancy leaned down, planting a sticky lip-glossed kiss on his cheek. She sat down on the sofa. 'Why did nobody tell me he was gorgeous?'

Owen Clancy sat beside her and fumbled with his notes while one girl combed his shock of black hair and another attached a microphone to his lapel.

'Three, two, one,' the floor manager counted down on her fingers. Oonagh crossed her legs and inflated her chest.

'Hello.' She gave the camera a dazzling smile. 'I'm Oonagh Clancy.' Her Dublin accent was gone.

'And I'm Owen Clancy.' Owen beamed. 'And you're welcome to OO *in the Afternoon*.'

They sat, smiling at one another while the jingle played.

'We put the "OOOH" in the afternoon.

We're there for YOU in the afternoon.

We're OO, OO in the afternoon!'

Owen Clancy had already been a newsreader when Nick was still young. He was in his fifties. Oonagh was twenty years younger. She'd started out as a weather girl on TV3 when Nick was living in the States.

The jingle was winding up.

'We're here from two and right THROUGH the afternoon.

It's OO, OO in the Afternooh-ooh-ooh-oon!'

'We've got a great show lined up for you, today,' Owen boomed. 'We'll meet the man who crossed Ireland backwards dressed as a woman.'

Oonagh's smile dissolved, seamlessly, into sympathy. 'We'll be talking to a young father about his harrowing struggle with bowel cancer.'

'And later on,' Owen winked, 'our chef, the lovely Ita Fox, will be sharing her luscious Double Chocolate Cupcakes.'

'But first,' Oonagh turned to Nick, 'let's meet our new coach on the couch, radio agony uncle Nick Dillon. Nick will be joining us every week to talk love, lust and making marriage last.' Oonagh beamed at him. 'Welcome to the show!'

'Thank you. My coaching is all based on honesty so I have to be truthful and confess that I'm pretty nervous. You guys make this look so easy.'

'Well, we do it twice a week.' Oonagh patted her husband's head. She leaned over and stage-whispered to Nick, 'I'd like to do it more but Owen's getting on a bit!'

'Just wait till I get you on your own,' Owen laughed. 'You are in so much trouble!'

'Is that a promise?' Ooonagh swatted at him with her notes.

Owen put his elbows on his huge thighs. 'So tell us about yourself, Doc.'

Doc? Nick wasn't a doctor but he didn't want to get side-tracked from the intro he'd rehearsed. 'Well, I grew up in Dublin but I've spent just over half my life in the States. I went to college in Washington and I worked in human resources in a finance company in New York for fifteen years, but people tend to bring their personal problems to work—'

'Tell me about it!' Oonagh rolled her eyes.

'So after I lost my job in the downturn, I retrained as a life coach, specialising in couples. I got married three years ago. So I have to walk the walk as well as talk the talk!'

'Nick has designed a relationship workout programme to help you,' Oonagh pointed at the camera, 'and me to get our relationships back in shape. It's called "We-Fit". After the break he'll be teaching our guest couple how to strengthen their relationship through "Soul Gazing" and a fun game for two called "Complimentition". Don't go away now!'

She dropped her D4 accent when the camera stopped rolling. 'Jaysus, you're a natural!' She beamed at Nick. 'Isn't he, Owen?'

Owen was fiddling with his mike and pretended not to hear.

Claire hadn't spoken to her agent since she'd walked away from Red Rows. At some point, she'd been passed on to his assistant Brenda, who handled extra work. She'd promised herself that she'd call Lorcan every single day this week but it was four o'clock now and she couldn't face being fobbed off by Brenda again.

She'd spent the previous day in RTE as an extra on *Fair City* and she'd been going home to have an early night but Ray had persuaded her to go out for 'one drink'. They'd ended up in Copper Faced Jack's till three in the morning drinking way too much cheap white wine and talking rubbish.

She was going to have to develop some self-control if she didn't want to let her promise slip away before she'd given it a proper shot. Ray only worked for a couple of hours a day so he had plenty of time to play and he was too damned good at it.

He'd book tickets for a movie he knew she wanted to see or a boat ride to Dalkey Island or a restaurant in Howth and then he'd claim it was too late to cancel. He'd talk her into driving to Sligo or Clare in a day. Once he produced her passport when they arrived in Rosslare and they ended up on a ferry to Le Havre. At night, he'd drag her off to Cassidy's for pints or to an obscure band in Whelan's or to a comedy club he'd heard was brilliant. If she refused to leave the house, he'd appear at her door with a pitcher of frozen margaritas and a DVD. It was like living downstairs from the Devil.

She poured herself another coffee and arranged herself and her hangover carefully on the uncomfortable chaise longue in the living room with a plate of toast balanced on her lap and switched on the TV, then jolted upright as her brother's face filled the screen.

'It's too late to make up for what we didn't have when we were children,' Nick was saying to the camera. 'We have to stop re-reading the early chapters of our lives and start over with a blank sheet of paper.'

Their dad didn't die of a broken heart, the way people did in stories. He just sort of disappeared. He stopped whistling while he shaved. He stopped eating proper meals. He stopped reading Claire stories and taking her around the garden to help him talk to his plants. He stopped going to work. The graphic design company he worked for sent briefs to the house by courier instead and he stayed up all night in his bedroom sketching illustrations and storyboards for TV ads.

He'd shuffle downstairs red eyed, exhausted, to make breakfast for Nick and Claire. Sometimes their plates would still be on the table when they came home from school.

Claire remembered a pair of shoes that pinched from September to Christmas because her feet had grown a size. Dust bunnies the size of hamsters under her bed. Her Care Bears duvet cover flecked with damp spores because her dad had put on a load of washing and forgotten to take it out.

Little by little, Nick took over. He buttered Claire's bread on both sides and put a separate triangle of Laughing Cow cheese, which was what she liked, into her lunchbox. He made her fried egg and spaghetti hoops and Findus Crispy Pancakes and Vesta

Chicken Supreme. He reminded her to do her homework and checked to see that she had clean clothes for the morning. He combed out the tangles in her hair. When she was seven and he was eleven, he had seemed to love her more than anyone in the world.

She lowered the volume and looked at his face on the screen. His white American teeth looked too bright in his pale Irish face. He had two deep horizontal lines on his forehead and a thinner vertical one between his eyes. There were tiny threads of silver in his sandy hair. He was still her brother but he was a stranger.

Her phone began to ring. She rummaged around the sofa, looking for it.

'Three years of radio silence and then suddenly you're calling me every day?'

'Lorcan!' Claire shot up, knocking her toast on to the rug. 'I don't mean to stalk you. I just wanted to let you know that I'm ready to start looking for proper acting work again.' Her voice was husky from shouting over the music in the club the night before. 'I won't turn down extra jobs for the moment but I'd like to in the long-term because—'

'Claire, slow down.'

She couldn't. She had to get it all out before she lost her nerve. '—Because the thing is, I have a plan. I've given myself a year to get my acting career back on track. So if there's something, anything at all, then please put my name forward.'

'Are you available for a day's shoot next Wednesday?'

She caught her breath. 'What?'

'And for another five days spread out over the next nine months?'

'Yes!'

'Good. Because you've been cast as a shepherdess in *The Spaniard*.'

'What do we write,' Oonagh asked Nick after the break, 'on this blank sheet of paper?'

'The things we all want from our relationships,' he ticked them off on his fingers. 'Honesty. Trust. Intimacy. Respect. Then we set time aside, every week, to *work out* together.' He was completely relaxed now. 'We need to work out our issues. We need to *strengthen* our communication. We need to *tone up* our intimacy. And we can start right now with the first exercise in the We-Fit programme. It's called "Soul Gazing".'

Anne and Dermot, the studio couple, were in their sixties and they had looked as if they had just had a huge row. After they'd sat on the sofa and gazed into one another's eyes for sixty seconds, they were still glaring at one another. Nick hoped this wasn't going to fall flat on its face on live TV. 'OK,' he said cheerfully. 'Now that you're warmed up, we can move on to our second exercise. "Complimentition". Did you know that we find fault with our partners, on average, fifteen times a day?'

'Is that all?' Owen smirked.

Nick held up a stopwatch. 'This is a competition to outdo one another with compliments. The sky's the limit and you have two minutes. Starting from now!'

Dermot sighed. 'This is ridiculous.'

'Just start with "I like your . . ."' Nick prompted, 'and add a word.'

Dermot looked at the floor. 'I like your . . . dress,' he said grudgingly.

'It's a skirt and top,' Anne snapped. 'I like your suit. Which I had to pick up from the dry cleaner's because you didn't bother. Your turn.'

'I like your hair long like that.'

'Really?' She touched her thin blonde hair self-consciously. 'I like your smile. If you just used it more.'

Dermot smiled. 'I like the way you did the dining room up.'

'Oh! Well I like the way you do all the little bits and pieces around the house.'

Nick looked at the watch. The hand was halfway through its second sweep.

Dermot looked at the floor again. 'I like the way you asked my mother to live with us after she had her stroke. I know it wasn't easy.'

Anne nodded. 'I like how good you were to her, Dermot. You were a lovely son.' Her voice cracked.

Dermot moved along the sofa and put his arm around her. 'It's OK, love,' he said.

'Well,' Oonagh fanned the sides of her eyes with her fingertips, 'you heard it here first. The couples that praise together stay together! Right, Owen?'

'What? Oh, sorry!' Owen winked. 'I was distracted by Ita's cupcakes which I hope I'll be sampling after the break.'

'Are they always like that?' Nick asked the runner who led him across a tangle of snaking cables and out into the corridor after his slot was over.

'Bitchard and Rudie? Yeah. They fight like cats and dogs on air then they make up,' she made a horrified face, 'in their dressing room.'

3

Actors in elaborate gowns and leather jerkins and hose were hanging around in the cobbled courtyard eating breakfast. The crew were buzzing about in their unofficial uniform of black, but it was the guy in the faded jeans and T-shirt that Claire noticed first.

He was tall with longish, light brown, curly hair, and he was standing at the half-door of a stable talking to a huge grey horse. It reminded her of the way her dad used to stand in the garden, before the accident, chatting to his delphiniums and his hollyhocks, persuading them to grow. She was looking over at the guy with a silly smile on her face when he glanced up at her and she turned away quickly and made her way over to the catering table. She was half expecting to hear a bolshy fourth AD yelling at her that this was 'actors only'. The extras' area was at the end of the long avenue, near the gates, with the generator trucks and the Portaloos.

The Spaniard was a new Irish-American co-production about the Armada, which was shipwrecked off the west coast of Ireland in 1588. Claire wasn't sure what shepherdesses wore back then but she was willing to bet that it hadn't been as minxy as the woollen skirt and calico bodice she'd been laced into. But who cared about historical accuracy? She had three lines of dialogue today and more to come. She'd get to fill the gaping hole in her CV and she'd even get a credit on IMDB. She poured herself a cardboard cup of iced coffee and reached for a chocolate croissant.

'Claire Dillon!'

She turned and there, in a low-cut, pale blue and gold velvet gown with ropes of pearls woven into her long, caramel hair, was Emma Lacey. Described by *VIP* magazine as 'the Irish Jennifer Aniston' and by Declan as 'the woman I've fallen in love with'.

'Listen,' Emma said, 'you're not really supposed be in here but if anyone tries to throw you out just get them to talk to me.'

Claire's shock gave way to childish anger. 'I've got a part!' She thrust out her two pages of script. 'I've got lines.'

'Oh!' Emma peeled off one long kid leather glove. 'I thought you were with the extras. Milo Daly told me he'd seen you lurking in the background on *Forensic*.' She looked down at Claire's costume. 'Are you a milkmaid?'

'I'm a shepherdess,' Claire said.

'I'm Lady Kathryn. We're in the same scene. It'll be just like the old days.'

The old days, Claire thought, which ones? The days at drama school when Emma had acted like her friend or the days when they were rehearsing *Cat on a Hot Tin Roof* when Emma kept 'borrowing' Declan for script consults over coffees and drinks and then decided to keep him.

Emma must have read her mind. A flush of colour rose into her cheeks beneath the ivory mask of her make-up. Good, Claire thought. She had dreaded bumping into Emma again but she wasn't the one who should feel embarrassed.

'You can't begin to imagine how hot it is inside this huge dress in all this heat.' Emma looked away and pretended to fan herself with her glove. 'I'm so glad I decided to go for a winter wedding next year.' The word hit Claire like a punch in the stomach. 'Oh!' Emma turned back with a sly little look. 'You do know that Declan and I are getting married?'

What Claire knew was that Emma always had to win and that this time she wasn't going to let her. 'Of course,' she said coolly. 'Congratulations!'

'What about you, Claire? Where are you living these days?'

'Carysfort Square.'

'In one of those Georgian houses?' Emma looked surprised. 'On your own?'

'With Ray.'

'Ray Devine.' Emma's small mouth fell open a fraction. She had tried, all through their twenties, to get Ray into bed. 'You two are together now?'

Claire couldn't resist it. She nodded. 'We are.'

'Excuse me.' A girl with a walkie-talkie was standing beside them. 'Emma, the first AD needs a word.'

Claire watched Emma picking her way across the cobbles. They were getting married. She tried to imagine Declan in a morning suit walking down the aisle of a church but his face was out of focus. She could hardly remember what he looked like any more. She scanned herself for pain but instead there was an unexpected feeling of lightness. She had been dreading this for three years but now that it had happened, she didn't have to dread it any more.

The location was a few miles away on a hillside above Avoca. Claire was shown to her first position on a grassy lane and she waited beneath the shade of a tree by a wooden gate while the crew buzzed to and fro setting up the generators and dolly tracks.

'Got everything you need?' a runner asked Claire as she hurried past and she nodded. It was lovely to be essential instead of extra.

An old Land Rover pulling an open trailer packed with sheep bumped down the lane then parked up, and the guy Claire had seen in the courtyard climbed out and walked over.

'You're Claire, the shepherdess? I'm Shane and these are yours.' He nodded at the sheep. 'Someone will be along to let them out just before the camera turns over.'

Claire had forgotten that there would be sheep. She looked at their strange bony faces protruding through the bars of the trailer and shuddered. 'Never work with children and animals, that's what they say, isn't it?'

He looked at her. Beneath his heavy brows, his eyes were so dark that they seemed to be all pupil. He was older than she'd first thought and taller. He frowned. 'Why do they say that?'

'I suppose because children and animals can't act.'

'Ah.' He nodded. 'That explains it.'

'What?'

'Why I like them so much.'

He leaned his arms on the gate, hooking his foot on the bottom bar, and looked away from her across the field. His light brown

35

hair came down below the collar of his T-shirt. His arms were tanned and he had a scatter of tiny scars on his hands. There was a faint white band on one finger of his left hand as if he'd worn a ring and taken it off.

Claire felt she had to justify herself. 'I had a bad experience. I'm scared of being bitten.'

He turned around and looked at her again, then lowered his voice. 'Watch out for the one at the back with the yellowy eyes.'

Claire whipped around and stared at the trailer. They all had yellow eyes.

His face cracked into a grin that lit his eyes, then he turned away and looked across the field again.

They stood there listening to the clunk and stutter of a starting generator and the sound of a plane passing overhead. After a while, a 4x4 with a horsebox pulled up on the other side of the field and Claire saw Emma in her elaborate gown getting down from the passenger side.

'Well . . .' Shane straightened up. 'Time to go. You guys be good now,' he said to the sheep as he passed the trailer. He sauntered slowly back up the lane, his hair catching the sun as he passed out of blocks of shadow and into the light.

Something beneath Claire's ribcage yawned and stretched. 'Ah,' she thought, 'so you're still in there. You survived after all.'

'Thank you,' Kelly gazed into Nick's eyes, 'for sharing.' They were sitting cross-legged on their bed Two-Listening. Candles flickered on the windowsill. Whale music played softly in the background. She waited for a particularly loud whale to finish before she went on. 'What I heard you saying is that the OO show has given you a sense of purpose and that you love the idea of helping people you've never even met.'

Nick squeezed her hands. 'Thank you for hearing me. Do you want to share?'

Kelly was getting pins and needles in her foot. 'Not tonight, honey, but I think that Clancy woman is right.' She waited for some dolphin clicking to cease. 'You're a natural in front of the camera.'

A single strand of Kelly's dark hair had come loose from her silver barrette and fallen over one bare shoulder. Nick tucked it behind her ear. 'I couldn't do it without you.'

Claire froze. Over the frantic hammering of her heart she heard it again. The squeak of the middle step that led down to the kitchen. There was an intruder in her flat! She got out of bed, pulled on a sweatshirt, grabbed the rainstick and crept quietly down the narrow dark hall. There was the shadowy silhouette of a man in the kitchen. The fridge door creaked open and the light came on. There was Ray wearing a Banksy T-shirt and pair of white boxer shorts, peering into her fridge.

'Jesus, Ray!' She came down the steps and switched on the fairy lights. 'I thought you were a burglar!' Even after all these years, it was still odd to find a person who she'd seen strutting around a stage in front of twenty thousand people at large in her kitchen.

'I need cheese.'

'I don't have any.'

'Sweet dreams are made of cheese!' he sang. 'Who am I to diss a Brie?' He was rummaging at the back of the fridge. 'What's going on in here? What's all this healthy stuff?'

Claire had decided that if she was going to get back into acting, she needed to get healthy. She was too broke to join a gym but she could ditch the takeaways and the drinking on week nights.

Ray waved a smoked mackerel. 'Who first looked at one of these and thought "Let's smoke him"?' He took the lid off a tub of hummus and sniffed it suspiciously.

Claire sighed and sat down. 'You can't keep wandering down here in the middle of the night. What if I was in bed with someone?'

Her mind flashed back to the shoot. After the director had called a wrap, when the crew were packing all the gear away, Shane had swung himself up on to the huge grey horse that Emma Lacey had been riding. Claire had always thought that the whole sexy-man-on-a-horse thing was an awful Jane Austen cliché but watching him galloping across the field to the horsebox she had changed her mind.

Ray put the hummus on the table and opened the cupboard. 'If you were in bed with someone that rainstick wouldn't be in your hand, it would be on the stairs, according to the rules of The Contract.'

The Contract covered everything from who controlled the remote control to who got the last Rolo. There was a Jolie Sub-Clause that obliged Claire to accompany Ray to every Angelina film as long as it wasn't animated and a Non-Exclusivity Rule that allowed either of them to blouse out of an arrangement if they got a better offer. The Do Not Disturb Protocol obliged Ray to leave his frisbee on the stairs if he had someone round. Claire was supposed to do the same with her rainstick but it had spent most of the last three years under her bed.

Claire had unpacked a box of acting books and they were scattered all over the tiny sofa. Ray grabbed a copy of a Lorca play and tucked it under the rickety leg of the table to stop it rocking, then he sat down on one of Claire's rickety folding chairs and spread some hummus on a cracker.

He loved Claire's pokey kitchen with its ancient gas cooker and open shelves of mismatched crockery and strings of fairy lights. Well, it was his kitchen, really. He'd bought the house after 'Asia Sky' went platinum. His loft-style living room upstairs had a modular sofa and a forty-two-inch TV and twenty grand's worth of recording equipment. His kitchen had poured concrete floors and polished steel units and a huge black glass light fitting that reminded him of a hovering insect. But he felt more at home down here, sitting on one of Claire's uncomfortable sofas, watching her tiny temperamental TV, trying to plug the draughts with her collection of knitted draught snakes.

'Why don't you get changed into something foxy and come out clubbing with me? Or we could open a bottle of wine and a box set.'

Claire pinched his cracker and took a bite. 'I can't do that stuff any more.'

'Why not?' he said petulantly.

She chewed slowly. 'Because when my mother was my age, she wasn't out clubbing every night or staying up till three in the morning watching box sets.'

'That's because box sets hadn't been invented.'

'I'm just trying to be more grown up,' Claire sighed. 'I wish you'd help.'

Ray looked down at his plate to hide his exasperation. It pissed him off that she was always comparing herself to someone she barely knew.

'What's with the pout?' Claire laughed. Ray's Liam Gallagher-esque fringe had fallen into his eyes. His bottom lip had a sullen jut. He looked like his own picture on the cover of *It's Not You, It's Me*.

He shook his head. 'I wish you wouldn't put your mother on a pedestal, that's all.'

'That's rich coming from someone who spent a good part of the last ten years on his own pedestal,' Claire licked her finger and picked up the crumbs from his plate.

Ray Devine had moved in across the street the summer that Claire turned fourteen, the year that her brother had gone to college in Washington. Nick had promised he'd call every week but the calls got shorter and the gaps between the calls got longer and Claire got the message. She missed him but he had moved on. He had escaped and left her behind.

The house was so empty without him. The friends she had made at school had drifted away when term ended. It rained every single day that summer. Claire spent hours curled up on her bed reading, while the boy across the road spent hours sitting on the wall outside his house beneath the dripping hedge listening to his Discman.

Claire would never have had the courage to talk to a boy who looked like Ray Devine at school but one day, when the steady downpour turned into a monsoon, she pulled on an anorak and ran across the road, dodging the puddles.

'Excuse me,' she said. His dark hair was plastered to his head. There were raindrops caught in his long eyelashes. 'Why don't you go inside?'

There was a yell from the open window of the house behind the wall and the sound of a door slamming. 'I'm cool.' His shoulders were hunched up by his ears.

'You don't look cool,' Claire said. 'You look frozen.' She stared down at his soaked sneakers. 'You can come over to my house if you want.'

At the door, she bit her lip and waited for the look that she'd seen on her friends' faces the only time she'd brought them home. The mixture of pity and curiosity. But Ray just trudged past her into the living room, his sneakers squelching, his hands tucked into the pockets of his damp jeans. 'Can we watch TV?'

They sat on the sofa all afternoon watching *Countdown* and *Grange Hill*. After a while, her dad came downstairs.

'I was just going to make an omelette,' he said. If he was remotely surprised or put out to find a strange boy in his living room, he didn't show it.

They ate, with plates on their knees, watching a documentary about Stephen Hawking, and the next morning Ray was sitting on the wall outside looking up at Claire's window when she opened her curtains. And that was how it began. He was like a brother but one who didn't nag her about her homework or tell her to tidy her room. He was way more fun than Nick had ever been. There was an engaging madness to Ray Devine.

'Let's cycle up to Enniskerry,' he'd say. 'Let's skip school and hop the train to Bray. Let's bring stuff down to Lennon's and reverse-shoplift. Let's play sweary Scrabble by the train tracks.'

Nick had never wanted to go the graveyard with her but Ray didn't mind. She'd bring scissors when she went there to trim back the grass from the headstone and she'd always leave something behind. A programme from a school play with her name printed in the cast list. A postcard of the Rock of Cashel she'd bought on a geography trip. A pebble in the shape of a heart. One Christmas, Ray had brought a set of battery-operated fairy lights. Claire could still see the tiny pinpricks of glitter in the darkness when they reached the gate and looked back.

People said there was no such thing as platonic friendship but Ray and Claire proved them wrong. When she didn't have a boyfriend to bring to her deb's dance, Ray had bought a tuxedo in Oxfam and hired a grumpy man in a Mercedes to chauffeur them to the hotel. When she finally did have boyfriends she'd still come home to find him sitting on the sofa watching TV with her dad.

After the band got their record deal and Ray moved to London, Claire thought she had lost him, the way she'd lost Nick, but he called her every week and emailed her and sent her kitsch post-cards from every city he played. He'd even written a song about her, which was sweet and kind of embarrassing. It had been Smoke Covered Horses' biggest hit.

'I can't eat any more of this hippy-dippy shit!' Ray pushed away the plate of hummus and crackers. 'Do you have any cereal?'

Claire went over to the cupboard and found a box of Straw-berry Clusters. 'Declan's getting married,' she said without turn-ing around, 'to Emma Lacey.'

Ray still enjoyed elaborate fantasies about killing Declan and Emma for what they'd done to Claire. She'd been in tatters when he persuaded her to move in here three years ago. He tried to keep his voice level. 'How do you feel about that?'

Claire picked a piece of freeze-dried strawberry out of the box and let it melt on her tongue. 'Better than I thought I would.'

'Fuck Declan Brady and Emma Lacey,' Ray said. 'Steve Soder-bergh is going to see you in *The Spaniard* and put you in *Ocean's Fifteen* and you're going to marry Ryan Gosling and have lots of little goslings and I'll never see you again. Don't do it, Claire.' He slid down on to the floor, crawled across the worn floorboards and grabbed her leg. 'Don't marry Ryan. I can't live here without you.'

'You won't have to.' She threw a cluster of toasted oats at him and he caught it in his mouth. 'You'll be out there on the Smoke Covered Horses' comeback tour, right?'

'Right.' He got up again. 'Course I will.'

She gave him a searching look. 'Any word from Chip?'

'Not yet. He's just taking his time crawling back.' Ray dusted his knees down and sat down again.

'Maybe you should get Paul Fisher to talk to him.'

'Mmmm.' Ray decided to move the conversation along. 'In other news, my cleaning lady, the lovely Lana, has gone back to Poland to open a pharmacy and marry a badger.'

Claire laughed. 'Are you sure?'

'That's what she said. Though I think she meant "a butcher". I hope so.'

Claire stared into the cereal box. 'I could do your cleaning.'

'What?'

'As part payment for the rent.'

'What?' Claire insisted on paying Ray five hundred euros a month for the basement flat. He always made sure it went back to her in dinners and lunches, movie tickets and petrol, but he wished she wouldn't pay him at all. 'Have you lost your little ginger mind? You don't have to pay me rent. I'm loaded. Every time "Asia Sky" plays on the radio I get fifty quid or something. I just resold the rights to the Japanese airline for an obscene amount of money. You are not doing my cleaning. You can make me a cup of tea, though.' He made a swipe for the cereal. 'No milk, two sugars.'

'I'd love to,' she said sweetly, 'but it's Tuesday. So according to The Contract, it's your turn.'

4

Kelly was due in Deansgrange at two o'clock to check on a
kitchen installation. She was queueing for a decaf in Sol on
Baggot Street when the rain started. 'Here we go again!' The
barista rolled his eyes. 'Will it ever stop?'

Three things about Dublin made Kelly mad. The awful coffee.
The incomprehensible one-way system. And the way everyone
acted as if wet weather was the end of the world. Apart from that,
she loved it, unconditionally. She'd loved it from the moment
she'd seen it from the plane. She remembered looking out the
window at the spread-out city between the patchwork of green
hills and the grey ripple of the sea and thinking, *This is where
we'll have our family*.

She loved the faded city squares and the little seaside villages
Nick took her to at the weekends. She loved that she could see
the Sugarloaf from their bedroom window and that it was dark
enough at night to watch the constellations wheeling across the
sky above their tiny garden. She loved the soft vowels and the
hard consonants and the way everyone talked to her, as if this was
a village, instead of a city. She paid for her coffee, went outside
and took off her sunglasses then opened the umbrella she always
kept in her purse. She'd grown up in Seattle, she was used to rain.

'The brilliant thing,' Kelly had told Nick when they'd finally
named the elephant that was their Tribeca apartment, 'is that
now that we're both freelance, we can live anywhere.'

The apartment was just one of a whole herd of elephants that
had stampeded through their lives after Nick had lost his job.
There wasn't time for him to build up a private business and they

couldn't afford to pay $4,000 dollars rent on her salary. The problem was that neither of them wanted to live in New York if they couldn't live in Manhattan. They sat by the Hudson on a hot summer evening playing Second Guesses where one person had to guess what the other one wanted.

'Boston?' Nick asked her. She shook her head. 'Chicago?'

'Think farther away.'

'San Diego?'

'Farther again.'

Nick laughed. 'Farther away than San Diego,' he pointed out, 'is Mexico.'

'I'm thinking Dublin.'

Nick stared at her for a long time. 'Are you sure?'

'It would be a fresh start and it's what I'd love, if you think we could be happy there.'

Nick curled his fingers around hers. 'I think we could be happy anywhere.'

Nick had meant what he said that day by the river but, sometimes, over the last year, he'd regretted saying it.

Starting a coaching business in a recession hadn't been easy. For the first few months he'd only had a trickle of clients. Then he started doing an agony uncle slot on Fish FM to build his profile but nothing much came of it. Now, after only two appearances on TV, his phone was ringing off the hook. This week, he'd been booked solid for private coaching sessions. If things kept going like this, he could seriously think about giving up Fish.

The radio slot hadn't worked out the way he'd hoped. Most problems just couldn't be solved in one minute. Dom Daly, the host of the show, treated the slot as a joke, and maybe it was just Nick's imagination, but since his two TV appearances he had been trying to make a fool of him.

This morning, along with a couple who were constantly bickering and a man whose fiancée was a compulsive liar, Nick had a caller who said that her boyfriend had 'a reptile dysfunction' and then hung up.

'Seeya later, alligator!' Dom laughed. 'Any advice, Doc Nick?'

'If Miriam thinks her partner has a *serious* problem,' he said patiently, 'she should tell him that.'

'Come on. There must be things your wife doesn't tell you.'

'No,' Nick said. 'We don't keep secrets from one another. We—'

'Going to have to cut you off there, *Doc*. That's all we have time for on "Problem Solved" today. The next song goes out to you and your lovely wife.'

It was 'Shiny Happy People' by REM.

It was pouring when Nick left the studio. He made a dash to the Drury Street car park, taking a short cut along King Street. It took him past the old Mercer's Street Hospital. It was an apartment block now but it still made him feel queasy, this pretty Victorian building. This was where his mother had been taken after the accident. He hurried past the doors, clutching his wet car keys in his clenched fist. How could he have thought that he could make a fresh start in a place that was so full of memories?

'Change partners!' the dance instructor yelled.

'I'm not changing you.' Nick kept one hand on Kelly's shoulder and the other on her narrow waist as the music started again. He looked at their reflections in the mirrored wall. The ordinary-looking guy with close-cropped sandy hair and the heart-stoppingly beautiful brunette smiling up at him. Dom at Fish was right. They were shiny, happy people.

'You look Brazilian in that dress,' he shouted over the sudden blare of salsa music.

Kelly gave him a mischievous look. 'I look Brazilian out of it, too.'

'You're full of surprises.'

'I have another surprise for you,' she grinned up at him.

'Change partners!' the instructor called, again.

'Later!' Kelly mouthed over her shoulder as she danced away with a man in a grey jumper.

Date Nights were Kelly's idea. One night out every month devoted to romance and honeymoon sex. She did the planning. Nick never knew whether he was going to wind up at a Thai cookery class or a French film or in the private steam chamber of a spa. He watched her now, dancing gracefully away from him and wondered what else she had up her sleeve.

'Hello.' A woman in her thirties with lank blonde hair was standing in front of him and he took her in his arms. 'I think you're amazing,' she yelled over the music, 'on TV.' He spun her round and she landed, heavily, on his foot. 'Sorry!' To his surprise, she looked as if she was going to cry.

'It's OK,' he said.

She shook her head and pulled away. 'I thought it would help if I could talk to you but it won't.'

They juddered to a halt and stood still in the circle of spinning dancers. 'What is it?' Nick asked her. She was taller than Kelly, they were almost eye-to-eye but she wouldn't look at him.

'I've been having some problems in my marriage.' She had to say it twice so he could hear her.

'You can work on that—' he began.

'I did everything I could and then—' The music stopped suddenly. 'I had an affair,' she shouted into the sudden silence. Every head turned in their direction. She flushed and bolted for the door.

Nick caught up with her in the hallway outside. She was tugging her coat off a peg. 'I'm sorry. I don't know why I told you that.'

'Have you told your husband?'

A tear ran down her cheek and dripped off her chin. 'If I did, he'd never forgive me.'

'If you want to keep your marriage, you have to take that risk. You have to be completely honest with him.'

'I have to go.'

'What's your name?'

'Roisin.'

Nick pushed his card into her hand. 'Come and see me anytime. On your own or with your husband. No charge.'

'Do you think this is going to happen a lot?' Nick asked Kelly as they got to her Beetle. This was the third time he'd been recognised this week.

Kelly tossed him the keys and slid into the passenger seat.

46

'Do I think what's going to happen a lot?' She crossed her long legs. 'You and I sneaking off to a hotel for hot sex?'

'You're kidding me?'

'Breakfast is not included but everything else,' she gave him a wicked smile, 'comes free.'

Claire parked Mossy outside the gate in case he got stuck in reverse and sat looking at her dad's house. It looked even worse than it had three weeks ago, on her birthday. The driveway was speckled with dandelion clocks and new shoots of ivy had crept across the living-room window and swallowed up most of the old surgery sign that still hung on the wall above the converted garage.

Mr Cunningham was in the garden next door deadheading his roses. Claire's heart sank. The Dillons had never got on with their neighbours. Her mum used to call them the 'Cunning Hams'. She got out and walked up to the front door as quietly as she could.

'Claire,' a voice behind her said while she was rummaging for her keys. 'Where do you live these days?'

She turned around. Mr Cunningham had walked over to the wall.

'Monkstown,' she said brightly.

'Do you have a garden?'

Ray had a Zen pebbly thing going on at the front of the house and she had a scraggy patch of nettles at the back. 'Sort of.' She shifted her bag to her other hand and scrabbled in her pocket for her key.

'Really? Would you like me to come around in the morning and jump over your wall and leave a huge turd on your lawn?' Mr Cunningham asked.

Claire stared at him. Was there a right answer to this? 'Um. No?'

'I didn't think so.' Mr Cunningham glared at her. 'But that's what your father's dog does on my lawn, Claire. Every single bloody morning. Maybe you'd have a word with him. He refuses to answer the door when I try.'

Claire's dad didn't like surprise visits but he hardly ever answered the phone and she worried about him more now that he was retired, so every couple of weeks she pretended that she was just passing and he pretended to believe her.

Sometimes, she just stayed for a cup of tea, but tonight they split an omelette and a plate of Jaffa Cakes, which was all her dad had really eaten for years, and watched TV. They sat through a long report about the impact of deregulation on the European postal system and in between statistics about universal service and uniform pricing Claire thought about all the questions she would never ask him. 'How did you and Mum meet?' 'Was it love at first sight?' 'What did you love about her most?'

Her parents had been married for eleven years when her mum died but they had still been crazy about one another. Her mum would pass her dad's chair and just drop into his lap and kiss him. He would get embarrassed but Claire loved to see them like that.

She remembered music from the record player floating up from downstairs long after she'd been put to bed. Once she crept down and saw her parents slow-dancing in the living room. Her father still had all his clothes on but her mother was barefoot and wearing only a tiny white slip. This was private, Claire understood, like her mum's surgery and the time she woke up to hear her mum giggling on the landing and saw her dad carrying her into their bedroom in his arms.

At exactly nine o'clock, there was a thud at the door and her dad opened it. Dog was so long that he seemed to enter the room in sections, like a bendy bus, carrying one of the leather slippers Claire had given her dad for Christmas in his mouth. He folded himself up on the carpet, dropped the slipper and stared at the television.

'I'm sorry,' her dad said, 'he has to watch the news.'

'Why?' Claire shuffled along the sofa to get as far away from Dog as possible.

'I've never been able to figure it out but even when I'm upstairs he comes up at six and at nine and makes me come down to switch it on.' Her dad changed channels as the intro ended and the camera cut to a newsreader with an impassive face and a helmet of blonde hair. 'I think he has a soft spot for Anne Doyle.'

Claire brought the plates out to the kitchen and went upstairs to wash her hands. The door to Nick's old room was open. Her dad had moved his drawing desk in here after Nick went to the States. There were hundreds of old storyboards mounted on stiff boards and stacked around the wall. Claire picked one up. It showed key frames from an ad for soup. Eight beautifully drawn illustrations of a family sitting round a dinner table, the boy and the girl smiling, the dad waiting with his spoon in his hand, the mum ladling soup into his bowl.

Her own mum had hardly ever been there at dinnertime. She'd go into her surgery first thing in the morning and sometimes she was still working when Claire went to bed. 'You'll see her in the morning,' her dad used to say. It was agony knowing that her mum was in the house but not being allowed to see her.

Sometimes, Claire used to make her own hospital in the hall in front of her mum's surgery door. She'd line her dolls up and cover them with toilet-paper sheets. Her mum had given her an old stethoscope to play with and she used to press the silver disc against the door, trying to hear her mother's voice. Once her dad came in from the garden and found her there. He squatted down till he was at her level. 'You know what private means, don't you?' he asked her quietly. 'It means you're not allowed to disturb your mother when she's busy.'

'I know.' As Claire tugged the stethoscope off it caught in her hair. 'But I miss her.'

He untangled the stethoscope, carefully. 'I'm planting sweet peas and I need someone to talk to them nicely so they'll grow.'

'I'm too busy,' Claire explained, 'with my patients.'

He looked at her dolls. 'I think they're asleep. Maybe you could leave them just for a minute.'

'Maybe.'

Her dad took her hand and they went out into the garden. She remembered how tall he had seemed then. The scratchy feel of his gardening glove. The way the bright sunshine made her eyes squinty. A robin flew down and perched on the lowest branch of the chestnut tree.

'You know what he's thinking about?' her dad asked her.

'Worms?'

'He's thinking that your finger is just the right size to make a hole for a sweet pea seed.'

He took her finger and showed her how push it into the damp earth. When she pulled it out, there were little black crumbs of soil stuck to her skin. He shook a seed into her hand and she dropped it into the hole. 'Now we have to think of the right thing to say to make it grow.'

Her dad had gone up to his room when Claire came out of the bathroom. 'Bye, Dad,' she called as she passed his closed door.

'Safe home now,' he said. It was what he used to say to Ray, when he was going back across the road to his house. 'Say foam!' Ray still said to her sometimes, and it always made her smile.

She went downstairs and found her jacket in the kitchen. Her dad had slipped an envelope with a hundred euros into the pocket. 'For your birthday,' he'd scribbled on the flap. She went back out to the car and switched on her phone before she started the engine.

Five texts from Ray, two missed calls from her agent, one voice message.

'Lorcan here. I was putting together some headshots for a hair care ad and I stuck in one of you and you've been picked as a featured extra. Somebody up there seems to be looking after you.'

'I'm not a machine.'

The man sitting in the cream armchair opposite Nick had shredded a Kleenex tissue into a hundred little pieces. 'I can't spend eight hours with the kids every day and just flick on the adult switch when you walk in the door. I don't work like that.'

'You don't work at all!' his wife shouted. 'I'm the one who's chained to a desk for ten hours a day while you're at home fucking finger-painting.'

Nick held a hand up. 'I don't think either of you can hear one another right now. If you can't seem *to listen,* what you have to do is *Two Listen.* One of you talks for two minutes. One of you listens and repeats, word for word, what's been said. Then you swap over.'

By the end of the session, it had all come out. All the little resentments first and then the underlying pain. His shame that he wasn't the breadwinner. Her fear that she was going to miss seeing her kids grow up.

Nick could tell they were afraid that the ceasefire would disappear as soon as they left the room. It happened. So he gave them three We-Fit assignments. Affirmations to say alone and together. A massage exercise. A questionnaire to fill out and share.

'Thank you,' they said together, as they left.

'It was a pleasure,' Nick said and he meant it. Nothing beat fixing other people's problems. It was the best feeling in the world.

Coming to live in Ireland was supposed to reduce her stress levels, Kelly thought as she closed her laptop, not increase them. She had spent the morning trawling around three architectural salvage yards trying to find a Belfast sink. She'd driven to Rathmines to pick up some fabric samples. Then she'd taken the M50 out to IKEA to return two rugs a client had rejected.

It was great that Nick's business was finally picking up because she was ready to take a break from all this. She closed her laptop, curled up on the sofa and switched on the TV to catch Nick's slot on the OO show.

Every time Kelly picked up an Irish magazine, Oonagh and Owen Clancy were plastered across a double page spread talking about his hair transplant or her body issues but the only body issue Oonagh seemed to have today was that she was wearing another dress that was at least one size too small.

'So! Let's cut to the nitty-gritty, Nick.' Oonagh was purring. 'What about sex? I mean, does it matter?'

Kelly felt a tiny twinge of possessiveness. Nick looked at Oonagh levelly. 'It depends. If you're having sex, it doesn't matter much. If you're not, it matters a lot.'

Kelly grinned. That was what she loved about Nick. He was just so straight down the line.

She had so nearly not met him that it scared her. Her roommate Haru had booked a self-help seminar called 'Your Future Starts Here', then she'd caught flu and given her ticket to Kelly instead. It was way over on West 34th Street and it turned out to be a lot of New Age waffle about how you create your own reality and how the only thing to fear is fear itself. Kelly planned to leave at lunchtime and kill Haru later.

'Let's do a little exercise before we break up,' the facilitator said. 'I want you to walk up to someone in the room and ask them any question as long as you're a hundred per cent sure the answer will be no.'

Kelly was seriously tempted to walk up to her and say, 'Can I get a refund?' when a guy came over and stood in front of her. He was older. Five or six years at least, and he wasn't her usual type. He looked Irish with those freckles and that sandy hair, but half the people in New York looked Irish so it was a surprise when she heard his voice.

'Will you have dinner with me?' It was the accent that did it.

'Um,' she said, looking into his eyes. They were warm and brown and direct. 'OK.'

He laughed. 'You were supposed to say "no".'

'Ask me something else.'

'Do you have any idea how pretty you are?'

'No,' Kelly lied.

She watched now while Nick taught the guest couple how to Hug Until Close and then do the Chakra Sexercise. Even Owen, who had been gazing at his fingernails since Nick started to speak, looked interested.

'*Do* try this at home,' Oonagh beamed to camera when he'd finished. 'Thanks to our coach on the couch, Nick Dillon. And thanks for all your calls saying how much you're enjoying We-Fit. Coming up next, Coco the psychic cocker spaniel and a disturbing report on human trafficking. Don't go away now!'

'Can you hang around?' The production assistant caught up with Nick in the corridor. 'She wants to see you on her own after the show,' her eyes widened, 'in their dressing room.'

A little ribbon of anxiety unravelled in Nick's stomach. He'd thought his slot had gone well but maybe he'd been wrong. 'I am calm and relaxed,' he told himself. 'All is well in my world.'

'Word of advice?' The runner made a face. 'Don't sit on the sofa.'

The room was tiny and chaotic. The dressing table was

cluttered with make-up bottles, empty paper cups and plates containing half-eaten snacks. Oonagh was sitting on the arm of the sofa, eating Ladurée macaroons out of a box. She was biting each one in half then dropping the other half into the bin.

'New diet,' she mumbled in her off-screen accent. 'Half the calories. Half the fat. Sit!'

Owen's suit was thrown over the only chair so Nick had no choice but to sit on the sofa beside her. He lowered himself down gingerly.

'I'm not going to bullshit you,' Oonagh said through a mouthful of macaroon. 'The bad news is you can forget about your slot turning into a regular thing.'

Nick's heart sank.

'It's not you. It's the whole show.' Oonagh sighed. 'The station budgets are about to take another hammering and I don't think we're going to escape. The good news is,' she picked out a pistachio macaroon and smiled at it, 'I've got a parachute. I've been talking to a UK production company about a really exciting new project. It's a reality TV show franchise that's going to roll out on Channel 5 next spring and, if it gets the ratings, it'll go to the States.'

Nick felt a prickle of irritation. He liked Oonagh but she was self-obsessed. It was just like her to ramble on about how great her own career prospects looked when he was about to be fired.

'The working title is *Relationship Rescue*.' Oonagh peeled off a strip of fake eyelashes from one eye and stuck it to the macaroon box. 'The idea is to reunite couples who have split and hook them up with counsellors and coaches to try to resolve their problems. At the end, they get to decide whether to make a go of it again. They approached me and Owen to co-present but the producers have gone off him big time. Would you be interested in coming on board?'

It took a second to sink in. Oonagh wasn't firing him. He thought she might be offering him a job. 'Wow! As what?'

'Co-presenter and lead coach? I won't have the final say but I'd like to put you forward to Clingfilms.'

He stared at her. Clingfilms was a huge UK production company. 'But I don't have any real TV experience—'

'You're a natural, Nick. People love you. We had three hundred emails after your slot last week. Our previous record was two hundred the time Owen got his back waxed live on air.' She peeled the eyelashes off her other eye. 'And most of those were complaints. What do you say?'

Nick was still struggling to take it in. 'I need to think about it.'

Oonagh laughed, expelling a cloud of tiny green crumbs. 'About what? The chance of getting the We-Fit message out to millions of people instead of the pathetic little *OO* show audience?'

Nick's mind was racing. A UK profile would give him an amazing platform for a series of We-Fit seminars. He could write a book. 'But what about Owen?'

'Oh, he'll go thermonuclear.' Oonagh sighed. 'But the truth is, he never really had a chance. He's sixty-three and, as you might have already noticed, he thinks any kind of therapy is,' she impersonated Owen's booming baritone, 'a pile of shite.'

'I thought he was fifty-five?'

'You haven't seen him naked,' Oonagh said, dryly. 'Are you interested or not?'

'I'll have to discuss it with Kelly—'

'You can't discuss it with anyone. I'm breaking my non-disclosure agreement even mentioning this to you.'

'I can't do that—' Nick began.

'Why?'

'Kelly and I don't have any secrets from one another.'

Oonagh bit into a raspberry macaroon. 'It would only be for a couple of weeks.'

'I wouldn't feel OK about not telling her.'

'Fine.' Oonagh closed the Ladurée box and licked her fingers. 'Let's just forget this conversation happened.'

Nick swallowed. An opportunity like this might never come along again. 'Hang on, just give me a second.'

'You have about twenty-nine,' Oonagh said, 'before Owen comes back from the canteen, finds you here and does his King Kong impersonation.'

Nick stood up. His heart was racing. 'OK,' he said, 'do it, put me forward.' Kelly was his biggest supporter. She'd understand.

5

Kelly opened the fridge to get a bag of salad leaves for lunch. The cake she'd made for Claire was still there, sitting on the middle shelf covered with Saran Wrap. She took it out and put it on the table. It was too pretty to throw away. She peeled the wrap off, picked off the black marzipan stiletto and remodelled it into a black daisy with a red centre then she wrapped the cake up again and got her laptop and her jacket.

Niamh and Rory had been Kelly's first Irish clients. They had hired Kelly to redecorate their Regency house in Blackrock. She had taken the ferry to Brittany with Niamh and spent three days scouring the markets and they'd bonded over sofas and tables and chandeliers. She was so close to Nick that there wasn't really room in her life for friends, but it was fun to have another couple to hang out with from time to time. She hadn't seen them much over the last three months. They had adopted a little Vietnamese girl and they'd had their hands full. Today, Kelly knew, was her third birthday.

Niamh's face lit up when she opened the door. She had finger paint on her face and flour on her wrap-around dress. 'Come in!'

'I can't. I just wanted to drop this over.' Kelly handed over the cake.

'Wow! Linh will love it. Just come in for a minute. I've been dying for you to meet her!'

A tiny figure in a tutu flashed past the kitchen door. 'I'd love to, sweetie,' Kelly said. 'But I've got a meeting.'

'Well, let's get together for a walk soon, the four of us.' Niamh's face broke into a happy smile. 'I mean the five of us. I'm still getting used to that!'

The bell gave a little jangle as Kelly pushed the door open.

'Do you need any help?' A girl smiled up at her from behind a Venetian mirrored desk.

'Just looking. Oh, this is lovely.' Kelly picked up a dusky rose crew-neck cotton sweater with tiny mother of pearl buttons.

'Isn't it?' the girl stood up. 'It's from the Autumn collection.'

Along with the rose there was a delicate oyster and a pale blue. Ten minutes later, the girl was wrapping all three in tissue and Kelly was handing over her business credit card. She regretted it the moment she left the shop. Her hand was clammy around the ribbon handles of the bag. They were supposed to be watching what they were spending. Nick would be horrified if he ever found out she'd blown nearly two hundred dollars like this. She'd have to hide the bag with the others.

Eilish was dancing around the tiny room that served as a kitchen, a living room and a study area for Holly. 'Hair we go! Hair we go! Hair we go!' She shimmied past the desk to light the candles on the mantelpiece.

'Stop!' Claire put her fingers in her ears. 'Enough with the awful hair jokes.'

'Sorry! I just can't get my head,' Eilish tossed her black bob, 'around the fact that we're both getting thirteen hundred euros for one day's work!' She salsaed into the kitchen, pulled a bottle out of the fridge and danced back to fill their glasses, then raised hers in a toast.

'You gave yourself a year to get your acting career back on track and look what you've done in less than a month.'

Claire smiled. 'You've done pretty well yourself!'

After Lorcan had told Claire she'd been cast in the hair care ad, Eilish had door-stopped him until he'd sent her headshot over to the ad agency and today she'd had a call to say she'd been cast too. So tonight they were celebrating with Aldi's finest cava and Eilish's notoriously decadent demerara meringues. But, first, they had to work their way through her Provençal onion tart and her salmon with sugarsnap peas and dill pistachio pastou.

Eilish leaned over the cooker and peeked into a sauté pan. 'Eat your heart out, Nigella! But slow-cook it in Coke first, then dip it in seventy per cent chocolate and don't forget to lick your fingers afterwards.'

Claire's phone rang halfway through the main course. It was Ray. 'I don't like Prosecco,' he said. 'Does that make me anti-secco?' There was a lot of clattering in the background. 'Come upstairs. I've got a little surprise for you. Actually, it's a sizeable surprise.'

'I'm over in Eilish's.' Claire put down her fork. 'She's made dinner to celebrate the hair thing.'

'You've eaten?' Ray sounded disappointed.

'We're eating now.' Claire made a pleading face. Eilish rolled her eyes and then nodded reluctantly. 'Do you want to come and join us?'

'No thanks. I have a . . . takeaway.' There was a loud crash in the background.

'What's that?'

It was Ray's takeaway. It had woken up and it was trying to get out of the sink.

Ray needed to find something really special to celebrate Claire getting the hair ad, and as he was walking along Chatham Street it hit him. A lobster. There was only one left on the pile of crushed ice in the window of the fish shop. It was huge and blue-black with glassy eyes on stalks and rubber bands around its massive claws. A leg that looked as though it was supposed to still be attached lay nearby.

The fishmonger picked it up and waved it at him. 'They like to scrap,' he said fondly. 'Tell you what, as you're a Smoke Covered Horse,' he winked, 'I'll give you five euro off and I'll throw in the leg.'

He whistled the opening bars of 'Wish You Were Her' as he wrapped the struggling lobster up in newspaper and moved on to 'Pretty Stupid' as he tried to wrestle it into a plastic bag. 'It's a shame you fellas decided to call it a day. I was hoping for a reunion.'

'Never say never.' Ray took out his wallet.

'Really?' The fishmonger looked pleased. 'That's not what Chip

Connolly said. I had him in here last week. He bought a lovely bit of hake.'

'Yeah?' Ray tried to sound casual. 'What did he say?'

'I said "Any chance of the Horses getting back together?" and he said "Over my effing dead body".' The fishmonger handed over the thrashing bag. 'Maybe it was "Over my dead effing body" but you get the general sense.'

The lobster had calmed down by the time Ray got it home, but while he was on the phone it had livened up again. It had torn its way out of the bag and managed to escape from the sink. It came limping towards Ray now across the draining board, one big claw held up, like Sylvester Stallone in *Rocky*.

'Got to go, Claire.' Ray hung up, threw a towel over the lobster and shoved it into the freezer. He'd read somewhere that was supposed to slow its blood down. He poured himself a glass of Prosecco. What was he supposed to do with the bloody lobster now? He didn't want to cook it, he felt too sorry for it. Could he keep it alive for the weekend and bring it back to the shop? What would he feed it? What did lobsters eat?

'Fish, clams, whelks and smaller, weaker lobsters,' according to Google. Ray looked at the abandoned leg in the sink. Maybe the lobster wouldn't know it was his own leg if Ray cooked it first.

'Promise me that the first thing you'll do when you get paid is get out of Ray's basement and get a place of your own.' Eilish refilled their glasses with the last of the cava. 'The whole *Upstairs Downstairs* thing is wrong on so many levels.'

Claire nibbled a sugarsnap pea. 'I feel bad about just leaving him there on his own.'

Eilish snorted. 'Do you think he'll feel bad about leaving you there when the band gets back together and he swans off for another seven years?'

Claire was beginning to wonder whether that was going to happen at all.

Eilish refilled their glasses. 'Look, I know Ray's charming and he's generous and he was there for you after you broke up with Declan but—'

'What?'

'Do you think that any self-respecting guy, say that gorgeous man you met on *The Spaniard*, is going to put up with an ex-rock star texting you every fifteen minutes and turning up in the middle of the night in his pants?'

'And a T-shirt.'

Eilish shook her head. 'It's Peter Pan and Wendy. As long as you have Ray, you don't need to have a relationship. You don't have to take risks or get hurt. Sometimes I wonder if you think you deserve to be happy at all.'

Claire stood up and went into the kitchen to get a glass of water.

'I'm sorry,' Eilish said softly. 'It's just that you're your own worst enemy, Claire. Look at the way you handed Declan to Emma.'

Claire wheeled around. 'They went behind my back.'

'You *let* him go off for all those little assignations with her. This is Emma Lacey who used to ice her nipples for auditions. Who'd get up on a cracked plate if she thought she'd get a credit.'

Claire flushed. She *had* known. But she'd felt the way she always did when something bad was happening. Frozen to the spot, powerless to stop it.

'It's been three years and you've had, what, two one-night stands?'

'One of them was a five-night stand, the other one was a three-night stand.'

Eilish twisted the stem of her glass and tiny prisms of light from the candles danced, like fireflies, around the walls.

Claire sighed. 'I thought this was a celebration?'

'All I want to say is don't waste another three years in that gloomy basement watching box sets and playing word games with Ray Devine.' She stood up. 'Lecture over. Now I'm going to wash out my mouth with demerara meringues.'

After he'd finished the second bottle of Prosecco, Ray opened the freezer door cautiously. Rocky was wedged between a frozen pizza and a bottle of Absolut. He glared out with his weird stalky eyes, the big claw raised defiantly. Ray sighed. This wasn't how he imagined tonight would turn out.

'Bit late to be building a sandcastle, isn't it?' the taxi driver said on the Merrion Road. Ray was in the back with Rocky and a bottle of Absolut in a bucket between his knees. He was too drunk to remember why he'd brought the spade but it had seemed like a good idea at the time.

'You can drop me here!' He pointed at the side gate to the park. The plan had been to release Rocky on the beach but this would do.

The park was deserted and the pond was silvered with moonlight. Nights like this reminded Ray of being young and staying up late with Claire. Nights when they'd drive her mother's clapped-out old car up the Dublin mountains with enough money for one pint between them. They'd sit on the bonnet for hours after the Blue Light had closed looking down at the glitter of the city. Anything had seemed possible on nights like that.

Claire was never interested in fame, performing was a kind of disappearing act for her, but Ray had known it was going to happen for him and it had. But what if it didn't happen again? What if the Horses never reformed? What was he supposed to do? Write jingles for the rest of his life?

He put the bucket and spade down and used the light of his phone to take a check on Rocky. 'Hang on in there, mate!' He took a mouthful of slightly fishy Absolut. The gate to the playground was closed but it wasn't locked. He left the bucket on the path and went in and climbed on to a swing, standing on the seat and looping the chains around his arms, the way he had on the cover of *Special and Different*. All the other Horses had been in the background, out of focus, on the roundabout.

Ray had been a mediocre guitar player but his gravelly voice and his looks made him the perfect front man and Chip Connolly knew it. He'd started 'No Horses' in '98 and they were still going nowhere when Ray joined in 2002. The first thing Ray did was change their name. Two years later, they had a deal, they were touring Asia and Australia, and the music press was calling them 'The Irish Goo Goo Dolls' and 'Forty Shades of Green Day'.

As far as Chip Connolly was concerned, he was the talent

and Ray was just the pretty boy. So right from day one, it pissed him off that Ray was the centre of attention, and he found hundreds of ways to show it. 'Death by paper cuts,' Claire used to call it.

'Our music is a collaborative process,' he told the *NME* once. 'I write the songs and wait for Devine to stop looking in the mirror long enough to sing them.' Ray particularly loved that quote because even though the Horses' second and third singles charted in eleven countries, it was the one song that Ray had written that everyone remembered.

It spent twenty-six weeks in the UK top fifty. It went platinum. It made Smoke Covered Horses famous and then, two years later, it broke them up. It was called 'Asia Sky' and he'd written it for Claire.

It had come from nowhere when he was on an AsiaSky flight from Tokyo to London after the 2006 Asian tour. The Horses had played twenty-four cities and Chip had made sure that Ray was miserable in every single one. Talking to Claire on the phone was the only thing that held him together. In Tokyo, he had booked himself through to Dublin and she had promised to get rid of Declan Brady for the night and meet him off the plane. At 35,000 feet, the words had come to him so fast that he had to scribble them on a cocktail napkin.

Bangkok and Tokyo
Another night. Another show.
6,000 miles of Asia sky,
That's all there is between us.

Gravity and atmosphere.
Suburban summers, teenage fears.
Friendship that has lasted years
That's all there is between us.

And I'm so glad I'm flying home to you.
AsiaSky takes off into the blue.
Till I'm so high that I can see it's true
The world is small when the world's just me and you.

'Oh Christ, this is bad,' Chip had sneered when Ray played it. They were back in London, locked into the studio, working on their third album. 'This is so fucking bad, James Blunt wouldn't even use it to wipe his arse.' He refused to have anything to do with it and Happy and Godot went along with him, the way they always did. So Ray went to Paul Fisher and got the go-ahead to record the song with session musicians. It was the first single from the album and it was the song the fans screamed for on the next tour. Chip used to turn his back when he was playing it. For Ray, that was a cut too far.

When the airline AsiaSky wanted to buy the rights to use the song in their ads, he sold them, just to piss Chip off. It worked. Chip had real tears in his eyes at the emergency meeting in Tarantula Records.

'You sold us out for a fucking advert! How could you do that? You had no right.'

'Yes I did!' Ray was lounging on Paul Fisher's leather sofa. He had exclusive rights. Publishing and recording. 'I offered you guys a split, but you told me where to shove it. Remember?'

Chip leapt to his feet and lunged at him across the glass coffee table, and Happy had to grab him to stop him punching Ray. 'It's over, do you hear me?' Chip yelled, struggling to get free. 'I never want to see you again, you talentless fame whore.'

Fisher had tried to get them all to sit back down and work it out but Ray had refused until he had an apology from Chip. He could take 'fame whore' but he wasn't taking 'talentless'.

The wooden seat of the swing creaked under Ray's feet. Way off, over the humpy hill of Howth, a plane was coming in to land like a slowly falling star. Ray had been waiting for Chip to say 'sorry' for three years now. Maybe Claire was right. Perhaps it was time to get Paul Fisher involved. He was flying to London for a meeting with Sounds Familiar on Monday. He'd call into Tarantula, let Fisher him take him out to lunch and ask him to broker a truce. This time next year, he could be back out there.

'Hello Blackrock,' he called, into the darkness of the deserted park, 'are you ready to party?'

*

62

Claire and Eilish were finishing their second helping of dessert when Eilish's phone pinged. She squinted at the screen. 'How sharper than a serpent's tooth it is to have a thankless child.'

'King Lear is texting you?' Claire grinned.

'It's Holly. She was supposed to be coming home this evening but she's staying over at her dad's. Again. I've hardly seen her this summer. I've only got one more year before she goes away and she hates me.'

'She doesn't hate you!' Claire picked up the hand-painted mug that Holly had made when she was seven. 'She thinks you're the "Best Mum in the Wold".'

'What is a "wold" anyway?'

'I think it's a grassy upland or a hill.'

Eilish sighed. 'I can't believe that she's the same age I was when I had her. Where did the last seventeen years go?' She stood up and began to clear the table. 'Promise me you'll have kids, Claire. And that you won't wait till you're forty and desperate and have to call on the services of Ray Devine. I'm sure you two have some kind of agreement about that.'

'We don't.' They did. It was called the Desperation Clause.

'God!' Eilish put the plates down again. 'I've suddenly had a vision of Ray Devine,' she began to laugh, 'as a dad. Can you imagine him pushing a buggy in his leather trousers and his sunglasses?' She stared at Claire. 'At a mums-and-toddlers group,' she squeaked, 'singing "The Wheels on the Bus!" with that pouty look he used to put on in the videos.'

Rocky was lying at the bottom of the bucket. He waved his claw feebly but the fight seemed to have gone out of him. Ray sang the Rocky theme tune, changing the lyrics to 'The Eye of the Thai Girl' as he lifted him out of the bucket. He put him carefully on to the shovel. As he slid Rocky into the pond, something huge and white detached itself from the far bank and propelled itself over to see what was going on.

It was a huge swan. It unzipped the moonlit water and bore down on Rocky, swiping at him with its beak. Ray grabbed the loose lobster leg and hurled it. The swan whipped around, distracted and behind it, Ray saw Rocky's claw raised in one last grateful salute before he sank into the water and disappeared.

Nick was involved in a complicated daydream about turning We-Fit into a series of seminars. He missed his turning and, before he realised what he was doing, he was taking the next left and saw, up ahead of him, the green-painted railings of his old school. Suddenly, he was eight years old again. He was rubbing the sleeve of his grey school jumper along the pebble-dashed wall, watching the other end of the road, waiting for his mum's green Citroën to appear, crossing his fingers that she wouldn't have brought Claire. Hoping that she wasn't going to honk the horn and flash the lights of the car when she saw him. Wishing she was like his friends' mothers. That she didn't always have to stand out.

He forced himself to focus on the bumper of the car in front. 'I put the past in the past,' he affirmed to himself. But affirmations didn't work so well, now that he was back in Dublin.

Kelly had laid the table in the garden. They sat outside eating Parma ham and fig salad and toasted flat bread and shared their day. So far, Nick had managed to keep his promise not to tell her about the Channel 5 show, but it was getting harder every day.

After dinner, Kelly went to work on some mood boards in the kitchen and he took his laptop into the living room to do the prep for the *OO* show he'd put off earlier.

It was a piece on resolving conflict. Kelly had come up with the idea of calling it 'Fight or Flight'. He typed up a quick intro. 'Instead of trading insults, imagine you are about to board a flight that's taking you and your partner into your future together. Imagine your luggage in the hold. What parts of your past would you pack? What would you leave behind?'

He stared at the screen but he was seeing himself and Kelly somewhere over Nova Scotia on a plane bound for JFK. Coming back to Dublin had been a mistake. He had grown up here but America was his real home. He missed the anonymity of the city and the contagious optimism of the country.

If he really had a serious chance of landing *Relationship Rescue*, it would be the perfect excuse to leave. The series would be shot in the UK. Kelly loved Dublin but she'd love London even more. And if the show was a success, if it went Stateside, it would be the perfect stepping-stone back to their old life in New York.

Kelly was so caught up in what she was doing that she didn't hear Nick come into the kitchen.

'Hey!' He put his hand on her bare shoulder.

She jumped. 'Nick! Don't creep up on me like that.'

'Sorry.' He put his arms around her. 'Are you OK?'

'I'm fine. It's just PMT.'

Nick had been hoping they could take a long shower and make love but this wasn't a good sign. 'Why don't we do a Chakra Connection? That'll relax you.'

'Sure.' She wriggled out from under his arms. 'I'll finish up here and see you upstairs in five.'

She waited till she could hear the sound of running water from the bathroom then she opened her laptop again and cleared her browsing history.

Nick put a finger on the crown of Kelly's head and she put her finger on his head. His hair was still damp from the shower. She stared into his eyes and wondered whether her Dundrum client's budget would stretch to Farrow and Ball paint. Elephant's Breath for the walls in the living room. Stony Ground for the skirting boards. Roman blinds. They'd hide the half-finished block of apartments on the other side of the street.

Nick moved his finger to her throat chakra and Kelly touched his Adam's apple lightly. It was sandpapery. He needed a shave. And she needed to get a bikini wax. She made a mental note to book one. She wondered if she had enough basil to make zucchini soup for tomorrow's supper.

Nick's hand drifted down to her heart chakra and she let her hand drop down onto his chest.

'Other side!' he whispered.

'Sorry!' she whispered back. If there wasn't enough fresh basil, she thought, she'd just use dried.

6

'Hey,' Kelly said as they drove down the tree-lined avenue to the river walk, 'what are you grinning about?'

Nick kept his eyes on the bumper of Rory's 4x4. 'I was just thinking about that trip we took up to New England to see the leaves.' He'd been thinking about the email Oonagh had sent him, this morning. Clingfilms had seen the tapes. They loved Oonagh and Nick's 'co-presenting chemistry'. They wanted to meet. It was probably just as well that Kelly had organized this walk in Powerscourt. He was so excited that, if they had been at home, he might have just blurted it out.

Still, his spirits sank at the thought of the next few hours. Niamh's heart was in the right place, but Rory was a pain in the arse. He had told Nick once that he'd cut his own balls off rather than go to a couples coach. 'If I'm going to be emasculated,' he'd snorted, 'I'd rather do it myself.'

But Rory didn't look like an ad for masculinity right now, squatting by the back door of his parked Lexus, trying to per-suade his toddler to get out of the car.

'Come on, sweetie,' he pleaded. 'Daddy drove all the way. All you have to do is take one ickle step.'

Linh peered down at the ground. 'Dirty!'

'They're just leaves, pumpkin.' Niamh wrung her hands. 'Do they have autumn?' she whispered to Nick. 'In Vietnam?'

'I wouldn't want to get *my* feet dirty if they were that pretty.' Kelly pointed at Linh's sparkly pink shoes. 'Tell you what? Why don't you let your daddy give you a piggyback?'

Linh looked at her imperiously from beneath her razor-sharp

fringe, but she put her arms up and let Rory swing her up on to his shoulders and they set out along the riverbank.

'You would not believe how heavy this child is,' Rory said to Nick, as if the weight of his daughter, like the square footage of his house and the size of his legal practice, was index-linked to his own importance.

Nick exhaled his irritation and imagined inhaling the beauty around him. The sunlight dappling the river, the silence of the woods, the squirrel darting down a tree trunk and crossing the path ahead of them.

'Doggy!' Linh shrieked, breaking the silence. She pummelled Rory's head with her tiny fists. 'Down!'

'It's not a dog,' Rory lifted her down but he held on to her arms. 'And it might have fleas.' She sank her teeth into his hand and broke free.

'Ouch!' Nick said.

Rory hid his wince under a smile. 'The funny part is Linh means *gentle spirit*.' He watched her chasing the squirrel. 'It's just the terrible twos.'

Wasn't she three, now? Nick remembered Kelly saying she'd dropped over a birthday cake. 'So how are you two coping with parenthood?' They looked exhausted, as if they hadn't slept for years.

'It's been hell for the last three months but, once she goes to pre-school, we'll get our lives back.'

'Right.' Nick remembered Claire wetting the bed when she was six. The nightmares that had woken her up every night for months when she was nine. The time, when she was ten, that she'd caught lice and he'd had to cut her hair. The mood swings when she was twelve. The months of tears when she was fourteen and he'd told her he was going to college in the States. You never got your life back when you had a child.

'How's show business?' Rory put his arm round Nick's shoulders.

'So far so good.'

'Should Doctor Phil watch his back? Niamh says you're pretty good but I'm not sure I trust her critical faculties.' Rory guffawed.

'She's at home all day. She probably means compared to the Teletubbies.'

Rory kept his arm draped over his shoulder as they walked along. Nick imagined it floating away and focused on Kelly. She was trying to distract Linh from the squirrel with a game of peek-a-boo.

'It's good to have the TV show as another string to your bow.' Rory kicked at some leaves. 'People are struggling to pay the mortgage. They haven't got money to throw away on therapy.'

Nick shrugged Rory's arm off. 'As a matter of fact,' he said, sounding angrier than he meant to, 'a drop in income means people can't afford to separate so they need couples counselling to keep their relationships on track.'

Rory guffawed. 'You tell yourself that, Doctor Nick, while me and all the other divorce lawyers laugh all the way to the bank.'

'I'm not a doctor,' Nick's heart was thudding under his sweat-shirt, 'and I didn't think anyone in this country was laughing all the way to the bank.'

'That's my point, pal. Kelly's business must be taking a hammering with the property slump. You might have to get the old breadwinner's hat out one of these days.' Nick felt his face heat up. He and Kelly had been living on her savings since they'd moved back to Dublin, she must have told Niamh. 'I'm just saying,' Rory spread his hands, 'it wouldn't hurt to be proactive. Write a book. Think about getting your own show.'

'I'm way ahead of you,' Nick snapped before he could stop himself. 'In fact, I might need you to look over a contract in the next couple of months.'

'Attaboy!' Rory grinned. 'Are we talking your own series?'

'I can't talk about it.' Nick said, before he could help himself.

Rory's eyes widened. 'Hang on! Is this something to do with a certain new relationship reality show that La Clancy might be hosting for Clingfilms?'

Nick shook his head but it was too late. He had a terrible poker face and Rory wasn't a lawyer for nothing.

'Have they put an offer on paper?'

'I haven't even spoken to them.' Nick tried, desperately, to backtrack. 'Look, I shouldn't have said anything. It's still up in the air.'

'My lips,' Rory mimed a zipping motion, 'sealed.'

Kelly linked her arm with Nick's as they walked back along the riverbank. 'Isn't Linh adorable?'

Nick watched the little girl running ahead of them, chasing a Highland terrier with a branch. 'She is,' he said, as an elderly woman with a walking stick stepped into Linh's path.

'Leave him alone!' she shouted. 'You horrible little girl.'

'Hey!' Rory jogged up to her. 'Don't talk to my daughter like that!'

She leaned down, picked the dog up and tucked him under her free arm.

'Want to play!' Linh stamped her sparkly foot.

'He doesn't want to play with *you*!'

'I told you not to shout at my daughter!' Rory squared his shoulders.

Nick hurried over. 'Let's just all take a deep breath here,' he said in a calm, even voice.

'This child is completely out of control.' The woman rounded on him. 'My dog has epilepsy and you,' a flicker of recognition passed over her face, 'are Doc Nick from television! I'm Mary.' She beamed. 'This is Twinkle. We think you're marvellous!'

'This keeps happening,' Kelly laughed after Mary had finally stopped telling Nick how marvellous he was and gone away.

'Better get used to that!' Rory grinned. Nick shot him a warning look but he pretended not to see it. 'It's going to get a lot worse when he's on Channel 5!'

'What I hear you say,' Nick said patiently, 'is that you feel hurt because I held this back from you. And angry because I didn't consult you before telling Oonagh I was interested in the show. And insulted because I told Rory about it and—'

'Betrayed.' Kelly picked at her salad. Her voice was so low he could hardly hear it. 'I feel betrayed.'

After they'd left Rory and Niamh, they'd driven over to Avoca for lunch. It was one of the places Kelly loved most and Nick was hoping they'd find a quiet table in the garden but it was buzzing with children and wasps.

'Betrayed,' Nick repeated. It was hard to remember all the things Kelly felt. *Offended. Upset. Shocked. Confused.* She had spent the last ten minutes listing them without looking at him at all, though the Two Listening exercise was very clear about maintaining eye contact. 'Is there anything else you want to share?'

She shook her dark head. 'I guess not.'

'I want to take full responsibility for all the pain I've caused you. We promised to tell one another everything. I broke the promise but I will never do that again.' He waited for a small boy who had crawled under their wooden table to emerge and run off before he went on. 'I'm sorry. Can you forgive me?'

Kelly nodded at the half-eaten avocado on her plate.

Nick felt a wave of relief and a prickle of excitement. It was out in the open now. They could talk about it. They could make plans. 'It's an amazing opportunity, you know. I mean, nothing might come of it but—'

'It is an amazing opportunity.' Kelly folded her napkin. 'But I'm not sure the timing is right.'

'The timing?' Nick said carefully. He didn't want to upset her again but what did time have to do with it?

'We have to factor our baby plans into the equation.'

They had agreed, when they moved to Dublin, that Nick would spend three years getting his career up and running before they started thinking about a family.

'I know we said that we'd wait three years before we started trying.' Kelly looked up at him for the first time since the river walk; her wide blue eyes were wet, she had a tiny smudge of mascara on one cheekbone. 'But everything has really taken off for you since the OO show. I think we should start trying right away.' She smiled at him.

A pulse of panic ticked in the back of Nick's throat. 'Can we look at the big picture for a second? This job would give us a chance to get our finances on the kind of solid footing we need before we start a family.' Her smile faded. 'This is a once-in-a-lifetime chance, Kelly. We've run through our savings. We're living in a rented house. We could afford to support a child at a stretch but if we wanted two—'

'Like we agreed.'

'Like we discussed, we could run into trouble.'

'But you're booked out with private sessions!'

'There are rumours that *OO in the Afternoon* is going to be cancelled, and if it is I'll be back to square one in the middle of a recession. People are struggling to pay their mortgages. They haven't got money to throw away on therapy.' He couldn't believe that he was quoting Rory.

A wasp landed on his hand. He wanted to swat it away but he sat perfectly still and, after a moment, it climbed on to Kelly's plate. She stared down at it, her lips pressed between her teeth.

'Honey, couldn't we just start trying anyway? In case we have a problem and we can't conceive.'

Nick leaned over and took her hand. 'You're thirty. We have all the time in the world.'

She nodded. 'Could you take the plates away before this little guy stings one of us.'

'Sure.' Nick kissed her fingertips, gathered their plates and carried them across the lawn to the café.

The wasp was circling a trickle of spilled salad dressing. Kelly picked up her water glass and turned it over, trapping it inside. She watched it fly against the glass, again and again, until, after a while, it stopped and began to crawl up and down the sheer sides instead still trying desperately to find a way out.

'Ray! My man!' Paul Fisher came out from behind his desk and gave Ray a bear hug. 'Looking good!'

'You too,' Ray lied. Paul was in his old rock and roll uniform. Faded jeans and Queens of the Stone Age T-shirt, but he still looked like an anaemic accountant.

Paul sat down again, his hand hovering over his phone. 'Can I get Carline to get you something? Coffee? A drink?'

'I'll wait till lunch, thanks.'

'Shit!' Paul smacked his forehead with his palm. 'You didn't get my message?'

Ray had switched his phone off in the Sounds Familiar meeting. 'No.'

'I've got a new signing coming in. Bloody boy band from Swindon. They're down in reception now. Whole building already stinks of Lynx.'

Ray shrugged. 'I'm around tonight. We could catch some dinner?' Paul shook his head. 'Or a drink.'

'No can do. I'll be with the kiddywinks.' Ray thought this might be the name of the boy band until he followed Paul's eyes to a framed picture of two small girls. 'I have twenty minutes, now,' Paul said cheerfully. 'What's on your mind?'

He fiddled with a paper clip while Ray explained. 'Listen, man. I'm all for a reunion. Have you seen the Facebook page? There's still a huge fan base out there, but I think the call would be better coming from you. Maybe if you got in touch with Chip and said sorry—'

'Sorry?' Ray got up and went to the window. Paul's office had a view of Soho that the clubbers never saw. Ray stared out at the chimney pots and the crooked lines of washing and the wilting pot plants in kitchen windows then he turned back to Paul. 'I didn't call *him* a "talentless fame whore".'

'You know what he's like.'

Ray did. Bitter, twisted, vindictive.

'You don't have to apologise if you don't want to, Ray. Just write another "Asia Sky",' he snapped his fingers, 'and I'll get you a solo deal. Simple.'

Except it wasn't. Ray had been trying to write another decent song for years and couldn't.

'Whatever you decide,' Paul stood up, 'my door is always open.' He was opening it now and Ray had no choice but to walk out through it.

Ray got into the lift and jabbed the button. He was shaking and his palms were clammy. The lift stopped at the fourth floor and a girl with a blonde pixie crop got in. Ray could feel her checking him out.

'It's you, isn't it?' the girl said. Why did they always have to say that? Of course it was him. Who else would he be? He gritted his teeth. 'I guess the disguise isn't working.'

She had a small, feline face that looked sort of familiar. 'It's Aisling,' she said. 'Ash. I work here. I mean . . .' She frowned. 'I did till about five minutes ago. I just quit.'

The lift stopped and they both got out and stood awkwardly in reception. A bunch of guys who looked about twelve years old were slouched on the sofas, watching music videos on a wall of old-fashioned Bush TVs.

'You don't remember me, do you?' The girl was staring up at him. 'I used to work in PR? I'm Ash. Irish Ash?'

A faint bell jangled in the back of Ray's head but he was too upset to hear it properly. 'Irish Ash!' he said. 'Course I remember you.'

Then, all of a sudden, he did. She used to have long hair. He had a murky recollection of going back to her flat once after a gig. He couldn't remember anything else except that her shower curtain had a pattern of very realistic goldfish. 'How are things?'

'Not so good. I'm just about to move back to Dublin.' She shook her head. 'It's so weird bumping into you, today, after all this time.' A tear streaked down her face. It hung on her chin for a moment and then dropped on to the front of her dress.

Jesus, Ray thought, this was all he needed. He put his hand on Ash's back and propelled her out through the glass doors on to Wardour Street. It was raining. She pulled a pack of Marlboro Lights out of her bag and her hands were shaking when he lit her cigarette for her.

Ray had thought he'd be unfolding a starched napkin and drinking champagne with Paul Fisher right now, not standing in the rain with some weepy girl he'd had a one-night stand with seven years ago. He needed to get drunk, he decided, very drunk. 'Do you want to get a drink?'

The pub was deserted and gloomy with a row of flashing slot machines. The beer-stained carpets stuck to the soles of Ray's shoes when he went to the bar. He ordered two double Jameson and Cokes and brought them over to where Aisling was sitting.

She picked out the straw and took a gulp of her drink. 'I'm just

73

having a bit of a weird time. I broke up with my fiancé last week. I resigned from my job, and now I have to go back to Dublin, where I know nobody, to live with my parents.'

Ray swallowed half of his whiskey in one sour gulp. 'You know me. I'll give you my number. We can meet up.'

She poked at the ice in her glass with a finger. 'Like you'll call me back.'

'Sure I will,' Ray said, though that was a lie.

'You didn't last time. I must have left about a hundred messages.'

Did she have any idea how many girls left messages on his machine back in those days? 'I'm sorry.' He finished his whiskey.

'I needed to talk to you.'

Ray signalled for another round. 'Talk to me now.'

She stared down at the greasy table while the barman made their drinks. A fly landed on the collar of her denim dress and then on the rim of her glass. She brushed it away. Then her eyes filmed over with tears again. She opened her bag. He thought she was looking for a tissue but she took out an iPhone and handed it to him.

The screensaver was a photograph of a kid, a little girl. 'She's beautiful.' Unlike most people's children, she really was beautiful with a heart-shaped face and a halo of dark hair and the most incredible blue eyes. 'Is she your daughter?'

Ash nodded. 'And yours.'

'What?'

'Her name is Willow. She's six.'

Ray dropped the phone onto the table. 'You tracked me down, to tell me *this*?'

'I had no idea till twenty minutes ago that I was ever going to see you again.'

Ray stared at her and then stared at the door. Imagining himself crossing the sticky carpet, pushing it open, standing out on the street taking a lungful of fresh air. But the whiskey had thickened his blood. He couldn't move.

'I don't even know why I told you.' Ash put her hand over her mouth. Her dark red nail varnish was chipped. 'I told her last week that my partner wasn't her real father. She asked me about you. When I saw you earlier it just seemed like, I don't know, fate or destiny or something.'

'Destiny?' Ray gave a hollow laugh.

Ash stuffed her phone back into her bag and stood up. 'Forget we met. Forget I told you.'

'How do I even know she's mine?' Ray called after her but she didn't turn around and he didn't need her to. There was only one other person he knew with eyes like the little girl in the picture.

Claire's second scene on *The Spaniard* didn't involve sheep or Emma Lacey but she was hoping that it would involve Shane. She spent most of the morning sitting in a shady spot in the courtyard waiting to be called, waiting for him to appear.

At lunchtime she finally saw him, sitting two tables away from her, eating on his own, his light brown head bent over a book. He didn't seem to notice her but she felt hyperaware of him, as if an invisible thread connected them.

When she was driven out to the location, he was the first person she noticed. He was standing by his Land Rover in a jumper and jeans, his tanned arms folded, talking to the first AD. She had just psyched herself up to talk to him when the director called her over to rehearse.

Her scene was short and simple. She had to stand at the door of a cottage and watch the actor who played her father being dragged away by two men. Her only line was 'He ain't here.' It was all over in four takes, but by then Shane had gone and it would be another five or six weeks before her next day on set.

She felt stupidly disappointed with herself all the way back to the base. 'Are you coming for a pint?' the wardrobe assistant asked when she was helping her out of her shepherdess costume. 'We all head up to Johnny Foxes on Fridays.'

All, Claire thought, pulling on her jeans and her T-shirt and slipping on her sneakers. 'Maybe.'

Johnny Foxes was halfway up the Dublin mountains. A rambling maze of interconnecting rooms jammed with antique Irish bric-a-brac. Claire finally found the cast and crew in the long bar down at the back. Shane was already there, standing against the far wall, in front of a display of scythes, talking to a group of rowdy actors. Claire fought her way into the crowd to the bar.

By the time she was served, Shane had moved away from the actors and was wedged into a corner between a rusty mangle and a Singer sewing machine, talking to a woman with her back to Claire. A woman with bare shoulders and a mane of honey-blonde hair. She stood on tiptoe to whisper something into his ear and Claire didn't need to see her face, she knew that it was Emma Lacey. Her heart did a queasy little flip, a kind of physical déjà vu. This was how it had all started with Declan. Little intimate chats, little whispered remarks. Claire put her untouched glass down and pushed her way through the crowd, then out into the corridor. She found an open door to the car park and sat down on a low whitewashed wall.

'Hey,' a voice behind her said. 'You're leaving in a hurry.' Shane was standing at the door of the pub. 'Are you OK? You're really pale.'

'I'm always pale.'

'Hang on, I'll get you a glass of water.' He went back into the pub.

She leaned back against the wall. He must have been watching her. He had come looking for her. Her phone buzzed; she slid it out of her pocket and read the text. 'Just landed. Need to see you. X-ray.'

She texted him back. 'Can't meet you. In Johnny Foxes—' Then her phone died before she could add an excuse.

'It's Claire, isn't it?' Shane was back. He sat on the wall and turned to look at her, the shadow of a smile at the corners of his wide mouth. 'I'm glad to see the sheep didn't leave any scars.'

She tried to think of something clever to say but all that came out was 'No.'

He looked away. 'Well, the view out here is definitely better than it was in there.'

'Yes,' she said. They sat for a while. Claire was used to the quickfire of conversations with Ray. The silence felt awkward and nervy. It made her aware of the sound of her own breathing and the muffled thud of her heart.

She looked out at the witch's-hat peak of the Sugarloaf and the distant navy ribbon of the Irish Sea and the criss-cross of jet trails in the fading blue sky, then she glanced down at Shane's hand. The band of white on his finger had faded a bit but it was still there.

His glass of Coke was almost empty and she had a horrible feeling that he might finish it and leave before she had a chance to let him know that she was interesting and interested. The best she could manage was, 'So you work with a lot of animals.'

'I grew up on a farm. What about you?'

'I'm not good with animals.'

'I meant does acting run in your family?'

'Oh! My dad's a retired illustrator. My mother was a doctor. My brother wanted me to do medicine but it didn't work out.'

Shane put his glass down on the wall. 'What does your brother do?'

'He's a life coach. We don't really get on.'

'Ah!' He looked at her for a second, then looked away. There was another long silence.

'What about you?'

'Parents, twin brother.'

'Are you close?'

Shane looked away. 'Finn was killed four years ago in a riding accident.'

'I'm so . . .' She used to hate it when people said this to her but now she realised there was nothing else to say. '. . . sorry.'

'Thank you.'

Claire looked at his profile in the dusk. 'But you still ride. I don't understand. How can you . . .'

'It's how I make sense of it.' He rubbed the palms of his hands on his jeans. 'How did you get into acting?'

'I used to be good at it.' Drama class had been like a holiday from herself. A few hours when she could lose herself in someone else's problems. She lifted her feet on to the wall and hugged her knees. 'I'm not sure I'm very good at it any more, though.'

'You looked pretty good to me.' He was flustered. 'In that costume.'

She pulled her sleeves down over her knuckles. 'I'm sure nobody wore anything like that in the sixteenth century.'

He kept his eyes on the view. 'If they did, I doubt they looked as beautiful in it as you did.'

Beautiful? Claire had missed beautiful by a series of tiny fractions that added up to a mile. The gap between her top front teeth, the little fleshy bump on the tip of her nose, the blur of her freckles, the obstreperous tangle of her hair. She had always felt awkward, all angles and edges, elbows and knees.

Unless she had a line of direction, she had never known what to do with her hands. She didn't know what to do with them now. She zipped her locket back and forth on its chain. 'Well,' she said, 'thank you.' She looked up and he was watching her. She saw his brown eyes move down to her mouth. She could feel his breath on her face. Her face was already tilting back, her eyes beginning to close when the door of the pub opened.

'What are you two doing out here in the dark?' It was Emma. She wrapped a pink pashmina around her bare shoulders and smiled at Claire. 'Hello, Claire. How's Ray?'

'Fine,' Claire mumbled.

'Claire's boyfriend is the divine Ray Devine. He used to be with that band Smoke Covered Horses. Remember them?' Shane shook his head slowly. A taxi pulled up over the road. 'Oh!' Emma said. 'Perfect timing! Bye!'

'Take it easy there,' the taxi man said.

'I'm cool.' Ray heaved himself out of the taxi and almost collided with a blonde dressed in pink.

'Well,' she said. 'It's the artist formerly known as Ray Devine.'

Ray snorted. 'It's Emma Lacey. The bitch formerly known as Claire's friend.' He sounded even drunker than he felt. 'Is she around?'

'She's by the side door.' Emma smirked. 'I don't think she's expecting you.'

'You have a *boyfriend?*' Shane blinked at Claire and then rubbed his chin, hard.

'No.'

He was already moving away along the wall, putting distance between them. 'I just told Emma I did because . . .' She didn't want to get into the whole thing about Emma and Declan. 'It's complicated.'

'Claire!' She looked up and saw Ray weaving his way unsteadily towards them, supporting himself on parked cars. 'Why is your phone switched off?' He sat down heavily on the wall and slung his arm around her neck then buried his face in her hair. 'Oh Christ,' he moaned.

'Ray.' She tried to push him away but he was a dead weight. 'What are you doing here?'

Shane was on his feet.

'Please!' Claire said. 'Don't go! You don't understand.'

'I think I do,' he said over his shoulder.

'Claire, wait!' Ray staggered after her, trying to catch up, but she was already at the car. She got in and started the engine then rolled down her window. 'Don't ever do that again, Ray.'

'Do what?'

'Act like you own me!' Her eyes were narrow and her mouth was set in a straight line. She crashed the gear lever into first. Exhaust fumes billowed around Ray, turning his stomach. How many whiskeys had he had? A dozen?

'Something really fucked-up has happened.'

'Get off the car, Ray!'

He thumped on the sagging soft top. 'I'm trying to tell you something. Paul Fisher wants me to apologise to Chip Connolly.'

Claire revved the engine.

'And I have a daughter!'

7

Ray was trapped in the dressing room of the Happy Go Lucky in Tokyo. He could hear the roar of the crowd as the band walked out on stage. The door was locked. He slammed his fist against it over and over but it wouldn't open. 'I'm supposed to be out there!' he shouted. 'Let me out!' But nobody could hear him over the thunder of applause as the Horses began to play their first number.

When he woke up, the sound of applause was still in the room. It was the rain, he realised, hammering on the fire escape outside. His T-shirt was soaked in sweat. He groaned, turned over on his back and lay there, looking at the ceiling, but all he could see was the face of the little girl on Ash's screensaver.

Someone couldn't just get into a lift with you and drop a bomb like that. That sort of shit only happened in the fucking soaps. He wasn't ready to be a father. He was still a big kid himself. He'd spent the last ten years sidestepping anything that lasted more than a couple of weeks. How the fuck had this happened to him? He pushed his thumbs into his eyes until he saw red fireworks in the dark behind his eyelids. And why couldn't Claire leave him alone?

She had been angry with him the other night in Foxes but she'd been like a broken record since. 'Did you get Aisling's number?' 'When is she moving over to Dublin?' 'When are you going to see the little girl?'

Ray didn't have the answers to any of these questions, except the last one. He wasn't ever going to see *Ash's daughter* because that's what she was. She had nothing to do with him.

Claire's whole life was built around worrying about her

screwed-up father and making excuses for her uptight brother and trying to live up to some crazy idealised version of a mother she'd never even known. But family meant nothing to Ray. His parents had been too busy trying to tear one another apart to care about him. Music was what he had instead of family, and that's what he had to focus on.

He had to forget he'd even met Irish Ash, just like she'd told him to. He had to keep well out of Claire's way until she stopped giving him a hard time and left him alone. He had to either write another 'Asia Sky' or swallow his pride and call Chip fucking Connolly. Paul Fisher's door was still open but it was closing fast.

Claire lay listening to the rain. It rattled on the metal fire escape and drummed on the wheelie bins and pinged off the rusting patio heater in her overgrown garden. Ray had bought the heater for her thirty-first birthday. His daughter would have been three then. All the time they'd been staying up drinking cocktails, taking off on road trips, behaving like teenagers, Ray had been a father. Claire tried to imagine a child with Ray's cheekbones and his incredible eyes. She had lost her mother and now this girl, this Willow, was about to find her father. There was a sort of cosmic rightness about it all.

She had tried to explain that to Ray but first he had refused to listen. He wasn't answering her calls and the frisbee had been on the stairs for days now, even though she was sure he was up there on his own.

She turned on her side and looked at the clock. Four a.m. She wondered if Shane was lying awake listening to the rain. She closed her eyes and she was back in the dusk sitting on the low wall outside Johnny Foxes. She saw his eyes move from her eyes down to her mouth. He'd been about to kiss her and then Emma had come out and she'd been caught out in that stupid lie. Before she'd had a chance to fix things, Ray had barged in. Now it would be weeks before she saw Shane again to explain, and even if she could he would think she was a fool for lying to Emma, and he would be right.

*

81

Nick wasn't on air today but he'd arranged to meet Oonagh for a coffee. She was in the corner of the station canteen, her hair in rollers, her head bent over a plate of chunky chips and a copy of *Grazia*. Nick had already drunk two coffees but he bought a third anyway just to use up more time before he had to admit to her that he'd broken his word. Kelly wasn't going to tell anyone about the Channel 5 show but Rory was probably standing on the corner of Grafton Street and Stephen's Green right now with a megaphone.

Oonagh pointed at a double-page spread as he sat down. 'Team Angelina? Or Team Aniston? I'd say you're more a Jen than an Angie.'

Nick took a breath. *Name it and tame it.* 'Look, Oonagh, I'll understand if you're angry about this—'

'I'm not going to kill you if you pick the wrong one.'

'I told my wife and a friend about the Clingfilms project.'

Oonagh dipped a chip in a pool of ketchup. 'I told Owen at the weekend. He kept asking me when we were going to London to meet the production team. I had to put him out of his misery.'

Nick exhaled a sigh of relief. 'How did he react?'

'When I told him they wanted a different co-presenter he just roamed around the house with a face like a smacked arse. When I told him it might be you, he started sleeping in the study.'

She licked her finger and began to thumb through the pages of the magazine quickly, then tossed it on to the next table. 'Honestly. Gorgeous younger woman,' she pointed at herself with a scarlet fingernail, 'left alone in the marital bed by a man who is about to qualify for his bus pass. You couldn't make it up, could you?'

She looked at her plate of chip halves wistfully then picked one up. 'This is what happens when I fight with him. I crave carbs. I've just had lunch and all I can think about is dinner. Hey!' she said. 'There's an idea. The four of us. You, me and the WAHs. I can have you at my place. Owen will have to stop sulking if your lovely wife is there.'

'WAHs?'

'Wives and husbands, Nick. You're going to have to be a bit

more au fait with popular culture when you're on a mainstream TV show. How's Saturday?'

'Look at us!' Eilish said, twisting the wing mirror of a generator van and peering into it. 'How hot are we?'

They had arrived at the set for the hair care ad at seven and it was now lunchtime. They had been in wardrobe and make-up for five hours. They'd both been fitted with beautiful satin brides-maid's dresses. Eilish's was a pale, peony pink with a tightly boned bodice that gave her Marilyn Monroe curves. Claire's was cut on the bias in an opalescent green. Layers of heavy make-up concealed her freckles and gave her cheekbones she didn't have. The feathery fake eyelashes that had taken nearly an hour to insert made her dark green eyes look enormous.

'We do look pretty good,' she admitted, checking herself out in the fisheye of the mirror. 'Apart from the hair.'

The half-dozen bridesmaids in the ad, the hair stylist had explained, *hadn't* used Vitalustre conditioner. The bride *had*. She was going to throw a bottle of conditioner instead of a bouquet and they were all going to try to catch it. So Claire's curls had been back-combed into a tangle of frizz and Eilish's bob had been combed through with baby oil to make it look lank.

'I don't care. They could shave my head for thirteen hundred euros,' Eilish said, cheerfully, as they joined the queue for lunch. 'And I'll catch anything,' she clutched Claire's arm, 'except salmonella from Greasy Pete.'

Pete Purdue's catering van was notorious. His salmon parcels had nearly killed a clapper loader on *Revenge of the Dawn*. He was in his late thirties with dark, greasy, waist-length hair and a massive crush on Eilish. He was waving at her now, but she pretended not to see him and, instead, steered Claire past the van to a table laid with cheese and fruit.

'Tell me more about Ray's love child,' Eilish said, spreading Brie on a wheat thin.

'Nothing to tell.' Claire sighed. 'I still haven't been able to talk to him.'

'It's bad enough him blundering in on you and that gorgeous

83

guy but not wanting to see his own daughter.' Eilish snipped some grapes from a cluster with scissors. 'That's just inhuman. But maybe it's better, he'd be a pretty awful father.'

'I don't know,' Claire said. Though the truth was, she did. She just hoped she was wrong.

'Everybody!' the first AD called. 'First positions please.' The bridesmaids lined up on the grass by the fountain. 'Turn over and action.'

The bride had a waterfall of shining blonde hair but she was a terrible shot. The Vitalustre bottle kept flying over the head of the bridesmaid who was supposed to catch it or falling short and exploding on the grass. Once it went sideways and the lighting cameraman had to duck out of the way to avoid being decapitated.

Claire jumped and jumped again. After twenty-two takes, sweat was running down the back of her neck and her calves were aching. Finally, on take twenty-three, the shot went like a dream. The bride tossed the bottle over her shoulder and it flew straight into the hand of the right bridesmaid. The crew cheered.

'We're just going to do one more shot for luck,' Desmond, the director, yelled from behind the camera. 'Bridesmaids, you're looking a bit limp.' He held up the Vitalustre bottle. 'I want you to look as if you want this more than you want George Clooney's babies.'

Conditioner had never worked on Claire's hair but she lined up with the other bridesmaids and got ready to jump one last time.

The bride threw the bottle and this time, it came straight at Claire. Before she could stop herself her hand shot up to catch it. She heard her own Maria Sharapova-esque grunt as her fingers closed around the bottle, then she heard a sharp 'crack' as her elbow connected with something soft, and when she looked down Eilish was on her knees with blood pouring from her nose.

'This is what I should have worn to my wedding.' Eilish gazed down at her ruined dress while they were waiting in A & E. 'It turned out to be a bloody mess too. I thought marriage was for life, but after Holly goes, I'll be on my own.'

84

'You'll meet someone.'

'I'm too cynical to let my guard down again.'

'Wedding brawl?' a man with a stab wound in the next chair asked, giving their dresses a once-over.

'Yeah.' Eilish held up her fists. 'You should have seen the bride.'

After she had finally been X-rayed, had her broken nose set and the half-inch gash over her eyebrow stitched up, Claire drove Eilish home to Sandymount and helped her out of her dress and put her into bed.

'I'm so sorry,' she said, handing over an ice pack. 'I'm officially the world's worst friend.'

'Emma Lacey is the world's worst friend. You come a close second. Now give me another one of those painkillers.' Claire handed one over. 'And a glass of wine.'

'Are you sure?'

'It's for the pain!' Eilish groaned. 'The terrible, terrible pain.'

Claire ran to the kitchen.

'Claire! I'm messing. It could have happened to anyone. We'll put it in *Eyelash and Eclair*. We'll still be laughing at it when we're ninety. Now hurry up and get that wine, "Wold's Second Worst Friend".'

The Clancys' house was on a pleasant suburban road in Sutton but it looked as if it had been airlifted in from the Hollywood Hills. It had a vast steel and glass extension with, bizarrely, a grass roof on it. When Kelly had seen it in *Irish Homes* magazine the grass had been neatly trimmed, but now it was like a meadow.

Owen answered the door with a tumbler of whisky in his hand. A naked baby was crawling along the Paul Smith runner behind him towards a steep flight of stairs.

'Oops!' Kelly darted past him and caught up with the baby as he was hauling himself up on to the first step. He looked at her for a moment and then began to cry.

A girl of about four in pyjamas with a plastic bag tied around her shoulders like a cape appeared above them on the suspended glass walkway. 'Excuse me!' she said politely to Kelly. 'Can you turn that baby down! We're trying to play.'

Oonagh Clancy came up from the kitchen in a clingy pink

velour tracksuit and high-heeled gold sandals. 'Oi, Oslo! Put a sock in it!' The baby stopped crying and bobbed his head round Kelly's neck towards her. 'You're Kelly, right?' She sounded different now that she wasn't on TV. 'Look at the state of me.' She planted a kiss on Kelly's cheek. 'The sitter called in sick. I haven't had time to get changed or change this yoke.'

'I'll look after him.'

'Are you sure?'

Kelly put her arms out, took the baby and held his warm weight against her chest. 'Just show me where everything is.'

'Paris! Vienna!' Oonagh called up to the mezzanine. 'Get the nappies and the wipes from the fertility room.' She smiled at Kelly. 'It's the utility room but it's where all the kids were conceived. Owen is scared to even look at the tumble dryer in case I get pregnant again. Darling,' she said over her shoulder, 'take Nick into the den and make him comfortable.'

'Glenmorangie? Dalwhinnie? Lagavulin?' Owen was standing, like a bouncer, in front of a cabinet full of single malts.

Nick didn't drink but he didn't want to refuse. 'Whatever you're having.'

'I'm having a double.' Owen pulled the cork out of a bottle and half-filled two tumblers.

Nick forced a sour mouthful of whisky down his throat. 'That's quite a view.' He went over to the window and pretended to look out at the stretch of beach and the patchwork green hill of Ireland's Eye. But it was hard to enjoy the scenery with Owen looming behind him.

'I remain confident and unaffected by negativity,' he told himself, under his breath. Then he turned around. 'Listen, Owen, I'm sorry if I've stepped on your toes.'

Owen frowned. 'If you stepped on my toes, you'd know all about it.'

The little girl Nick had seen from the hall ran into the room holding the edges of her bin-bag cloak with her fingertips.

'Oslo's spitted up all over the lady!' she said, delightedly. 'And it's orange.'

*

'Aargh! I know there's Vanish in here somewhere.' Oonagh slid open the lacquered doors of the floor-to-ceiling units. She had changed into a low-cut white jersey dress while Kelly was changing the baby.

I want this, Kelly thought, and she didn't mean the Eileen Gray table or the Arne Jacobsen chair or the Stuart Haygarth chandelier. She wanted the jumble of plushie toys and LEGO on the floor and the bottom half of the pair of pink pyjamas that had been abandoned at the door of the bathroom and the dusting of baby powder on her fingertips.

'What are we going to do about your dress?' Oonagh frowned.

'It'll come off with baby wipes.' Kelly handed Oslo over to Oonagh and opened a packet.

'You'd better not puke on Mummy, you little tinker.' Oonagh lifted the baby up and kissed the powdery folds of his fat thighs. 'Or she'll take you back to the shop!'

Kelly blotted away the stains on her dress, wiped her hands carefully and put them out to take Oslo again.

'Gorgeous *and* an earth mother!' Oonagh gave her a calculating look and Kelly looked right back. She had met plenty of women like her. If Nick had been a different kind of man, she'd have been worried.

Oonagh handed Oslo over. 'No wonder your husband is impervious to my charms.'

The two little girls were planted in front of a DVD in their bedroom, but Kelly insisted on holding on to the baby. She ate with one hand while he sat gurgling on her lap. Owen barely spoke. Oonagh and Nick talked non-stop about Clingfilms. Kelly tried to look interested but every time Oslo turned his head and pressed his warm cheek against her face she felt her heart softly implode.

'That was a wonderful meal,' she said when Oonagh was clearing the plates. 'Who does the cooking?'

'The Butler's Pantry in Howth. When you have three kids everything except chicken nuggets and spaghetti hoops goes out the window.' Oonagh sighed. 'You two lovers probably had breakfast in bed this morning and a candlelit dinner last night.'

Nick smiled at Kelly.

'Who needs breakfast in bed?' Kelly ruffled Oslo's fuzz of sticky-up hair. 'When you have this sweet little monkey to wake up to.'

'Sorry, love,' Oonagh laughed, 'but I think you're talking through your ovaries.'

Even after he'd brushed his teeth, Nick could still taste the whiskey on his tongue. It turned his stomach. The whole evening had made him feel nauseous. Dinner had been awkward. Oonagh hadn't seemed to notice how rude Owen was being and every time he tried to talk to Kelly she was fussing with the baby. Afterwards they'd moved to some uncomfortable sofas around a rock and gas fire. Owen had finished off the bottle of whisky and dozed off. Then, just when he thought they could leave, Oonagh had produced an iPad and spent the next hour and a half showing Kelly photographs of her children.

When he came out of the bathroom, Kelly had lit candles and put on a relaxation CD. The bedroom sounded as if it was full of bickering birds.

She was sitting cross-legged on the bed, her dark hair caught up in a loose ponytail, wearing tiny white cotton shorts and a camisole. They hadn't planned to have sex. Nick wasn't sure he was up to it. 'I know tonight was awful,' he said. 'Thank you for being there for me.'

She smiled. 'I'd like to share something with you.'

Nick hauled himself on to the bed, sat cross-legged opposite her and took her hands.

'I know how much you want this Clingfilms job and I'm here to support you every step of the way.'

'What I hear you saying—' he began.

But she put a finger on his lips. 'I don't want to Two Listen,' she said gently. 'I just need you to hear me.' He nodded. 'I know we agreed to wait until I'm thirty-three to try for a baby but I want to be sure that, when we do, it'll happen.'

'Of course it will.' Nick was having trouble keeping his eyes open.

'It didn't for Rory and Niamh,' Kelly said. 'And it would really help me if we went to a doctor to get checked out, both of us.'

'But—'

'I went to dinner tonight because this job matters to you. This matters to me.'

He nodded slowly. 'OK.'

'Thank you.' She kissed him on the mouth and he slipped one of the little ribbon straps off her shoulder.

'If, for any reason, everything isn't OK,' she whispered, 'I'd like us to agree to start trying right away. Promise?'

'Promise,' Nick mumbled into the little hollow between her collarbones.

8

'You tuck into those olives,' Eilish said. 'I just need to consult my porn collection.' She rifled through the old-fashioned dresser packed with cookery books then pulled one out. ' "Nigel Slater Tarragon Chicken" OK with you? I'll make extra so you can bring some home.'

'I don't deserve it.' Eilish had a swollen nose, a gash above her eye and a psychedelic bruise running from her eyebrow to her cheek.

She fluffed out her vintage red prom dress. 'I think it's kind of an edgy look. *Stepford Wives* meets *Fight Club*.'

'But what about work?' Lorcan had waived both their fees for the Vitalustre ad and Eilish wasn't going to get any extra work while she looked like this.

Eilish put down the book. 'Sorted. Greasy Pete needs someone to help out in his catering van.' Claire almost choked on an olive. 'I'm starting on Monday. Six weeks on location for *Emerald Warriors*. It's some *Rome*-style thing about Irish legends. Don't look at me like that, Claire. I have to work. The money's good. I'll be able to stash away a couple of grand for Holly's uni fund and, to be honest, I'm looking forward to it. Extra work's not the same without you. I miss *Eyelash and Eclair*.'

Her mobile rang. 'Hello,' she said in a robotic voice, 'you've reached Teenage-Line. Press one if you think your mother is a bloody cow for not letting you get a tattoo. Press two if she embarrassed you by wearing an orange velvet catsuit to do the shopping in Lidl. Press three . . .' She sighed. 'Oh, go on. What have I done now?' She frowned down at the chopping board and then she looked up at Claire.

'Apparently we're on YouTube! We've had nine thousand hits.'

The clip was called *Desperate Bridesmaids*. It was an out-take from the Vitalustre advertising shoot, cut to the music from *Pulp Fiction*.

'How did it get there?'

'Someone must have nicked it when the rushes were being processed.'

'Play it again,' Claire whispered, through her fingers.

The shot had been slowed down to fifteen frames a second. The bride threw the conditioner bottle over her shoulder and the camera followed it as it headed straight for the red-haired bridesmaid in the pale green dress. She jumped to catch it, her brow furrowing with concentration, her back-combed hair rising up into the air like a wonky halo. And there it was in horrible slo-mo, the look of comic-book surprise on Claire's face as her elbow connected with Eilish's cheekbone and she doubled up on the grass.

Ray was watching reruns of *Modern Family* when Claire put her head around his door.

'Jesus!' he said. 'What are you doing up here? I'm working and the frisbee's on the stairs.' Too late he realised that these two statements contradicted themselves but Claire didn't seem to notice.

'I have to show you something.'

He got up and followed her down the stairs.

Whoever had thought of the *Pulp Fiction* soundtrack was a genius, Ray thought; it turned a moderately funny clip into comedy gold. But mentioning that might be a mistake. 'Ouch!' he said, instead. 'Is Eilish OK?'

'I broke her nose,' Claire said, miserably. 'Now I'm breaking it all over the internet.'

'Have you asked your agent to get it taken down?'

'He's trying to get hold of the Vitalustre people but they won't be back in the office till Monday.' She refreshed the page. 'It has twenty-nine thousand four hundred and fifty-two views!'

'Well, you know what they say, "there's no such thing as bad publicity".'

'Did they say that when Chip Connolly told that Dutch journalist that you made Ronan Keating look like Captain Beefheart?'

Ray burst out laughing. Nobody made him laugh like Claire Dillon did.

'It's not funny.' Claire shook her head. 'I was just beginning to get my acting career back on track. This makes me look like an idiot.'

'It'll be gone by Monday. Someone will come along with *Fainting Goats* 2 or a *Surfing Squirrel* and it'll be history.'

She pulled at her frizzy cloud of hair. 'Are you sure?'

He wasn't but she looked so desperate that he nodded. 'Now, you know what you need? You need a Perfect Day.'

'No, I don't!'

'Come on,' Ray said. 'It'll be fun.'

A Perfect Day was supposed to cheer them both up as long as they followed Lou Reed's lyrics to the letter. They had to drink sangria in the park. Feed at least one animal in the zoo. Watch a movie. And go home.

Claire shut her laptop. If she stayed here she'd just be checking the view count every ten minutes. And she'd been trying to get hold of Ray for days. This would give her a chance to persuade him that he had to see his daughter.

Ray spread his jacket on the damp grass in the Phoenix Park and they sat in the wind and the drizzle, drinking mini-bottles of Shiraz by the neck because they couldn't find any sangria in the off-licence and Ray had forgotten to bring plastic cups.

'I've got a good one for you.' Ray began to sing 'Rhinestone Cowboy', changing the words to 'Like a nine-stone cowboy.'

'You're recycling, Ray.'

'Maybe. But we haven't had this one.' He pointed at a herd of deer grazing near the obelisk. 'The antlers, my friend, are blowing in the wind,' he sang in a gravelly Dylan drawl, 'the antlers are blowing in the wind.'

Two women in their twenties power-walked past with strollers. They looked over and Claire felt mortified. This was knacker drinking, she realised. You could call it a Perfect Day, but that didn't change it.

The zoo was deserted. The wind rattled the Plexiglas walls of the chimps' enclosure and howled through the grasslands where the lions were supposed to be. Claire was wearing Ray's jacket over her own corduroy one but she was still shivering. 'Can we just skip this bit and go to the movie? I'm freezing.'

'You know it won't work unless we feed the animals first. I'll just get some bananas.'

Claire huddled on a bench. After a minute, a blonde woman came along with a girl of about ten in a blue bobble hat. They stopped at the meerkat enclosure and the little girl started to read the information plaque out loud.

'The meerkat is a small ma-mmal belonging to the mon-goose family. Meerkats live in the . . .'

'Kalahari,' her mum prompted.

'. . . the Kalahari dessert. A group of meerkats is called a "mob" or "clan" . . .'

Other people's mothers had always been extra nice to Claire. There was always someone wanting to bake extra fairy buns for cake sales or make her costume for the Christmas play. When she was older they tried to draw her out, to talk to her about clothes and boys and periods, but it always made Claire feel awkward and uncomfortable because they were sorry for her.

The woman with the blonde hair and the little girl with the blue bobble hat were standing hand in hand, looking at the empty meerkat enclosure, and Claire saw they didn't mind that it was cold and raining and that the meerkats had all sloped off inside to their heat-lamps. She didn't know which one of them she wanted to be most. The little girl who had a mother or the mother who had a little girl.

Ray had very nearly kissed Claire once, over by the kiosk between the tapir enclosure and the reptile house. It was the day after he'd written 'Asia Sky'. He'd been up all night, drinking duty-free booze in the kitchen of the flat Claire shared with Declan Brady. She was supposed to go to a rehearsal the next morning but she told Declan she was sick and they had a Perfect Day. Ray had sung 'Asia Sky' to her on a bench by the kiosk, his voice all screwed up because he hadn't slept for seventy-two hours. When he was finished, her pale face had turned bright pink.

'It's shit, isn't it?' he'd said.

'It's not that.' She pulled her sleeves down over her hands. 'I'm just a bit mortified because you wrote a song about me. It's a bit, you know,' her narrow shoulders floated up to her ears, '*boy-friendy*. It's really good though.'

'Really?'

'Really, really good.' He knew from her eyes that she wasn't bullshitting him. And it was just the jet-lag and the relief but he suddenly wanted to kiss her, but he didn't. Because he knew what would happen if he did. The same thing that happened whenever he kissed anyone. He'd start looking for an escape route and when he found one he'd lose his best friend.

A few weeks later, on the phone, he'd added a 'One Kiss Clause' to The Contract. It meant that if they did kiss, even once, they had to try being a couple for three hundred and sixty days. Claire had thought it was the most ridiculous thing she'd ever heard.

Ray waited until the official-looking guy in Pets' Corner had turned his back and then slipped a HobNob to the pygmy goat. 'Result!' He grinned at Claire. 'We have fed the animals in the zoo. Now we can get out of the rain and go to the movie or we could cheat and watch one on Apple TV. What would Lou do?'

'Ray.' Claire took his arm and steered him towards the café. 'We need to talk.'

'I just wonder,' Claire picked at the monkey sticker on her place mat, 'if you're having some kind of a mid-life crisis.'

'You think I'm going to die when I'm sixty-six? Thanks a lot.' Ray was trying to catch the waitress's eye.

'You've been locked away upstairs since London pretending that this little girl doesn't exist . . .'

Ray opened the menu. 'I don't want to start something I can't finish.'

'How can you not be curious?'

94

Ray opened the menu. 'You of all people should know that I'm not father material.'

'Ask me what I'm doing on Sunday,' Claire said.

Ray squinted at the starters. Why did they have to make the print so small? 'Hitting me with more emotional blackmail? You tell me.'

'I'm going to pretend to be passing by my dad's house and I'm going to practically force my way in so I get to see him. This is my father who never taught me to tie my shoelaces or to ride a bike. Who never came to a single parent/teacher meeting or a sports day or a school play.'

Ray's dad had never done any of those things with him either. As far as Ray knew, he hadn't listened to a single song he'd ever recorded. But Ray didn't care. That was the difference between him and Claire. He had left his past behind. She was still stuck in hers.

'When I was small, I used to have terrible nightmares.'

Ray sighed. 'I know.'

'I used to drag my duvet across the landing and curl up outside my dad's door. I didn't knock or go in. Just being closer to him stopped me being afraid.' Claire remembered the honeycomb print the carpet left on her cheek. The ribbon of light where the door met the floor. The faint sound of the BBC World Service and the scratch of the Rapidograph pen he used to sketch.

'My dad is not father material, Ray,' she looked up at him with those steady green eyes. 'But he's still my father. Nothing can change that.'

Ray closed the menu. 'I'm getting semantic satiation. And that's not an appetiser, Claire, it's what you get when someone repeats something over and over and over again.'

'Will you just see her once?'

'If I do, you have to swear that you won't hassle me about this again.'

'I swear!'

The letter 'P' on Claire's laptop had been broken for months now so she had to compose her email to Lorcan without 'p's then copy and paste them in afterwards, one by one.

'Dear Lorcan, I a_ologise for _estering you about this but can you _lease s_eak to the _eo_le at Vitalustre about the YouTube cli_? I am ho_ing it can be taken down as soon as _ossible.'

The clip had three hundred thousand views now and Claire was a national joke. She couldn't go into her local petrol station because the guy behind the counter kept throwing things for her to catch – toilet rolls, packets of Jaffa Cakes, tubes of Pringles. Worse still, the clip kept coming up at auditions. This morning, a director had gone off into a long rant about copyright violation and completely forgotten she was in the room.

'What about copyright violation?' Claire said, when Lorcan finally got around to reading her email and called her.

'The copyright belongs to Vitalustre and they don't want to take it down. It's free advertising, Claire.'

'What am I going to do?'

Ray had hoped that Ash would be hard to find but it took him less than a minute to track her down on Facebook. Aisling Glennon. Her profile picture was a *Mad Men* cartoon of a vamp in a tight red dress with a cigarette holder and a cocktail glass. Her information was private but he sent her a message with his phone number in it.

'I think we were both pretty upset the day we talked in London. If you're back in Dublin, it would be good to meet and talk again. R.D.'

Four days later, she called him. She was back in Dublin but she wasn't happy to hear from him. Eventually, he persuaded her to meet him for a coffee. She was pretty hostile, but Ray laid on the charm and, eventually, she thawed very slightly. And when he said he'd like to see Willow she said she'd have to think about it.

Ray was hoping that was it. But two days later Ash called again. She said she needed a babysitter on Saturday afternoon so if Ray was free to look after Willow for four hours, he could if that wasn't too much of an imposition on his precious time.

'Shouldn't I be police cleared or something?' Ray asked, suddenly nervous at the idea of meeting a six-year-old.

'You already have been,' she said crisply. 'My brother's a Garda.'

*

There were five men in the small waiting room, their heads bent over magazines they weren't reading. Irish men were so self-conscious, Nick thought, walking straight up to the desk. He should come up with a programme to help them. *No More Mister Shy Guy.*

A woman with spiked black hair and a slash of crimson lipstick was on the phone. 'Excuse me,' Nick began. She held her hand out and he had to wait until she'd finished her call. 'I have a three o'clock appointment.'

'Name?'

'Dillon. Nick.'

Her face lit up. 'Doc Nick. My friends are going to be so jealous when I tell them I met you. We watch you every Thursday.' All the men in the room were watching Nick too and now he was the one who was self-conscious.

He took the small sealed paper bag and the leaflet and found an empty chair. He still wasn't sure what he was doing here. If Kelly were thirty-five, he'd understand the rush. He caught himself thinking she was being neurotic and made himself do a We-Fit exercise he called Positivi-Three. 'For every one negative adjective you think about your partner, think of three positive ones.'

One: she was a perfectionist. She wanted everything to be just right. From the mixer tap on a bath to the brand of maple syrup she liked on her French toast. She carried a Moleskine notebook in her purse and made neat little lists of anything she thought might improve their lives.

Two: she was honest. If she had a problem, she didn't hide it. She came right out and said what she needed.

Three: she was incredibly sexy. Nick had a flashback to the date night they'd had last week. They'd gone to a movie then skipped dinner and gone home to bed. She had made it pretty clear what she needed and, the next morning, she made it pretty clear that she wanted it all over again.

'It's me!' Oonagh said. 'Where are you?'

Nick's mind went blank. 'I'm at the . . .' He looked at the poster of the cartoon sperm on the wall of the waiting room. '. . . bank.'

'Can you talk?'

'Not really.' He glanced at the bent heads around him. 'There's a queue.'

'The OO show has been nominated for a TV Media award. It's our first one and it's all down to you and your fabulous ratings!'

'That's great news.'

'Oh, who cares about a crappy old Irish award,' Oonagh said, scornfully. 'The exciting part is that I've booked a table and invited Curtis Young, the head of Clingfilms. He's flying over to meet you!'

Ray checked himself out in the hall mirror. White Gap T-shirt. Baggy jeans. Biker boots. Grey beanie. His skin looked kind of washed out. That serum stuff he was using wasn't working and there was a short grey hair poking straight up out of his fringe. It suddenly hit him. If his daughter had a child when she was sixteen, he could be a *granddad* at forty-four.

The bell rang and he forced himself to open the door. Ash was standing on the front steps holding a little girl by the hand. She was wearing a Little Miss Lucky T-shirt, a skirt with a pattern of rabbits and carrying a backpack, also shaped like a rabbit.

'Hi!' he said, in a big fake voice. She looked up at him as if this was the stupidest thing she'd ever heard then retreated behind her mother's legs.

Ash squatted down. 'This is Ray. Remember? He's your biological daddy. The one that the sperm came from.'

Willow whispered something into Ash's ear and she stood up. 'She'd like to use your loo.'

Ray had remembered the framed Helmut Newton nudes in the hall at the last minute and bunged them in the downstairs bathroom along with a dusty bong he'd only used once and all his *GQ* and *Maxim* magazines. So he had no choice but to lead them both up the stairs through his bedroom to the en suite.

Willow went inside and Ash looked around, taking in the black sheets on the bed and the zebra-skin rug. 'So this,' she smirked, 'is where the magic happens?'

'There hasn't been much magic around here for the last few weeks.' Ray crossed his arms.

Ash sighed. 'Living with my parents is driving me around the bend. My mother has booked me in to see a marriage guidance counsellor this afternoon. She wants me to take Willow back to London and try to work things out with my ex.'

'Probably not a bad idea.' Not least, Ray thought, because Claire couldn't hound him if Willow lived in another country.

'Ray is going to call Granny if you decide you want to go home, OK? He has my number.' Ash kissed the top of Willow's head and went down the steps and out of the gate.

'So,' Ray said, rubbing his hands for some reason. 'Here we are!' He closed the door and they went into the living room. Willow perched on the edge of the modular sofa and looked at him expectantly.

'Would you like to watch TV? Or play with the iPad? Or the Wii?' Ray said. She shook her head. 'Do you want some ice cream?' All children liked ice cream. She shook her head again. 'Well, is there anything you would like?'

'Will you do some magic?' Willow's voice was husky and her accent was English, which, for some reason, Ray hadn't expected. 'Please,' she added.

'I can't do magic.'

She frowned. 'Mummy said this is where magic happens.'

'I can juggle.' He grabbed a couple of oranges out of a bowl and tossed them into the air. One of them hit him, quite painfully, in the eye.

'Shit!' he said. 'I mean *sugar*.'

Willow stared at him 'Why are you wearing a hat indoors?'

'I didn't know I had it on.' Ray pulled it off. 'Well, I wonder where Claire is?'

Willow brightened. 'Is she your girlfriend?'

'Yes,' Ray lied.

'Can I try on all her clothes?'

'You'd have to ask her.'

'Mummy was your girlfriend before,' Willow told him, 'when you put me in her tummy.'

'That's right,' Ray lied again.

*

'Willow,' Claire kicked off her shoes and kneeled on the floor, 'I don't know if anyone told you this but,' she leaned over and whispered, 'there's a bunny on your back!'

Willow's eyes which were Ray's eyes in her tiny face, widened. 'I know!' She shrugged her rabbit backpack off and slid down on to the floor beside Claire. 'There's another rabbit,' she hugged her knees, 'inside.'

'Can I see?' Claire tried to catch Ray's eye but he was slouched on the sofa doing something on his iPad.

Willow unzipped the backpack and pulled out a very grubby rabbit toy with one blue eye and one green one. 'This is Bowie.'

Ray looked up. 'After David Bowie, the singer?'

Willow looked unsure about this. 'I don't know him.'

'You've never heard of Ziggy Stardust? Scary Monsters, Super Creeps?'

'They're not really scary monsters,' Claire said quickly.

Ray jumped up and went over to his stereo. 'But you've heard of Lou Reed, right?'

They listened to some early Bowie from Ray's precious vinyl collection and then to some rare Lou Reed. Then they went outside and caught a taxi. Ray sat in the front and chatted to the driver about Smoke Covered Horses and Claire and Willow sat in the back and played 'I Spy'. Willow had Ray's ears, small and close to her head, and his sallow skin, dusky and golden, even in winter. She even had his eyebrows, in miniature. All of this made Claire feel woozy with amazement but it seemed to be going right over Ray's head.

They got out at Merrion Square and walked across to the Natural History Museum. 'Me and Claire used to mitch from school and come here all the time,' Ray said to Willow over his shoulder, 'it's really cool. There's a weird, badly stuffed giraffe called Spoticus and a hairy-nosed wombat.' He pushed open the heavy door and they were hit by the sickly-sweet smell of formaldehyde.

'Look up!' Ray pointed and Willow's head tilted back to take in the whale skeleton that was hanging from the ceiling. 'Do you know what that is?'

'It's bones,' she said quietly.

'I'm not sure this is a good idea,' Claire hissed.

'Give it a chance!' Ray hissed back.

They trailed behind him up the stairs and along the wrought-iron walkways while he walked from display cabinet to display cabinet wearing a hole in the words 'wow' and 'cool'.

'Excuse me.' Willow tugged Claire's sleeve and pointed at a grim tableau of three stuffed rabbits being stalked by a snarling, stuffed fox. 'How did they all die?'

'Of old age.' Claire hurried her past. 'In their sleep. After long, happy lives.'

'This used to be my favourite burger place when I was a kid,' Ray said as they climbed the stairs to Captain America's. 'It's got all this great authentic retro comic book character stuff.' Claire guessed that comic book to Willow meant Little Kitty and Dora the Explorer, not an eight-foot snarling Superhero. Things got worse when the waitress brought the menu.

'Ash never said you were a vegetarian!' Ray said.

'I'm a vegan,' Willow said quietly. 'Is there any tofu or quorn?'

'We have *corn*,' the waitress said, doubtfully.

Ray closed the menu. 'She'll have that. And chips. Why don't you go and look at those cartoon strips?' he asked Willow. 'Jesus!' he said when she was out of earshot. 'I should never have let you talk me into this!'

'Ray, calm down,' Claire said. 'Stop trying to impress her. This isn't a date. And take off the sunglasses.'

'I'm leaving the shades on.' He picked up a spoon and re-arranged his fringe in its stainless-steel surface. 'I don't want her to see the fear in my eyes.'

'So why don't you eat meat?' Ray asked Willow after he'd paid the bill.

'Because animals have feelings.'

'That's just cartoon animals,' Ray scoffed. 'Cows and sheep don't have feelings.'

'Sheep have friends,' Willow scoffed right back. 'They can remember sheep they haven't seen for years. It's on the internet.'

Their eyes narrowed. Their mouths were set into the same sulky line. They looked so alike that Claire had to pretend to be busy putting David Bowie back in Willow's backpack to hide her smile.

'Can I wash my hands?' Willow asked Claire when they were sitting in Ray's living room, waiting for Ash to arrive.

Claire took her into the downstairs loo and dropped a towel over a bong that Ray, for some reason, had left in the middle of the floor.

'Who are *they*?' Willow pointed at the framed picture of Smoke Covered Horses.

'That's Ray and his band. He used to be . . . I mean, he is a singer.'

'Is that lady a singer too?' Willow pointed at the print of the woman wearing a leather corset that was leaning against the wall.

'No!' Claire turned it towards the wall quickly. Willow lifted her arms to have her sleeves rolled up. Claire filled the basin with water and soaped her hands carefully then she sandwiched them up in a towel and patted them dry. She remembered her mum doing this for her once in the bathroom of a restaurant. 'There,' she said, rolling down Willow's sleeves again. And Willow said, 'Where?' just the way she used to.

'Well, that,' Ray called from the kitchen over the rattle of ice, 'was a complete disaster.' He came in with two large vodka gimlets. 'Is there any *tofu*,' he put on a polite little English voice, '*or quorn*?' He slid on to the sofa beside Claire and held out a glass.

'I don't want a drink,' she said.

'Fine. Invisible Mike can have it.'

He took a sip out of one glass and then the other. 'Did you see the way Little Miss Frosty froze me out in the hall?' Willow had kissed Claire goodbye but she wouldn't kiss him.

'She's a vegan. You took her to see a lot of dead animals and then to a burger restaurant. And you told her I'm your girlfriend. Why?'

'I don't know. She freaked me out. The whole idea of having a child at all freaks me out.'

'You'll get used to it.'

'Nope.' He shook his head.

Claire turned and stared at him. 'You're not going to see her again?'

'Ash is probably bringing her back to London anyway.'

'There are flights to London every day.'

'We had a deal, Claire, remember?' Ray flicked on the TV and channel-hopped till he found a soccer match.

'Ray, look at me.' She took the remote and muted the volume. 'You have a chance to be part of this little girl's life. I'm not going to let you throw that away—'

'You're not going to *let* me?' His dark eyebrows came down below his fringe. His eyes hardened. 'What am I? Your *bitch*?'

She put her hand on his arm. 'She's six, Ray. When I was six, I lost my mother and—'

'Your mother! Here we go a-fucking-gain.' Ray shook her hand away. 'You have to drag her into everything, don't you? Every single thing has to come back to your mother. Jesus, Claire, you're pathetic. You're a broken record, do you know know that? This is not about you and your misplaced guilt complex about your mother. This is about me,' he was shouting now, 'and a kid I didn't even know existed until a couple of weeks ago.'

Claire shrank away from him and put her hands over her face.

'Jesus!' Ray lowered his voice. 'Forget I said all that. I can't take this on. I've got to focus on my music career and—'

'What music career?' Claire lifted her face. There were two high spots of colour on her cheeks. 'You're a *jingle* writer.'

'Until I get my shit together.'

'You keep telling yourself that.' Her voice was flat and icy. 'Go right ahead, waste your life writing snappy little tunes for gravy and dental floss and drinking your way through the cocktail alphabet and hitting on girls who'll sleep with you because you used to be famous.'

Ray tried to interrupt her but no words came out.

'That little girl is the most important thing that's ever happened to you!' Claire stood up. Her legs were shaking. 'But you're too vain and shallow to see it.'

Ray finally found his voice. 'I don't need to listen to this shit.' He reached for the remote control but she snatched it away.

'I'm not finished.' She glared down at him. 'You can forget about the Desperation Clause, Ray. You were right, you're not father material.' She threw the remote down on the sofa. 'You're not friend material either.'

9

'I just think,' Nick tried to keep his voice neutral, 'that we need to freshen the phone-in format. Why don't I just take one caller each show and work through exercises to solve their problem?' Dom and his producer Tara exchanged a comic eye-roll across the tiny control booth. 'Guys, this works on TV. The OO show has been nominated for an award—'

'Well, I'm sure it'll look lovely on your mammy's mantelpiece,' Tara said, tartly, 'but our listeners want "Dear Deirdre" not "Sigmund bloody Freud".'

'But in my experience—' Nick began.

'What experience?' Dom snorted. 'A couple of months on the telly and suddenly you're a media guru?'

The show that followed was a nightmare. Dom kept trying to wind Nick up. Cutting across him and making smart remarks. By the time the last caller phoned in, Nick was exhausted. Her voice sounded weirdly familiar.

'I have a problem, Doc. There's a guy I'm seeing *right now* and he has a very big head and I'm finding it very hard to keep him satisfied.' Dom swallowed a chortle. Nick looked up and saw Tara, with a phone to her ear, grinning at him from the production booth.

There was nothing he could do except pretend that their juvenile behaviour didn't push his buttons. He fumed through two private coaching sessions and after his clients were gone he was so busy thinking of all the things he should have said that he completely forgot that he'd arranged to meet Kelly and he was already fifteen minutes late.

'I release my anger,' he told himself when he'd finally managed to catch a cab. 'And fill my mind with calm and harmonious thoughts.' But his mind was filled with thoughts of the look he might see on Dom's face when Nick resigned from the show and told him where he could shove Fish. He closed his eyes and tried some Seven-Eleven breathing.

'Having sympathetic contractions back there?' The taxi driver grinned as they turned off Mount Street. 'You wouldn't be the first. Here we are.' He pulled over outside the National Maternity Hospital. A couple of pregnant women in dressing gowns were smoking on the steps in the late September sunshine.

'I think you've got the wrong address,' Nick said. 'I'm looking for the Wilton Clinic.'

'Oh! Sorry! When you said Mount Street I presumed . . .' The driver gave him a pitying look. 'The Fertility Clinic's number twelve, two doors up.'

Fertility clinic? Nick thought the driver had made a mistake. But the words were there, in discreet italics, on the brass plaque outside the door. He rang the bell and went up the stairs to the waiting room just as Kelly's name was being called.

'Honey!' She stood up. 'I thought you weren't going to make it!' She grabbed his hand and he had to follow her back out into the corridor.

'I don't understand,' he said. 'I thought we were just having everything checked out.'

She was already tapping on the door of a consultation room. 'That's exactly what we *are* doing.'

Dr Brown Bastiman was glamorous and very brisk. 'Gillian!' she shook their hands across her cluttered desk. 'I've just been looking at your sperm count,' she announced to Nick before he had sat down. 'Your motility is just below average but that wouldn't worry me overmuch. It's your blood work, Kelly, that's the real issue here. Your FSH level has been hovering around fourteen for nearly a year now which is very high for a woman of your age. I can see why you might be concerned about your chances of conception.'

Nick frowned.

'Sorry, Nick,' Gillian looked up from her notes, 'I should explain, a high level of Follicle Stimulating Hormone means your wife is probably not ovulating.' Nick knew all about FSH. He'd coached a couple once who were having trouble getting pregnant. What he didn't know was that Kelly had been having her hormones tested. He squeezed her hand and tried to catch her eye but her attention was completely focused on the doctor. He might as well not be in the room.

'So,' the doctor closed the file, 'I'd usually suggest trying for a year before offering any treatment but given these results, I think we should start a course of an ovulation stimulation drug right away.'

'Like Clomid?' Kelly asked.

'Exactly.' She uncapped a fountain pen and began to scribble on a prescription pad. 'Let's try six cycles and keep our fingers crossed.' Kelly let go of Nick's hand to cross her fingers. 'Any questions?'

Kelly had a list. They were all numbered and written neatly in one of her Moleskine notebooks.

'What about side effects?' she began.

'Hardly any at all, I'm happy to report.'

Nick's head was reeling by the time they left the room. He waited out in the hall while Kelly went to pay the receptionist. She took his arm but he gripped the wooden banister and refused to move.

'Why didn't you tell me you were having your hormones tested?'

She shrugged. 'Sweetie, I don't bother you with every little detail of my cycle. It's been a bit irregular so the GP suggested a couple of tests. It wasn't a big deal.'

'It wasn't a couple of tests. It was a year of tests. And we're supposed to tell one another everything.'

She bent her head and her dark hair fell over her face. 'You didn't tell me about the Clingfilms job,' she said quietly.

'I know but that's . . .' *Different*, he wanted to say. But was it? He felt too dizzy to figure that out. This was all happening too fast. One minute they were having a few general health checks, the next they were trying for a child. What about going back to their old life in New York? Where would a child fit into that? 'I'm just not sure what we're even doing here,' he said, lamely.

Kelly looked up at him. There was something in her eyes that needled him. Amusement or accusation. 'You promised that if there were any problems we could go ahead and start trying.'

'I know but I just wish you'd told me about those tests.' His voice was loud and it echoed around the stairwell. 'I felt so stupid in there.'

'Nick!' Kelly said.

'Please let me finish,' he said sharply. 'It's disrespectful to interrupt—'

'Nick!' She nudged him and he saw the couple hesitating in the hall below. A clammy wave of shame broke at the back of his neck. An hour ago he'd been on national radio telling a man from Dun Laoghaire that he should never raise his voice to his girl-friend, now here he was, shouting at his wife in front of complete strangers.

'I'm so sorry,' he said, when the couple had climbed the stairs and disappeared into the waiting room. 'That was inexcusable. This is just all happening so fast but I can see how much it matters to you.'

'Thank you,' she said softly.

'I just love what we have.' He put his hands on her shoulders. 'I waited so long to meet you. I don't want anything to change.'

'Nothing's going to change.' She smiled up at him. 'I promise. Whatever happens, we'll still be us.'

Claire was trying to show Lorcan how serious she was about getting back into acting. She arrived fifteen minutes early for her audition for the Noel Coward play at the Gate, even though she'd heard that the part she was reading for was already cast. She had learned the lines she was supposed to read. She should have been running over them and trying to come up with smart retorts to the inevitable questions she'd get asked about the YouTube clip but all she could think about was the row she'd had with Ray. They had bickered before, hundreds of times. Once, when he'd been obnoxious to Declan, they hadn't spoken for two weeks. But this was different. *'You have to drag her into everything, don't you?'* Ray had said. *'Every single thing has to come back to your mother.'*

They were both eighteen when Claire had told him about the accident. They were celebrating the end of the Leaving Cert by the overgrown railway track on an overcast summer's day wearing petrol station sunglasses and passing a bottle of Monte Alban tequila between them. There was a worm in the bottom of the bottle. Ray was planning to eat it because it was supposed to be hallucinogenic but Claire was already feeling spaced out after the first few gulps of alcohol.

She could still remember the scratchy feeling of the parched grass on her bare legs and the oily burn of the tequila and the sticky sweetness of the Jelly Babies they were eating between gulps.

Ray was propped up on his elbows, his dark fringe so long that he had to keep pushing it away from his sunglasses, firing out random questions. 'What's the most disgusting thing you've ever eaten?'

'Liver.'

'Who's the most embarrassing person you've ever fancied?'

'Jamiroquai.'

'What's the worst thing you've ever done?'

Claire had stared down at the worm in the bottom of the bottle. Did they kill it first, she'd wondered, or put it in alive and let it drown?

She closed her eyes and took a gulp of tequila as Ray bit the head off a green Jelly Baby and passed it to her. But instead of putting it in her mouth, she held it, tightly in her fist. She could feel the icing sugar melting against her damp palm as she battled with herself. Wanting to hold onto her secret, wanting to let it go.

'Oh no!' Ray groaned. 'You're going to barf, aren't you?' He sat up and moved his denim jacket out of the way.

She shook her head and looked up at him. The grass and the trees and the sky and her own face, telescoped to a pale dot, were reflected in the lenses of his sunglasses. 'I just don't know if I can trust you.'

'Trust me to what?' He lifted his fringe up and wiggled his eyebrows like a cartoon villain.

Claire started to laugh and then she started to cry and before she could stop herself, she told him the truth. She'd told him the worst thing she'd ever done.

Ray was the only person apart from her dad and her brother who knew what had happened the day of her sixth birthday. And that was what hurt so much now.

Her phone began to vibrate in her bag. Her dad's number was flashing on the screen. Why was he calling her? He never rang. She'd only seen him a week ago.

'Dad,' she covered the phone with her hand, 'is everything OK?'

'Oh, hello, Claire. This is Caroline Cunningham from number twenty-two. I'm afraid there's been a bit of an accident.'

'An *accident?*' Claire's heart pushed itself into a corner of her ribcage.

'Brian found your father in the garden. He'd fallen off a very high ladder.' Mrs Cunningham said, importantly, 'We wouldn't have known he was there at all if that dog hadn't been barking all night.'

Claire stood up. The floor seemed to be tilting. She had to hold onto the back of her chair to stop herself falling. 'Is he badly injured?'

'He went to St Vincent's in an ambulance about two hours ago. I just popped in to lock that dog up and I found your number by the phone.'

'*Please!*' Claire whispered over and over as she ran from the room to the car park and through the rain. '*Please!*' Her lungs burned as she ran up eight flights of stairs to the top floor where she'd parked Mossy. '*Please!*' she whispered at every traffic light and every pedestrian crossing between Drury Street and the Merrion Road. '*Please. Don't let him die.*'

Her dad was on a trolley in the corridor in A & E. His jeans and shirt were soaked through. There was a gash on his head leaking blood and he was lying awkwardly, half on his side covered with his old raincoat. The belt had come undone from the loops and the buckle had a crust of dirt where it must have trailed on the ground. But his face was the worst part. It was clenched and pale, his teeth gritted, his jaw set, his eyes squeezed closed against the pain.

'Dad, it's me.' Claire wanted to touch his hand but she knew he would hate that so she lifted the buckle instead and squeezed it. 'What happened?'

He gripped the sides of the trolley. When he could breathe again he whispered, 'Just a little fall. I'm fine.'

'You were out there all night in the rain! You could have . . .' She pressed her lips between her teeth. 'What were you doing up on a ladder?'

'The television reception went. I couldn't get the news. I went up to check the aerial. They'll sort me out here. You go home now. I'll call you if I . . .' He squeezed his eyes closed to let a spasm of pain pass, '. . . need anything.'

A young doctor with a white coat over a crumpled shirt and jeans came over.

'Tom, we've just had a look at your X-rays. The good news is the trauma to your head is minimal, though we'll need to keep you under observation.' Claire exhaled. 'The bad news is you've really done a job on that right hip. I'm going to write you up for some pain relief now and we'll take you down to theatre first thing in the morning.' He turned to Claire. 'Are you his daughter?' She nodded. 'You'll need to pack a bag for him. He's going to be staying with us for a while.'

Claire followed him out through the curtain. 'Is he going to be OK?'

'It's a very complicated break. It's going to be a long surgery and he has an irregular heartbeat which increases the chance of complications.'

'Complications?' Claire repeated.

The doctor gave her a meaningful look. 'Your father fell the best part of thirty feet, from what I understand. He's lucky to be here at all.'

When she went back into the cubicle, a nurse was slipping a needle into her dad's arm. After a minute, his face unclenched and his eyes closed. The nurse slid a dental plate with four teeth out of his mouth and put it into a ziplock bag, then she took off his watch and his wedding ring and gave them to Claire.

Claire sat on a plastic chair beside the trolley with her phone in her hand. Ray was the first person she had called when she got glandular fever. When she aquaplaned and smashed Mossy into a wall. When Declan told her he was in love with Emma. She stared down at his number on the small screen and then she called Nick.

Nick patted Claire's back and tried to think of an affirmation for being overwhelmed but he couldn't so he just kept repeating, 'He'll be fine, he'll be fine,' until she finally opened her arms and let him go.

He moved to the other side of the trolley and she told him what the doctor had said. 'They gave me his false teeth. I didn't even know he *had* false teeth.'

Nick nodded. There were a lot of things Claire didn't know. He stared at the streaked lino and the rip in the flowery cubicle curtain, anywhere except into her panicky eyes. What was he doing here? Why had he ever left New York? If he was three and a half thousand miles away, this could all be dealt with in a phone call.

'I have to go and get him some things.' She was kneading the buckle of the old man's coat between her hands. 'Will you stay here with him till I get back?'

He nodded. What else could he do?

The house looked different. Naked, Claire thought, exposed. The heavy swags of ivy that used to cover the exterior walls had been hacked away. The windows looked oddly bare. The old surgery sign had been uncovered. It hung, cracked and lopsided above the garage. A dozen bulging green garden sacks were lined up by the wall like dumpy prisoners waiting to be shot. There was a note Sellotaped to the front door.

'*There have been a lot of complaints re. the state of the garden so I have taken the opportunity to mow the lawn, trim the ivy and put down some weedkiller etc. Brian Cunningham.*'

'Bastard!' Claire whispered under her breath. He couldn't wait till her dad was out of the way before interfering. It took a second before her hand stopped shaking enough to put the key in the lock and turn it. She grabbed a shopping bag from the hallstand and went upstairs to her dad's bedroom.

The faded swirly navy carpet was still thick on one side of the bed but it had worn away on the other. One bedside table was empty, the other had on it a small travel clock and a pile of books.

The top two drawers in the mahogany built-in dressing table were still full of her mother's underwear and scarves. Claire opened the third drawer and found a clean pair of her dad's pyjamas. She unhooked his plaid dressing gown from the hook on the back of the door and looked under the bed for his slippers and then, with a jolt, she realised that he wouldn't be needing them. His hip was shattered. She saw her own reflection in the dressing table mirror, one hand to her mouth, and forced herself to move over to the built-in wardrobe.

Her dad's things took up a dozen hangers; the rest of the space was still packed with her mother's clothes. Claire ran a finger along the line of wooden hangers, stopping at the things she thought she remembered. The blue cheesecloth summer dress. The chamois leather skirt. The yellow pussycat bow blouse. The red coat with the missing button.

Her father rarely left his room after the accident, but sometimes, when he went downstairs, Claire had taken some of her mum's clothes into her own room and laid them out on her bed. The grey angora jumper and the black wool mini skirt. The dark green pinafore dress inside the red coat. The Aran scarf looped around the neck, the way her mum used to wear it. Claire would lie down carefully beside each outfit and press her face against a lapel or a sleeve and imagine that her mum was really there.

She opened her bag now and took out her father's watch and his ring. He must have stood here with her mother's rings all those years ago, before he put them in the crystal ashtray where they'd been ever since. Claire slipped his ring in beside her mum's and put his watch beside the ashtray on the shelf. She took out the false teeth in their little Ziploc bag. What was she supposed to do with them?

*

The porter wheeled Nick's father's trolley along a network of identical corridors, in and out of two lifts, and into the orthopaedic ward. The old man slept through it all. His mouth looked caved in without his front teeth and his unruly grey hair was matted with dried blood. Nick shook his head. What was he even doing up a ladder at his age? Of course it was rotten, like everything else in that house.

A Filipina nurse came and filled in all the gaps that Claire had left. If the surgery went well, the old man would be home in a month, she told him. He wouldn't be able to fully weight bear for another couple of months but, if he made an effort to do his physio, she said, he could make a good recovery.

An effort. Nick wasn't going to put any money on that.

He left the old man in his bed by the window, went out into the corridor and called Kelly again.

'I'm so sorry, honey,' she said. 'My cell was switched off. I was at yoga class. I got your message. How's your dad doing?'

'It was a bad fall but he'll be okay,' Nick said gruffly.

'That's such a relief. What about his dog?' Kelly said. Nick had forgotten about all about the dog. 'Do you want me to find a kennel that will pick him up?'

'That would be great.' Claire was scared of dogs and she'd only turn the whole thing into a drama.

'Do you want me to come?'

'No. I won't be long. I just have to wait for Claire to get back.' Nick checked his watch. Why was it taking her so long to pack a few things into a bag?

After the call he went to the bathroom and washed his hands. The front of his white shirt was smeared with streaks of Claire's mascara. They made him feel queasy. He knew he was Pattern Matching, overlaying the past on what had happened today, but seeing Claire so needy had rattled him.

He had been ten when his mother died but Claire was barely six. Way too young to understand what had happened. It would slip away from her and she'd be fine for weeks and then the bad dreams would start again or she'd wet her bed and he'd find her curled up on the landing, her pyjamas damp, her duvet wet. He was the one who had to change her covers and find her dry things and bring her back to bed and read to her until she went back to sleep again.

He had thought that the old man would snap out of it and start looking after Claire, start looking after *him*, but he hadn't. While boys in his class were playing soccer and computer games, he was making Claire's dinner and helping her with her homework and making sure she had a clean jumper for school.

'Why didn't you go to an adult for help?' his therapist in the States had once asked him. But there was nobody to go to. None of his grandparents were alive. His mother had been an only child. His father had two brothers but they lived in Australia. There were neighbours but they had never been friends. And even if they had been, always at the back of Nick's mind was the fear that, if anyone found out how bad things really were, he and Claire would be taken into care.

Nick sat on a chair beside the old man's bed and stared down at a dog-eared copy of *New Scientist*. He was halfway through an article about astrophysics when he heard a ragged gasp. The old man was trying to sit up. His eyes were wet and his face was crumpled into a grimace of pain.

He had never seen the old man crying before, not even after the accident.

'It's okay,' he said gently. 'I think the morphine's wearing off. I'll call the nurse to give you another shot.'

'No!' the old man groaned. 'It's fine.'

''Course it is,' Nick said, hearing the hardness in his own voice. 'Everything's always fine, isn't it?' He picked up the magazine and forced himself to begin reading again.

Claire had already closed the front door when she remembered the dog. She went back inside and opened the kitchen door nervously and jumped back as Dog exploded into the hall in a coat hangery tangle of legs. He hauled himself up the stairs. She heard him thundering around up there, blundering into her dad's bedroom, clattering around the bathroom. After a minute he came crashing back downstairs again and stood in the hall, panting, looking at her worriedly from beneath his tufty white eyebrows.

Her father always spoke to Dog as if he were a person. 'Dad is at the hospital!' Claire said slowly. Dog put his huge grey head on one side and lifted one big grey paw to take a step towards her. 'Stay!' she shouted. She backed through the kitchen and opened the back door and he hung his head, trotted down the hall and went out into the garden.

The air smelled of wet grass. The hedges had been trimmed and the lawn had been freshly cut. The wooden ladder had been propped up against the wall behind the chestnut tree.

Claire's mum used to climb that tree, kicking off her shoes, swinging herself up, gracefully, as if it was the easiest thing in the world. Later, when Claire was big enough, she used to climb it too. It was where she used to hide, when she was upset and she didn't want Nick and her dad to find her. She would scramble up into the tent of leaves and disappear.

Dog circled the garden slowly, stopping to sniff every leaf while Claire looked up at the roof and down at the grass, trying to figure out where her father had landed when he fell. He had been lying out all night. He would still be there if Dog's barking hadn't annoyed the Cunninghams.

'Good dog,' she whispered. Dog lifted his head and looked at her warily. 'Good Dog.'

Part Two

10

One evening, when Claire was sitting by her dad's bed in the stuffy ward, he reached out and took her hand. She stared down at the wrinkled skin over the blue veins on his wrist, his swollen knuckles, his thickened nails. It was the first time he'd held her hand in twenty-seven years. It was probably just the morphine but in those awful days after his operation, it felt like a sign.

The surgery was supposed to take three hours but took eight. The surgeon had to insert a seventeen-inch pin in her dad's femur to hold the shattered bone together. He had lost a lot of blood and had to have a transfusion. Claire sat on a plastic seat in the foyer of the hospital all day, afraid to even go outside to put money in the parking meter in case something happened.

For the first week she spent every minute she was allowed to in the ward. Nick made excuse after excuse not to visit but she juggled visits between auditions, bringing Jaffa Cakes he didn't eat and books he couldn't read. She had seen more of him in the last three weeks than she had in the last three years.

It was strange to see her dad away from his solitary life, being chatted to by cheerful nurses and teased by the tea lady. It made her wonder if maybe he could be part of the world again, instead of cut off from it. She looked at him now, propped up in bed, with the *Irish Times* spread out on the cover; his eyes had an out-of-focus morphine glaze. 'Do you want me to read that to you?'

He sighed. 'You should go now, Claire. I'm fine.'

Fine was a bit of an overstatement but the worst was over. He was beginning to learn to walk again using a Zimmer frame. In just two weeks, he'd be allowed to go home.

Nick stood in the hall and looked up the stairs at the faded wallpaper that was worn away at hand level, the chipped wooden banisters and the dust motes that swirled in the weak light from the landing window. He hadn't set foot in the house for years but nothing had changed.

'I have moved on from my past,' he said out loud. 'I live in the now.' His voice sounded thin and unconvincing in the empty house. He picked up a roll of bin bags and went into his mother's old surgery. He had been allowed in here sometimes when he was very small. He remembered sitting on his mother's lap. The way her long hair tickled the back of his neck. She'd shake the anatomical doll she kept on her desk so that all the tiny plastic organs fell out and help him to slot them all back into the hollow body. But that was before Claire came along and everything changed.

The old man wouldn't be able to climb the stairs for months so the surgery had to be made into a bedroom for him. If it was up to Nick, the clear out would have been done by the handyman Kelly had organised to paint the room and lay the carpet, but Claire had insisted on doing it herself and he knew if he left it to her she'd agonise over every little thing and it would take forever.

He'd arranged to meet her at ten but he'd come an hour earlier. With any luck, he could get most of it done before she arrived. He pushed past boxes full of books and bags of old clothes and set up his portable shredder on his mother's old desk, elbowing a pile of medical journals out of the way to make space. He shook out a bin bag, held it under the windowsill and swept everything in. Dried-up pens and rusty paper clips and paperweights with drug company logos. A plastic ashtray with tear-shaped scorch marks in the bottom. He shook his head. A doctor who smoked at work. It was hard to believe now.

He moved on to the desk and began to go through the drawers quickly, tossing prescription pads and patient files into a pile for shredding and binning the rest. In the bottom drawer he found a printed flyer for a nativity play he'd been in when he was seven. He had been a reindeer who, for some reason, had been present at the holy birth. He'd worn cardboard antlers and a brown polo-neck and a painted table tennis ball cut in half for a nose. He remembered the old man in the front row with Claire, who must have only been four, on his knee. His mother hadn't turned up. He had looked for her in the audience, knowing that his father would say, if he asked him, that she couldn't come because she had to work.

The rusty yellow skip was half full by the time Claire pulled into the driveway. It was mostly big stuff, a rolled-up rug, a couple of old chairs, a broken electric fire, but Nick should have waited. They were supposed to be doing this together. He was bent over a box of magazines when she entered the old surgery. 'I thought you said ten?'

'Did I?'

'I brought coffee.' She held out two paper cups.

'I'll take a rain check, thanks.' Nick could have used one but he didn't want to stop. He crushed an empty box and turned to the built-in shelves. He was going though the piles of drug information leaflets, stuffing them into a bag, when something fell on the floor. He picked it up. It was the little plastic anatomical doll. He dropped it into the bag, too.

'You can't throw that away!' Claire put down the coffees and came over.

This was exactly what he'd been dreading. Claire was sentimental. She'd want to examine every little thing. 'Fine.' He fished it out of the bag. 'You keep it.'

They worked in silence. Nick gathered up all the drug samples in a box to be dropped off at the chemist. Claire emptied a drawer full of blank stationery then tackled a shelf of medical directories and textbooks. In among them, she found a library book in a plastic cover – *Couples* by John Updike. She remembered the one time she had disobeyed her dad and opened the surgery door. She must have been about five. It was bedtime and she'd desperately wanted to see her mum. 'She's busy but she'll come in and kiss you goodnight when you're asleep,' her dad had said. But Claire couldn't wait. She had turned the brass handle slowly and pushed the door open just a crack, and she had seen her mum curled up on the examination table reading a library book. It might have been this one.

She handed it to Nick. 'What should we do with this?'

He opened it. 'It was due back on July twenty-fourth 1984.' He laughed. 'So the fine will probably run into six figures!' He went back to taping the lid on a box.

Claire watched him out of the corner of her eye. He had laughed so maybe he wouldn't bite her head off if she asked him a question.

Nick could sense Claire watching him, fiddling with that locket she still wore. It was mawkish. He should never have given it to her. The old man had gone to identify the body. Afterwards, he had sat in a chair in the kitchen with his fist clenched, and his face had been empty as if he were gone too. Nick had seen the glitter of the chain dangling from his hand and later he found the locket on the floor and put it around his sister's neck, the way his mother used to when Claire was upset.

'Do you remember the sing-songs?' she said. 'We used to sing the "Na na" bit of "Hey Jude".'

'Not really.' Nick wrote: 'Caution! Poison!' on the side of a box. The old man was shy. He'd hated singing but he did it anyway. There was nothing he wouldn't do for *her*.

'And Mum and Dad used to sing that old song that Johnny Cash does.' Claire was still looking at him. ' "If You Could Read My Mind". It was her favourite.'

'Was it?' Nick said vaguely. With Claire there had always been two layers. The things they were talking about and the thing they couldn't talk about. He picked up two bags of rubbish and went outside to chuck them into the skip. What he remembered was wanting his mother to be the way she'd been before Claire was born.

He felt the past, like a familiar weight settling over his ribs, pressing down on him, the way it had when he was a child. He stood in the pale autumn sunshine and took lungfuls of crisp air. In for a count of seven. Out for a count of eleven. But the air didn't make it past the hard knot in his chest, the one he thought he had dissolved years ago.

*

Claire was sitting cross-legged on the floor, sorting through a pile of medical journals, when he went back into the surgery. 'I'm sorry.' She looked up at him. 'I know it's hard for you to talk about her. It's my fault.'

'We've been through all of this!' Nick ran his hand over his hair. 'It's not your fault. You have to stop re-reading the early chapters of your life.'

'I heard you saying that on TV.' She bent her head so her hair fell over her face. 'But it's not as easy for me as it is for you.'

'I can't do this.' Nick held up his hand. It was grimy, he saw, there were black crescents of dust under his nails. 'Maybe you need to talk to someone but it's not me. A therapist or a counsellor, OK?'

Claire nodded. She still had the badly photocopied fact-sheet that the counsellor had given her when she was in her twenties. *'Moving Beyond Survivor Guilt'. 'The idea that you could have stopped what happened is more attractive to you than the idea that life is random and senseless,'* it began. The last page had a list of cheery bullet points. *'It's OK to delight in being alive! Give yourself permission to be happy. Self-sabotage is your enemy. Don't let it stop you living fully. Think of your life as a gift.'* But Claire's life still felt like something she had stolen.

Nick turned his back and began feeding paper into the shredder. 'Why don't you make a fresh coffee? Let's push on here. I want to get home for lunch.'

Home to Kelly, he thought tiredly, who would want to read him the latest conception advice she'd found on the internet. The house would smell of the Chinese herbs she boiled that were supposed to increase their chances. She had said that trying for a baby wouldn't change them, but it had already changed her. Everything revolved around this baby that didn't even exist. And when it did she might change even more, the way his mother had after Claire was born.

Claire filled the kettle and found two mugs. Nick had been so kind to her for so long, she couldn't resent him because he'd stopped. When she was eight, he used to take her to the cinema in Rathmines every Saturday morning. He was twelve then, far too old for all the films she wanted to see but he watched them with her. *The Care Bears. The Never Ending Story. The Princess Bride.*

She had hated going shopping for shoes and clothes after her mum was gone. He had tried to make it fun. They'd get the bus to Dundrum, buy jeans and sweatshirts and T-shirts and shorts in Penney's and afterwards they'd have cream cakes in Bewley's. Then, when she was thirteen, everything changed.

Claire remembered the day it had happened. She had wanted to go into Dublin to pick out something for her Christmas present. Nick had trailed around Miss Selfridge and A-Wear after her while she flicked through rails of sparkly tops and flimsy dresses.

In Switzer's, he had waited for her outside the fitting room while she tried on a green jersey dress with shoulder pads that she knew he was going to say was too old for her. But when she came out, he wasn't there. She pulled her clothes on and searched the whole floor but he was gone. She had never been in town without him before and she didn't have any bus fare. She got to the bus stop as a bus was pulling over and saw him in the queue. She darted across the road, between the lanes of traffic.

'What happened?' She had a stitch from running and she was out of breath. 'Why did you leave me like that?'

He wouldn't look at her. 'I can't do stuff like this for you any more!' He shoved some money into her hand. 'You have to start looking after yourself.' She watched him getting on the bus, waiting for him to turn around, to come back and explain. But he didn't so she waited for the next bus home.

Claire put the plastic anatomical doll into the cupboard under the sink. She looked around the kitchen. At the old Formica cupboards, the ancient gas cooker, the scuffed lino, the peeling styrofoam ceiling tiles. This had once been their home, but some day this room would be cleared out too and people would move into this house and start all over again. She hoped that they would be a family and that they would be happy.

The surgery was almost cleared. The last thing to tackle was the filing cabinet. The top drawers were packed with hanging files. Nick pulled them out and handed them to Claire and she dumped them on the floor beside the shredder. The bottom drawer was jammed closed. He wedged his foot against the desk and jerked it until it opened with a rattle. It contained three empty vodka bottles.

Claire's hand went to her locket. 'Do you think Dad was drinking when he fell off the ladder?'

'The ladder was rotten,' Nick said.

'But—'

'These have been in this drawer for years.'

'How do you know?'

'I put them in here.'

'But you never drink.'

'I used to.' He took the bottles out, one by one, and dumped them into a bag. 'When I was in my teens. I had a lot to deal with back then. Let's not make a big drama out of it, OK? It all happened a long time ago.'

11

The noticeboard in the waiting room of the ultrasound suite was covered in pictures of babies. They were smiling and crying and sleeping and nursing, and all of them belonged to other people. Looking at them made Kelly ache with longing. All those tiny, beautiful babies had been born to couples who'd had fertility treatment. Every single one of them was a miracle. She looked at Nick. Some day soon their little miracle might be up there too.

It was day sixteen of her second cycle of Clomid. It hadn't worked the first time round but at least she'd had a proper period so she'd been able to time the second cycle properly.

She'd been terrified that the drugs wouldn't work again. She wanted to feel close to Nick but he hadn't been there for her, not the way she'd hoped. She had tried to support him since his dad's fall. He had been busy with his coaching sessions and strategy meetings with Oonagh Clancy so she had organised kennels and painters and furniture and interviewed live-in carers to look after his dad when he came home. But every time she wanted to talk to him about this amazing journey they were supposed to be taking together, he just withdrew. He had been tense since Tom's fall. She guessed it was stirring up stuff from his past but he didn't want to talk about it. He had moved away from her and she wished he'd come back. This was the most exciting thing they'd ever done. She wanted to feel that they were doing it together.

Nick was flipping through a magazine so he didn't have to look at the notice board. The pictures reminded him of Claire, when she was a baby. She hadn't learned to talk till she was two and a half. She hadn't needed to. She'd just grunt and point and he would get whatever she wanted. He remembered her first real words. They were sitting at the kitchen table, having Sunday lunch and Claire had suddenly said, 'The bin is on fire.' They'd all stared at her, astonished. And then the old man had jumped up because the bin really *had* been on fire.

Kelly squeezed Nick's hand and smiled at him. Ten minutes ago, she'd nearly taken his head off because he'd driven past a free space in the car park. She had been on a hormonal roller coaster for nearly two months now.

'I have a really good feeling about this,' she whispered.

'That's great but try not to get your hopes up too high,' he said quietly. 'You were so upset when the last cycle didn't work.'

'You were upset too, right?' She frowned at him. 'You're trying to have a baby as well.'

'Of course.'

She sighed. 'I can't help wanting to be hopeful. There's so much riding on this.'

Nick nodded. There was a lot riding on the Channel 5 show too but he couldn't share that with Kelly. He'd tried to reduce his stress by giving up the weekly slot on Fish FM but Oonagh wouldn't hear of it.

'It's good for your profile.'

'It's tacky and—'

'Nick!' she'd laughed. 'A two-page feature in *Gossip* magazine about my addiction to nail extensions is tacky, but it keeps me top-of-mind. We want Clingfilms to think you're hot stuff. Unless you're just about to open your bedroom doors to *VIP* and tell the world that you and Kelly are the new Sting and Trudy, Fish stays.'

'Let's see.' The ultrasound technician moved her wand. 'No follicles in the left ovary.' Kelly gripped the edge of the bed and stared at the blurry black and white screen. She couldn't bear to go home with nothing. The image fuzzed up as the wand moved around inside her. 'But look at this!' The technician pointed at the screen. 'We have three mature follicles on the right ovary.' She clicked on a dark grey blob and took a screen grab. 'Twenty millimetres, twenty-two millimetres and twenty-four millimetres.' She smiled. 'That's exactly what we're looking for.'

Kelly was already down to her underwear by the time Nick had climbed the stairs. She pulled off her pink lace bra, grabbed his tie and dragged him in to the bedroom. He had never seen her want sex so much and he'd never wanted it less. The sight of the cheerful technician squirting lubricant on her wand and the nurse's mortifying instruction to 'have plenty of intercourse' had not left him feeling sexy. 'Could we just reconnect before we do this—'

'Seriously?' She let go of his tie. 'OK. Sure. What?'

'Maybe we could meditate together for a bit?'

'Fine.' Kelly pulled on her dressing gown.

He found his iPod and they lay side by side on the bed with one earphone each, listening to a podcast.

'Now take another long, slow deep breath,' the spaced-out woman in Kelly's left ear said, 'and imagine your body is filling with orange light.' She sounded like Kelly's high-school friend Jennifer after she had smoked too much grass. 'Honey,' she pulled her earphone out, 'I'm sorry, would you mind if we just skip the starter and cut straight to the main because timing is kinda critical here.'

Nick sat up. 'I'm just not sure I'm ready.'

'You're not ready to have our baby?'

'Of course I am,' Nick began, 'what I meant was—'

'Because every month that goes by decreases my chances of conception with or without the Clomid, so I need to know we're on the same page here.'

'We are,' he said soothingly. 'But I need a minute before I—'

'Oh!' She smiled. 'You just lie back and leave everything to me.'

'What about you?' Nick said when they were finished.

'I'm good, thanks.' Kelly fluttered her hand as if she were turning down a side order of fries. She pulled her dressing gown on again, slid on to the floor, then swung herself up into a yoga headstand. Her dark hair pooled on the carpet. 'Gravity is supposed to help the sperm swim in the right direction,' she gasped.

'I'd better get back to work.' And do what? he wondered. He'd cancelled all his face-to-face sessions for this afternoon so they could have a romantic lunch before they went home to make love.

'Nick,' Kelly called after him when he was halfway down the stairs. 'Sweetie, will you come home early so we can do it again?'

No TV. No emails. No phone calls. No internet. No alcohol. No sex. Not until he'd written a decent song. Ray had made the rules and he was going to stick to them.

The blinds were drawn. The laptop was open. His guitars – acoustic and electric – were tuned. The table was piled with takeaway cartons, pizza boxes and Sapporo cans. The rug was littered with scrunched-up balls of paper and trodden-in Bombay mix.

He had done this before, why couldn't he do it again? He tried to think himself back into the mindset he'd been in when he wrote 'Asia Sky'. What had made it so special?

He'd been miserable when he got on that plane in Tokyo. Great, he was miserable now. He'd been angry with Chip. Snap! Now he was angry with Claire. '*What music career? You're a jingle writer.*' He still couldn't believe she had said that. Even Chip, at his worst, hadn't been that vicious.

He picked up a ball of paper, smoothed it out on the table and read the scribbled lyrics.
*'Time flew like an arrow
To pierce our tomorrow.
I'm left here to wallow—'*
He picked up another page:
*'She got an agenda
Put my life in a blender,
Return to sender—'*
And another:
*'Too rich, too thin.
My favourite sin.
You have skin.
You smell like—'*
'Like what, Ray?' The voice in his head was Chip Connolly's. 'Gin?' 'Vim?' 'A bin?' He sat biting his knuckles. He needed a drink but it was half past four in the morning and when he'd

made his rules, he'd poured everything in his cocktail cabinet down the sink. He went into the kitchen to check the freezer for vodka. There was nothing in there except the faint smell of lobster and his frisbee.

He crept down the stairs, skipping the step that creaked, and opened the door to Claire's flat. It wasn't her flat, he reminded himself, it was his. He could go wherever he liked. She might not even be down here. She'd been coming and going at weird hours for the last couple of weeks.

He made his way silently to her kitchen and opened her fridge. It was packed with food but there was no alcohol. He cursed and began to search the shelves and, at the back of the cupboard above the sink, he finally hit the jackpot. A dusty bottle of sake he'd given Claire in 2006.

The heat from Ray's laptop woke him up. It felt like it was burning a hole in his thighs. He sat up and the hangover hit him between the eyes, like a samurai sword. He vaguely remembered finishing the last of the sake and then he must have watched a DVD or, he glanced down at the screen of his laptop, *written an email*. Cold fingers of shame crept up his spine. It wasn't just an email. It was *an apology* to Chip Connolly.

'Hey Chip,' it said, 'it's been a while. Thinking about a Horses reunion and thought it was about time we buried the old hatchet. Just wanted to apologise for all the shit that went down when I sold "Sky" to the Japs. Sorry, man! I know that cut you up, big-time. Anyway, if you ever want to get together for a jam, you know where I am. Rx.'

Ray put his face in his hands and groaned. It was the 'x' that got him. That was how he always signed his texts to Claire. It made him sound like a teenage girl.

Claire was at the hospital and Nick was doing a double coaching session so Kelly offered to go to his dad's house to pick up the dog and let the live-in carer in. She had chosen the carer herself. Nick had said it was the kind of thing Claire would be useless at so Kelly had advertised online, made a shortlist and interviewed three women. None of them seemed particularly caring to her but

Sinead, a neat woman in her sixties with a grey perm, seemed to be the most capable.

The woman from The Pet Hotel was already waiting by the front door with Dog. He looked thin and thoroughly wretched. 'This is the first time he hasn't barked his head off in a month,' the woman said, hurriedly taking Kelly's cheque. 'He howled the place down and he wouldn't eat. I would have asked you to take him back but I knew you were stuck. He's really too old to be in a kennel, you know. At a certain point, it's not kind to put an animal through that.'

Kelly patted Dog's head. He made a long low moaning noise and buried his head in the folds of her coat. 'Poor old thing,' she said. Nick was allergic to dogs but she liked them. If they had a boy, she thought, they'd get one of those terriers that didn't shed. There was something about little boys and dogs that went together.

Dog followed her around the house while she checked everything. The surgery was freshly carpeted and smelled of paint. The locker she'd bought in IKEA had been assembled and the hospital bed had been put together. Sinead was to sleep in Claire's old room. Kelly wondered what Claire's friends had made of it when she was growing up. It had a bed, a desk and a dressing table but there were no girly touches. She'd bought new linens, some throws and a rug in soft pinks and greys, and added a velvet chair and a reading lamp.

It was just staging really, but the room looked warm and cozy. It used to give Kelly a thrill to be able to do this, but nothing mattered now except getting her body to do what it was supposed to do. She stood on the landing and hugged herself. Dog was lurking at the top of the stairs, afraid to let her out of his sight. Dogs were supposed to sense when a woman was pregnant, she'd read that somewhere. They picked up on the change in body chemistry. She couldn't feel it, but maybe he could tell that her cells were dividing and multiplying, right now, doing the oldest algebra in the universe. Making a baby.

'I'm sorry,' Sinead pursed her lips and picked her travel bag up again, 'but this is not what we discussed.'

When Irish people started their sentences with 'I'm sorry', Kelly thought, wearily, it always meant that *you* were going to be sorry. *'I'm sorry but that rug is too beige.' 'I'm sorry but I thought your fee included VAT.' 'I'm sorry but those are not the taps I ordered.'*

She put on her most professional smile. 'But I told you there was a dog at the interview. You said that wouldn't be a problem.'

Sinead folded her arms. 'That's not a dog, that's practically a donkey.'

'He's very gentle and I can organise someone to walk him. You won't even notice that he's here.'

The line of Sinead's mouth tightened. 'An animal like that roaming around a patient who has just had surgery is an accident waiting to happen. This is not about me, it's about the welfare of the patient.'

'He belongs to the patient,' Kelly began, 'the patient loves him, but if it's a matter of money—'

'I'm wasting your time.' Sinead pulled her gloves on. She wasn't bluffing, Kelly saw, and there was no back-up.

'Please,' she said, 'don't go. I'm sure we can work something out.'

Claire opened the front door and the ambulance men wheeled her dad up to the porch then carried him into the hall.

'How are you going to get this thing up those stairs?' he asked.

'They won't have to because you're in here.' Claire opened the door to the revamped surgery. Her dad looked past her into the neat room, taking in the new oatmeal carpet, the new wall-mounted TV, the hospital bed with its pulley.

'Who did this?' he whispered. 'What have you done with all your mother's things?'

'Most of it was just old medical records, Dad, and—'

'Is that a thirty-two-inch telly?' one of the ambulance men interrupted.

The other one guffawed. 'You need your eyes tested. Got to be a thirty-six at least! What do you think, Tom?'

'Please, bring me upstairs to my own room.' Her dad looked from one of them to the other.

'You won't be able to walk for months.' Claire bit her lip. 'How are you supposed to get up and down the stairs?'

'I can just stay up there.'

'What if there was a fire?' One of the ambulance men tried to smooth things over. 'You'd be toast.'

Her dad didn't speak while the ambulance man helped him into the bed, then he turned, awkwardly, on to his side, away from her.

'I'll just go and get Dog,' Claire said to his back.

Kelly was standing in the doorway. 'I'm not sure,' she said quietly, 'that's a good idea.'

'He'll have to go back to The Pet Hotel.' Claire sighed when Kelly explained that the carer wouldn't stay unless Dog went.

'They won't take him. They said he's too old.'

'I don't want him going to kennels,' Claire's dad said to the wall. 'Bring him to the Cats and Dogs' Home.'

'The pound?' Claire stared at his back. 'You don't mean that!'

'*You're* not going to take him. Nicholas is allergic. I'm not leaving him in a cage for six months. At least this way someone might give him a proper home.'

But this was his home, Claire thought. Dog and her dad were inseparable. 'You need to think this through.' She wished he would turn around to face her. 'You don't want to make any decisions you might regret.'

'All I want,' he said in a small, broken voice, 'is to be left alone.'

Nick had just spent a double session with a couple who were on the verge of breaking up. He had managed to get them to commit to living in the same house for another week, but it hadn't been easy and now he felt utterly drained.

'Just do what the old man wants,' he told Claire. 'At least this gives the animal a chance to be re-homed.'

Claire looked at Dog, who was curled up nose to tail in the corner of the kitchen. He was trying to make himself disappear but he was too huge to pull it off.

'Nobody's going to take an ancient dog that looks like that,' she whispered. 'They'll put him down, after three days. I saw a programme.'

'Look, are you going to do this or not?' Nick's voice was sharp.
'I'll do it,' she said quietly, and hung up.

Nick sat staring at the phone. Why did she always bring out the worst in him?

After the accident, *he* had been the one taking Claire shopping for clothes. There was nobody else to do it. The old man was barely able to leave the house.

They usually went to Dundrum, but when she turned twelve, Claire started wanting to go into town and he'd gone with her, until that day just before Christmas, when he was seventeen. It had started out OK. She had dragged him around every bloody girly shop on Grafton Street. She'd disappear into the fitting room and come out in half a dozen different dresses, and he was supposed to tell her which one was the nicest. He hadn't a clue. To him, she looked best in what she always wore, T-shirts and jeans.

'This is the last shop, promise!' she said when they went into Switzer's. She disappeared into a fitting room with an armful of clothes, and he was waiting outside, trying to decide whether they'd go for a pizza or a burger afterwards, when he felt a hand on his back.

'How old are you?' It was a saleslady with a blonde perm and glasses and she was glaring at him.

'Seventeen.'

She nodded. 'How old is that little girl in there?' She pointed at the fitting-room curtain.

Nick flushed. 'She's thirteen.'

She folded her arms. 'You should be ashamed of yourself.'

Nick was so angry that when he opened his mouth to explain that Claire was his sister no words would come out. Five or six other women were looking over now.

'Look at the guilty look of you!' The saleslady shook her head. 'Get out before I call security.'

So he did. He just walked out and left Claire there. He knew she'd panic when she came out and found he was gone but he was too humiliated to go back.

12

The closest animal pound was Rathfarnham. It was only four miles away but the idea of being in an enclosed space with a dog even for a short time made Claire feel sick with anxiety. She wanted to call Ray but wouldn't let herself.

Kelly put some ham on Mossy's back seat and Dog climbed in stiffly but he didn't even look at it, he wouldn't take his eyes off the house.

Claire opened the driver's door and edged carefully into the seat. Her back tensed and she waited to feel his breath on her neck, but he just sighed and folded himself up, nose to tail, on the slippery leatherette behind her.

'Stay!' she said as she drove slowly up Hawthorn Drive.

The fuel needle was hovering just below empty, which either meant that Mossy would go for another fifty miles or else that he would conk out at the next set of traffic lights, so Claire decided to stop in Blackrock for petrol. Dog lifted his big head and stared out, bewildered, at the brightly lit forecourt. Claire felt like the woodsman going into the woods to kill Snow White.

She went inside and queued for the till. She couldn't take him to the pound. Maybe she could find an estate where kids lived and let him out, but it was kids who had tied him to the shopping trolley all those years ago. She stood at the window, looking out at the car, trying to think of a way out of this. Then she saw it. The wooden sign outside the house on the other side of the road. 'Barnhill Veterinary Surgery'. She could pretend Dog was a stray. Somebody would take him home.

She opened the back door. 'Out!' she said to Dog.

Dog climbed out stiffly. His grey fur was flattened on one side where he'd been lying on it. He looked miserable. He still had his lead on. Claire held it at arm's length, and dragged him across the road. He started shaking at the gate but she herded him into the garden. At the door, she unclipped the lead. There was a little metal disc on his collar with her dad's phone number on it. With shaking hands, she took that off too, then stuffed the collar into her bag.

The tiled waiting room had an empty row of metal chairs and a display stand stacked with bags of pet food. There was a receptionist in a white coat behind a desk.

'I just found this dog,' Claire said. 'I think he's a stray.'

'Name?'

Was this a trick question? 'I don't know,' she said.

'*Your* name.'

'Oh, Claire Dillon.'

'Number?'

The receptionist wrote it down. 'Take a seat. We're just closing but I'm sure the vet will see you.'

'I don't need to stay, do I?'

'It'll only take a minute.'

The receptionist went through a swing door and Dog sank down on to the floor, dropped his head down on to his huge paws and let out a pitiful, low whine.

'This is your best chance,' Claire whispered.

'You'd tell them your whole life story, wouldn't you?' The receptionist was back. 'You can go on through now.'

The surgery was small and white and windowless with a computer and an examination table.

'Who do we have here?' a voice behind her said.

She turned and there, in green scrubs and trainers, was Shane.

'I though you were an animal wrangler,' she stammered.

'Did you?' His dark brown eyes under his heavy brows looked indifferent. 'What are you doing here?'

'I saw this dog, outside, on the road, and he looked as if he was a stray.'

'I thought you were terrified of dogs?'

'I am but . . .' Claire thought, hard. '. . . he seemed even more scared than I was.'

136

Shane looked down at Dog. 'Good boy, good dog,' he said softly. At the sound of his own name, one of Dog's ears popped out and revolved like a hairy satellite dish. Shane ran his hands over him. 'He's pitifully thin. He hasn't eaten properly for a couple of weeks at least. And look at this.' He showed her the mark the collar had left around Dog's neck. 'Someone just took his collar off and ditched him. He's got to be thirteen or fourteen years old. Who'd do a thing like that?'

Claire swallowed.

'Well, whoever did it is going to be sorry!' Shane began rummaging in a drawer.

'What do you mean?'

'If he's microchipped, I can trace the owner.' He picked up the phone. 'Sandy, I need the scanner. Can you see if it's in Patricia's office?'

'Will that do any good?' Claire said, nervously. 'Wouldn't you be better off finding someone who wanted to keep him?'

The receptionist knocked and handed Shane a small white plastic device.

Claire held her breath while he scanned every inch of Dog.

'No luck,' he said softly.

Claire swallowed a gasp of relief. 'What will you do now?'

Shane put the scanner away. 'I suppose I'll fax his picture around all the other vets and let the Gardaí know, but he'll probably go to the pound in the morning.' He shook his head. 'Do you know how many dogs were put down in this country last year?'

'No.'

'Five and a half thousand. This guy will just be a statistic three days from now. He's way too big and way too old to be re-homed.' He slipped a lead around Dog's neck and opened a door to another windowless room with a wall of cages. Dog looked around frantically for a way out.

'I'd take him home with me, tonight,' Shane said. 'But I don't know how he is with cats.'

'Not good!'

'How do you know?'

She stared at Shane, willing her mouth to move. 'Just a feeling.'

'You're pretty intuitive around animals for someone who's afraid of them.' His eyes had warmed a little. 'I don't suppose you'd take him?'

'I would but I don't have a garden. It wouldn't be fair.'

'You're right.' He opened the door of a cage. Dog splayed his long legs trying to stand his ground, but Shane gently manoeuvred him inside.

Dog peed himself as the wire door closed then slunk down to the back of the cage. Claire couldn't bear to look at him. He had always seemed so big to her but now he looked pitifully small.

She followed Shane back out to the waiting room. The receptionist was gone. The floor had been mopped with strong bleach that made her eyes water.

'Thanks for bringing him in.' Shane folded his arms.

'How much?'

He shook his head.

'I feel I owe you an apology for that night in Johnny Foxes. I lied to Emma. That guy in the car park isn't my boyfriend, he's just a friend. I'm not even sure he's a friend any more.'

Shane frowned. 'It doesn't matter. I shouldn't have . . .' But he didn't finish his sentence. 'The thing is,' he rubbed his chin, 'I'm not really in a position to—' He stared up at the fluorescent strip light. 'My marriage broke up a few months ago.'

Claire glanced down at his hand.

'I think I told you that my brother died. It's hard to explain but something like that changes everything.'

'I know.' She could see that he didn't believe her.

'Right.'

'My mother drowned when I was six.' She felt disgusted with herself the moment she said it, for just blurting it out like that. 'I'd better go.' She turned away quickly and swung her bag on to her shoulder and the sound of Dog's lead jingling inside it made her feel even worse.

The nightmares always began differently. In this one, Claire was driving Mossy. Dog was in the back and, suddenly, she realised that the car was underwater. She held her breath and lay across the passenger seat and kicked the door open. She turned around for Dog but he was gone. She pulled herself out of the car. It was dark but she could see light way above her on the surface. She tried to fight her way up to it but the current was too strong. It sucked her down as if it were swallowing her. With every foot she sank, she felt more of the fight going out of her. Her breath escaped and bubbles fizzed past her face. She woke up gasping, her T-shirt clammy, her face wet.

She got out of bed and went down to the kitchen. She had hardly been drinking since her row with Ray but she opened a bottle of wine and sat at the table shivering. The nightmares always ended the same way. Every time she had one, the day her mother died came flooding back.

When Claire went to bed, she was only five. But when she woke up, she was six. She was going to have a party tea with Nick and pin-the-tail-on-the-donkey and a special present, though she didn't know what it was yet.

Her teacher, Miss Keane, made a fuss of birthdays. She would write 'Claire' on the blackboard first thing and, before the lessons started, they would all have to guess as many words as they could beginning with 'C'. At lunchtime, Claire would get to wear the gold birthday crown while everyone sang the birthday song.

Her mum was going to take her to school as a treat but they couldn't find Claire's sandals and by the time they did, the big hand on the kitchen clock was pointing at nine and that meant that they were already late.

'Nobody should have to go to school on their birthday,' her mum said. 'You can stay with me. We'll have fun!' She made French toast and turned on the TV so Claire could watch cartoons and when that didn't stop Claire sulking, she folded her arms and pretended to be stern. 'I can't have you in my surgery with a grumpy face like that!' Claire had never been allowed into the surgery before. She thought it would be even better than school, but it wasn't.

Her mum made a cave under her desk with a blanket and Claire brought in her dolls and pretended they were sick people. Only one real sick person came. An old man with a red face. Claire peeped out to watch her mum putting a black band on his arm and pumping it up and then letting the air out with a long, snaky hiss. After he was gone, nothing happened for a long time and Claire started whingeing. She didn't want to, but she couldn't stop. Her mum let her sit in her swivel chair and gave her the plastic anatomical doll to play with but, at twelve o'clock, she gave up and put the 'Closed' sign on the surgery door and they went into the back garden for a birthday snack. Milk for Claire and Coke for her mum and a whole plate of chocolate biscuits to share. Claire wasn't hungry. Her mum lit a cigarette and exhaled in a little grey puff of exasperation.

'Would you like to go to the park to see the deer? Or to Howth to feed the seals? Or to town for a proper grown-up lunch?' Claire shook her head. 'What is *wrong* with you, Claire?' Her mum looked at her over her sunglasses. And even now, twenty-seven years later, Claire didn't know why she had been so difficult that day.

'How about a magical mystery drive?' Her mum stood up. 'We can take a picnic!'

The wicker basket was one of Claire's favourite things. There were blue gingham napkins and little knives and forks and plastic goblets. Everything packed neatly into its own little compartment. Her mum made tomato sandwiches and filled a flask for herself and put in some bricks of cold Kia-Ora for Claire. Then she made Claire close her eyes while she wrapped her birthday cake in tinfoil. But at the front door, Claire hung back. 'I don't want to go,' she pulled at the skirt of her mum's yellow dress, 'unless Nick and Dad can come too.'

'Your dad's at work and Nick's at school, you know that, Claire.' Her mum sounded exasperated. 'But we can go anywhere you want.'

Anywhere? Claire thought hard. 'I want to go to the sea to learn how to swim.'

Nick had started swimming classes in school but she wasn't supposed to start for another year.

'It's a deal.' Her mum ran upstairs to get her swimsuit before she changed her mind.

The little green car zipped along the country roads. Usually Claire was in a good mood on mystery drives but today the smell of her mum's cigarettes made her head hurt. They stopped in Wicklow town and her mum bought her a yellow bucket and spade and a pink blow-up swimming ring with an inflatable Dalmatian head.

The long beach was quiet. They spread out the plaid rug near a ruined bathing hut and her mum helped Claire to put on her navy swimsuit. She had forgotten her own bikini so she took off her yellow dress to sunbathe in her bra and pants.

A man passed by smoking a cigarette and her mum asked him for a light. She poured Claire's juice into a little plastic goblet and filled her own goblet from her flask and they had a birthday toast and Claire began to feel a bit better.

Her mum lay down on her stomach on the rug and opened her library book. 'Why don't you make a sandcastle,' she said, 'while I have a little read?'

Claire tried but it was hard without Nick to help. She was supposed to be learning to swim but her mum had fallen asleep so she decided to practise herself. The water was icy and it fizzed and hissed and nibbled her toes, but she stepped into her ring and waded out until the water lifted the frilly white skirt of her swimsuit.

A wave curled and swept past her and she felt it tugging at her knees. The next wave lifted her off her feet. She held on to the Dalmatian head and kicked her legs. She was doing it. She was swimming. After a minute, she looked back to see if her mum was watching her but the beach was so far away that all she could make out was the little postage stamp square of the rug.

She tried to turn herself around but her legs were too tired to kick any more. Two seagulls standing on a floating plank watched her with sharp eyes. A really big wave came rolling towards her and then she lost her grip on the slippery Dalmatian head and slid through the ring and the sea closed over her like a silvery trap-door. Water rushed into her nose and down her throat. She managed to hold on to the ring and came up coughing, her eyes stinging with salt. The beach was gone now and Claire was surrounded by walls of grey water. The sea gulped her down and spat her out again and again, as if this was a game. Then, just as she was getting too tired to hold on to the swimming ring any more, she felt an arm lock under her chin and her mum was swimming beside her, churning the water up, pulling her in.

When they got to the beach, she fell on the sand on her hands and knees and her mum patted her back till she coughed up some sea and then lifted her up in her arms. 'It's OK,' she said. 'You're safe.'

If Claire had known those were the last few moments that she would ever have with her mother, she would have tried to learn her by heart so that she would always remember her. But instead, she bucked and struggled until her mum put her down. Then she put her hands over her face and started to wail.

'It's your fault!' she sobbed. 'You were supposed to teach me but you fell asleep. You ruined my birthday.'

Claire felt wrung out when she woke. She stood in the shower with her hand on the tap wondering whether to turn the water on. If she had a shower, it would make her hangover headache better. But then the pipes would start their banshee shrieking and right now even the sound of her own breathing made the headache worse.

Her phone rang; she put her hands over her ears then tiptoed into the kitchen. 'Hello,' she whispered.

'Claire? Shane O'Neil.'

'Oh! Hello!' she said too loudly, setting the hammer of her headache off again. Her heartbeat joined in. 'How did you get my number?'

'You gave it to the receptionist. Is this a bad time?'

She caught a glimpse of herself in the mirror and realised she was completely naked. 'No.'

'Good. I'm going to call over.' He sounded different, business-like, busy.

'When?'

'Now.'

Claire's kitchen swam into focus. The empty wine bottle on the table. The dishes she had left in the sink. The pile of laundry waiting to go into the machine.

'Could we meet somewhere for a coffee instead?'

'No.' His directness was unexpectedly sexy. A feather of excitement fluttered down her spine. 'I'll be there in twenty minutes.'

The washing machine was full so she stuffed the laundry into the dishwasher, then she realised that she had nowhere to put the dishes so she just shoved them back, still dirty, into the cupboard. She sprayed perfume everywhere and washed herself at the bathroom sink – she didn't want the pipes to be wailing when he arrived. She put on a brown wrap-around dress and a pair of high black boots and she had just managed to brush her hair and put on mascara when the bell rang.

Shane was leaning on the doorframe when she opened the door. His old Land Rover was double-parked in the laneway. He gave her a fierce look that she mistook, for a few glorious seconds, for passion, then she realised that it was anger.

'What are you like?' he asked her coldly. He walked over to his car, opened the back door, lifted Dog out and put him gently on the ground.

'My partner at Barnhill, Patricia Conway, is your father's vet. She saw me faxing this old guy's picture round this morning and recognised him straight away.'

Claire felt a flush creep up her neck into her face. 'The thing is,' she stammered, 'Dad had an accident and he has to have a live-in carer and she wouldn't stay if Dog stayed so he told me to bring him to the pound and . . .'

Shane looked over her shoulder at the patch of nettles by the path. 'And you don't have a garden, right?'

'I'm afraid of dogs.'

'What are you afraid of? That this poor defenceless animal is going kill you? Oh, hang on, that's what you were going to have done to him. You're a pretty good actress, Claire. You had me fooled for a while back there.'

He took a loose page from a notebook out of his jeans pocket. There was a number scribbled on it: 530. 'You know what this is? It's the number of animals I've had to put down since I started practising. I keep count of every one so I never get blasé about what I do. But I'm not counting this one. 'This one's on your conscience.'

*

The hangover was back. It pounded on the inside of Claire's skull while she huddled on the sofa, her knees drawn up to her chin, wondering what to do with Dog. He was pacing back and forth in the tiny kitchen on his huge grey paws, making a high, whistling, whining noise and stopping, every now and then, to lick the floor. Claire got up and edged over to the sink. 'Stay!' she warned him. His bushy grey eyebrows came together in a kind of frown as he watched her filling a saucepan with water. He waited till she had retreated to the sofa and then lapped it all up and went to the back door and looked out. He was so enormous that he could see the garden through the bottom pane. He looked over his shoulder at her with his sad, orangey-brown eyes.

Claire had been told, at school, that God saw everything, but he must have been looking the other way the day her mum had drowned. She had waited for something really bad to happen to her, something that would punish her for what she'd done, but it never did, so she punished herself. She held on to her guilt as tightly as she'd held on to the swimming ring. It was there now, as Dog folded himself and put his head on his paws and looked at her, mournfully, waiting for her to decide his fate.

'We both know what you're going to do,' his eyes seemed to say. 'Why don't we just get this over with?'

13

'I don't think I can face this.' Eilish surveyed the heaving crowd beneath the massive chandeliers in the Rococo Bar. She had dragged Claire out to cheer her up. 'Can we go to Neary's instead?'

'Someone will recognise me.' Claire had given up going to actors' pubs after she'd broken up with Declan; now she couldn't go because the YouTube clip had made her a laughing stock.

'La Cave?' Eilish suggested. 'Someone would need infrared goggles to recognise you in there.'

They sat at the bar in the tiny, candlelit restaurant and ordered two glasses of wine and a cheese board. 'This is more like it,' Eilish said. 'I'd rather die alone and get eaten by my own cat than hang around a glitzy pick-up joint waiting for someone to hit on me.'

'You don't have a cat,' Claire pointed out.

'And *you*,' Eilish forked some Brie on to a cracker, 'have a dog. How's that going to work? You're terrified of dogs.'

'I don't know.' She had decided to keep Dog till her dad got better. Last night she had barricaded him into the kitchen with a chair and this morning she'd locked him out in the garden. She was too scared to take him for a walk in case he bit her when she was putting on his lead.

'You're better off with an old canine than you were with Ray Devine. At least he isn't raiding your fridge in his pants.'

Claire didn't want to talk about Ray.

Eilish touched her scar with her fingertip. It was beginning to fade. Her nose was still swollen but the bruises around her eyes had gone. 'I'm sorry about Shane,' she said. 'But if he was in

145

the middle of a messy marriage break-up, then maybe it's just as well.'

Every time she thought about the lecture he'd given her, she cringed with shame. She was dreading seeing him on *The Spaniard*; thankfully she didn't have another call-out till November.

'I know it's hard at the moment,' Eilish was saying, 'but this is going to be your year, you promised, remember?'

'Can we not talk about me for a bit? How have you been coping with Greasy Pete in the Van of Death?'

'I spent two days scrubbing the van out. It's spotless now and Pete is actually quite nice. Plus Holly appreciates me way more now that I'm only around at the weekends.' She shook her empty glass. 'Want another?'

'Just water.'

Claire hadn't told Eilish about the bottles in the filing cabinet. Poor Nick. He'd been so young and under so much pressure. Something had to give.

Claire had finally worked up the courage to take Dog out for a walk. She held her breath while she put his lead on then herded him into Mossy and drove him to Dun Laoghaire pier and walked him all the way down and back. Apart from the fact that he steamed up all the windows in the car then peed on every inch of the pier, it had been OK.

He was curled up in the back of the car when her phone rang. She pulled Mossy over to take Lorcan's call. 'Good news! The YouTube clip is coming down.'

'Thank God!' Claire drew a smiley face in the dog-breath condensation on the windscreen. 'I was starting to think it was going to ruin my career.'

Lorcan laughed. 'There's even better news. The Vitalustre people are shooting a new advertising campaign.'

'But they just shot an ad.'

'They're binning it. The *Bridesmaids* clip has boosted sales. They're going to shoot three new viral-style spots and release them on YouTube. They want you to star in them.' Claire stared at the smiley face. 'And they're offering to pay you a flat fee of twelve grand.'

The cute blonde in the denim shorts and stripy tights stuck her gum on the side of her can of Red Bull and put on the headphones.

'OK, lads,' she said in a squeaky little voice, 'I'm good to go.'

Ray stared at Donal, the sound engineer. 'I asked for a Lady Gaga sound-alike, not a Tweetie Pie impersonator.' The Mocca Place demo Ray was recording was supposed to be with Sounds Familiar by this afternoon; he didn't have time to screw around.

Donal grinned. 'Hold your fire. OK, Gemma, let's go for a take.'

She opened her mouth and a wave of sound hit him. Her voice was incredible. It was 'Poker Face' – well, almost.

'*Come and try, come and try, come and try Mocca Place! Mocca Place!*'

What Ray wanted to do right now, he thought, watching Donal mixing the demo, was to hang out with Claire, to sit on her lumpy sofa watching *Deadwood* or playing sweary Scrabble, or to go for gimlets in the No Name bar, but he couldn't and that was her fault. She was the one who'd forced him to see Willow and seeing Willow had caused that terrible row. He'd said some awful things, he was willing to admit that, but he was done with apologising. That grovelling email he'd sent to Chip had used up his lifetime supply of 'sorries'. Claire had been pretty harsh herself. If she wanted to make up, she knew where he was. A few feet above her stubborn little ginger head.

Two hours later he was in the No Name bar with Gemma and she was giving him a lecture about the music business. He had started out bigging her voice up, telling her that he had a couple of record company contacts, but pretty soon he realised she didn't need any encouragement. She already had an ego the size of a cruise liner.

He sipped his fourth gimlet and listened to her banging on about her MySpace strategy, managing fan databases and trading tracks for re-tweets. Why was this session singer talking to *him* as if he was the wannabe? Only one person at this table had gone platinum eight times and they weren't wearing tiny denim shorts.

He had been going to bring her home but now he just couldn't face it. When she finally took a breather to go to the bathroom, he asked for the bill and checked his phone to see if Sounds Familiar had listened to the demo yet. He had one new email. It was from Chip.

There was an address and a date and a time and there were just two words.

'You're on.'

If Chip Connolly hadn't turned down the rights to 'Asia Sky', he could, Ray thought, have been able to afford something a bit more rock 'n' roll. He knocked on the door of the tiny terraced house and Chip's wife, Helena, opened it. She was a Welsh girl with long, dyed red hair and she was the only Horses fan who had turned Ray down for Chip, which was probably the reason Chip had married her.

She looked up at the sky. 'Thought there'd be pigs doing a fly by!' she said.

'Never say never!' Ray shrugged.

'Go on through, the boys are out the back.'

Ray walked through the cluttered kitchen, past a dozing toddler strapped into a buggy and out into the back garden. There they were, the band that had played the Bowery in New York and headlined the Beierenlaan Fest in Rotterdam and caused a riot at a Tokyo TV studio. They were standing at the door of a garden shed with mugs of coffee, eating chocolate digestives.

'Looking good, Ray!' Happy grinned then looked flustered when Chip glared at him.

'You too.' That was a lie. Ray did look good in head-to-toe black and RayBan Aviators. The other Horses looked like a convention of geography teachers. Happy had put on two stone. Godot's hair was receding. Chip's ratty little face was lined and he was getting a potbelly.

If the Horses were going to re-form, Ray thought, there were going to have to be a few serious changes. He shoved his hands in the pockets of his jeans and followed them into the shed, which stank of creosote and engine oil. Two microphones, a drum kit, a keyboard and a couple of amps had been squashed in between a lawnmower and a sawhorse.

'So,' he folded his arms and leaned on a lawnmower as casually as he could, 'what's been going on?'

Chip turned his back and plugged his guitar into an amp and Happy began to jabber nervously. Chip had a two-year-old son and was a stay-at-home dad. Godot had eighteen-month-old twins and was back working in IT. Happy was a rep for a pizza franchise, which explained the weight gain. His girlfriend was due in three months. 'What about you?' Happy jammed another digestive into his mouth. 'Kids?'

An image of Willow staring up at the stuffed giraffe in the Dead Zoo floated past Ray's eyes, then disappeared. 'Nope.'

'Explains why you look so good. Either that or you have a portrait in the attic.'

'A portrait of Michael Bublé,' Chip said over his shoulder. 'So what have you been up to, Raymondo? Apart from jingles for breadcrumbs?' He strummed the intro to Gnarls Barkley's 'Crazy' and began to sing 'Gravy!' 'That's one of yours, isn't it? I do love that one.'

'Glad to hear it!' Ray snapped. He had been man enough to say 'sorry' but that didn't mean he had to take any of Chip's shit.

'Are we going to jam or what?' Godot slipped his bass over his shoulder and Happy squeezed himself in behind the drum kit. Ray took off his shades and put them on top of a plastic box labelled 'drill bits' then stepped behind the mike.

Chip went straight into a rusty version of 'Wish You Were Her' and the lush wave of sound from his guitar, the deep, gut-quivering punch of Godot's bass and the kick of Happy's drums hit Ray behind the knees. He'd missed this with every cell in his body. He grabbed the mike, closed his eyes, opened his mouth and began to sing.

They segued straight into 'Get Your Coat' and then 'It's Not Me, It's You'.

'It's not me, it's you.
You want him, then join the queue.
They stick to him like Superglue.

We're through. And it's not me, it's you.'

They played four tracks from the first album, three from the second and two from the third. Ray threw himself at the words as if he was drowning and they were saving his life.

When they took a break, Ray took out his laptop and balanced it on the sawhorse.

'Something you want to share with us?' Chip sneered. 'Another "Asia Sky"?' Ray shrugged. 'No? Well, I've got something.' Chip began to play a melody on his old red Stingray. Godot joined in. Happy picked up his sticks and Ray had to stand there, like a moron, while Chip sang the lyrics.

'*You threw away what you had before.*

You got to face it or waste it.

Use it, or lose it.

It's up to you to choose it.

If you're not too deluded.'

Chip's weedy little voice ruined it but it was a good song. Ray set his laptop to record and, when they started over, he kicked in, deep and husky, closing his eyes to shut out the dreary shed and Chip's pinched little face.

They went over it again and again, changing it, tweaking it. Then Godot's mobile rang. 'Got to go,' he said. 'Girlfriend's going to a hen party and I've got to look after the ankle-biters.'

Ray checked his watch. Two hours. Was that it? 'You want to hear the last track back?' he asked the others.

'Nah.' Happy pulled on his jumper.

'I thought it sounded pretty good.' Ray turned to Godot.

'It's better than anything you could write.' Chip snorted. 'But then "Asia Sky" makes "Bob the Fucking Builder" sound like "Smells Like Teen Spirit".'

Even after a three-year break, Chip's sarcasm made Ray feel like a tongue-tied teenager. 'Fuck you!' he said.

'Fuck you too!' Chip jerked his little chin at Ray.

'Yeah,' Happy said, nervously. 'Especially the Edge. I hate that stupid little beanie.' It was an old Horses joke but nobody was laughing.

'Why do you have to be such a bitter little shit?' Ray glared at Chip.

'Same reason as you have to be a talentless sell-out!' Chip spat back.

Ray put on his sunglasses and looked around the shed. 'It this what talent buys you, Chip? A two-up, two-down in fucking Fairview and a ninety-nine-euro shed from Aldi?'

Chip lunged at Ray but Happy stepped between them.

'Why?' Ray heard Chip spitting as he walked away. 'Why did we let Fisher talk us into this? I'd rather go on tour with Jedward than re-form the Horses.'

Everything about Dog seemed designed to freak Claire out. His strange black rubbery lips, the single snaggle tooth that stuck out when he was asleep, the horrible yellowy-grey tangle of his beard. The way he burst out of the kitchen at exactly six o'clock and nine o'clock in the evening, just as the news came on the TV. The way he howled along with the banshee wail of the pipes every time she had a shower.

She had started walking him to the park every morning. Ten minutes there, ten minutes back, twenty minutes round the jogging path, trying to stay as far away from the pond as possible. The one thing that scared Claire more than dogs was water, but Dog wouldn't do what Eilish called his 'dog bidness' on the lead. Instead, Claire had to follow him around the football pitch at a respectful distance until he had selected exactly the right spot. Eilish had given her a box of disposable kitchen gloves and a roll of pink polka-dot poo bags. Claire double-gloved and double-bagged but every time she reached down to pick up one of his warm turds, she thought she was going to pass out.

And while she was distracted, sprinting, bag at arm's length, for the bin, Dog always made a beeline for the pond. He was obsessed with the swan. He stood by the edge of the water whinnying at it while Claire yelled at him to come back. His obsession was not reciprocated. The sight of Dog seemed to infuriate the swan. It inflated to twice its size and shot across the pond hissing and flapping its huge wings. Every morning, Claire had to run over and clip Dog's lead back on and drag him away before he was attacked. She wasn't sure which would come off better in a snout-to-beak smack-down but, if she had money to put on it, she'd put it on the swan.

At home, she had tried to lay down clear boundaries. 'Yours!' she'd said, waving at the kitchen, the garden and the blue draught snake she'd given him so he'd leave her stuff alone. 'Mine!' She pointed at her boots and the washing basket and her bedroom door. He just raised his tufty grey eyebrows and looked at her as if she were unhinged and then, when she wasn't looking, he made off with anything he could find that was made of leather.

She cradled the phone against her ear and lowered her voice so he wouldn't hear her. 'I tried to cure him of the leather fetish. I put all my shoes on top of the wardrobe but then he went into the washing basket and when I came back from the hairdresser's, he was lying on my purple suede skirt and that cashmere hoodie that Ray gave me that never fitted.'

'Sounds like Dog's putting together a capsule wardrobe.' Eilish laughed over a clatter of pans. Claire could hear Greasy Pete in the background, whistling. 'Maybe he's planning a little trip?'

A huge grey shadow passed by her bedroom door. 'Hang on!' She poked her head out. Dog was fleeing down the hall with an ankle boot she'd just taken off dangling from his mouth. She chased him into the kitchen.

'Drop!' She stood a few feet away from him and windmilled her arms. 'Eilish, he's drooling all over my boot! What will I do?'

'Give him ham.'

Claire opened the fridge and took out a slice. Instantly, a gleam came into Dog's eyes, his mouth opened and the boot fell out and hit the floor. He took the ham delicately from her fingers.

'Wow! That's the first food he's had since he arrived.'

'It sounds like he's pining for your dad. Give him a hug from me.'

'This is purely a business arrangement.' Claire shuddered. 'I didn't sign up for hugging.'

'Have you told your dad that you didn't bring Dog to the pound?'

'Not yet. That horrible carer woman says he doesn't want to see me.'

The hospital with its set visiting hours had given Claire an excuse to see her dad every day but, now that he was home, she hadn't seen him for nearly a week. She called every day but Sinead kept insisting that he wasn't ready for visitors.

'You can't let that woman keep you out of your father's house,' Eilish said.

'I'll figure out a way around it.' Claire ran her hands through her hair and then stopped. 'Aaah! You should see what they've done to my hair. I look like I've been dunked in a chip pan.' She'd spent the morning in a hairdressing salon having a three-month blow-dry. She wasn't even supposed to comb it until she got on set tomorrow.

'Speaking of hairdos,' Eilish laughed, 'I gave Pete a short back and sides back at the B&B last night. He looks quite presentable! Got to go. Good luck tomorrow. Break a leg!'

It was never going to happen. The Horses were never going to re-form. Those two years of stardom had just been a brief, bright blip.

Ray had wanted to curl up in a foetal position with a bottle of tequila, but instead he'd had to listen to Andy from Sounds Familiar giving him shit.

'The client hated that chick you used for the Mocca Place jingle. She sounded way too Lady Gaga.' Andy had sounded pissed off. 'You know the rules. What you come up with has to sound the same but—'

'Different.' Ray tried to sound upbeat. 'I'll give it another shot.'

'Forget it. We sorted it in-house. Just don't let me down on the Bentley's Bagels brief. It's a big one. The deadline's Friday. Enough time?'

'Absolutely,' Ray had said.

But it was Monday now and he was still hitting the same brick wall. Andy had already left five messages this morning; he had to crack it by the end of the day.

It wasn't the money that was at stake here, it was his confidence. If he couldn't write a jingle for a bloody bakery product, how could he write a decent song?

He stared at the hypnotic red and green and blue sound-waves on the Pro Tools screen. He'd wasted the last six hours fiddling around with 'Heaven Must Be Missing A Bagel' and it still sounded like shit.

He watched the silent rough cut of the Bentley's Bagels TV ad again. A half-naked couple were rolling round in bed. The guy was trying to take playful bites of the girl's bagel. As you would, Ray thought bitterly, if you woke up with what looked like Rosie Huntington-Whiteley's younger, prettier sister.

He racked his aching brain. 'Bagel in a Centrefold'? 'Bagel Eyes'? Then it came to him. 'I'm Loving Bagels in Bed'. It was perfect! Thank you, Robbie Williams. All he had to do now was rework the track so it wasn't too close to the original. He mailed the mpeg at exactly twenty-nine minutes past five. Three days over deadline but he'd pulled it out of the bag.

The thought of sitting around the apartment worrying about what he was going to do for the rest of his life made him feel like ending it, so he had a shower, got dressed and headed out.

Ray grabbed a basket at the door of Fallon & Byrne and stood around in the organic vegetable section, looking clueless. Embarrassingly, this tactic usually worked well, but tonight, for some reason, it didn't. Finally, a dark-haired girl in a tight red coat smiled at him. 'Is this a celeriac or a Jerusalem artichoke?' he asked her.

It was squash and her name was Edel. She was a twenty-four-year-old trainee solicitor with a tongue piercing and a feeling that she'd seen Ray before. He watched her trying to work it out.

'Why do you look so familiar?' she said when they were sitting down in the wine bar sharing a bottle of Merlot. 'Have you killed anyone? Sued anyone? Are you getting divorced?'

Ray shook his head and looked mysterious. It was always better to let them do the work themselves.

Edel had green-painted toenails and a tattoo on her hip. 'Best Before April 30th 2008?' Ray said, afterwards. 'What's that about?'

'Should have gone to Specsavers!' She got out of bed and wrapped herself in a towel. 'It's *2018*. My thirtieth birthday. It's all downhill after that. Oops!' She smirked, seeing his face. 'Did I touch a nerve?'

'It's different for boys.'

'You keep telling yourself that.' She leaned over and pinched his thigh. 'And ask Santa for some anti-cellulite cream because all the skincare stuff you have stashed in your bathroom doesn't work.'

Ray flushed. 'It belongs to my sister.'

'Tell your *sister*,' Edel's smirk got even bigger, 'that *my sister* is a model and the only thing she uses is Preparation H.'

'On her face?'

'It tightens skin anywhere.'

Ray picked up his guitar and began to play the Bentley's Bagels track he'd composed earlier. It still sounded pretty good.

'What's that?' Edel was zipping up her black pencil skirt.

'Just something I wrote.' He was going to add 'for you', but he didn't. She wasn't the kind of girl who was going to buy that.

'Sounds like "Loving Angels Instead".' She stepped into her shoes.

Ray's fingers froze on the strings. 'Really?'

'Really. The firm I work for specialises in copyright theft.'

Ray did a quick bridge into Chip's song, the one they'd fooled around with on the day of the jam. Edel looked over her shoulder. 'Now *that's* good. Did you write that one all by yourself?'

He nodded.

'I'm impressed!'

Ray didn't have to give Edel the speech about being too focused on his music to get involved, etc., she was in too much of a hurry to listen.

'I know how I know you!' she said when she was on the step outside his front door.

Ray smiled. 'Busted!'

'You were in my yoga class a few months back. You hooked up with the teacher afterwards.'

Ray had a blister on his tongue from Edel's tongue piercing and a panicky feeling that she was right about the Robbie Williams track. He ran back upstairs and opened Pro Tools and got to work again. An hour and a half later, he was typing another email to Andy.

'Sent you the wrong demo earlier. Robbie Williams sound-alike I ruled out. This was the one I meant to send. It's an original track but I think it works pretty well. Ray.'

He still had the recording of Chip's song on his laptop.

'*You threw away what you had before.*

You got to face it or waste it.

Use it, or lose it.

It's up to you to choose it.

If you're not too deluded.'

Ray hadn't had time to do much with the arrangement but he'd dashed off new lyrics and recorded them himself.

'*Try Bentley's Bagels, you'll want some more.*

You can toast them or bake them

Just wait till you taste them

You won't want to waste them

Just remember to share them.'

14

Desmond, the director of the original Vitalustre ad, swooped into the hair and make-up department in Stealth Studios, kissed Claire on both cheeks, then punched her, painfully, on the arm. 'You and me really ruffled a few feathers with that YouTube viral,' he said, as if the whole thing had been his cunning plan all along instead of a huge mistake. 'I don't think you met the Vitalustre marketing director, last time, did you? This is Richard. Your biggest fan.'

'It's true.' Richard was in his thirties with fair hair and the most immaculate grey suit Claire had ever seen. She wished that her hair wasn't hanging over her shoulders like overcooked spaghetti. 'Your comic talent has single-handedly redefined the Irish hair care sector.'

'You mean *single-elbowedly*,' Claire said with a half-smile.

'You see?' Richard laughed. 'That's what I'm talking about!'

Everyone else laughed too. Desmond, Lily the hairdresser, Nicky and Fiona the make-up assistants, and the snotty costume designer whose name was almost certainly not 'Vogue', and Claire laughed along. She'd been an extra on enough ad shoots to know that the client was always the star of the show.

Vitalustre were using the budget they'd been going to spend airing the original ad on TV to make three new spots that they hoped would go viral. The scripts were fine but Claire wasn't sure they were funny enough for people to share on their Facebook walls. But that, as Eilish would say, was not her fish to fricassee.

In the first script, Claire played an airport security guard frisking a gorgeous model who had a bottle of Vitalustre strapped to her thigh. When the model wouldn't hand it over, Claire had to elbow her and run off with it. The next script had Claire leaping out of a locker in a gym to elbow a second model so she could grab her Vitalustre. In the final script, she was a sexy cat burglar who blew a hole in a hotel room wall then elbowed yet another model who came at her with a pillow. All the spots ended with Claire tossing her hair and saying: 'I'd do anything to get my hands on the Vitalustre shine.'

While her hair was blow-dried into an impossibly shiny sheet of copper silk, Claire tried to work out her motivation. If her character already had amazing hair, why did she need the conditioner at all? As the last fake eyelash was glued into place, she found the answer. Her character was an ordinary woman, her victims were all models. No matter how much conditioner she had, she was never going to be as gorgeous as they were.

'Wow!' Desmond said, when he finally called a wrap, ten hours later. 'That was absolutely brilliant, Claire. You should think about acting.' She didn't know whether to laugh or cry.

She had a rash on her back where the towel had been glued to her skin in the second script. The smoke from the fake dynamite had given her a sore throat and the leather cat suit had cut off the circulation in her calves. She staggered back to Wardrobe, and Vogue, whose name it turned out was Grainne, released her from the cat suit and she tugged on her jeans and sweatshirt. Her phone was dead. She had no idea what time it was but she knew it must be late. She had forgotten all about Dog.

She stuffed the rest of her things into her bag and ran out into the car park, where the crew were packing the lighting equipment from the sets on to lorries. Richard was standing by a car talking to two of the models. Claire felt about a hundred and fifty years old but he looked as crisp and fresh as he had at seven a.m. He probably had a whole wardrobe full of freshly laundered shirts at home and a freshly laundered girlfriend waiting for him, Claire thought, instead of a huge and possibly incontinent dog.

'Hey!' he called. 'You going to join us for a drink?'

Ray had told her once that a dog's intestine was seven times longer than its body. Dog was three feet long. That was twenty-one feet of intestine. He hadn't eaten much this morning. Maybe there was time for a quick drink? She stole a look at Richard's wrist. Ten to eleven. 'I'm sorry,' she said. 'I can't.'

Richard saw her looking at his watch. The models had drifted away now and it was just the two of them standing in the dark car park in a rectangle of light from the open studio door. 'That watch comes with an interesting story,' he said. 'Why don't I tell it to you over dinner sometime?'

Dog was curled up by the cooker when Claire came in. He had surrounded himself with a world of leather. Two handbags, a pair of boots, a belt and three shoes. But the floor was clean. He opened one eye and looked at Claire accusingly. 'I'm sorry but I have a life,' she said, 'which doesn't revolve around your intestines.'

She stood back so he could get out the door without touching her. She didn't feel quite so terrified of him now but she tried to minimise actual physical Dog-on-Claire contact. She watched him climbing the steps then doing an arthritic circuit of the garden. Richard wasn't strictly her type. But who was? The string of actors she'd dated in her twenties who treated her more like an audience than a girlfriend? Declan, who had said he loved her then proved he didn't? Or Shane who thought she was a cold hearted liar?

Dog was snuffling around the nettles. 'Be careful of those,' she hissed. 'They sting.'

'It's going to be a great show today, right, Owen?' Oonagh put her hand on Owen's thigh and gave it a friendly squeeze.

'That's right, Oonagh.' Owen lifted her hand and dropped it on to the sofa between them as if it were something dead that was going off. The camera was too high to catch it but a ripple of tension ran around the studio.

'Coming up,' Oonagh's smile wobbled but she managed to steady it, 'we have the Clontarf woman who found the face of Jesus in a tea towel.' She turned to Owen. 'Should she sell it or send it to the Pope?'

'And we'll be meeting the ex-politician who has opened

Ireland's first bubble tea café. But before we get to the interesting stuff, we have Doctor Nick and We-Fit.' He yawned.

'You can't be tired.' Oonagh slapped him on the wrist with her notes. 'You were tucked up in bed last night at half-nine!'

Owen folded his arms and raised an eyebrow. 'How would you know?'

'This seems like the perfect place,' Nick jumped in, 'to discuss conflict resolution. On the last show we talked about big issues, like sex and money, that drive couples apart. Today I want to talk about the little irritations that can end in divorce.'

Oonagh turned her back on Owen. There was murder in her eyes.

'What we have to watch out for is the catalogue of day-to-day complaints we build up about our partners.' Like his own re-actions to Kelly's hormonal highs and lows, he thought ruefully. Last week she'd cancelled their date night for the second time in a row and he had screened her calls for the next two days.

'What can we do, Doc,' Owen was saying, 'when we're just sick of the sight of our partners?' Oonagh flushed.

'Today I'm going to teach our guest couple three We-Fit exercises designed to return us to a space of love and intimacy. The "Bicker Buster", "Positivi-Three" and "Naming the Ele-phant".'

Owen turned around and prodded Oonagh's corseted stomach. 'We could call her "Oonagh".'

'I don't care what happens after we sign the contract with Cling-films,' Oonagh groaned, 'but we're going to have to manage Owen somehow or he'll derail the whole thing.'

'*If* we sign!' Nick reminded her.

They were sitting in an empty row of seats in the back of the studio after the show, drinking takeaway coffees. 'Oonagh,' Nick said, carefully, 'I think there are issues here that you and Owen need to face. I think you're in denial.'

'I'm the queen of denial.' She sighed.

'I'd be happy to coach the two of you if that would help.'

'You just love fixing other people's problems, don't you?' Oonagh kicked off her shoes and swung her legs over the seat in front. 'What about your own?' Nick shrugged. He and Kelly used to sit down every week and discuss their problems, but that was easy when nothing much was going wrong. 'You look wrecked, Nick. I want you looking good for Clingfilms. It's a shame we don't have time to do anything about that scar.'

'What scar?' Nick mumbled.

'I've been looking at you under the lights for months now.' She leaned over and ran a finger along the fine white line on his forehead. 'How did that happen?'

'I fell out of a tree.'

'Whoever stitched you up should be shot. I know a good plastics guy in the Mater Private. When we get the go-ahead, I'll book you in.'

'*If!*' Nick laughed.

She leaned back farther and unbuttoned her tight jacket. 'I have a good feeling about it. Once Curtis meets you, it's a no-brainer. They're talking about shooting *The Ex-Factor* pilot before Easter.'

'*The X-Factor?*' Nick turned to look at her.

'With an "e" and an "x". Fabulous, isn't it?'

'What happened to *Relationship Rescue*?'

'Oh,' Oonagh tossed her takeaway cup on to the floor, 'that was just a working title.'

'But it doesn't make sense.'

'Not with the old format, but they've revamped the whole idea. There'll be open castings to find the most bitter divorced couples. Each couple will be managed by a coach and a celebrity.' Hadn't Rory mentioned celebrities? Nick remembered. 'And there'll be a public vote every week.'

'But it sounds just like—'

'I know!' She grinned. 'TV gold! Clingfilms have got buy-in from one of the American networks. If it takes off, the show will go directly to the States with the UK presenters on board!'

'What?'

'I could be the white Oprah! You could be Doctor Phil with hair!' She laughed. 'Say something.'

Nick was speechless. Clingfilms hadn't just reformatted the show, they'd reinvented it. But if people got something from it, if watching other couples sort out their problems taught them how to fix their own, then the ends justified the means, didn't they? Especially if it meant that he could go back to the States with a job that would set him up in the coaching business for life.

'Your jaw just dropped,' Oonagh grinned. 'Are those veneers?'

The chemist was frumpy and wore medical-looking shoes. 'I'm looking for something for cellulite,' Ray whispered.

He'd tried to check himself out in the bathroom mirror in the morning but the lighting in there was moody. It was surprisingly difficult to get a good look at your own arse.

The chemist came out from behind the counter and he followed her over to a shelf of bottles and boxes.

'It's a gift,' he said.

She picked out a box. 'I think we both know,' she pursed her lips, 'that this is not a gift.'

Ray swallowed. 'Do we?'

'Perfume is a gift.' She handed him a box. 'A scented candle is a gift. This is an insult.' She turned on her sensible heels and stalked off.

Ray trailed her back to the counter. 'Do you have any,' he lowered his voice, 'Preparation H?'

'Yes,' she beamed. 'Do you want me to gift wrap it?'

Five years ago, when 'Asia Sky' was still riding high, Ray would have caused a riot if he'd gone into a café full of teenage girls, but now the girls in Starbucks in Dundrum looked through him as if he didn't exist. He was the same but everyone else was different. The girls were so loud that he almost didn't hear his phone ringing, and he had to go outside into the shopping centre to take the call. It was Andy from Sounds Familiar.

'Bentley's Bagels are loving their jingle.'

'Great, but I need to tidy it up a bit before they go into production.' Ray was going to have to change it so it didn't sound like Chip's track. He could fly in a new baseline, add a second guitar, suggest a female singer instead of a male one.

'No need,' Andy said. 'They want the demo as is and they want to pay you handsomely for your vocal.'

Ray felt a wave of panic lap at his knees. If he didn't change it and Chip *heard it* . . . 'I can't let it go as it is. It's just too raw.'

'It's perfect, Ray. Everyone in here's been singing it non-stop.'

'Just give me half a day—'

Andy's voice was sharp. 'Ray, I'm not going to tell the client they can't have the track they love.'

The teenage girls were spilling out of Starbucks in a squealing throng. 'I'm sorry,' Ray began, 'but you can't—'

But Andy only heard the first two words. 'Apology accepted. Where are you anyway? The zoo?'

While Richard was studying the Japanese menu, Claire had a chance to study him. Short blond hair. Neat nose. Nice mouth. He looked like Rob Lowe's younger, blond brother. His light blue cotton shirt was the exact colour of his eyes. She caught herself thinking of Shane's dark eyes instead. She had spent an hour getting ready and now here she was, trying to sabotage the evening before it had even started.

'So . . .' Richard looked up and smiled at her. 'I'm a horologist. I hope that's not going to be a problem.'

Claire smiled right back. 'Isn't it a bit early in our relationship to be admitting that?'

'Very funny. I'm into clocks and watches. My granddad used to have one of these.' He rolled up his sleeve. 'It's a Rolex Sub-mariner. Water resistant to a thousand feet. Unidirectional rotating bezel.' He shook his head. 'I lost you at "unidirectional", didn't I?'

'You lost me at a thousand feet,' Claire shot back.

The waitress arrived with the wine list.

'What wine do you recommend,' Richard asked her, 'with a sushi plate?'

'I don't,' she said frostily. 'Japanese food and wine don't mix.'

He handed back the menu. 'Good advice. I'm Richard and you are . . .' He smiled at her broadly.

'Your waitress for the evening,' she said, then her icy expression dissolved. 'Naomi.'

'Beer OK with you, Claire?' Claire nodded. 'Two Sapporos, Naomi.

'Anyway, my granddad left me some money in his will so I decided to buy a Rolex for myself. I was seventeen. I got the bus up from Wexford in my school uniform and headed into Weir's on Grafton Street.'

'That was a pretty brave thing to do when you were seventeen.'

'There was this manager tearing strips off a guy my age because he hadn't polished a display cabinet so I waited till he was free and I went over and asked him to show me the Swatches. Then I said I'd maybe look at something a bit more expensive. So he showed me the Timexes and then the Omegas and then the Tag Heuers.' He topped up Claire's beer glass. 'Finally I asked to see the Rolexes. He thought I was having him on. You should have seen his face when I said I'd take this one.'

Claire laughed. 'He thought he'd sold a guy who came in for a Swatch a Rolex. You must have made his day.'

'Didn't cost me anything to do it. Anyway, enough about me. What makes you—'

'Don't say it!' Claire groaned.

He grinned. 'Tick?'

He was easy to talk to. Light and funny, and Claire began to enjoy herself.

He chatted about his family home in Wexford. His bohemian mother and his strait-laced father and his two wild younger sisters. 'What about you?' he asked, when they were sharing a slice of very un-Japanese cheesecake. 'Does your family live in Dublin?'

'My dad and my brother do.' Claire felt the shadow of the past fall between them, the way it always did. 'My mother died when I was young,' she said lightly.

'Oh.' He put his glass down and looked at her. He was imagining cancer, the way people always did when she said that. The family around the deathbed. Tearful goodbyes. And she let him. She had told Shane too much. She wasn't going to make that mistake again. 'I don't really like to talk about it.'

He nodded. 'Did I thank you for your brilliant performance the other day?'

'Three times since seven o'clock.'

'When I saw that viral on YouTube, I knew you were comic

gold. The board wanted to take it down but I stood my ground. When sales went up by nineteen per cent they had to admit I was right. I had to fight tooth and nail to get those old dinosaurs to buy the viral idea, but when they see the new campaign, they'll know I was right again.'

'I hope so,' Claire said.

'Why haven't I seen you in *Fair City* or *Love/Hate*?'

'I haven't been focusing on my career for a while.' A piece of cheesecake slid off Claire's spoon on to the front of her dress. She dipped her napkin into her water glass and blotted it.

'You missed a little bit there to the left. I mean stage left. Here.' He leaned over, and dabbed at the neckline of her dress.

'Richard Thomas Doyle!' A tiny girl in her late twenties with Audrey Hepburn hair was standing by their table. She planted her hands on the hips of her short sequinned dress. 'Groping a lady-person in a public place! Who is this flame-haired temptress?'

'This is Claire.' Richard put his napkin down. 'Claire, this is Helen, my little sister.' The girl slid on to the wooden bench beside him and made a swipe for his beer glass. He moved it out of her reach. 'My least annoying little sister. If you can believe that.'

Helen squinted at Claire from under her dark fringe. She was very pretty and very drunk. 'Do you work with Richard? You can't be going out with him because you're way too cool and you're not wearing a hair band or a twin set or anything from Lalph Rauren.' She frowned. 'That doesn't sound right! Hang on. I need to see your shoes.' She ducked her head under the table.

'Sorry about this,' Richard whispered.

Helen popped back up again, her face flushed, her bun lop-sided. 'Ooh! You're wearing slushy shoes. I mean slutty shoots. Is this a date?'

'No it's not!' Richard said.

'Oh my God! It's a date. You're *so* not his type. This is fabulous!' Helen rummaged in a tiny, sequinned bag and took out her phone. 'I have to take a picture! I need evidence for Mum and—'

Richard grabbed her phone before she could do it. 'OK, show's over. Time to go back to whoever you're with, Helen.'

'I'm on my own. I was supposed to be meeting bloody Aine but she never showed up. So I had to drink about a gallon of sake on my own. If I'd known you were a few tables away groping some glammy ginger, I would have been over like a shot! Hey! Shots! That's a great idea! Let's get shots!'

'No shots!' Richard said firmly.

Helen pointed a wobbly finger with a sparkly purple nail at Claire. 'Wait a minute! I know you! You're that girl with the mad hair in the *Desperate Bridesmaids* thing. Where are all your lovely curlies?' They had been smoothed into submission by the twelve-week blow-dry. No matter what Claire did to it, her hair looked perfectly sleek. 'Are you a comedienne?'

'Claire's a serious actress,' Richard said. 'She has nineteen credits on IMDB.' Claire stared at him. 'I'm sorry.' He looked embarrassed. 'I Googled you.'

She laughed. 'It's OK.'

Richard got the bill and they managed to walk Helen outside even though she insisted on stopping to embrace a life-size statue of Buddha just inside the door. 'I love the Dalai Lama,' she murmured to it. 'He's just so real.'

'I'm afraid we're going to have to take a rain check on that drink.' Richard looked up and down George's Street for a free cab. 'I can't send her home to her apartment. It's by the canal. She'll fall in. She can stay at my place.'

'I don't want to go to your place.' Helen grabbed on to Claire to keep her balance. 'It has too many clocks. Tick! Tick! Tick! And you iron everything. Don't let him iron me!' she pleaded with Claire.

A cab pulled up and they manoeuvred her into the back and Claire got in beside her. Richard sat in the front.

'Is she going to hurl her cookies, boss?' the taxi man said. 'Because if she does—'

'I'll pay for a full valet,' Richard craned to read the licence taped to the dashboard, 'Frank.'

It was only nine-thirty, way too early to be going home. Claire felt disappointed. The whole evening had been going so well.

'Richard is the white sheep of the family,' Helen told Claire in loud stage whisper. 'We think our mother might have played offside with a German tourist. He's the only one with blond hair.'

'Don't listen to anything she says!' Richard said from the front.

'I need to take a picture of your shoes now!' Helen said. 'Hold this,' she handed Claire her phone, 'while I look for my phone.' She rummaged in her bag. 'I can't find it. You'll have to come to Wexford for Sunday lunch so I can show you to my mother and my sister. My sister is a fruit loop, but you'll like her.' Her head sank down on to Claire's shoulder and, immediately, she fell asleep.

The taxi parked at the top of the laneway with its hazard lights on and Helen snoring inside. Richard walked Claire to the door in the lane. She jiggled the key in the lock and then gave the door a little kick to get it to open.

'Well, goodnight.' She turned to look at him. It was the first cold night of the year and their breaths met in a little white puff between them. 'Thank you for a—'

He put his hands lightly on the shoulders of her red coat and kissed her. It was a short kiss but long enough for her to see a couple of stars.

He wound a strand of her hair around his finger. 'I'm going to be away in Germany for ten days but why don't you come to Wexford on Sunday week for lunch? To my folks' place? Helen will forget she asked you but I think it's a great idea.'

'OK.' Claire remembered Dog. She couldn't leave him on his own for a whole day, not again. 'We might have company.'

'Do you have kids?'

'I'm looking after a dog.'

'No problem. I'll pick you up on Sunday week. At about eleven, and I'll bring some WD40 for that lock.'

Claire let herself into the kitchen. Her lips were still tingling from the kiss.

'I'm home,' she called. She had started talking to Dog as if he were a person, she realised, the way her dad did. After a second, she heard the faint 'thump, thump' of his tail on the floorboards in the hall, as if he was talking back.

15

There was something weird, Ray felt, about a guy going to a film on his own in the middle of the afternoon, but it was better than sitting around the apartment trying to digest the terrifying truth that he was never going to have another shot at fame. Perhaps Claire had been right, maybe he was just a jingle writer after all. His phone buzzed so he got up and went outside into the cinema foyer to take the call.

It was Ash; she sounded upset. 'Can you take Willow for a couple of hours on Friday?'

Ray examined his face in the window of the ice-cream concession. He'd been using the Preparation H but the lines by his nose looked just the same. 'I thought you'd gone back to London to work things out with your boyfriend.'

'Fiancé. Ex-fiancé.' Her voice was shaky. 'I did. But I'm back in Dublin. I have to get a job and get Willow into a school. I have an appointment to see one on Friday afternoon so I wondered if you'd look after her.'

'Look,' Ray said carefully, 'she didn't have a very good time with me.'

'I know but it'll only be for a couple of hours. Please, Ray. My parents are going to a wedding. I'm really stuck.'

'Can't you get a friend to do it?'

'I don't have friends here.' Ash sighed. 'Not any more.'

'Snap,' Ray sighed.

'What?'

'Just say when.'

*

Two grubby boys of five and six were standing on bottle crates at the table decorating gingerbread men with icing and Smarties. They watched Kelly shyly while she measured up the kitchen.

'Thanks, Pauline.' Kelly closed her notebook. 'I think I've seen enough.' Years of running her own business had given her a sixth sense for window shoppers. Pauline seemed nice but she didn't look like someone who had a spare twenty grand to extend the kitchen and put in new units. 'I'll be in touch with some estimates next week.'

'There's no rush.' Pauline pushed her hair out of her eyes. 'We'll have to save up to get it done. I lost my job so I'm at home all day with the boys now and we spend most of our time in here. It's such a mess.'

The lino was grotty and worn. The tiles above the sink were coming away from the wall. There was a leak behind the dishwasher. The smell of damp hit the back of Kelly's nose and her stomach did a queasy flip.

Could this be morning sickness? she wondered with a flutter of excitement. Her period wasn't due for another week but maybe one of the blurry grey dots she'd seen on the ultrasound screen was turning into a baby.

'You mentioned you might want to take a few pictures,' Pauline was saying.

Kelly forced herself to nod. She'd already wasted an hour, another five minutes didn't matter. She took a few random snaps of the kitchen then opened the back door and stepped on to the patio. Her heel caught in the wheel of a discarded tricycle and suddenly she was pitching forward and the broken paving stones were flying up at her face. She managed to break her fall against the pebbledash wall.

Pauline came running out. 'Are you OK?'

The heel of Kelly's hand was grazed and beaded with blood. 'This garden is a death trap!' Her voice was shrill. 'I could have lost my baby!'

'I'm so sorry!' Pauline took her arm and brought her back inside.

Why had she said that she was pregnant? Kelly tried to think of a way to take it back but couldn't.

'Please, sit down.'

'I can't.' Kelly was due in a carpet showroom in Dun Laoghaire in under twenty minutes, then she had to stop by an attic conversion in Monkstown. How was she supposed to act as if she cared about underlay and dormer windows when a baby might be growing inside her? She felt her eyes prickle with tears.

'Let me clean that up.' Pauline guided her into a chair opposite the boys. 'I'm guessing this is your first?'

Kelly nodded. Did a nod amount to a lie? she wondered.

'I was terrified when I was pregnant with Finn.' Pauline rummaged in a drawer and found some cotton wool and a bottle of TCP. She cleaned the gravel off Kelly's hand and wrapped it in a tissue. 'I did lots of things wrong but it all worked out.' She smiled at the two little boys who were picking Smarties off the floor and sticking them back on to the gingerbread men.

'You're so lucky,' Kelly said.

'Two rounds of IVF for Finn. Three for Dan.' She laughed. 'We'll still be paying the loans off when we retire.'

'I'm on Clomid.' Kelly stared down at her hand. 'Second cycle.'

'Ah yes, Clomid!' Pauline made a face. 'The wonder drug with absolutely no side effects except that it turns you into a complete psycho.'

'I don't care if I turn into a psycho as long as it works.'

'So you're not pregnant?' Pauline looked confused.

Kelly bit her lip. 'I don't know why I said that. It scares me how badly I want this . . .'

Pauline smiled. 'I bet it scares your husband too, right?'

Kelly nodded. 'I think it does, a bit.'

'Won't Greasy Pete mind you giving me all this food?' Claire watched Eilish ladling coq au vin on to a foil tray.

'I've got him eating out of my hand. He thinks I'm Nigella Lawson's younger, prettier sister. Bless!' Eilish tried to squash the tray into Claire's tiny freezer but it wouldn't fit. 'Why don't you bring some round to your dad?'

'He won't eat it,' Claire said. 'But that's a good idea. It would give me the perfect excuse to get past the bloody gate-keeper.' Sinead was still insisting that her dad didn't want to see anyone.

'You could bring Dog!' Eilish said.

Dog was stretched out under the table, his legs and enormous paws protruding at odd angles. When he heard his name, he rolled over, revealing a squashed sandal.

'I wish he wouldn't do that!' Claire went over and retrieved it.

'Let's see which he prefers.' Eilish spooned some chicken on to a plate. 'Jamie Oliver or Kurt Geiger?' She took the sandal and put it on the floor beside the plate.

Dog looked from one to the other, the mobile tip of his long black snout twitching, his eyebrows doing a little dance of indecision, then he wolfed down the chicken.

'Enough Dog talk!' Eilish said. 'I want to know all about this Richard person!'

Claire filled her in on the date with Richard. 'He's picking me up on Sunday. We're going to drive down to his parents' house. He's going to fix my rusty lock.'

'I bet he is!' Eilish smirked. Claire didn't even want to think about going to bed with anyone. Her lock had probably seized up by now. 'So is he a keeper?'

Claire forced herself past the tiny little ache of regret she had about Shane. 'It's early days but—'

'You like him?'

'I think I do.'

'Woo hoo!' Eilish got up and did a salsa round the table. Dog stood up so she grabbed his sideburns and planted a kiss on his shaggy head. 'She likes you too. She's still a bit scared of you, but she'll get over that!'

'It's like living with a teenage boy.' Oonagh planted her elbows on the bar and her face in her hands. 'A sixteen-stone teenage boy with a hair transplant and a persecution complex. I have to take Clingfilms' calls in the loo. I couldn't even tell him I was coming to meet you. I said I was going for a bikini wax,' she sipped her wine, 'not that he'd notice.'

Nick hadn't told Kelly where he was going either. She'd been weepy and edgy all week. Her period was due. For the first time since they'd met, they weren't celebrating Thanksgiving. The turkey he'd bought had been shoved to the back of the freezer. It was nice to be away from the clenched atmosphere of the house, to be sitting in a dark quiet bar doing something useful.

'Owen's just stonewalling,' he told Oonagh. 'It's a very male way of dealing with his upset. You just need to connect with him.'

'I need to connect him to the national grid and run a couple of million volts through him.' Oonagh signalled at the barman for another drink. 'Or tell some journalist that we're getting divorced – that might jolt him out of it.'

Nick shook his head and laughed.

'What are you laughing at?' Oonagh snapped in her off-air accent. '*Whaddaya laffin ah?*'

'Oonagh,' he handed the barman his empty Ballygowan glass, 'the whole premise of *The Ex-Factor* is that relationships can be saved. How's it going to look if you and Owen break up?'

She sighed. 'You try acting like you're happily married when you've got Owen Clancy looking at you over his Sugar Puffs like a wounded stag.'

'Did you try homework? The Two Listening? The Soul Gazing? The Positivi-Three exercise?' Nick had been trying to help Oonagh to sort things out with Owen for weeks, but nothing had worked. They were the most dysfunctional couple he'd ever come across.

'He doesn't speak to me unless we're on air.'

'You can work on this alone if he won't co-operate by making a Partner Gratitude List. Come on.'

'Do I have to?' She sighed. 'I'm grateful that Owen is twenty years older because he'll always look worse than me first thing in the morning. I'm grateful that he had a hair transplant for me because bald men look like giant babies—'

'Oonagh!'

'I'm grateful that he had kids with me even though he already has kids from his first marriage and could have done without any more thank you and . . .' She put her fingers under her eyes. 'Now you've made my mascara run.' Her voice was shaking. 'He's the crankiest old bastard on the planet and I love him.'

'I know.'

'But I grew up in a council flat in Ballymun. My mam cleaned offices so I could go to college. She's not around to see it but this is her dream coming true and I'm not going to let anyone destroy it.'

'Your father really isn't up to visitors.' Sinead planted herself in the doorway.

'I was just passing,' Claire said. 'I thought I'd call in.' Sinead looked at the catering saucepan she was holding as if might contain human remains. 'It's coq au vin. I thought if Dad had some proper food—'

'—I've been cooking him proper food,' Sinead said crisply. 'But he won't eat it.' She stood back, reluctantly and followed Claire down the hall to the kitchen.

The Cunninghams were sitting at the table drinking tea. Claire nearly dropped the saucepan. Did her dad know they were here?

Mrs Cunningham bobbed her frosted head. 'Oh, Claire! You're the image of your poor mother with your hair like that. Isn't she, Brian?'

Mr Cunningham grunted and cut himself a slice of Battenberg.

'Brian and Caroline have been marvellous,' Sinead said. 'Telling me when to put the bins out. Driving me to Superquinn. There's nothing like good neighbours, is there?'

'Sinead was just telling us that your father isn't making any effort to get back on his feet. It often happens with the elderly. They just give up.'

Elderly? Claire glared at her. The Cunninghams were at least ten years older than her dad.

'What's in the pot?'

'It's coq of some kind,' Sinead raised one thin eyebrow, 'apparently.' She took the pot into the utility room.

'I've brought Dog,' Claire followed her. 'I thought if Dad saw him it would give him a reason to do his physiotherapy.'

'I can't let you bring that enormous animal into the house. It's not safe.'

'I'll just bring him in here. We can close the door so he doesn't get into the kitchen.'

Claire opened Mossy's back door and Dog poked his long snout out and sifted the air. An expression of pure joy crossed his hairy grey face. He made a noise like an espresso machine and tried to lick her face.

'If you're happy now,' she grinned pushing him back, 'wait till you see Dad!'

The grin was still on her face when she opened the door of the old surgery but disappeared when she saw her dad. Slumped awkwardly in the armchair in front of the TV, he looked more like an invalid than he had even straight after the operation. The TV was switched on but he was staring at the floor, chewing his lip, his pale face clenched with pain. She put her hand to her locket. 'Dad.'

He turned to look at her. His chin was unshaven and there was a greyish stain on the front of his dressing gown. 'What have you done to your curls?'

'I had my hair straightened for a job. It's so good to see you. I brought you some coq au vin.' She perched on the edge of the bed. 'You need to start eating proper food and taking your painkillers so you can do your physio. And Dad,' Claire picked at a thread on the bedspread, 'I brought Dog.'

He stared at her. 'What?'

'He's in the utility room.'

As if on cue, Dog let out a plaintive howl.

Her dad flinched. 'I told you to bring him to the Cats and Dogs home.'

'I couldn't, they would have put him down. I'm going to look after him until you're well enough to walk him again.' Her dad covered his face with his hands. 'I thought you'd be pleased.'

His voice was muffled and broken. 'The only thing that would please me is if you'd get rid of that woman, Sinead, and help me up the stairs to my own bloody room.'

When Claire opened the door of the utility room, she found Dog lying beside the saucepan with a glazed look in his eyes. He had demolished the coq au vin. He'd even eaten the tinfoil lid.

'At least someone enjoyed it.' Sinead stood in the doorway, watching Claire clip on his lead.

'Don't let anyone into this house unless Dad invites them,'

Claire glared at her. 'Especially not the Cunninghams. Is that clear?'

Sinead's mouth was set in a thin line. 'Crystal.'

Nick and Claire never had friends over to the house but, when Claire was fourteen, she'd asked him if she could have a sleep-over.

'It's a bad idea, Claire, but you can do what you like.' He had been distant since the day he'd walked away from her in town. She knew that he had applied to go to college in America in the autumn and it felt as if part of him had already gone.

She had invited Amy Kelly, Lucy O'Donnell and Ruth Kinsella but she knew, from the moment she opened the door and saw them looking past her into the shabby hall, that it had been a mistake.

Everything was wrong. She saw her bedroom through their eyes and she felt ashamed of how bare and boyish it was. There was a horrible skin on the top of the hot chocolate. There was no open fire to toast the marshmallows.

The girls took tiny sips of their chocolate and left it. They nibbled round the edges of the marshmallows and put them back on the plate. Claire had bought a set of sparkly nail varnish at the chemist and they painted their nails but the atmosphere was flat and awkward. Then Amy got up and went over to Claire's bedside table.

'Is this your mother?' She picked up the photograph in the silver frame, the one of her mum playing cricket in the garden. The other girls got up and went over, bending their heads over the picture.

'She's so pretty!' Lucy sighed.

'Her hair is the same colour as yours, only it's straight.' Ruth pulled away the scarf that Claire had draped over the lamp so she could see it better. 'She died, didn't she?'

'What happened?' Amy's eyes were shining with curiosity.

Claire was still kneeling on the rug. She moved a marshmallow from one side of her mouth to another. 'It was an accident,' she mumbled.

'What kind of accident?'

She shook her head.

Ruth came over and hugged her. 'Claire doesn't have to talk about it if she doesn't want to.' After a minute, Amy and Lucy came and hugged her too and she was enveloped in a cloud of watermelon lip-gloss and the biscuity smell of other people's hair.

'Your mum was a doctor, wasn't she?' Amy wouldn't let it go. 'Did she work in a hospital?'

'No. She had a surgery downstairs.'

'Can we see?' The flatness was gone from the room now and the air was charged with anticipation. Everything else had been a disappointment and there were hours and hours to fill before they went home. Claire wanted to say 'no' but she couldn't.

She reached up to switch on the landing light but Amy stopped her. The girls giggled and bumped into one another on the dark stairs. Claire put her hand on the surgery door. This room still felt out of bounds though it had been eight years since the accident.

The girls pressed around her in a jittery knot and stared into the surgery. Pale moonlight leaked in through the broken Venetian blind. Her mother's desk and examination table had already been eclipsed by junk. Cardboard boxes of books and bags of clothes. A bicycle without a saddle. A broken electric fire.

'It's spooky,' Lucy breathed.

'I'm getting goose bumps,' Amy whispered.

Claire was getting them too. The tiny hairs on the back of her neck were standing on end and her throat was dry. Part of her wanted to see her mum's ghost but another part of her was scared. What if she was angry?

She saw the shadowy figure in the old swivel chair just before Amy screamed. Then the girls were pushing past her, shrieking and squealing.

'Sorry, Dad,' Claire said softly. 'I didn't know you were in here.'

He sighed. 'I just came in to sit for a while. Go back upstairs to your friends now.'

But after that, they weren't really her friends any more and Claire never brought anyone home again except for Ray.

She hauled Dog back to the car. He clambered in and collapsed on the back seat in a blissful food coma. She drove carefully so she wouldn't wake him. The longer he slept the longer it would be before he woke up and realised that he wasn't going home.

Claire woke with the feeling that she was being watched. She opened her eyes and saw a huge grey, whiskery chin looming over her head.

'Out!' She pointed at the door.

Dog's eyebrows came together as he looked at the door then at her and then at the door again.

'Oh,' she sat up, 'you want to go *out* out.'

She pulled on a sweatshirt then followed him down into the kitchen and opened the back door. He brushed past her as he went out but she was used to him now. He picked his way down the path, stopping to sniff enquiringly at some weeds. It was a beautiful November night. The garden glittered with frost and the moonlight was reflecting on the tiny glittering facets of quartz in the garden wall.

This was the one thing Claire liked about looking after Dog. She got to see things she normally wouldn't. The sky turning pink before a five o'clock sunset. The last few yellow leaves clinging to the trees in the park. A cloud of starlings dissolving and re-forming in the sky above the pond. She had promised herself, back in June, that she'd try to be healthy. She had hardly exercised for years but now she was taking a long walk every day. Maybe she'd keep doing that, after he was gone. But where was he going to go? What was going to become of him if her dad really didn't want him back?

There was someone in the garden. Ray could hear them crashing around. He jumped out of bed and lifted his bedroom blind. He'd left it down for weeks now because he was ignoring Claire. He thought now, that he was having some kind of complicated hallucination. There was a huge dog in her garden. If she saw it, she'd freak. He forgot the row. He forgot that they weren't speaking. He pulled on a pair of jeans, yanked up the sash window and climbed out on to the fire escape.

'Hey!' he shouted. 'What are you doing down there!'

The dog was squatting in the nettles looking up at him, wearing a tragic expression like a martyred saint.

'How did you get in?' Ray hurried down the metal stairs.

A girl in a sweatshirt with bare legs and long, straight hair appeared on the moonlit path. It was Claire with different hair. 'He lives here.'

'That's news to me.' Ray had reached the bottom step.

'I'm sorry.' She tugged her sweatshirt around her and looked up at him. 'I should have asked you if it was OK for him to stay. It's only temporary.'

She looked different without her obstreperous halo of curls. Sophisticated, slightly intimidating. 'What have you done with your hair?'

'It's a twelve-week blow-dry thing.'

They stood in an icy pool of moonlight, Ray bare chested, Claire bare legged, their breaths coming and going in tiny white clouds in the frosty air.

Ray peered at the dog lurking in the nettle patch. He had a beard and whiskery sideburns and a bizarre tuft on the top of his head like a wonky wig. His dark grey legs had an extra curly layer of light grey fur that made him look as if he was wearing dog trousers. 'Hey! It's him! Your dad's dog!'

'I'm looking after him till Dad gets better.'

'Better at what?'

'Dad had an accident,' Claire pulled at her sleeves, 'six weeks ago. He won't be able to walk for a while.'

Ray sat down heavily on the cold metal step. 'Jesus! What happened?'

'He fell off a ladder. He was in hospital for a month.'

'A month?' Ray stared up at her. He felt as if the cold had slowed his brain. 'Your dad was in hospital for a month? Why didn't you tell me?'

She shrugged and the things they'd said to one another the night they rowed came back to him.

'Jesus, I turn my back for a minute and you acquire a dog.'

'I turned my back for a minute,' Claire said dryly, 'and you acquired a daughter.' She was shifting from bare foot to bare foot on the path, and he knew she must be frozen. She hated the cold.

'I'm sorry about the things I said. Especially the things I said about you and your mum. I didn't mean any—'

'Let's not go back there. But I'm sorry about the things I said about you too.'

'Still friends?'

Claire's hair fell over her face and he couldn't see her expression. 'I don't know, Ray.' He swallowed. 'I know that's awkward. Do you want me to move out? It might take a while to find a landlord who's willing to take Dog.'

'You can both stay for as long as you like.' Ray's teeth were chattering now and Claire was shivering but he didn't want her to go back inside. 'I'm seeing Willow again, like you said I should. I'm looking after her on Friday.'

'She's so lovely and I hope . . .' He wondered if she was remembering that he'd told her it was none of her business. 'I hope it works out.'

'Why don't you come along? We could have a Perfect Day or—'
'I can't.'

'I could change it to Saturday.' He looked at her profile behind the sleek curtain of her hair. 'Sunday?'

'I'm going away.'

'Where?'

'To Wexford. I met someone.'

'The guy from Johnny Foxes?'

'Someone else.'

Ray picked up a pebble and threw it at the rusting patio heater marooned in the patch of nettles. He missed. 'Is he nice?'

Claire nodded.

He felt the icy trickle of a raindrop on the back of his neck and then another one. 'But we can still hang out sometimes?'

Claire shivered. 'I think I need some space.' It was raining properly now and there was a touch of sleet in the rain.

'The question is,' Ray said, 'are we talking the space between the prongs of a cake fork or the space between Alpha Centauri and Polaris?'

'I don't know.'

Dog, who had been dreamily sniffing a nettle, looked up at the sky and retreated to the back door. Ray's face was wet. 'I can't stand Lorraine,' he sang softly to the tune of 'I Can't Stand the Rain'.

'I'd better go in,' Claire said. 'I think Dog is getting cold.'

''Night, Claire.'

''Night, Ray.'

The light in Claire's kitchen went off and then, after a minute, the light in her bedroom went off too. Ray sat on the step watching the garden through the silver threads of sleet. It took a long time but finally it happened, the way it always used to when he was young. He stopped feeling cold and he just felt numb.

Claire lay in the dark beneath the duvet, shivering, waiting to hear Ray's footsteps going back up the fire escape, but the garden was quiet. She knew he was sitting out there in the rain the way he had been that first day she'd spoken to him. Part of her wanted to go out there and bring him in again but another part of her was still wounded by the things he'd said. And she had seven months to keep her promise to herself. Things had only just started with Richard. If she really wanted a relationship, Eilish was right. She was better off without Ray.

16

After the day that Claire took him back to her dad's house, Dog seemed somehow diminished. He was scared of things that hadn't bothered him before. The hairdryer, the kettle, hot-water bottles. He backed away from the Hoover and squeezed himself into the narrow space between the fridge and the cooker. He was like descriptions of houses written by estate agents that said 'deceptively large', Claire thought. Except, inside, he was deceptively small.

'I have to do this!' She switched on the Hoover. Richard was picking her up in the morning and she wanted to make the right impression. 'I'll be as quick as I can.' She would have been quicker if Dog didn't shed so much. Grey tumbleweeds were drifting around the hall and the bedroom carpet had a fine blur of fur. Dog wasn't technically allowed in there but none of the doors in the flat closed properly.

He was still tucked in beside the fridge after she'd washed down all the floors and polished the mirrors and bleached the loo and the bath. He looked so dejected that she gave him the portion of Eilish's garlic and tarragon chicken that she'd defrosted for herself.

He licked the bowl clean then lay staring at the back door as if he was waiting for her dad to burst in and rescue him at any moment. He might, Clare thought sadly, be waiting a very long time. At exactly six o'clock, Dog got up and went into the living room and sat in front of the TV. Claire followed him in and turned on the news. She looked around, trying to see the room through Richard's eyes. Her cluttered bookshelves, her yellow velvet chaise longue, her collection of junk-shop mirrors and her flower fairy lights. 'Is it shabby chic?' she asked Dog. 'Or just shabby?' But he didn't look at her, he was mesmerised by Anne Doyle.

Richard was standing in the laneway holding a can of WD40. He sprayed it into Claire's lock. 'Try it now.'

Claire slipped her key in and the lock turned with a velvety click. 'Wow!'

'Wow yourself!' He looked at her short grey dress and then put his hands on her shoulders and kissed her. Nobody had kissed her properly for three years. She had forgotten how nice it felt. If Ray looked out of his window, Claire thought, he'd see them. Then she stopped herself thinking and concentrated on kissing.

'We should go,' Richard said, pulling away, 'before I decide I want to stay.'

Dog wagged his tail when he saw Richard. He liked men. He was always checking them out in the park.

Richard did a double-take. 'OK! I was expecting a Paris Hilton handbag number. What is that?'

'He's a hairy lurcher,' Claire said. 'But he's not mine. He's my dad's. I'm just minding him for a while.'

'Does he have to come along?'

'I think a day out might cheer him up.'

'Would you mind if we took *your* car?' Richard said. 'I've just spent the morning cleaning mine.'

Claire had done her best with her flat but Mossy might as well have a neon sign on his roof – visible from space – that read: 'Claire Dillon's life is a mess.'

Richard picked up a broken wiper from the floor. 'Do you mind my asking what you do if it rains?'

'It still works.' Claire didn't look at him. 'You just have to use it manually.'

'You're joking.' Richard started to laugh.

She was trying to see out through the rear-view mirror but Dog was standing up on the back seat and all she could see was a wall of grey fur.

'Down!' she said. Dog pretended not to hear her and tried to nibble the back of Richard's hair.

'Down!' Richard said in a deep voice, and Dog crumpled as if he'd been shot. 'It's a pack thing.' He grinned. 'You have to show them who's top dog.'

'I saw some rough cuts of the viral campaign on Friday,' Richard said when they were on the N11. 'But they weren't right. I've told the agency to go back and re-edit.'

'Oh God!' Claire said, crashing into fourth and hoping that Mossy was going to keep his car BO in check. It got worse in higher gears. 'That doesn't sound good.'

'It's fine. I've seen the rushes. We've got what we need. You did an amazing job.' He put his arm along the back of her seat. 'So I suppose we should get the history thing out of the way. What's your longest relationship been?'

'Nearly three years.'

'Mine too. Three years exactly. I'm still good friends with all my exes, though. How about you?'

'Not really.'

'I get that.' Richard flipped down the sun visor. A piece of moss from the soft top fell on to his leg. He brushed it off. 'It would be hard for a guy to just be friends with you. He'd always want more. How long have you been single?'

'Three years.'

'Snap. Do you share your place?'

'I live on my own.' Claire was relieved that she didn't have to explain that her best friend was an incredibly handsome guy who used to be famous and that he lived upstairs and that there was a connecting door.

Richard's parents lived in a farmhouse just outside Wexford town. There were some strange tubular sculptures on the lawn. A collection of chipped statues of the Blessed Virgin Mary were gathered, in a menacing cluster, around a pot-bellied stove in the porch. The massive chandelier in the hall was made out of tarnished silver cutlery. Claire followed Richard down some steps into the kitchen. It was huge and low ceilinged and every wall was covered with paintings. There were big abstract canvases, shimmery watercolours and scribbled pen and ink sketches. A charcoal drawing of a large naked man hung above the range. Richard's mother, in jeans and a blue T-shirt, was at a wooden table hacking at a leg of lamb with a blunt carving knife.

'Thank God.' Her long, dark hair was shot through with silver. She pushed it out of her eyes. 'Can you fix this bloody knife?'

'This is Jean,' Richard said, 'my mum. This is Claire.'

Jean wiped her hands on a tea towel. 'We've all been dying to meet you.' She came over and hugged Claire. She smelled of roasting meat and L'Air du Temps. 'You were a huge hit with Helen. I have to warn you, she's already named all your future children.'

'Where's the knife sharpener?' Richard was rummaging in the drawer. He noticed the drawing above the fireplace. 'God! Is that—?'

'Frank Murphy.' His mother nodded. 'He's our next-door neighbour,' she said to Claire. 'Amazing physique. You'd never know it if you saw him with his clothes on.'

'Oh, Mum!' Richard said. 'Do we have to?'

'Leave me alone,' she grabbed the knife back, 'and go and nag your sisters. I told them to lay the table but they're probably just laying into the wine.'

Aine was two years older than Helen, but they could have been twins. They were sprawled across two sofas in the cluttered living room, their dark heads bent over the Sunday papers.

Helen jumped up. 'I was going to apologise for being so pissed the last time I met you.' She sighed, tragically. 'But there's no point now. We're already on to our second bottle of white. This is my big sister Aine. This is Claire, the actress of the slutty shoes.'

'She does look like a young Julianne Moore.' Aine stared at Claire approvingly.

'Now if I could only act like her,' Claire said, 'I'd be sorted.'

Jean gave Dog the lamb bone and he carried it off reverently to a corner of the kitchen while the rest of them went into the living room where the table had finally been laid. They barely fitted around it. Jean, Richard, Claire, Aine and Helen, Richard's dad –

Sean – and Andreas, Helen's boyfriend, who looked like a Greek god and spoke hardly any English.

Helen and Aine were a rowdy double act. They grilled Claire all through lunch. About her job, her flat, her shoes, her encounter with Jonathan Rhys Meyers and her preference for wearing skin illuminator under or over her foundation. When they ran out of questions, they turned on Richard.

'Richard couldn't sleep,' Helen speared a potato off his plate, 'if his CDs weren't all in alphabetical order. I used to swap around Backstreet Boys and Right Said Fred and he'd have nightmares for a week.'

'I don't even know who Right Said Fred is,' Richard scoffed.

'Oh yes you do.' Aine smirked. ' "I'm too Sexy for My Shirt". You used to sing it into a hairbrush in the bathroom mirror.'

'Helen's room was a no-go area.' Richard refilled Claire's glass. 'It looked like a bomb had gone off in an underwear factory.'

'True. Aine once sent me a postcard from Irish College,' Helen snorted, 'addressed to Helen Daly, Knickeragua.'

'Nicaragua?' Andreas frowned at Helen.

'She doesn't mean the place, sweetheart!' Helen said. 'She means my room was full of knickers.' She pulled up her skirt. 'Pants!'

'Helen!' Jean rolled her eyes. 'Can we get through one lunch without seeing your underwear?'

'Seriously, Claire, you need to know what you're getting into here,' Aine said. 'Richard has lost two grandparents, three cats and a gerbil—'

'A hamster,' Richard interrupted.

'—but I've only ever seen him crying once, when he caught Helen using his razor to shave her legs.'

Helen lifted one leg up and pretended to shave it with the handle of her fork.

'What do you both do?' Claire said. 'When you're not trying to embarrass your brother?'

'Touché.' Aine grinned. 'I'm an engineer and Helen's a chemist.'

'I work for Big Pharma and Andreas is a sheep farmer in Crete.' Helen ran her hand up the back of Andreas's shirt. 'It's perfect!'

'Before we get into the Helen and Andreas show,' Aine said, 'I need to point out that Richard did have his uses. He could do a brilliant forgery of Mum's handwriting when we wanted to mitch and he makes the world's best full Irish breakfast.'

Helen rolled her eyes. 'That's because he timed the ideal cooking length for every ingredient in a fry – mushrooms, eggs, bacon, sausages – and made a little chart thing with symbols. Mum still has it somewhere.'

'Anything else you'd like to add?' Richard pushed his plate away. 'Or have you finished destroying my character?'

'There is one other thing you need to know,' Helen said to Claire. 'He likes to fix things. It's kind of a compulsion.'

'I think that's pretty nice,' Claire smiled, 'as compulsions go.'

'Good for you,' Jean said. 'It is nice.'

'Speaking of fixing things,' Richard's father said, 'the motor mower's on the blink, Rich. We've been waiting for you to come down to sort it.'

Other people's families had always been a mystery to Claire. The rough and tumble and noise of them, the way they squabbled and made up. The mantelpieces of framed photographs – holidays and graduations and twenty-firsts. She had always felt as if she was on the outside, looking in. But around the crowded table, she felt included, part of a real family, one that couldn't have been more different from her own.

Meals at home, even when Nick was still there, had been silent. Her dad would have one earphone in his ear and his small radio tucked into his pocket. Nick would read a book. After he had gone to the States, Claire and her dad would eat in front of the TV. There had been love at home, but it had gone underground when her mother died and it had never found its way back up to the surface.

After lunch, Richard, his father and Andreas went outside with a box of tools and Dog sloped out after them, keeping a respectful distance.

'Call Sky News!' Aine gasped. 'Richard is playing with a dog. He hates dogs.'

'He doesn't,' his mother said. 'He hates germs.'

Aine started laughing. 'Remember Dutch?'

'Dutch was our sheepdog when we were growing up,' Helen said. 'Richard would only touch him when he was wearing Marigolds.'

'She means when Richard was wearing Marigolds,' Helen clarified. 'Not the dog.'

They stood at the window, watching Richard throwing a frisbee which Dog dutifully retrieved.

'Well, that's it.' Helen opened another bottle of wine. 'I'm buying a hat because he must be seriously into Claire, to do that.'

Mossy wouldn't start. Claire turned the engine over and over until she smelled it flooding. Richard tried to jump-start it then called the AA.

'Why don't you stay the night? We have plenty of room,' Jean said when they were all back in the living room with the fire lit.

'I've got to fly to Glasgow in the morning,' Richard said.

'You could drive up first thing?' Jean said. 'With the girls.'

They all looked at Claire. She couldn't face the whole thing about who was going to sleep where. It was only a second date. 'I've got an audition in the morning.'

'That sounds so glamorous.' Aine sighed.

'It isn't.'

'Do you do any of those radio ads?' Helen asked. 'Terms and conditions apply. Prices may rise as well as fall.'

'No. But I'm planning to do a demo tape and sent it around some advertising agencies.'

'I'll get the guy who records our radio ads to handle all that for you,' Richard said.

'Watch this space!' Aine waved her glass.

'*Listen* to this space,' Helen groaned. 'Told you she was a fruit loop,' she mouthed at Claire.

'You told her *what*?' Aine snorted. And they were off again.

One minute Claire was sitting in the overheated tow-truck cab, listening to Richard and Ronan, the driver, talking about battery posts and starter switches, and the next, Richard was shaking her gently and they were pulling over at the top of her laneway.

Ronan lowered the ramp and let Dog out of Mossy. He hadn't been allowed to travel in the tow-truck. He climbed down stiffly and gave Richard a wounded look. Claire put the key in the lock and it turned with a silky 'click'.

'I'll get Ronan to drop me home then leave the car with my mechanic,' Richard said. 'When I get back from Scotland, I'll get it sorted.' He kissed her lightly on the lips. 'You were a big hit today. They all loved you.'

She smiled; the afternoon had left her with a hazy glow of warmth. She had loved them too.

Kelly tugged at the zipper of the cream sequinned dress but it was stuck fast. She caught her breath and looked at her reflection. She was half in and half out of the dress, her dark hair caught up in a ponytail. She put her hand on her belly. Was it slightly swollen? She opened the velvet curtain and called over an assistant. 'I need the next size.'

'That one's perfect on you!' the girl said. 'I can help you get the zip up.'

'No!' Kelly insisted. 'Get me the ten.' Her phone rang.

'Did you catch the show?'

'I missed it.' Did Nick seriously think she had time to sit around watching TV? She'd had to cram two meetings into the morning so she had time to come to Dundrum to find something to wear for his awards dinner.

'I had a lot of feedback from the two conflict pieces so I did a slot on the three things couples most row about. Money, sex and in-laws. Oonagh came up with a name: "the good, the bad and the ugly". Pretty smart, eh?'

'I guess.' Kelly sat down on the stool; she was beginning to get very tired of hearing about how smart Oonagh was.

'What time are we meeting tonight?'

'Tonight?' Kelly had to go and check on an extension in Ranelagh later. It would be dusty and the builders would be difficult. She'd been looking forward to going home and getting into a hot bath.

'It's our date night, remember?'

'Are you sure?'

'You put it in my diary after you cancelled the last one.'

With a sinking heart, she realised he was right. 'Why don't you book something,' she snapped. It wouldn't kill him to organise it for once. She did it every month.

'Sure.' He sounded hurt. 'There's a French film festival at the IFI.'

Subtitles. Kelly felt like sliding down on to the floor at the very thought of them. There was a rough edge on Kelly's thumbnail where she'd caught it on the zip. She pressed it against her cheek. 'Text me the time and I'll meet you at the cinema.'

'Perfect!' he said too cheerfully. 'We can have supper afterwards.'

Then he'd want to make love, Kelly thought, after she'd hung up. And she didn't want to. She knew it was stupid, the kind of thing a teenager thought, but she was afraid that if she was pregnant, sex might somehow mess it up.

Nick leaned back in his leather chair and stared at the wallpaper on his iPhone. It was a photograph of Kelly taken back in May. She was in the garden in a tiny brown flower-print sundress and a wide-brimmed straw hat with a blue ribbon.

Kelly had a special camera smile, a way of turning slightly to the side and looking over her shoulder, that she thought made her look pretty, but she was laughing in this shot and when she was happy, she didn't just look pretty, she looked beautiful.

He knew how much she was hoping that the Clomid would work. But he was hoping just as much that it wouldn't. She had rushed him into this without giving him a chance to share his feelings. He wasn't even sure that he could share them. How could he explain what it had been like struggling to bring Claire up, on his own? Nick remembered a photograph of his sister that he put up on his locker in his dorm at college. She was about ten. When he looked at it, he didn't see the sweet red-haired girl with the shy smile, he saw the gap that should have been fixed between her top front teeth. The way her navy school jumper was worn at the elbows. The pinkish tinge that all her shirts had because he kept forgetting to separate the colours from the whites.

He stared back down at the photograph of Kelly. He missed the laughing girl in the garden. He would have given anything to sit next to her in the cinema and hold her hand in the dark.

Ash was already waiting outside the Stephen's Green Centre when Ray got out of the cab. She was wearing a belted black coat and high black boots, her roots had grown out and her eyes were puffy.

'Thanks,' she said.

'Any time,' Ray said, automatically, then wished he hadn't. He didn't mind helping her out this once but he didn't want it to become a regular thing.

'Hi,' he said to Willow.

'Hello.' She stared gloomily down at her tiny blue All Stars. She was obviously looking forward to this as much as he was.

However, Ray had done his homework this time and found a new vegan-friendly restaurant called the Happy Cow. He and Willow queued on the stairs in silence, and by the time they were seated at a table, he was starting to feel exhausted. He pointed at her rabbit backpack. 'Have you got David Bowie in there?'

'Bowie was dirty.' Willow was tearing little bits off the paper place mat. 'Granny wanted to wash him so I brought my Sylvanian family instead.'

Ray opened the menu and stared at it, but the print was too small to read. He had put off getting glasses for years on the grounds that they'd ruin his rock 'n' roll image but unless he wrote another 'Asia Sky', he thought grimly, he wouldn't have to worry about that any more.

A cute Australian waitress in black shorts and a T-shirt that said 'Meat is Murder' came to take their order. She beamed at Willow. 'What are you going to have, missy?' Willow asked for a vegetarian stir fry and an orange juice. 'What about your dad?'

'He's not my real dad,' Willow said. 'He's bi-logical.'

'Right!' The waitress looked at Ray. She was smiling now but there was pity in her eyes.

'Do you have any meat?' Ray asked. 'At all?'

'No.' She pointed at the logo on her apron. 'If we had meat the cow wouldn't be happy, would he?'

'Cows were female, last time I looked,' Ray said. He pointed at something on the bottom of the menu. 'I'll have that.'

'Are you sure?' The waitress's smile turned into a smirk.

'Yes,' Ray snapped. 'I'm positive.' Her smirk turned into a grin and then into a laugh. He glared at her. 'Is there a problem with that?'

She shook her head helplessly. 'So that's one vegetarian stir fry and one Function Room: Available for Private Parties. How would you like that done, sir?'

Ray sighed. 'Just bring me whatever she's having.'

'Do you really look at cows?' Willow asked when the waitress was gone.

'It's just an expression.' Ray sneezed. He wondered if he was coming down with something after the drenching he'd had on the fire escape.

'Bless you!' Willow said.

'Thank you.'

'It's just an expression.' Willow shrugged off her backpack and began to unpack some tiny rabbit figurines.

'More rabbits.' Ray blew his nose.

'Sylvanian rabbits. They're called the Babblebrooks,' Willow said. 'They have five children.' She lined them up on the table. 'Richard, Judy, Bubba, Breezy and baby Coral.'

It was going to be a long lunch.

Willow ate slowly, very slowly, chewing everything carefully and taking lots of breaks to fill Ray in on the complex family dynamics of Sylvanian families. There were Buttercups, Blackberries, Dappledawns and Cottontails. And that was just rabbits. Other animals were involved. Penguins, hedgehogs, ponies. Ray lost count.

'The Barkers are my second favourites. They're dogs but I left them in my house in London,' Willow looked sadly at a piece of tofu, 'with Maurice.' She said it the French way, *Mo-reece*.

'What's Maurice? A badger? A skunk? A duck-billed platypus?'

'He's Mummy's boyfriend.'

Ray pictured a weedy Belgian hipster with complicated facial hair. 'And what does this Maurice do?'

'He's a singer in a band called In Your Dreams.'

A bean sprout went down the wrong way. 'Maurice DeVeau?' Ray spluttered.

Willow nodded.

Maurice DeVeau was a legend. He'd been on the cover of *Rolling Stone* twice. Ray tried to cough up the sprout but it was stuck. He grabbed his glass and drained his orange juice.

Willow put down her fork. 'Your eyes are very sticky outy.'

He nodded and coughed again.

'Do you want me to do the Heineken manoeuvre?'

'The,' he spluttered, 'what?'

'It's where you stand behind someone, and—'

Ray laughed so hard that the bean sprout shot out and landed by Willow's bowl.

She looked at it for a moment. 'You're supposed to chew it seven times before you swallow it.'

'I was a singer in a band, too, you know,' Ray said, when he caught his breath.

'I saw a picture,' Willow was arranging the Babblebrooks around the bean sprout, 'in your toilet.'

'We were called Smoke Covered Horses. Claire had come up with the name of the band by mistake. She always got the lyrics of songs wrong. She'd thought that one of the lines in "Lucy in the Sky with Diamonds" was "the girl with colitis goes by".'

'I don't understand.' Willow frowned. 'Why are the horses covered in smoke? Are they on fire?'

'There's this song called "Smoke on the Water" by Deep Purple, who are, by the way, a seminal rock band.'

'What's seminal?'

'Never mind. I played the song for my friend Claire and she thought it sounded like "Smoke Covered Horses".'

Willow shook her head. 'But it doesn't.'

'It does if you hear the song. It's like,' Ray picked a pea off his plate and began to sing, 'all we are saying, is give peas a chance.' Willow stared at him as if he'd grown a second head. He pointed at his rice and drummed a reggae beat on the table with his cutlery. 'Get up, stand up, stand up for your rice!'

'But I'm sitting down.'

Ray racked his brains for one she'd get. 'OK. When I was your age, we had this hymn at school called "Gladly, the Cross I'd Bear". But I thought it was a song about a bear named Gladly—'

Willow nodded. 'With crossed eyes.'

'Yes. But it's about Jesus's cross.'

'Why is Jesus cross with a bear?'

Ray had been right. It was going to be a long afternoon, but he was beginning to enjoy it.

17

Claire did great first-sex nerves. She'd been doing them for years and had perfected them at this stage. There was the underwear dilemma. Sexy, which meant she had to live up to it, or virginal, which meant that she wasn't up for it. The amount of alcohol she should consume – just enough to relax her but not enough to make her pass out. The lighting conundrum – energy-saving bulbs brought out the blue in her pale skin and made her look like a corpse but candlelight was a bit stagey and there were other downsides, too. Once, when she was in bed with Declan, they'd knocked over a nightlight. He'd mistaken her screams of alarm for passion and, by the time she managed to explain to him what was happening, the rug had caught light.

She usually managed to work herself into a frenzy of anxiety for days before the actual sex itself, but, with Richard, she didn't get the chance.

He had asked her to go for a hike in Glendalough the Saturday after he got back from Scotland. Nothing Claire owned was hike-appropriate so she drove herself to 53 Degrees North in the zippy little yellow Yaris that Richard had organised. He had talked his own car insurance company into lending it to her until Mossy was fixed.

Claire missed Mossy but the Yaris had its upsides. Central locking and electric windows and heat that worked without filling the car with smoke and the smell of grilled mackerel.

She went mad in 53 Degrees North and bought waterproof trousers, a bobble hat, a polar fleece, a shiny down jacket and a pair of walking boots that could, the assistant said, take her up K2.

She handed over her credit card without the familiar lump of dread in her throat. Vitalustre had paid Lorcan and, even after he'd taken his commission, Claire had nearly nine thousand euros in her account.

She had arranged to pick Richard up at his apartment. It was raining when she coaxed Dog into the Yaris but she didn't care. She was wearing waterproof mascara and rain-proof clothes. She had wipers. She had hair that made her look like Julianne Moore and walking boots, she realised looking down at them, that made her look like Inspector Plod.

Richard's apartment block was in a new development off Booterstown Avenue. There was a cheery 'For Sale' hoarding showing a woman in a black lace slip and a judge's wig smiling suggestively under a headline that said, 'I'll see you in Dromoland Court.' It was all a bit close to the bone, Claire thought, given that the developer who'd built the apartments had just declared himself bankrupt in the UK.

She texted Richard to say she was outside and he texted back. 'Come up for a sec. Rx.' She opened the window a crack for Dog then took the lift to the fourth floor. Afterwards she wondered if she'd misread Richard's text and what it had really said was 'Come up for sex, Rx', because that, when she was least expecting it and dressed for a polar expedition, was what had happened.

Richard opened the door wearing a grey towelling dressing gown and a grin.

'Oh,' Claire said, 'am I early?' The hall had at least twenty clocks, but before Claire had a chance to check the time, he smiled, took her hand and led her down the hall and into the bedroom.

'Wow!' She looked around at the dark wooden floor, the big window, the shelf of family photographs. 'This is nice.'

He kissed her.

'Are we . . . ?' she said through the kiss. 'Is this . . . ?'

Richard unzipped her anorak and pulled her down on the bed. Then he took off his dressing gown and it most definitely was it.

The blind was open. Anyone in the block opposite could have seen them – the naked man and the woman dressed like Sir Ernest Shackleton rolling around Richard's king-sized sleigh bed.

'Well,' Richard said, afterwards, smiling down at Claire and taking off her bobble hat.

'Well,' Claire's blood was coursing with feel-good chemicals, 'that was unexpected.'

'Not really.'

'You planned this?' Claire stared up at him.

'We were heading there so I thought I'd take the pressure off.'

'But I bought boots!'

'Well, put them back on again and let's get out there.'

It was still cold but the rain had stopped and they strolled arm in arm through the forest with Dog trailing behind on his extending lead, stopping to sniff every fern and tree trunk. She should take Dog more places, Claire thought. It would take his mind off her dad.

Most of the other walkers were neatly paired. Young, good looking, with children or without. All wearing performance clothes and Inspector Plod boots. This was what other people her age had been doing on Saturday afternoons, Claire realised, while she'd been hanging out with Ray drinking margaritas and eating party packs of Manhattan popcorn and watching *Mad Men*.

Ahead of them, Claire saw the lake spreading out, grey and silver, beyond the trees, and she felt her stomach tighten with fear. She held on to Richard's arm and kept her eyes on the path so she didn't have to look at the water. She didn't want that old darkness to be part of today.

'Ever been lake-swimming?'

Claire couldn't swim.

'There's a lovely lake a few miles from my parents' place. And the sea's pretty close. I'll take you there the next time you're down.'

'Maybe,' Claire said vaguely, taking a fork in the path that led back up into the forest. She would cross that bridge when she came to it.

'You look cute in all that outdoor stuff,' Richard said when it was getting dark and they were walking back to the car. He took a photograph of them on his phone and handed it to her.

The flash had turned the trees behind them to monochrome, picking up the gold lights in Claire's red hair and the pale blue of Richard's eyes. They looked good together. They looked like a couple.

In the car park, a man with a little girl riding on his shoulders stopped to admire Dog. 'Can my daughter say hello?'

'Sure,' Richard said, yanking the lead to reel Dog in. 'What's your name?'

'Britney-Rose,' the girl said. Her dad leaned down so she could pat Dog's head. He sniffed her hand, his whiskers quivering with excitement. He liked kids, Claire thought, nearly as much as he liked men.

'His beard tickles. What's his name?' the little girl asked.

'Dog,' Richard said.

'That's a very stupid name!' She giggled.

People in glass houses, Claire thought, looking at Britney-Rose, shouldn't throw names.

Willow was watching the swan on the pond while a redhead doing warm-up stretches by the playground was watching Ray. He opened Willow's book and frowned down at it, as if it were *A Guide to Top-Down Cosmology* and not *The Werepuppy*.

Ash had rung to say that Willow wanted to see him again. He wondered if this was just another cover-up to get a free babysitter but he was between jingle jobs and having Willow took his mind off his misery about the Horses. Plus it might give him an excuse to accidentally bump into Claire. He hadn't realised, till he'd seen her the other night, how much he'd missed her.

Willow had brought *Toy Story* 2 in her rabbit backpack and he'd put it on then sat near the window in case Claire went out into the garden. He was laughing so much at the out-takes in the credits he didn't hear the back door opening and, when he looked out, she was disappearing into the laneway with the dog.

It had taken ages to get Willow back into her coat and her backpack and, by the time they got downstairs, Claire was gone. Ray had stationed himself by the gate in the park but so far there was no sign of her.

'You're Ray Devine, aren't you?' A shadow fell over the book.

The redhead was in her late twenties and pretty. At another time, Ray might have been interested, but not when he had a six-year-old chaperone.

'Yeah,' he began, 'but—'

'Is that your little girl?' She pointed at the pond. Ray nodded. 'Is she OK?'

He twisted around to look. Willow was squatting at the edge of the pond in her red coat holding out a crust of bread for the swan. Ray dropped the book and ran across the grass. He grabbed Willow just as the swan lunged at the bread, beak snapping.

'Jesus!' He put her down carefully. 'What were you doing?'

'I was trying to speak swan,' Willow whispered. 'But he didn't understand me.' Her bottom lip was trembling. She looked as if she was going to cry.

'I know a lobster,' Ray said breathlessly, trying to distract her, 'who lives in that pond.'

'Really?' Willow said.

'His name is Rocky and he only has one claw.'

'You dropped your book.' The redhead was waiting at the bench when they got back. 'That swan is dangerous. Someone should lock him up,' she said and jogged away.

Ray brushed some breadcrumbs off Willow's coat.

'I didn't think he would eat me,' Willow said, 'because swans are vegetarians.'

'I got a fright.'

'Me too.' Willow was pale.

'You know what we need?' She shook her head. 'A Perfect Day.'

They had apple juice with cut-up bits of banana and apple instead of sangria. Ray wanted to feed an apple to the elephant in the zoo but Willow wouldn't let him because there was a sign saying 'Don't Feed The Animals.' So they watched the keeper feed a giraffe some straw instead. Then they went home and watched *Toy Story* 2 again.

'We had a perfect day, Mummy,' Ray heard Willow telling Ash in her polite little English-girl voice as she bunny-hopped down the steps. They had. It was just like Lou said. She had made Ray forget himself. He'd thought he was someone else, someone good.

Cooking wasn't Claire's strong point so she'd just defrosted a couple of portions of Eilish's tarragon chicken and served it with some fancy salad leaves.

Richard put down his fork. 'Is there anything you're not good at? Except for all the practical stuff.'

'I'm practical!' Claire protested.

'You're creative, like my mother. You shouldn't have to worry about fixing locks and taps and computers.' Richard had fitted new washers on all Claire's taps and his IT guy had sorted her letter 'P'. 'Anyone can do that stuff. Though I'm not sure,' Richard folded his napkin, 'if anyone can fix that decrepit car of yours.'

'Oh!' The thrill of the Yaris was wearing off and Claire missed Mossy.

'The mechanic is working on an estimate but I wouldn't hold your breath.' He saw her face. 'It's only a car, Claire.'

Claire twisted a strand of her hair. 'He was my mother's car.' Every time she put her hands on the wheel she felt connected to her mum.

'Come here.' Richard took her hand and pulled her on to his lap. 'You miss your mother, don't you? Was she sick for long before she . . .'

Claire shook her head. She didn't want to talk about the accident. She still regretted telling Shane about it. What had come over her? Why had she confided in a complete stranger? Her face burned just thinking about it. She had seen him on the set of *The Spaniard* a week ago and he'd blanked her completely.

'Hey.' Richard tilted her chin with his finger. 'Would it cheer you up if we took your dad out for a pint some evening? I'd love to meet him.'

'He's not well. He had a fall and broke his hip.'

Richard massaged her shoulders. 'We could go round to him then.'

Claire sighed. She hadn't been to see her dad since the day she had taken Dog over. 'He doesn't want to see anyone. I'm not even sure I'll be able to spend Christmas with him this year. I don't know what I'm going to do.'

'Come to Wexford with me.'

'I couldn't. We've only known one another a few weeks and your family is so close.'

'When are you going to get how special you are? How am I going to get that into your head?' He knocked on her temple, lightly, with his knuckle. 'My mum is already asking if you'll come skiing with us at Easter.'

Claire laughed. 'I'm not sure I'd last thirty seconds on skis.'

'Skiing is acting. It's all about confidence. You have that, you can do anything.'

Claire had just drifted off to sleep when the squealing began.

'Christ!' Richard sat up. 'What's that?'

'It's the tank refilling. Did you have a shower?'

'A quick one after you fell asleep.'

There was baleful howl from the kitchen as Dog joined in with the pipes.

'You know what you need?'

'A plumber?' Claire had to shout to be heard over a high-pitched shriek.

'Someone to take care of you.'

'I can take care of myself!'

He shook his head. 'You're such a girl.'

'I'm a woman!' Claire hit him with her pillow.

He ducked and wrapped his arms around her. 'Well, I'm not,' he grinned, 'going to argue with that.'

Claire must have fallen asleep again because she was woken by a blood-curdling shout and hissing. Her eyes snapped open. Richard was standing in the middle of her tiny bedroom, naked, wielding her rainstick like a samurai sword.

Claire sat up. 'What?'

He pointed at the door. 'Noises in the hall. I thought we were being burgled.'

Dog was cringing by the door, his head low, his ears flat, looking at the rainstick with terror in his eyes.

'Oh, come on!' Claire sat up and pulled the sheet around her. 'Nobody's ever done anything to you with a rainstick.'

'What?' Richard put the rainstick down.

'I was talking to Dog.' Claire swung her legs over the bed. 'I think he needs to go.'

Richard shook his head. 'That's such a relief. I didn't want to say anything but I'm not a dog person.'

Claire bit her lip. 'I mean he needs to go out into the garden for a pee.'

'Today I feel so happy, so happy, so happy,' the crow puppet sang, and Willow and the rest of the audience sang along with it.

'Ray, why aren't you singing?' Willow whispered. 'Did your voice break?'

'About twenty years ago.' Ray liked singing but he drew the line at the crow song even if Willow seemed to be enjoying it. He had the hang of keeping her amused now. The secret was to keep their get-togethers fresh. Find something unexpected to do. Animals of all kinds were a success just as long as they weren't dead. Last week, he'd taken her to a 'Meet the Pigs' experience in Wicklow. The smell still haunted him. It was worse than Mossy on a hot day.

After the puppet show was over, they walked up Grafton Street playing Weird-Would-You-Rather-Be? A game Willow had invented.

'Would you rather be a hamster or a verruca?' she asked him.

'What's a verruca?'

'It's on your foot.'

'A hamster. Would you rather be a hamster or a lobster?'

'A lobster! Would you rather be a lobster or a toaster?'

'Toaster. Would you rather be a toaster or a roller coaster?'

They passed a man smoking a joint outside Stephen's Green. 'Smoking is bad!' he said to her. 'You know that, right?' Were there other things he should tell her? About drink and drugs?

'What did Maurice do when you hung out with him?' he asked her, casually. In Your Dreams had a fairly wild reputation and the idea of anyone getting wasted in front of Willow worried him.

'He did a lot of space pigs.'

'Space pigs?' Ray's mind boggled.

Willow trailed her hands along the railing. 'It's where you swing someone around by their hand and their foot? You know?' Ray didn't. It sounded dangerous. 'And he tells funny jokes.'

'What kind of jokes?'

'I don't know. Jokes disappear into my head. Do you know any jokes, Ray?'

He must have heard millions. But they disappeared into his head too.

'You know your band,' Willow said when Ray was putting her Quorn sausages on to a plate. 'The Slow Covered Horses.'

'Smoke!' Ray speared his sausage and put it on her plate. He could eat later. 'They're covered in smoke not snow.'

'Yes,' Willow said, patiently. 'But did you sing any famous songs?'

'Didn't your mummy tell you about "Asia Sky"? It went platinum in the UK.'

'Oh!' She wiped her fingers on a napkin and put her plate back on the coffee table. He could tell she had no idea what platinum was but she probably didn't know what the UK was either. 'Will you sing it for me?'

'OK.' Ray picked up his guitar and sat down on the sofa. For some reason, maybe because she was watching him so intently, he felt embarrassed and he sang the chorus from the Asia Sky jingle instead of the song.

'*Anata ni furainguhōmu.*
AsiaSky ga takaku tobu
Sore wa hontōdesu.
Sekai wa anatadesu.'

Willow frowned. 'What's a "sicky wa"?'

'It's Japanese.' He began to sing it in English.

'*AsiaSky takes off into the blue.*
Till I'm so high that I can see it's true
The world is small.
When the world's just me and you.'

She made him sing it again in Japanese, joining in, mangling the words and the tune. She had the worst voice that Ray had ever heard, apart from Claire's.

'I saw Claire's dog!' Willow said when Ray was helping her to put on her backpack. 'He was in the garden before. Can we go down and see him?'

'Not today.' Ray buttoned her coat. 'Claire and me are having a break.'

'Like Mummy and Maurice,' Willow said sadly.

Ray wanted to give her a hug but he wasn't sure they knew one another well enough so he pulled her hat down over her dark curls. 'Knock! Knock!' he said.

'Who's there?'

'Boo!' He remembered a joke now.

'Boo who?'

'Don't cry!' he said. 'It's only me!'

She fell laughing back on to the sofa, with her backpack and her coat on and her hands over her face.

Maurice DeVeau may have been on the cover of *Rolling Stone* magazine twice, but Ray was willing to bet that he had never made Willow laugh like that.

18

The door to the en suite was open and the splash of water on tiles and the peppery musk of Nick's body wash drifted into the bedroom. After weeks of avoiding him, Kelly suddenly wanted to unzip her sequinned dress and step into the shower with him right now, but if she did, her hair and her make-up would be ruined.

She remembered her friend Molly in New York telling her how incredibly turned on she was all the time she was pregnant. Maybe it was a sign. She was a week late. She wasn't allowed to do a pharmacy test. The hormone drugs could give a false positive reading. But this could be it!

She zipped up her dress. Most women would have given anything to fit into a size eight but she couldn't wait to fill her wardrobe with loose dresses and maternity jeans. She was going to love every stretch mark, every pang of nausea, every backache.

'Why are these things so fiddly?' Nick came in, barefoot. He was already wearing his black tuxedo trousers and a white shirt with a black dicky bow hanging loose from the collar. He went down on one knee so she could tie it for him.

'Will you have dinner with me?' he asked her.

'Yes.' Those were the first words he'd ever spoken to her.

'Will you marry me then?'

'Sorry,' she laughed, 'I'm already married!'

'Happily?' She nodded. 'Really?' He looked so doubtful that she felt a pang of remorse. The last few months had been a hormonal head wreck but if they had managed to make a baby then it would all have been worth while. 'Really.' She kissed him hard on the mouth.

Nick kissed her back then broke away and checked his watch.

'I'd like to take you up on that but I need to print out the invitations. Can you be ready in five?'

'I'm ready now.' She stood up.

'Beautiful dress. But what's that?' He pointed at the stool.

Kelly looked over her shoulder. There was what looked like a rose petal on the padded blue silk cover. A wonky heart shape. Crimson with a touch of soot at the edges. The roses in the vase on her dressing table were pink. It was blood.

Poor Kelly. Nick wished they could just cancel but tonight was incredibly important. He only had one chance to impress Curtis from Clingfilms. Oonagh had been rehearsing him for weeks. He was primed to deliver impressive nuggets on audience selection criteria and editorial control.

He stopped to straighten his tie in the mirror in the hall. Had the relief he'd felt when he'd seen the spot of blood shown in his face? He stared at his reflection. The old man had become a father at twenty-eight and then gave up on it when he was thirty-eight, just a few months older than Nick was now. He felt too young to have a child and, confusingly, he felt he'd left it too late.

He checked the study for his laptop then he remembered that he'd left it in the boot of the car. His feet were bare and his shoes were still upstairs. Kelly's MacBook was on the sofa in the kitchen. He could log into his email and print the invitations from there. He perched on a stool and flipped it open. A banner at the top of the page caught his eye. It was pink with a headline in white:

'SHARE YOUR INFERTILITY ANGST WITH OTHER BROODY LADIES.

Would your DH rather talk about the FTSE than the patter of tiny feet? Welcome to the BroodyGals bulletin board. A safe, anonymous space where you can share your hopes and fears.'

Nick smiled. Apart from Niamh, Kelly didn't have any friends in Dublin. It was good for her to have a place to connect with other women. He scrolled down the page and scanned the posts.

'SadGal-11
Joined 1.02.2011
ME 37

DH 37

TTC 6 months

Help! Before we were TTC my DH couldn't keep his hands off me. Now he runs a mile when I ovulate. What is wrong with guys??? And why can't my DH understand why I want a baby soooooo much. Grrrrrrrrr.'

'Mum2BSoon

Joined 19.10.2010

ME 40

DH 38

TTC 1 year

@SadGal-11 Grrrrrrrrr. Lol☺ My DH is not exactly champing at the bit either. My advice is stay away from emotional stuff and stick to the science bit. Put your DH in charge of your temperature chart. Men love graphs. Hang on in there! Hugs.'

TTC must be 'trying to conceive', Nick guessed. 'DH' was 'dear husband'. The next post looked like a reply from Kelly.

'BroodyKelly07

Joined 15.08.2008

ME 30

DH 37

TTC 3 years, 1 month.

@SadGal-11. I was TTC for 3 years and my DH had no idea.'

Nick stared at the screen. Kelly had been trying to get pregnant for three years without telling him.

'My advice is don't tell your DH you're ovulating! Plan a sexy date night every month and act like you can't keep your hands off him! He's not going to ask questions! My DH didn't.'

'Do I look okay?' Kelly was standing in the doorway in a black dress. Her long dark hair was pinned up and the tiny diamond he'd given her as a wedding present was flashing at her throat. She looked like a complete stranger.

Nick had no jacket, no phone, no shoes and nowhere to go. He had driven to the hotel on automatic. Now he had no idea what he was doing there. He pushed through the awards guests milling around the foyer and ducked into the empty, wood-panelled bar. He leaned on the polished counter and put his head in his hands.

'What'll you have?' A barman was standing in front of him.
'Vodka. A double.'

The familiar, sharp, sickly smell of it turned his stomach. He wasn't sure it would go down but he put the glass to his lips and poured it down his throat until he felt the ice rattling against his teeth.

His mind had shut down in the car but it began to race now. Moments came flooding back to him. Times when he and Kelly had Two Listened and Soul Gazed. Their Honesty Box. Their Open Heart Policy. Their Complaints Journal. Every day he met couples who deceived one another in a hundred different ways. He had thought they were different.

'Nick! Why aren't you answering your phone?' Oonagh was wearing a fitted pink dress that had relocated her cleavage to just beneath her collarbone. Her face was a smooth mask of make-up. Something iridescent glittered in the corners of her eyes. 'Where's your dinner jacket?'

'Your accent sounds comple . . .' The vodka had muddled his head and he couldn't find the word. 'Totally different when you're not on TV. Did you know that?'

'Jesus! What have you got on your feet?'

Nick had left the house in his bare feet then remembered, at the last minute, that there were trainers in his gym bag in the boot. 'There was a break-in,' he said. 'I got locked out of the house.'

This didn't make sense but Oonagh was too angry to notice. 'Why didn't you call me? Curtis is already here. Everyone's at the table.' She looked at his empty glass. 'You're not drunk, are you?'

He shook his head. The room swung around him in a dizzy whirl. 'Just got a scare.'

Oonagh grabbed his arm and dragged him out into the empty foyer and into a ballroom packed with circular tables. A dozen pillars of coloured light bounced overhead. He followed her through the labyrinth of tables. She stopped at one directly beneath the stage. He took in the faces. Ita Fox and a man who must be her husband. A fashion designer and his boyfriend. Owen, looking like a beefy James Bond, and a very young, very skinny guy with longer hair than Kelly. The guy bounced up and gave

207

Oonagh a hug. He was wearing leather jeans and trainers with his dinner jacket.

'Curtis, this is Nick Dillon, Ireland's go-to guy for couple trouble.' Oonagh pushed Nick forward and Curtis pumped his hand. He had a scarily firm handshake. 'Snap!' Curtis grinned, nodding at Nick's trainers and then at his own.

Oonagh sat opposite Nick and launched into a lively discussion about the challenges of reinventing reality TV for an audience that had seen it all. Nick was supposed to join in but all the sound bites she had taught him, all the statistics he had learned, were gone. All he could think about was the message board.

'*I was TTC for 3 years and my DH had no idea.*' Kelly had been lying to him since pretty much the day they got married.

'Red or white?' The waitress was hovering at his shoulder.

People drank to forget, Nick remembered. How drunk did you have to get to do that? 'Both.' Dinner was a blur. He didn't touch his food. The wine, both kinds, tasted like vinegar but he drank them anyway and asked for refills every time the waitress came around.

Curtis tried to engage him, asking questions about Fish and We-Fit and his private coaching sessions, but after a few mono-syllabic answers, he gave up.

Nick was vaguely aware of Owen smirking at him from behind a centrepiece of silver helium balloons and Oonagh mouthing indecipherable things and telegraphing frantic messages with her fake eyelashes. But all he could think about was those date nights. They had seemed spontaneous but they had been planned like military manoeuvres around Kelly's cycle. He had thought she wanted him but she hadn't, she wanted him to make her pregnant.

There was a break between the meal and the awards and Nick stood up, unsteadily, to go to the bathroom. Oonagh grabbed his arm as he passed her chair and pulled him down to her level. 'For Christ's sake, sober up!' she hissed. 'Or don't come back!'

He locked himself into a cubicle. Lies and secrets. Secrets and lies. He'd grown up with them. He'd crossed the Atlantic to get away from them. Now they'd caught up with him again. He leaned his head against the flimsy cubicle partition. Way off in the distance, he could hear the muffled jabber of an announcement, the boom of music then the machine-gun fire of applause.

He had to get back. Oonagh needed him in there. He staggered out of the cubicle, went to the sink and washed his hands. His face, above his white dress shirt, was clammy and chalk white. He ran his finger along the raised ridge of the scar on his forehead. Oonagh was right. If it had been stitched properly, it might have become invisible now.

'Let me give you a helping hand there, Doc.' Owen Clancy was standing behind him.

'I'm not a doctor!' Nick tried to say, then suddenly he was back at the table, leaning on Owen's arm. He was vaguely aware of a circle of horrified faces looking up at him as Owen steered him into his seat.

'I told you to put him in a taxi,' Oonagh hissed as he reached for someone else's glass of red wine. It tipped over and a puddle of red bloomed on the white cloth and he saw the stain on the stool in the bedroom again.

On the stage, a woman in a shimmering dress was making an announcement. 'The award for best Lifestyle Magazine programme,' there was a stagey pause, 'goes to *OO in the Afternoon*!'

A spotlight swooped and dived on to their table. Oonagh and Owen stood up. Curtis bounced to his feet clapping. Nick stood up too, confused by the blaze of light and the waves of applause. The fashion designer's boyfriend had to pull him back down into his chair to stop him staggering up on to the stage to collect the award.

Claire was beneath an oak tree in the park, double-bagging her hand, when Sinead rang.

'I've been trying to call your sister-in-law but she's not picking up. I'm afraid there's been an incident.'

Claire's heart lurched. She straightened up. 'Is Dad OK?'

'It's Brian Cunningham you should be worried about. He very kindly mowed the back garden this morning and—'

'Wait a second!' Claire cut across her. 'I told you that the Cunninghams were not to be invited into the house.'

'He wasn't in the house. He was in the garden when your father threw the teapot at him. Luckily it just broke the window but the poor man could have been killed. It's the final straw. Your father is monosyllabic, he's uncooperative and he's made it quite clear that he doesn't want me here.'

This was just the excuse Claire needed to see her dad again. 'I'll talk to him, Sinead. I can be round in an hour.'

'I won't be here. I have a taxi waiting. You can send on a cheque for what I'm owed.'

'You can't just walk out. Dad can't live without a carer.'

'Your father doesn't need a carer. If you want my professional opinion, I don't think that he cares whether he lives at all.'

Nick woke with his head stuck at an odd angle. Everything hurt. For a moment, he wondered if he'd been in an accident. Then his brain produced a word. Hangover. He opened his eyes. There was a mug on a coaster on the coffee table, steam rising from it in wispy trails. He heaved himself into an upright position, stood up carefully and walked slowly into the kitchen.

Sunshine was pouring in the window. Kelly was at the island in a grey tracksuit and a pink T-shirt that said 'Keep Calm and Carry On'.

'Hi.' She smiled, opening a carton of free-range eggs. This is what his mother used to do when he was angry with her, pretend that everything was just fine. 'I'm making breakfast but we could Two Listen first.' She came over and took his hand. A lemony tendril of her perfume wafted towards him, cutting through the sour smell of his clothes and his stale breath. Her hand was cool, the skin unlined, the nails painted a delicate pink.

'Honey, I want to say that I'm sorry. I should have told you I was trying to get pregnant all this time. It was wrong of me. I forgot to bring my birth control tablets when we were on honeymoon and then, when we got back, I just kept not taking them.' She shook her head. 'After a year, when nothing had happened, I was too scared to stop. I wanted to tell you but I just couldn't. There was nobody I could talk to.'

Except hundreds of people on the internet, Nick thought. He

was supposed to repeat what she'd said but he couldn't. Hearing it once was enough. He stood up.

'I just need a time-out.'

She nodded. 'OK.'

'Have a break, not a breakdown', that was what he told couples every day. He sat on the sofa staring at the clumps of dried mud on the pale grey rug. He remembered, hazily, that it had been raining last night when he came home. At least his car wasn't in the driveway. Someone must have put him into a taxi. He had been completely out of control. After a lifetime of carefully managing himself, he'd lost it completely in front of four hundred people. Shame broke over him in a sticky wave. When he had cleaned up this mess with Kelly, he'd have to call Oonagh. He had blown his chances with Clingfilms; he just hoped he hadn't blown hers.

He could hear Kelly in the kitchen. Taking things out of the fridge. Setting the table. He had to go back in there and save his marriage. That was his job.

The table was set with a jug of fresh orange juice, a bottle of maple syrup and a bowl of blueberries. Kelly was standing at the cooker, beating eggs with a balloon whisk.

'I'm sorry,' Nick began. He wanted to say he was sorry for staying so long in the living room but Kelly cut in before he could finish.

'I forgive you. All that matters is that we love each other and that we're going to have a baby together.'

She forgave him? 'I think we need to put the baby plans on hold,' he said evenly, 'just for a while.'

She stopped whisking. 'How long a while?'

'We could go back to our original timeline.'

'And wait another two years? Are you crazy? We can't stop! We're infertile! And we have another three cycles of Clomid to go.'

'Please,' he shook his head, 'I'm trying to be calm. I need to process all this . . .'

She was twisting her ponytail in one hand, staring around the kitchen, her eyes panicky. 'But if the Clomid doesn't work then we need to start thinking about IVF—'

'That is not going to happen.'

The house phone began to ring. They stood on opposite sides of the kitchen listening to it.

Kelly put down the bowl. 'You never wanted a baby, did you?'

'I have concerns . . .'

Her face was pale. 'And I have the FSH of a woman in her forties. I want a child I can love and nurture and if you aren't prepared to give that to me, I'm going to have to find someone who will.' She took off her rings and threw them down on the worktop, then she picked up the bowl and flung it across the kitchen. It flew past Nick's head and smashed against the wall behind him.

'Don't be here when I get back.' She grabbed her bag. 'Don't even think about coming back unless you change your mind.'

The front door slammed. Nick heard a spray of gravel as Kelly reversed, too fast, out of the drive. He stood listening to his own broken breathing, feeling the tightening of the skin on his cheeks where streaks of egg were drying, then he went upstairs to pack a bag.

19

Claire answered the door. She had done something to her hair and now she looked so like their mother that Nick caught his breath.

'You're sure you're OK to do this?' Claire pulled his case up the step.

He couldn't look her in the eye. 'I'll just stay for a couple of days until we can sort out a new arrangement for the old man.'

'Kelly won't mind?'

'She's away for a week on a course.' Nick bumped his suitcase upstairs and along the uneven carpet on the landing. He opened the door of his old room and stared in at the office chair, the drawing board and the shelves of art supplies. He was so overwhelmed that he'd forgotten that his room had been turned into a drawing studio after he moved out. He opened the door of Claire's old room, where the carer had slept, but the colour scheme of soft greys and pinks reminded him too much of Kelly.

He dragged the case into his parents' old room, closed the door and leaned on it. He hated this room most. It was a shrine to the past. The candlewick bedspread. The tangerine curtains. The wonky wicker and glass bedside cabinets. The heavy built-in wardrobe still jammed with his mother's things.

He thought, with longing, of an anonymous room, soothing and bland, devoid of any personality. He imagined crawling between laundered sheets and sleeping for a long time. But he couldn't go to a hotel. He was 'Ireland's go-to guy for troubled couples'. How was it going to look if he booked in without his wife only a few miles from where he lived?

*

'Thank you, Claire.' Her dad's face still looked gaunt and pinched but at least he wasn't ignoring her.

She put his tea down on his bedside table. 'I had to make this in the cup. The teapot is in pieces.'

'Is that woman gone?'

'Yes. Nick's here. He's going to stay with you for a few days, till we can find another carer.'

'I don't want another carer. All I need is a hand back upstairs.'

Claire wanted to shake him. She had never raised her voice to him before, but before she could stop herself she was shouting. 'You can't go upstairs until you can walk! And you won't walk again unless you start taking your pain medication and doing your physio! It's your choice, Dad!' She crossed the room and slammed the door behind her.

Claire had lined up a row of pill bottles on the kitchen table. 'Sinead said Dad hasn't been taking any of these but he's going to have to start. He's supposed to take a Difene first thing but he can't take it on an empty stomach.'

Nick folded his arms and leaned against the cooker.

'He needs to take these Ixprim twice a day after that. He's not going to be able to put weight on his leg if he's in pain and he needs to start moving even if he only goes as far as the kitchen and back.'

'I'm staying for a couple of days,' Nick said through gritted teeth. 'I'm not going to be his nursemaid.'

Her green eyes were glittering with anger. He'd heard her shouting at the old man. It had almost made him smile. 'If you can't do this then just say so. I'll move in myself.'

'Go on,' he said. The sooner she got through this, the sooner she'd be gone.

She held up a blister pack. 'These are sleeping tablets. One every night, after he's in bed. These are OxyContin,' she held up a brown bottle, 'for emergencies, in case the pain gets too bad to handle.'

She stood up. 'I'll try and organise a new carer as soon as I can.'

'I'll do it,' Nick said, quickly. 'Kelly has a dozen CVs on file from the last time. I'll sort through them. I'm just going to move the car.'

Why did he need to move his car? Claire wondered. What was he even doing here? He had only shown up at the hospital once. He hadn't spent more than a couple of hours in this house for nearly twenty years.

Nick parked the Volvo in the laneway at the back of the garden where it wouldn't be seen. Claire was gone when he got back. He went into the kitchen and found the OxyContin bottle. He swallowed one with a mouthful of water from the tap. Then he stood at the window looking out at the chestnut tree.

His mother had gone up first, hiking her long skirt up and swinging herself easily into the tangle of branches.

'Come on!' Her red hair was framed by a canopy of leaves. 'What's the matter?' She pulled off a twig and dropped it on his head. 'Too scared to climb a little tree?'

'I can climb it!' Claire patted the trunk.

'No!' Nick squatted down. 'You're too small.'

'Come on, Nickers!' His mother took off her cardigan and dangled it like a rope. 'I double, treble dare you.'

He reached up and grabbed the sleeve of the cardigan. His feet swung clear of the ground as she lifted him, there was a sharp tearing sound and then his hands were clawing the air, trying to grab branches as he fell. Don't let me fall on Claire, he remembered thinking just before his forehead hit the ground.

His mother took her locket off and gave it to Claire to stop her crying but Nick hadn't cried at all. Not even when she was stitching the cut.

'Not a single tear. You're a brave boy, do you know that?' His mother had nipped the thread with her teeth and then tickled him until he laughed. And he hated her and himself.

He had no idea how long he had stood at the window but he slowly became aware that it was gone. All of it. The memory of what he'd read on the message board. The pain. The anger. Even the hangover. He put his finger up to the ridge of his scar again, half expecting to find that it had gone too.

He knew he should call Kelly. They were adults, they needed to sort this out. But if he called her, the pain would come back and he didn't want to let go of the OxyContin blur. Not yet. He went into the living room and switched on the ancient electric fire then took his old place on the worn brown corduroy sofa on the far end, near the window.

He watched a medical drama about some good-looking surgeons with complicated love lives performing a liver shunt. The news came on. After a while he realised he was hungry. He hadn't eaten anything since lunchtime yesterday. He went into the kitchen and wolfed down half a packet of Jaffa Cakes and drank most of a carton of milk. Then he climbed the stairs, got undressed and slid in between the cold sheets of his parents' bed and fell into a deep and dreamless sleep.

Kelly had always loved the pier in Dún Laoghaire but today the sea was wild and a sharp wind blew sheets of icy spray into her face. Her hair and clothes were soaked when she got back to the car. She sat, watching the waves pound the harbour, putting off going home. Afraid that she'd find Nick there. Afraid that she wouldn't.

When she got back, the bowl was still in fragments on the kitchen floor. A scrawl of dried egg yolk looped up over the island, across the hand-painted wooden cabinets, up on to the ceiling.

She went upstairs and saw the cleared shelf in the antique bathroom cabinet, the empty drawers in the bedroom, the dozen bare, cedar-scented wooden hangers in his wardrobe. Seeing them sent a trickle of fear down her back.

There were no missed calls on her phone. She tried Nick's number but all she got was his message. *'This is Nick Dillon, couples counsellor. Leave your number and I'll call you right back. Have a good day.'* She sat on the bed hugging her knees, praying for him to call and when he didn't she called Niamh.

'Not a great time,' Niamh said. 'Linh is shouting the house down. Rory reversed over her Little Mermaid.'

'We had a fight,' Kelly whispered. The shrieking in the background died away as Niamh moved into a different room.

'You two never fight. What happened?'

Kelly picked at a congealed blob of egg on her arm. Niamh

knew that she was trying to conceive but not that she'd been trying for three years. 'He doesn't understand.'

'Join the club!' Niamh snorted. 'I spend the day running around after Linh then Rory comes home and expects me serve him a gourmet dinner and do the dance of the seven veils. Get used to it, Kelly. Once kids enter the picture, the whole perfect couple thing goes out the window.'

It was an hour, maybe two, before she could bear to face the kitchen. She swept up the splinters of bowl, cleaning away the egg as best she could. Two of the cupboard doors would have to be repainted and a dozen tiles in the splashback would have to be regrouted. She washed her hands, took out her notebook and started to make a list.

'Kelly?' She pushed her sleep mask up and looked at the clock on the bedside table. It was nine in the morning. She'd overslept. 'It's me. I'm at the old man's house. I meant to call you last night.'

'Don't worry.' She swung her legs over the bed, turning her back on the empty space where he should have been lying. 'I got the message.'

Nick rubbed his eyes. His head was still foggy from the Oxy-Contin. 'What?'

'The message that you don't want to have a family with me.' Kelly's voice was cold. 'If you'd changed your mind, you would have called.'

'Look, let's try not to fall into the Blame Game Trap.' He'd talked about this on the OO show only last week. 'I'm going to give the old man his breakfast then organise a temporary carer and then I'm coming home.'

'Don't,' Kelly said, 'unless you're happy to keep trying to have a baby.'

'Kelly, can you at least acknowledge that we have some issues to sort out before we commit to having a family—'

'No!'

'You're saying that if I don't make you pregnant, we're over?'

'I'm saying that if you stop me trying to have a child, I'll stop loving you, and we'll be over anyway.'

*

Nick had a pitiful shower under the frayed rubber hose that attached to the bath taps. He had a session booked with a couple at eleven and a meeting with Oonagh at one. He had called her after he'd called Kelly. She had been short but at least she was prepared to see him, without conditions, which was more than his wife was.

He got dressed then went down to the kitchen and made an omelette and some tea and brought them into the surgery with the Difene. The old man was already in his chair, his face grey and clammy from the effort it had taken him to get there. 'Need a hand getting dressed?'

'No, I'm—'

'Fine,' Nick said. 'Claire says you're to take this.' He shook a pill out on to a saucer.

'I don't need it, Nicholas. Why don't you just go home now?'

'This is my home,' Nick snapped. 'I grew up here, remember?'

Oonagh was sitting on the sofa in her dressing room in a black slip eating a Snickers bar. 'Did Owen pay you to screw up the Channel 5 job?' She was fully made up but she still looked pale. 'I can't think of any other reason for what you did the other night.'

Nick had swallowed the pill the old man had left on the tray with a cold mouthful of tea. It wasn't as strong as the tablet he'd taken last night but it blurred the edges. 'I can't apologise enough, Oonagh. You put so much work into this and I let you down. Maybe it's just as well. I'm not sure I would have been any good at presenting anyway.'

She scrunched up the Snickers wrapper and dropped it on the floor. 'Spare me the mock humility and the sincerity act. I've seen how much you love being in front of the camera and how much the camera loves you. You wanted this as much as I did!'

'I just want to help people.'

'Help me!' she shouted. 'I had a call from Curtis this morning. Turns out Clingfilms have a Plan B. An American couple. Husband and wife. We were the number-one choice until you blew the whole thing out of the water.'

'Sorry. Again.'

'Sorry isn't good enough! I talked Curtis into letting you explain what happened. He's giving us ten minutes on Skype at one fifteen.' She looked at him with real desperation. 'There is an explanation, isn't there? If there isn't I am in deep, deep shit. Things are bad with me and Owen. The *OO* show is on its way out. I have to get this Channel 5 job. You have to make this right.'

'Hey, Curtis!' Oonagh beamed at the laptop screen. She had back-combed her blonde hair and poured herself into a very tight green dress.

'Hey, gorgeous!' Curtis was in the back of a moving car. Nick could see the road disappearing in the window behind him. He was wearing a T-shirt that said 'You lost me at "hello"'.

'Nick.' He flashed Nick a tight little smile. 'How are you feeling, mate?'

Nick forced himself to smile. 'Better, thanks. Listen, about the night of the awards—'

'These things happen,' Curtis said distastefully, as if they only happened to other people.

'You must have thought I was out of my mind, but the thing is . . .' Nick swallowed and said the first thing that came into his head. 'I was on really strong painkillers. My back was in spasm. I could barely walk. I should have just stayed at home but it was such a key meeting that I didn't want to miss it.'

Curtis blinked. 'Bad back? That figures. You looked way too strait-laced to wear sneakers with a tux. What were you on?'

'What?'

'What painkillers?'

'OxyContin.'

'Hillbilly heroin!' For some reason, Curtis seemed impressed. 'You and half of Hollywood.' He narrowed his eyes. 'You don't make a habit of it? You're not an alkie or a druggie?' Nick shook his head. 'You're happily married? No skeletons in the closet?'

Oonagh snorted. 'Nick and his wife are so happily married they'd make you throw up.'

Curtis nodded. '*The Ex-Factor* has to take the moral high ground. We can't have you pulling a Charlie Sheen or an Angus Deayton. Hey,' he said to someone in the front seat of the car, 'we should put Charlie and Angus on our list of celebrity judges.' His mobile started to ring. 'Got to go. Good meeting. I'll be in touch.'

20

Ray wasn't spying on them. He just happened to be looking out of the window at the exact moment when they came into the garden from the lane. Claire in a black jacket and a sparkly black beret hanging on to the arm of the suit who had practically moved into the basement. The suit was definitely not, Ray thought, an actor. He was too well dressed and he didn't have a goatee or sideburns. He watched them disappear under the fire escape and went back to his desk and opened Pro Tools.

He was supposed to be working on a new brief from Sounds Familiar. A five-second music sting for You Alone ready meals. They'd given him 'Mmmh, Danone' as a reference but he couldn't make it work. A monkey could write this with his hands tied behind his back, he told himself, in Chip's weedy sneer. He went into the kitchen to get a beer. Did monkeys have hands, he wondered, or paws?

He picked up the iPad and Googled. Hands. That sorted that out. He stared at his own hands. Willow's were miniature versions of them, down to the slightly crooked knuckles on his little fingers. Ray wouldn't have minded looking after her today but Ash had taken her down to her uncle's house in Cork for a few weeks. They wouldn't be back till New Year.

He picked up the remote control and put it down again. He didn't want to put the TV on in case he saw the Bentley's Bagels ad again. It wasn't even supposed to be on in Ireland. Ray had written it for the Canadian market. But Bentley's, it turned out, were now available in Superquinn. Sounds Familiar had lodged a generous payment for the extra market in his bank account and now the ad was running in every break. The guy trying to bite the girl's bagel, Ray singing on the soundtrack he'd stolen straight from Chip.

'You can toast them or bake them
Just wait till you taste them!'

Ray didn't want to think about what Chip was going to do to him if he heard it. He'd probably toast him and bake him right before he killed him.

Willow had left her copy of *The Werepuppy* behind. He picked it up and flipped through it, putting off working. A business card slid out from between the pages. 'Izzy Heffernan. Art Attack Print Gallery.'

He was about to bin it when he remembered the redhead from the park! She must have slipped it into the book before she handed it back to him. He shook his head. That was a smooth move. He should call her and tell her that.

Nick lay awake, staring up at the styrofoam tiles on the ceiling and listening to the old man groaning in his sleep in the room downstairs. The pain was worse at night. He sounded as if he was in agony but it was his own fault. He had eighteen inches of metal in his leg but he wouldn't even take a paracetamol.

Nick swore under his breath. How long was he going to have to lie here and listen to this? He had thought that, after Kelly cooled down, she'd agree to meet, but he had been wrong. He'd only managed to get her on the phone once and she had refused to Two Listen or Dissolve the Story or Retie the Bond unless he agreed to continue trying for a baby.

'We had a deal,' she said. 'You were going for the Channel 5 job. We were going to try for a baby.'

'But I've lost the Channel 5 job—'

'That doesn't change anything, Nick.'

What was he going to do – Nick fought a wave of panic – if she didn't change her mind? Where would he go if he couldn't go home?

His old therapist would have a field day if she knew he was sleeping in his parents' bed. They had decided together, over two years of painful weekly sessions, that some things just couldn't be fixed. Sometimes you had to just close a door and walk away. But when Nick had moved back into this house, the door had opened again and all the feelings he thought he'd worked through had flooded out. Guilt. Helplessness. Claustrophobia.

He had tried positive affirmations, meditations and calming visualisations. He had flipped through every self-help book he owned but nothing worked, so he just kept taking his father's tablets.

It wasn't a huge decision. He just put them on the plate every day and when the old man left them there, well, he swallowed them himself. At least the painkillers took the edge off the panic and the sleeping tablets meant he got a few hours' sleep every night before the old man's groans woke him up again.

There were pregnant women everywhere. At bus stops. In shops. There were two of them at the next table in Cake Café sharing a slice of Victoria sponge. Kelly felt achy with envy just looking at them. 'I'll take the butternut squash soup,' she told the waiter, 'and I'll have it at a table outside.'

'You do know it's December out there?' He shook his head. 'I'll make you a hot-water bottle to keep you warm.'

'Thank you.' His kindness made Kelly want to cry; she was always on the verge of tears now.

She went out into the tiny courtyard, sat on a damp cast-iron chair and put her shopping bags carefully on the chair opposite. How much had she spent? she wondered with a little jolt of panic. Five hundred dollars? Six?

'All set for Christmas?' One of the pregnant women was standing under the awning trying to light a cigarette. She pulled her loose blue cardigan around her bump to keep the cold out. Pregnant and smoking. Kelly's heart squeezed itself into a tight knot of resentment.

'Why am I even doing this?' The woman shivered and clicked her lighter again. 'I've been trying to give these things up.'

Kelly made herself smile. It was a professional smile, about as real as a two-dollar bill, but the woman smiled back and Kelly felt her resentment begin to soften. It wasn't the woman's fault that she was pregnant and that Kelly wasn't. 'When are you due?'

The woman blinked at her through a cloud of smoke. 'Due what, love?'

'Oh!' Kelly said. 'Oh! I'm so sorry. I didn't mean to . . .'

The woman flushed, dropped her cigarette and crushed it under her heel. 'I'm not pregnant,' she said, quietly, 'but apparently I'm fat.'

'I know he's hopeless and unreliable,' Claire pulled on a red suede boot, 'but I'm not sure I can live without him.' Mossy's gearbox was on its last legs and something called his floorpan had to be replaced. It was going to cost the unbelievable sum of five thousand euros. Richard had sweet-talked his insurance company into letting Claire keep the Yaris for another few weeks, but she was going to have to decide whether to keep Mossy or let him go. Her mum's car!

Eilish picked up a shoe, looked at the price tag and dropped it as if it were on fire. 'Look, Claire, I know Mossy is more than just a car but he is falling apart and five grand is a lot of— ouch!'

Claire pinched her arm. 'Shh!' she whispered. 'That's my sister-in-law!' Nick had told Claire that Kelly had gone to the States for Christmas but there she was, on the other side of the Brown Thomas shoe department, stepping off the escalator wearing a cream coat and carrying half a dozen shopping bags.

She caught Claire's eye then turned away quickly and hurried over to the lift. 'I don't get it!' Claire turned to Eilish. 'If Kelly is in Dublin, why is Nick still at my dad's? Do you think I should try and talk to her?'

'Too late!' Eilish said as Kelly stepped into the lift and the doors closed. Claire hobbled back to the sofa to put her own boots back on again and they went back down to the ground floor so she could finish her shopping. Her dad had told Nick he wasn't up to 'any fuss' this Christmas and 'fuss' seemed to include Claire coming over for dinner, so she was spending the day at Richard's parents' house. Eilish was going to look after Dog.

Claire had already picked up a panettone in Carluccio's and a side of smoked salmon in Wright's. She had bought Richard a black cashmere scarf and a pair of soft brown leather gloves. She'd found a book of Carol Ann Duffy poetry for his mother and a Douglas Kennedy novel for his father. That just left his sisters, and five minutes at the Benefit counter sorted that.

'Come on,' Eilish said when they were finished. 'I need a killer outfit for the *Emerald Warriors* wrap party.'

'I'm so glad you're finishing up. I've missed you.' Claire took her arm and they went outside to join the river of shoppers flowing along Grafton Street beneath the canopy of Christmas lights. 'I can't wait for you to be back in Dublin full time.'

'I won't be back just yet. Pete's just won the contract for the second series of *Warriors* so I'll be on location for most of the spring.'

'But your face is healed. I thought you were going to start trying to get back into acting.'

'I will,' Eilish steered Claire round a group of carol singers, 'when this contract is over. But I can't let Pete down. That van would be closed down by the HSE if it wasn't for me.'

'Deja Vus' was where Eilish made all her best vintage finds. She flicked through the rails and pulled out a short yellow and green pinafore with a narrow orange belt. 'What do you think?'

'Mmmmm,' Claire said tactfully. 'It's kind of Zooey Deschanel.'

'Right. If Zooey was blind drunk or partially sighted.' Eilish turned to a rack of shoes and boots. 'Christmas with the parents, that's pretty momentous. Does this mean that Richard might be,' she held up a pair of white stilettos like quotation marks, ' "the one"?'

Claire remembered the night she'd seen her parents dancing in the living room. Her mum's face pressed against her dad's chest. Her eyes closed as she swayed against him. The tender look on her dad's face that time Claire had seen him carrying her mum in his arms into their bedroom. 'How are you supposed to know?'

'I don't know but I wouldn't hang around for sky-writing. They phase that out when you hit thirty.' Eilish pulled out a pair of seventies wooden platforms with 'love' in different languages carved into the wedges. 'Richard certainly seems to be crazy about you.'

'I just wish he was crazier about Dog.' Richard hated the way

Dog's fur got on his suits or the way he tried to burst into the bedroom at inappropriate moments and he hated having to watch the news on RTE instead of Sky.

'Claire!' Eilish slipped her feet into the shoes and looked at herself in a speckled mirror. 'You're doing it again!'

'What?'

'Finding a way to sabotage yourself. You weren't Dog's number-one fan yourself till a while ago.'

Claire sighed. 'We've just reached an understanding.'

Eilish kicked the shoes off, picked them up and checked the price sticker.

'Well, I'm going to invest fifteen euros in these lucky "love" shoes to bring you good luck because I think that you, Claire Dillon, might be falling in love, "l'amour", "amore", "liebe" and,' she squinted at the words carved into the wooden wedges, "zamilowanie".' She shook her head. 'And they say Polish isn't a romantic language.'

Aine popped a chunk of smoked salmon in her mouth.

'You're an animal!' Richard tried to pull it away from her. 'Claire is going to make smoked salmon and scrambled eggs.'

'I don't mind!' Claire was quite happy to skip making breakfast on Christmas morning. Eilish had talked her through it but she was terrified she'd burn the eggs or undercook them and give Richard's entire family salmonella.

Helen came running into the kitchen with tinsel around her neck and a set of battery-operated fairy lights in her hair.

'Let's go swimming.' She planted a set of antlers on Richard's head.

He groaned. 'Can't we just skip it this year? It's minus two out there!'

'Exactly!' Helen said. 'It's minus you two! Come on, you big chicken!' She rolled up a slice of salmon and posted it into Andreas's mouth.

'Is chicken?' He chewed it. 'It tastes of the fish.'

'We're going to have to do it,' Aine sighed, 'or Helen will keep this up all night. It's a Christmas Eve tradition,' she explained to

Claire, 'you only have to get into the sea for a few seconds. I can lend you a bikini unless you want to skinny-dip.'

Claire swallowed. 'I might just stay here, if that's OK.'

'We have a Lidl wetsuit!' Helen took her arm. 'You can have that!'

'I don't think so—'

Helen grabbed her other arm. 'We'll let you off 'cos it's your first year. But you have to come and watch!'

Richard drove. Helen had brought the salmon, wrapped in tinfoil, and a hip flask of brandy that she passed around the car. Claire hated brandy but she took a few mouthfuls to try to settle the trembling in her stomach.

They drove along winding country roads between bare trees and grey hedgerows, then Richard took a sharp left along a narrow track and, there, ahead of her, was the wide grey expanse of the Irish Sea. Claire's heart jumped up into her throat. Richard pulled over and parked a few feet away from where the beach started. She had never been on a beach holiday. Never been to a swimming pool. Never taken a ferry. This was as close to the sea as she had been since she was six.

The others were giggling and struggling out of their clothes in the back. Richard got out and undressed, folding his sweater and his jeans and putting them neatly on the driver's seat. Through the open door, Claire could hear the roar of the surf. The muffled thump of breaking waves, the clatter of the shingle.

'Richard, don't go in, please.' Her hand was shaking when she put it on his arm. 'It's not safe.'

'It's not heated. That's the problem.' He leaned in and kissed her.

'OK, people!' Helen took a final gulp of brandy. 'Let's do this thing!'

They grabbed one another's hands and raced, whooping, across the sand to the sea. Helen in a pink bra and knickers with a tattoo of angel's wings on her back, the tiny lights in her hair sparkling in the dusk. Aine in a gold halter-neck bikini with a tinsel halo. Andreas in black Speedos and reindeer antlers. Richard in Hawaiian shorts.

Claire closed the window then closed her eyes so that she didn't have to see them running into the sea. She counted under her breath to keep herself calm. She was at nine hundred and four when they all fell back into the car, soaked, shivering and laughing.

'Wow!' Richard's face was flushed and his goose-bumped skin was silvered with drops of water. He grabbed Claire and kissed her. His lips were so cold that she had to force herself not to pull away.

Richard went into the pub to get the drinks while the others waited on the village street under red and white Christmas lights with bags of hot, salty chips. Claire couldn't eat hers. Her palms were clammy and she was shivering, even though Richard had given her his sheepskin jacket.

'Come in, planet Claire!' Helen jabbed the air in front of her with a chip. 'I was asking if Richard's invited you to come skiing with us at Easter.'

Claire nodded.

'Mum will be devastated if you don't.' Aine licked salt from her fingers. 'She's probably at mass right now begging the Baby Jesus not to let the white sheep let you slip through his fingers. Hooves. Whatever sheep have.'

'Dear God.' Helen sank to her knees in the street and gazed up at a flashing neon Santa over the pub door. 'In your infinite wisdom, grant the Byrne family the gift of the lovely Claire. And lead us not back into the dark days of the Celtic Tiger when we had to put up with Foxrock Fannies in head-to-toe Max Mara who thought we were a shower of muckers because we didn't have our "hoor" styled by Dylan Bradshaw or have jobs in "morketing". Amen.'

The queue outside the chip shop applauded and Helen got up and bowed, then made Claire bow too.

It was another Byrne family tradition that everyone had to be in bed by midnight on Christmas Eve and, to Claire's relief, they all went along with it, even Helen. At ten to twelve she turned off the fairy lights in her hair and went to make everyone hot-water bottles.

Richard's dad had insisted on separate rooms for the guests but Claire was glad that she'd be sleeping on her own in the tiny single bedroom under the eaves. She'd done her best to try to be bright and chatty while they sat round the fire playing charades but she just wanted to be on her own now.

''Night, Claire!' Richard kissed her outside the bathroom on the landing. 'Sweet dreams.'

Richard's mother put her head around the door. 'You can sneak into Richard's room if you like. I don't think Sean will do a midnight raid.'

'It's OK,' Claire said. 'I'm happy to be on my own.'

Jean came in and sat beside her on the bed. Her hair was caught up in an bun with a wonky chopstick. She was wearing a grey man's dressing gown and there was a little blob of moisturiser by her ear. 'Are you missing Christmas at home?'

Claire nodded. She wasn't missing the strained, awkward Christmases, when she and her dad ate a roast chicken at the kitchen table then watched TV in front of the electric fire. She was missing the Christmases when her mum had made hot punch for Santa Claus and sung 'Happy Birthday' to Jesus when she brought the turkey to the table.

Jean sighed. 'Christmas is a tough time of the year, when you've lost someone. Richard told us that your mother died when you were very young. What happened?'

Claire pulled her sleeves down over her knuckles. 'She drowned.'

'I'm so sorry.' Jean's eyes went to the watercolour on the wall above the bed, a seascape with storm clouds. 'That must have been so hard. Who looked after you?'

'My brother did a lot.'

'It's not the same.' Jean shook her head. 'Girls need their mothers. I should know, I have two daughters. What was she like, your mum? Are you like her?'

'We look a bit alike,' Claire bit her lip, 'but we're not really. She'd done so much by the time she was my age.'

'And you think that matters? That you haven't done all the things she did?'

Jean's eyes were so kind that Claire had to look away. She stared down at the floor. 'It does matter,' she said quietly. 'Because she saved my life and then she drowned.' It was more than she had told anyone except Ray but it still wasn't the truth. Not the whole of it. She could feel Jean's eyes on her face.

'What a heroic thing to do. She sounds like an amazing woman.'

Claire touched her locket. 'She was only thirty-three.'

'Look at me.' Claire couldn't, so Jean took her hands. 'Listen to me. Your mother gave you life twice and the best thing you can do is live your life.'

'I'm trying to be more like her—'

'Don't do that,' Jean said. 'Be true to yourself.'

'I don't know how.'

'This is going to sound like a Hallmark line, but all you have to do is listen to your heart.' She put her arms around Claire and hugged her. She smelt of Nivea and marzipan. 'But you have to listen very carefully,' she said, 'because, most of the time, your head is shouting so loudly that you can't hear your heart whispering.'

Claire wanted to sleep but when she closed her eyes, she was on the beach again. Her mum's long red hair had turned brown and separated into thin tails. Her face was red and she was panting. She bent over and spat up a mouthful of sea water. She tried to pick Claire up again but Claire struggled out of her arms. Her mum shook her head in frustration. Drops of water flew in glittering arcs from the ends of her hair. A trickle from her locket ran down between her breasts. 'It's OK, nothing bad is going to happen!' She squatted down and put her hands on Claire's wet, shaking shoulders. The whites of her eyes were criss-crossed with tiny red lines. She looked ugly. 'What's wrong with you, Claire? You've been like this all day. What is it?'

It was at the back of Claire's head like the headache she got after eating too much ice cream, or a wobbly tooth that her tongue was too frightened to touch. She didn't know what it was, just that it was there. She began to sob, tears mixing with the water that ran from her own wet hair.

'What is it?' her mum asked her. 'Tell me!' Claire had to say something but she couldn't, so she pointed at her swimming ring instead. The waves had picked it up and it was ten or fifteen yards away from the shore now. A small, cheery pink circle against the dark wall of grey.

'I lost my swimming ring!' she whispered.

'Is that all? We'll get you another one.' Her mum smiled. 'We'll buy one on the way home in Wicklow.'

Claire shook her head. She meant, *no, that isn't what it is*. But her mum didn't understand.

'Fine! I'll get it.' Her mum stood up and waded back into the sea. She swam in a perfectly straight line, lifting her face to breathe and then plunging it back in again. But every time she reached the ring, the wind picked it up and it skipped away again.

Claire sat on the cold sand, her breath coming in shallow little gasps, her fingers digging into the damp grit, watching the dark dot of her mother's head grow smaller and smaller.

She heard something behind her, and when she looked over at the picnic rug, she saw the big yellow dog. He knocked over the flask and stuck his nose into the picnic basket then pulled out the birthday cake her mother had wrapped in tinfoil. Claire wasn't afraid of dogs, not back then. She had asked for a puppy for her birthday.

She ran over and grabbed his collar and pulled the tinfoil package out of his mouth. He pulled his lips back over his teeth and jumped at her. She felt his teeth snap at her fingers, then she fell, face first, into the sand.

When she sat up, her mouth was full of grit. The dog had run back up into the dunes and the beach was empty. Way out at sea there was a tiny smudge of pink, one bright bead in a dark grey ribbon, but her mum was gone.

Richard tapped on Claire's door then came in bringing the smell of churchy cologne and roasting meat. He was already dressed.

'Mum said to let you sleep in.' He sat on the bed. 'You must have been really tired. It's nearly twelve. I missed you last night.'

Claire sat up and put her arms around him and held on to him tightly. Jean was right. She had been blaming herself for what had happened for nearly twenty-eight years but it hadn't brought her mum back. The only thing she could do was live her own life. Live it enough for two.

'Happy Christmas.' Richard took a small duck-egg-blue box out of the pocket of his shirt and handed it to her. Inside was a tiny gold disc on a fine chain with the words 'Believe in You' engraved on one side.

'It's lovely,' Claire said.

'Are you going to put it on?'

Claire pressed her mum's locket between her thumb and her index finger. She had been wearing it ever since she was six. 'Can you help me?' She lifted her hair and Richard undid the clasp.

Ray opened one eye and saw a tumble of curls on the pillow beside him. For a surreal moment, he thought he was in bed with Claire, then he remembered she didn't have curls any more. The head on the pillow beside him belonged to Izzy, the girl from the park.

'Oh. My. Goodness.' She turned around and sat up, leaning her head on her hand. 'There *is* a Santa and he's finally answered that letter I wrote him when I was fifteen and brought me *Ray Devine*!'

Kelly had found the decorations but she hadn't had the heart to put them up. The delicate frosted baubles and stars she'd spent hours choosing last year were in a pile on a chair and the lights were in a tangle on the living-room carpet. Some of the bulbs had broken. There was a dusting of glass on the floor that crackled under her shoes when she crossed the room.

She had meant to wrap the clothes. She had bought paper. But in the end, she just arranged the bags in a little circle around a potted palm. The half-dozen bags she'd brought home from town and the dozen or so more she'd dug out of the back of the hall cupboard. She'd been hiding them there from Nick but she didn't have to do that any more.

On Christmas morning, she went downstairs in her bare feet

and made egg nog; then she put on a radio station to listen to the carols and drank a glass in the kitchen. She poured a second glass, gathered up the bags and carried them back upstairs.

She spread them out on the duvet and opened them one by one, untying every ribbon, unfolding the tissue paper carefully, shaking the clothes out to get rid of the creases. She took her time looking at every single thing. The white cotton onesies. The tiny summer dresses and shorts and T-shirts. The heavy down-filled snowsuit with the snowflake embroidered on the back. The little cotton sweaters with their mother-of-pearl buttons in rose and oyster and pale blue. The dozen Peter Rabbit burp cloths. The baby Uggs. Everything she needed except the thing she needed most.

Nick carried a tray into the surgery. The old man was ignoring Christmas and, for once, Nick was happy that he was living in denial. He had called Kelly over and over yesterday and she'd finally answered. 'Can we meet for an hour tomorrow?' he'd asked her.

'You'll just try to change my mind and I can't let you do that.'

'I don't understand.'

'You will when you hold our baby in your arms.'

'How could you lie to me for three years and then act as if I'd done something wrong?' He sounded like his clients did when they came to see him first – whiny and insecure. 'All those date nights, I thought you wanted me—'

'I did want you. I want you now.' Her voice broke.

'Then let's meet. It's Christmas!'

'I can't.'

Claire's scrambled eggs with smoked salmon were perfect but the turkey was burned to a crisp. Helen and Andreas had been in charge of it but they had slipped upstairs while it was cooking.

'It's your fault, Dad!' Helen picked off a piece of charred skin. 'If you'd let us sleep in the same room, we wouldn't have to sneak around.'

'The rule is you can sleep in the same room when you're married,' Richard's father said. 'Not before.'

232

'What about engaged?' Helen grinned. She held up her left hand. A solitaire sparkled on her ring finger. The kitchen erupted into shouting and cheering and kissing and hugging. By the time they sat down to eat, the turkey was cold as well as burned, but they'd had so much sparkling wine that nobody cared.

Richard and his sisters bickered all the way through dinner. About how to spell 'disconcerting', how many legs a fly had, which episode of *The Office* had made Aine pee herself and whether or not Santa was a pervert.

'He's a grown man,' Helen said. 'Who breaks into houses! And how does he know if you've been good or bad? Because he's a creepy stalker!'

'Santa is happily married!' Richard insisted.

Aine knocked his paper hat off. 'Why doesn't he have children, then? I bet he's gay. I bet Mrs Claus is his beard!'

Richard's mother shook her head. 'I'm sorry, Claire, you must think we're a bunch of savages.'

'Oh God!' Aine pretended to fall face first into her plate. 'My little sister is getting married before me!' She pointed her fork at Richard and Claire. 'You two better not be next. I don't want to be the bloody spinster in this family.'

'Can't make any promises.' Richard put his arm around Claire and Aine threw a sprout at him.

'This family is way past the stage of food fights,' Jean said. 'The boys can clear up and the girls can make coffee and we'll have it by the fire.'

She smiled and Claire stood up, her heart expanding. She was one of the girls. She was part of the family.

Kelly put it off until she couldn't put it off any longer, then she sat up in bed and dialled the number. 'Hi, Mom! Happy Christmas!'

'Kelly-Anne, what a wonderful surprise,' her mom said, as if this really was a surprise and not a carefully choreographed once-a-year call. 'Happy Christmas, sweetie! How's the weather over there? Do you have a white-out?'

Her mother seemed to have confused the climates of Ireland and Iceland, and Kelly hadn't bothered to correct her.

'Yep!' she said, looking at blinds she hadn't opened.

'A white Christmas, oh my! It's raining here, of course. How's Nick?'

'He's good, Mom. But I can't talk for long. We're just going to visit his dad.'

'Oh.' A tiny awkward silence opened up between them and then her mom rushed in to fill it. 'Well, you know you and Nick can visit us any time, honey. Christmas or not. I know you're busy but you're always welcome here. Your dad is still in bed but I know he'll want to wish you a happy holiday.'

Kelly heard her mom cross the black and white tiled kitchen she had only been in a handful of times since she left home. She heard her mom's footsteps on the stairs and then she heard her dad's sleepy voice.

'Is that my little girl?'

She closed her eyes and her throat tightened, locking her voice under a sticky glob of egg nog. They weren't bad people. They'd tried to do their best, she knew that. But they'd taken something from her. She had tried to forgive them for that, but she couldn't.

Part Three

21

It had been raining all night and the lawn was drenched. Nick's shoes were going to be soaked if he went across the grass but he couldn't risk leaving by the front door at eight in the morning. He didn't want the neighbours to see him.

If the papers found out that the *OO in the Afternoon* couples coach had broken up with his wife and was hiding out in his father's house, they'd tear him apart. Maybe he had it coming to him but he'd put Oonagh through enough. She was still clinging to the hope that Curtis was going to hire them, though it looked less and less likely now. Nick was sorry for her but he was also relieved. He just wanted the whole thing to go away.

He glanced around to make sure that nobody was watching from the upstairs window next door then opened the back door and stepped out on to the soggy grass.

'Hello, Nicholas.' Mrs Cunningham appeared at the wall. She was holding a weed spray, though it was far too early in the year to be spraying weeds.

Nick felt like he had when he was twelve and he'd been waylaid by neighbours bringing the washing to the launderette or walking home from school with a bag of shopping from Superquinn. They'd swoop on him, masking their nosiness with concern. His skin crawled now the way it had back then.

'Lovely morning, isn't it?' She wiped rain off her glasses. 'How's the patient?'

'Well, thank you. I was just dropping in to make him break-fast.'

'Aren't you very good?' The rain was really coming down now, soaking his jacket, flattening Mrs Cunningham's frosted curls.

Nick was due at Fish in twenty minutes. He didn't have time for this. 'You've always been so good to your father and your sister, Nicholas. I often say to Brian, "That poor boy had no proper childhood."'

Nick pulled his phone out of his pocket and stared at the screen. 'Sorry, I have to take this.'

She frowned. 'I didn't hear it ring.'

'It's on vibrate. Hello?' He clamped the phone to his ear. 'Yes,' he said, pretending to be listening to someone on the other end. 'Yes.' He nodded. Suddenly the phone did ring. Nick fumbled with it, trying to press 'answer' with his wet finger. Mrs Cunningham was watching him with a tight little smile.

It was Oonagh. Her voice was fizzy with excitement. 'Curtis just called. Clingfilms want us! We're going to Channel 5. We're going to be presenting *The Ex-Factor*! Congratulations!'

Nick's heart plummeted, like an out-of-control lift, past the painkiller he'd taken half an hour ago, down through his wet shoes into the lawn.

'Bad news?' Mrs Cunningham said when he'd hung up.

He nodded. 'Yeah.'

Kelly slipped a Fionn Regan CD into the car stereo so she didn't have to listen to Nick's radio show. Hearing his voice would make her miss him even more than she already did. She couldn't risk that. She had to stick to her ultimatum.

'Be Good Or Be Gone' began to play. She fumbled for 'eject' and the radio came on.

'I'm afraid that I can't talk about it,' Nick was saying. 'I'm sorry.'

Kelly froze.

'Oh, come on,' Dom cut in. 'Put us out of our misery! He's shaking his head, folks. He's keeping his cards close to his chest, and what a lovely chest it is, if I may say so. Someone left Doc Nick out in the rain and we can see right through his shirt, ladies. As clearly as we can see that he's too coy to admit that he'll be heading up a new UK relationship reality TV show with the lovely Oonagh Clancy.'

'That's not official—' Nick tried to cut in.

'But it's all over Twitter!' Dom chuckled. 'Check it out, tweeps!'

Kelly stared out at the rain that was hammering down on the windscreen, turning the car in front of her into a blurred blue and silver watercolour. Nick had told her that he'd lost the Channel 5 show but that had obviously been a lie just to get her to stop taking the Clomid.

'If you've got a problem,' Dom was saying, 'call in now and give the great Doc Nick one last chance to solve it before he departs for greener pastures.'

Kelly switched the radio off. She did have a problem. She had an ultrasound next week and, if there were any viable eggs, she was supposed to have sex. Maybe Dom Daly was right. Maybe she should give Nick one last chance.

If Claire had known, back on her birthday, how much her life would have changed by the new year, she would have been astonished by the progress she would make.

There were the small things. The fact that she was drinking less, going to bed earlier and getting more exercise than she had for years.

There were the medium-sized things. The fact that she hadn't done a single extra job in months. The fact that she had had four days' work on *The Spaniard*. The auditions she was showing up to every week. The voice-over demo she'd finally made.

There were the large things. The fact that she wasn't broke all the time. The fact that her long friendship with Ray, a friendship she'd thought would never end, seemed to be over. And the fact that, for the first time since Declan, she thought she might be able to trust someone again.

When Richard wasn't away on business, they spent every moment together. They had driven down to Wexford for Helen's engagement party and taken Aine to a comedy gig and met his parents at a rugby match. When his family talked about skiing in France at Easter or a trip to Achill in May or a wedding in Crete in the summer, they didn't ask whether she'd be there or not, they just presumed that she would.

*

Richard came into the bedroom, wrapped in a towel. 'What do you fancy doing today?' He had to yell over the squealing of the pipes. 'The usual thing,' Claire yelled back. She hugged herself as she made the barefoot dash past the various freezing draughts blowing around the hall to the bathroom. Having a usual thing to do was still new, still wonderful.

They walked Dog in the park then sat outside the Insomnia coffee shop in the January sunshine reading the papers. Then they drove into town and wandered around the bustling farmers' market in Temple Bar. They bought wild salmon cutlets for dinner and Richard kissed Claire beside the flower stall while she kept one eye open and picked a little tuft of Dog's fur off his shoulder. Then they went to Heaven. They didn't have a booking but Richard had a word with the manager and in less than a minute they were seated at a table by the window overlooking the square.

'How do you do it?' Claire shook her head in wonder. 'You just act as though everything will be easy and then, somehow, it is.'

'It's just confidence.' He smiled. 'It's like it says on the necklace I gave you, "Believe in you". You can do anything, Claire. You have so much talent. You could be huge.'

'I will be huge,' she closed the menu, 'if I keep eating as well as this.'

'There you go again!'

'What?'

'Avoiding a compliment. Finding a way to put yourself down. Speaking of compliments, Noel from Beacon told me your voice-over demo was absolutely brilliant and he's already recommended you to a couple of advertising agencies.'

'I wouldn't have done it at all if you hadn't organised it for me.' She sighed. 'You're going to have to stop doing all this stuff for me, Richard, I'll only get used to it.'

'I want you to get used to it.' He grinned. 'That's my evil plan!'

A waitress came with bread and olive oil and Richard introduced himself and asked if he could put their salmon in the restaurant fridge while they ate.

While he was in the kitchen, Claire looked through the huge window. Out in the square, a man and a pregnant woman were queueing at the fish stall. Suddenly, the woman grabbed his hand and pressed it against her belly. They both smiled. Some day, Claire thought, she might be standing somewhere in the winter sunshine with a man who loved her smiling into a certain future. She watched Richard, as he made his way back to their table, and she wondered if it might be him.

'Listen, why don't you come and stay over at my place tonight?' Richard said as they pulled into Claire's laneway.

'What about Dog?'

'He'll be fine for one night and we wouldn't be, you know, interrupted.'

Dog liked to lurk out in the hall when they were making love. Sometimes, the door would open a crack and his long, grey snout would appear at passionate moments. Richard found it off-putting.

'OK,' Claire bit her lip. 'But I'll have to be back early in the morning to let him out.'

'Can't you leave him with your dad or your brother, instead? I'll make you breakfast in bed.'

Claire shook her head. She had been around to her dad's twice since Christmas but he had barely spoken to her. Nick was avoiding her too. When she had cornered him to talk about organising a new carer, he'd said that Kelly had decided to stay in Seattle for another few weeks. Nick was the one with an elephant in the corner of the room now. Claire wondered when he was going to name it.

Dog lifted his head when Claire came into the kitchen. The tip of his long tail moved in a slow wag.

'I'm going to be gone all night so you have to have a pee now,' she told him.

He got up stiffly then stretched and walked over to the door. Relations had warmed between them but he still gave Claire plenty of personal space. He looked out to see if it was raining before stepping into the garden. He had a thing about getting his ears wet.

Richard had arranged to have the garden cleared as a surprise for Claire. The nettles had been cut back and the rusty patio heater had been dismantled and taken away but somehow that made the garden look worse than it had before. Dog seemed to like it though. He trotted around the bare earth, sniffing everything, and took a long pee before he came back inside and lay down again.

'I'll leave the TV on and the living-room door open. Anne Doyle will be on in about fifteen minutes,' she told him. 'She might even be on again at nine, if you're lucky.'

'Listen to that,' Richard said after they'd made love in his huge bed and he'd come back from having his shower, wrapped in a thick, white towel.

'What?' Claire sat up.

'The sound of silence!' He sighed.

'Except for the ticking of thirty clocks!'

'You don't hear them after a while.' Richard swatted her with a takeaway menu. 'And they're a hell of a lot quieter than those groaning pipes of yours. Have you thought about moving? It's kind of a weird set-up you have with that door that connects your place to the landlord's. I don't know what you're paying him but it's probably too much. I play squash with an estate agent. I could ask him to look out for something for you before it comes on the rental market or,' he put the menu down, 'you could always move in here with me.'

Claire was suddenly very wide awake. 'What about Dog?'

'I'm asking you to live with me and all you can talk about is the *dog*?'

'It's just that I couldn't leave him and Dad can't take him and Nick is—'

'We can figure something out when the time comes, which I hope it does,' he pulled the towel off and slipped back under the duvet, 'very soon indeed.'

Ray heard the bang of the door to the laneway and went to the window. He could see the dog's long, bony grey back and the top of Claire's head below. There was no sign of the suit.

'Hey!' He pulled the window up and hopped out on to the fire escape. 'Wait.' She turned to look up at him, reluctantly.

'I just wanted to ask you how everything is.'

'Everything is fine.'

'Your dad?'

She shrugged. 'He's fine.'

'And your new guy. What's his name again?' Claire hadn't told him his name.

'Richard. He's fine.'

'How was Christmas?'

'You know . . .'

'Fine?'

She nodded. 'I'd better go in.'

'Maybe we could all hang out together,' Ray said. 'You, Richard, me and Izzy.'

Claire peered up at him in the gathering dusk. Her hair seemed to be absorbing all the remaining light. 'Who?'

'My girlfriend. Izzy. I've been seeing her for a while now.' It had been weird to be in restaurants and at movies with a girl who wasn't Claire. Weird and kind of boring.

'You think she'll make it past your twenty-six-day record?' Claire asked him.

'Got my fingers crossed.' He crossed them and showed them to her. 'So why don't we all have that drink some time?'

'I don't think that's such a great idea.' Claire put her key in the door. It was on a key ring that Ray had brought her back from Tokyo. A yellow sunburst with the words 'warking on sunshine' written on it in red.

'Willow came up with a great misheard lyric the other day, all on her own,' he said. 'She heard "Blowing in the Wind" and she thought Dylan was singing "the ants are my friends".' Claire didn't turn around but she laughed. Ray had missed that laugh. 'Why don't you call up the next time she's over?'

She turned and looked at him. She was still smiling but her eyes were serious. 'I'm sorry, I'd love to but I just can't. I don't want to complicate things.'

'So you need a bit *more* space.' She nodded again. 'Aye aye,

Captain!' Ray said in a terrible Spock voice. He uncrossed his fingers and made the Vulcan 'V' sign instead. 'Live long and prosper!'

Claire and Richard were both up at five-thirty in the morning. He had to fly over to London for a meeting and she had to be on set at six-thirty for her last day on *The Spaniard*.

'Did you move my shoes and my watch?' he called from the bedroom. Claire froze under the reluctant trickle from her shower. She had a pretty good idea who might have. She made a naked, dripping dash from the bathroom past the bedroom and into the kitchen to retrieve them from under Dog. One shoe was a bit squashed and the watch strap was damp where he'd been licking it. She ran back to the bathroom and put the shoes on the floor and laid the watch on the side of the sink. 'You left them in here!' she called.

Richard appeared in the door. 'Did I?' He picked them up. 'Why is my watch strap wet?'

'Steam from the shower.'

Dog was in Richard's bad books because he had eaten an entire cooked chicken he'd brought for their supper, including half of the foil bag and all of the bones.

He was in Claire's bad books, too, because yesterday, while they were in the park, he'd taken a dump in front of six people doing t'ai chi. Then, while she was clearing that up, he'd sloped off to enjoy his daily stand-off with the swan. When she was trying to get him away from the pond, without actually looking at the pond, a shouty old man had appeared waving a walking stick at her.

'Get. Your. Dog. Away. From. That. Swan!' he'd bellowed at Claire, over and over until she thought her ears were going to bleed.

No matter how many times Claire had seen it, she never got over the magic of fake snow. One corner of the wet, muddy Wicklow field had been transformed into a pristine sparkling triangle of winter. The snow was two feet deep. Every branch of the bare tree above her was dusted with a glittering crust of white. Two of the crew were testing out the snow machine and a few flakes were already whirling through the air from the blower. Claire had to stop herself from sticking her tongue out to catch one the way she had the night she'd sat out in the garden with her mother when she was a little girl.

A rusty Land Rover pulled up and Sháne got out. Something woke up in Claire's chest and she forced it back to sleep again as he walked straight past, without looking over, and started chatting to the actor who played the Earl. Claire felt herself flush beneath her thick make-up. He might not hate her so much if he knew she hadn't brought Dog to the pound in the end, but she had no way of telling him. And anyway, why should she? She was involved with Richard now. She stared down at her script and pretended to be studying her dialogue. She had almost a full page of lines.

It was her last scene and her longest one so far. The shepherdess was trying to rescue her sheep in a blizzard and the Earl, who was riding past, stopped to help her. Then, while they sheltered from the snow, she broke the promise she'd made to his wife, Lady Kathryn, and told him she'd seen the Spanish ship. He 'looked at her for a long moment' and touched her cheek and told her she was a 'loyal wench' before he rode off again to confront his wife. There was something satisfyingly karmic about the idea that Claire was having a 'moment' with Emma's husband, even if he was only a fictional one.

Claire was pouring herself a coffee to try to get rid of the soapy taste of all the fake snow when Emma came floating across the courtyard in a pale grey velvet gown and matching shoes. 'Claire, how are you? I haven't seen you for ages. Are you still keeping a low profile after that awful YouTube thing?'

Claire gave her a level look. 'I've just been busy.'

'Oh, me too! It never ends.' Emma picked up an apple and looked around for a knife. 'They have me here around the clock. I'm literally in every second scene. I had to pull a sickie last week just so I could sneak off to London to do an audition for a sitcom. Don't tell anyone. It's a secret. But let's just say that Becky Martin, the woman who won a Bafta for *Peep Show*, might be directing it! Denise!' She grabbed the arm of the runner who was passing by. 'Can you be an absolute angel and get me that knife over there? I don't want to ruin my shoes.' She turned back to Claire. 'How's poor Eilish, by the way? I heard she's horribly scarred. Will she ever be able to work again?'

'She's fine—' Claire began.

'Here you are, Miss Lacey!' The runner came back with a knife.

'Oh, I wouldn't wave a knife at Claire!' Emma giggled. 'She got into a fight with another actress a few months ago and broke her nose!'

The only card game that Willow could play was Go Fish, which was incredibly boring, so Ray changed it to 'Go Horrible Sea Creatures', bringing a bit of creative madness to it.

'Do you have any sixes?' Willow stared at him over her cards.

'Go smelly brown skunk fish!' Ray said. Willow picked up a card, giggling. 'Do you have any sixes?'

Willow shook her head. 'Go giant slithery squid!'

'That's Atlantic pollocks. I know you have at least one.'

'That's rude!'

'Pollocks?'

She fell back on the sofa shrieking with laughter.

'Babe!' Izzy looked up from the sofa where she was flipping through a magazine. 'My head!'

She was hung over. They both were. They'd been the last to leave the VIP area in Lillie's Bordello last night. Ray's head felt as if it had been used as a spacehopper. If Willow hadn't been there he would have been on his third Bloody Mary by now.

'Do you have any eights?' she giggled.

'Why don't you look out the window,' he told her, 'and see if it's still raining cats and dogs.' She trotted over and he went over and lay down beside Izzy. He'd spent the whole morning trying to keep them both onside. It was exhausting. They'd got off on the wrong foot after Izzy went out for the paper and came back with three bacon bagels.

'Willow's a vegan,' Ray warned her as she was unwrapping them.

She licked some ketchup off her finger. 'I'll have hers, then!'

'Not sure you can eat meat in front of her. I don't want to upset her.'

'But you don't want to upset me either, right?' Izzy gave him a ketchuppy kiss. 'It's my hangover cure. We just won't tell her what it is. It'll be fine.'

Willow's little nose wrinkled as soon as Ray carried the plates in. 'Ray,' she said, 'what's that funny smell?'

'It's just a teeny, tiny bit of bacon.' Izzy put the coffees down.

'Bacon is another word for pigs,' Willow said, sadly.

'I had no idea!' Izzy pretended to look horrified, then she went back into the kitchen and they heard her noisily scraping a plate, but Ray could see her scoffing the bagel behind the door.

'I had a good time last night,' she whispered, winding her long, strong legs around his. 'Mr VIP! Do you want me to come back later, when Little Miss Sunshine is gone?' That was his hangover cure, Ray thought, sorted.

'It's only raining teeny drops,' Willow turned from the window, 'but that big grey dog is in the garden. Can I go down and say hello?'

'No!' Ray sat up. 'But I know the Japanese for dog,' he said, to distract her. 'It's "inu".'

Willow smiled. 'I know the Irish for dog. It's "madra".'

'Do you know the Irish for two dogs?' Izzy's eyes narrowed a fraction.

'Yes.' Willow didn't miss a beat. 'It's "madra, madra".'

After Izzy had gone, Willow and Ray took the DART back to Ash's parents' house. Ray hadn't been on public transport for years but Willow loved trains.

It was a ten-minute walk from the station to the house. On the way, she told him a long story about the time she fell off a swing and got a 'fraction' in her arm.

'Which arm was it?'

'I think it was this one.' She put one small hand on his and then frowned. 'Or maybe it was that one. They all look the same.'

The sun came out. Their shadows appeared on the pavement in front of them. The tall figure and the tiny one, joined at the hand, and suddenly, it hit Ray properly for the first time, even though it was so obvious. She was part of him. The length of each eyelash, the spiral of each dark curl, the glitter in her eyes when she'd faced Izzy down – none of it could have existed without him.

Long after his looks, his voice, even his life had gone, Willow would still be here. The sun went in. Their shadows disappeared and they walked on. But that feeling of amazement tucked itself into a corner of Ray's heart and stayed there.

22

Nick had read enough Freud to understand the concept of regression. Was that what he was doing by living at home? Temporarily reverting to his childhood so he didn't have to face the fact that his adult life was in meltdown? Except that perhaps this wasn't temporary at all, maybe this was his new reality.

He had cancelled all his private coaching sessions. How could he tell other couples how to save their own relationships when he had no idea how to save his own? Some of his clients were justifiably annoyed and he felt terrible lying to them that he'd come down with a mystery virus. Now he had to find a way to admit to Oonagh that he had to turn down *The Ex-Factor*. She wasn't going to be annoyed, she was going to be destroyed. But that wasn't why he was putting it off. The truth was, he couldn't face admitting to her or even to himself, that his marriage was in trouble.

The old man was still refusing to take painkillers or see the physiotherapist or to let Nick help to wash or dress him or tidy his room. This morning, while he was in the tiny bathroom off the surgery, Nick had used the time to clear up, shutting out the awful grunts and gasps of pain that were coming from behind the door. He was halfway inside a fresh duvet cover, struggling to get it on to the duvet, when his phone rang.

'Is this a good time?' Kelly said. There was a hint of warmth in her voice. He had called her dozens of times but this was the first time she had called him.

The duvet cover settled over his head. 'Yes,' he said.

'I was hoping you could meet me, today.'

'At the house?' The old man had a check-up at the hospital, later, but Claire could drive him.

'Not the house . . .' He heard the hesitation in her voice and his heart lurched with longing.

'Just say where and when. I'll be there.'

There was a long pause. 'At the clinic. I have an ultrasound at three o'clock.'

Nick closed his eyes. 'Kelly. Don't do this to me—'

'Please. I'll wait for you in the café across the road. Just say you'll think about it.'

Nick finished making the bed and washed the dishes. He took the old man's Difene with a mouthful of cold tea. He bagged up the laundry and drove to the shopping centre in Dun Laoghaire, where he wasn't likely to bump into any of the neighbours. He left the bag at the launderette then wrestled a rusty trolley from the bay in the car park and jolted it into the supermarket. It had a squeaky wheel and leaned heavily to the left but he didn't have the energy to go back for another one.

He picked up three dozen eggs and six packets of Jaffa Cakes. That was the old man sorted. He forced the trolley, against its steely will, through a section called 'Get Fresh'. Nick hadn't eaten a fresh vegetable since he'd moved home. He looked at the complicated lettuces, the feathery bunches of carrots, the wild mushrooms, the ten different kinds of tomatoes. What was the point of all of them? His father had lived on a diet of eggs and biscuits for twenty-seven years and he was still alive. If you could call it living.

Nick did a squeaky turn back into frozen foods, loading up on stuff for himself. Packets of potato waffles, frozen pizzas, cottage pies. All the things he'd bought for himself and Claire when they were young. As he was squeaking back down the aisle, he saw a familiar figure, a tiny girl in a red coat leaning into a chill cabinet on her tiptoes, a halo of freezing-cold air hovering around her dark head. It was Linh. Her parents were right behind her, arguing beside the freezer cabinets.

'It wouldn't kill you to buy me a few flowers from time to time,' Niamh was saying.

Rory snorted. 'I was up at five o'clock this morning reading Roald bloody Dahl. You should be buying *me* flowers.'

Nick's trolley refused to turn so he reversed it instead. It squealed like a dying rabbit. He nearly got away without being seen, then Linh blocked his way. She smiled delightedly up at him from under her black fringe and pointed at the trolley.

'Make the noise again!'

'Nick? Is that you?' Rory came striding over. 'Niamh told me the news!' Nick swallowed. Kelly had promised not to tell anyone that they were living apart. Rory grabbed him and pulled him into a hug. To his horror, Nick felt tears come into his eyes and he had to stop himself collapsing against Rory's chest.

Niamh appeared, beaming. 'Congratulations!'

'What?' Nick pulled away.

'On getting the *Ex-Factor* job! Kelly hasn't been answering my calls but I read about it in the paper.'

'Oh.' Nick nodded, trying to pull himself together. 'Yes. Right. Thanks.'

'So,' Rory said. 'Have you seen a contract yet?'

'Not yet.'

'Listen,' Rory said, 'I want you to swear to me that you won't sign anything till I've seen it. Come down to the office and we'll go through it with a fine tooth comb. OK?'

Kelly was the only customer in the Karma Café. She sat at the window and stared out at the steps of the clinic on the other side of the street. Two-thirty came and went. Then three o'clock. She pulled the raisins out of her uneaten scone and lined them up on the rim of her pink plate like dead flies.

She had missed her appointment now but she still sat there, watching the clinic door opening and closing, willing Nick to arrive. And even after she'd given up, she stayed where she was, trying to summon up the energy to stand up and leave.

A couple came out and crossed the busy street to the café. The woman had long dark hair and a cream coat like Kelly's. The man was fair and slightly taller than Nick, but he had the same build. They came in on a cloud of cold air and pure happiness. The man ordered a latte and a decaf.

'You want them here or to take away?' the waiter asked.

They grinned at one another. 'Take away,' they both said together.

'I've been talking to the team.' The orthopaedic consultant was in his sifties, a stern-looking man with a shock of grey hair and a rugby player's build. 'We're very concerned about your father's recovery. The physiotherapist says he's cancelled six appointments in a row. I was hoping to talk to him about that, today.'

'We tried to make him come in,' Claire sighed, 'but he wouldn't.'

She had tried, Nick thought; he had sat in the car outside the house with the engine running, watching the clock on his dashboard, trying not to think about Kelly lying on her own in the darkness of the ultrasound suite.

'You need to talk to him about this, as a family,' the consultant frowned. 'Because every week that goes by gives him less of a chance of living an independent life again.'

'He was right, you know?' Claire said in the car. 'If Dad doesn't snap out of it soon he might never get better.'

'Does everything have to be a drama?' Nick shot through a red light as a double-decker bus pulled out and swerved past them, clipping the wing mirror and snapping it off. The sound ripped through the interior of the car, loud as a gunshot.

'Pull over!' Claire yelled. She sat, with her shaking hands in her lap while Nick parked and put on the hazard lights, then she turned to him. 'Now what's going on, Nick? Why are you still living at Dad's?'

He gripped the steering wheel and shook his head.

'Are you and Kelly arguing about this job in the UK? Does she want you to turn it down?'

'Yes,' he lied.

'Well, do it, then,' Claire said softly. 'She's your family now. You have to do whatever it takes.'

Richard came into the kitchen buttoning up his cuffs. 'Have you seen my watch?'

Claire was taking off Dog's lead. 'Did you look in the bath-room?'

While he went back in to check she picked up Dog's rug and shook it out. A slightly gnawed leather belt fell out but there was no sign of the Rolex. She got down on her knees and peered under the cooker while Dog watched her, his hairy head cocked to one side, his ears pricked up with interest.

'What the hell have you done with it?' she hissed at him.

Richard was standing in the door looking surprised. 'I really thought I left it on the bedside table,' he said, sheepishly.

'I didn't mean you.' Claire blushed. 'I meant . . .'

He walked over and tilted her face upwards with the tip of his finger. 'You do know that talking to yourself is the second sign of madness.' He looked at Dog. 'You don't think he took it, do you?'

'No.' Claire stood between them. 'I'm sure it's just under the bed or something.'

'I've looked everywhere. I wanted to wear it today for luck. I'm presenting the final cuts of your virals to the board.'

The ads were being recut for the fifth or sixth time, Claire had lost count by now. She was starting to worry that there might be something very wrong with them that Richard wasn't telling her.

'Fingers crossed.' She crossed her fingers, kissed him on the cheek, then uncrossed one hand and picked one of Dog's long grey hairs off Richard's starched collar.

Dog was circling a tree in the park, sniffing the trunk carefully. 'What happens if a watch goes through a dog?'

'Hang on a sec!' She could hear the clatter of pots and the sound of Greasy Pete whistling 'Once, Twice, Three Times a Lady' in the background. After a minute Eilish came back. 'Is the watch waterproof or water resistant?'

'It's water resistant to a thousand feet.'

'Well, that's got to be good news, right?'

'I hope so. Richard will be broken hearted if anything happens to his Rolex.'

Dog was doing the little foot to foot thing he did before he squatted, like a golfer getting ready to tee off. 'I think he might be about to go! How will I know if Richard's Rolex is in there?'

'You'll know, Claire, trust me. Those things weigh a ton.'

'Any sign of my watch?' Richard looked tired.

Claire shook her head. 'How did the meeting go?'

He shrugged his coat off and ran his hand through his short, blond hair. 'Badly. The board is like bloody Jurassic Park. Those old guys just can't get their heads around the social media thing.'

'They're not going to run the virals, are they?'

'Not in this market, which is incredibly frustrating, but it's not the end of the world. There's a meeting of international Vitalustre marketing directors in London on Monday. I'm going to present the virals over there. If two or three other markets buy them we'll break even on the production spend.'

'But if they don't?' Claire wondered whether she should offer to repay her fee. She still had eight thousand euros left in her account.

'They will. The rest of the world gets digital. We're just in the Dark Ages over here!' He pressed his thumbs against his eyes. 'Can we stay over at my place tonight? I'd just like to get into bed with you without that dog bursting in on us for once. It's been a long day.'

Claire had had a long day too. She had brought Dog to the park four times and watched him like a hawk. She had turned the flat upside down. Then she had Googled 'my dog ate my watch'. If the battery leaked, Dog might get very sick. The advice was to feed him lots of soft food and watch for any signs of discomfort. She had already given him an entire packet of cooked pasta shells and she was defrosting a shepherd's pie. 'Do you mind if we stay here? I just don't want to leave Dog on his own.'

'Honestly, Claire. Sometimes I think you care more about him than you do about me.'

'I don't even like dogs.'

'Well, drop him over to your father for the night.'

'I can't. Nick's allergic to dogs and he's living there for a while.'

'Really?' Richard had been trying to arrange a meeting with

Nick for weeks now, he loved his show. 'I thought he had his own place in Donnybrook.'

'He does but he's having problems with his wife. I don't think he wants anyone to know.'

'That's a bit ironic, isn't it?'

'What do you mean?'

'Well, your brother, the relationship guru, is all over the TV and radio lecturing the rest of us about how to have trouble-free relationships. That's kind of misleading.'

Claire snapped before she could stop herself. 'About as misleading as giving me a twelve-week blow-dry and pretending my hair looks this good because I use Vitalustre!'

Richard put one hand up. 'Whoa! What's going on here?'

'Sorry. I'm just worried—' she looked at Dog, 'about your watch, that's all.'

He stood up. 'Maybe we should just call it a day.' Claire stared at him.

'I love you,' he said, 'but I'm just not a dog person.' He picked up his briefcase. 'I've asked the office handyman to come and fix the pipes on Friday and I'll get him to put a couple of new locks on the doors in the hall while he's here. I'm working late tomorrow but I'll see you Saturday. We're going to a movie with Helen and Andreas, remember?'

Relief washed over her. This was a proper grown-up relationship. It had ups. It had downs. It was going to be fine. He kissed her lightly on the lips. 'Sorry, Claire. Today was tough. I just need some time out.'

She saw him to the door to the laneway and then walked, in a daze, back into the house and closed the door and leaned on it.

'Did he just say he loved me?' she asked Dog. His stomach rumbled ominously. 'Oh no!' Claire reached for her coat. 'Here we go again.'

While Oonagh was introducing Nick's segment on 'Five Steps to Overcome Jealousy', Owen pulled off his microphone and wandered, out of shot, over to the kitchen set where a table had been laid with dishes for a Valentine's dinner.

'Nick, I think we all know, first hand,' Oonagh said, pointedly, 'how much damage jealousy can do in a relationship.'

'Absolutely.' Nick had decided that today was the day to be straight with Oonagh. He'd taken an extra painkiller to give him courage but it had just made him feel out of focus. 'A certain amount of jealousy is normal but, if it gets out of hand, it can lead to increasingly irrational behaviour.' Behind her, he saw Owen tucking into a plate of oysters, while the floor manager tried, in mime, to reason with him.

'Thanks, Nick, you were great, as always!' Oonagh's bottom lip was wobbling but she did her best to smile for the camera. 'Coming up after the news, liposuction, the man who wants to breastfeed his baby and an irresistible Valentine's supper.' She waited till the camera stopped rolling then she stood up and fled. Nick caught up with her in the corridor. 'Oonagh, wait, I need to talk to you—'

She turned and flung herself at him, burying her face in his chest. 'I know what you're going to say. You're going to say that I have to think of three good things about him or something. But I can't. I'm sick of him, Nick. He's jealous of us! He just can't bear that you're getting this job and he's not.'

He patted her blonde curls. They were stiff and sticky with hairspray. 'I wasn't going to say that. What I was going to say was that Kelly and I are—'

The floor manager stuck his head round the door. 'Oonagh, Owen's laying into the Valentine's cocktails. You need to get back in here fast.'

Ash was heading off to London for twenty-four hours. Ray guessed that she was packing up the last bits and pieces to move back to Dublin for good but he didn't want to be nosy. She'd asked him to look after Willow overnight and then deliver her to a fancy dress party.

'You've got the address?' Ash asked him for the third time on the steps. 'And the stuff to make the Rice Krispie buns?'

Ray had double-checked that the chocolate was vegan and

picked up a packet of paper chef's hats too. Willow was going to love those. 'Yeah. You have a plane to catch, remember?'

'Is Izzy coming?' Willow asked him as soon as Ash left.

'Nope.' Ray hadn't beaten his four-week record for a relationship. It hadn't been pretty to watch a grown woman trying to compete with a six-year-old. Especially when the six-year-old won. 'OK, let's get these crispies on the road.'

Willow was at the window. 'Can we just go down and pat Claire's dog first? Please? If we wash our hands afterwards. He's in the garden.'

Ray was unfolding his chef's hat. 'With Claire.'

'No, he's with a man.' Willow pressed her forehead against the window. 'The dog is going for a walk and the man is throwing money in the bin.'

'Money?' Ray walked over to the window. Richard, in weekend casuals, was closing the lid of the recycling bin. He wiped his hands carefully on a tissue.

'Will you promise me something?' Ray asked Willow.

'It depends.'

'Will you promise me you'll never trust a man who wears moccasins?'

Claire pushed open the door of Weir's and crossed the thick carpet, past the cabinets of glittering silverware and cases of trophies. An assistant was polishing the countertop with a duster.

'Can I help you?'

'I'm looking for a Rolex Submariner,' she said, 'with a unidirectional thingy and it has to be waterproof.'

Weir's didn't have Richard's watch in stock. They could order one in but Claire couldn't afford to buy it. Dog's little snack had cost five and a half thousand euros. She would have to try to track down a second-hand one on eBay.

There was a missed call from Richard on Claire's phone when she came out of her audition. 'The dog is missing!' he said when she called him back. 'The handyman must have left the gate open and he got out.'

Richard had already been to the beach and the playing fields

257

behind the school looking for Dog but he went back again just to be sure while Claire walked around the park. She asked everyone she met if they'd seen a huge grey dog but nobody had. She should have had him microchipped, she realised, too late, but at least her dad's phone number was on his collar. If someone found him, they'd call his house and Nick would let her know.

'He'll turn up,' Richard said when they met back at the flat. 'Now sit down and eat something. I got you a coffee and a muffin.'

'I'm not hungry. I have to find him. Tell me what happened again.'

He shook his head, helplessly. 'I got here at about three to let the handyman in. He was fixing the locks in the hall and I was checking my mail on the laptop in the living room and when I went into the kitchen at four Dog was gone. The gate was open when I looked out. The guy went out to get some tools from his van and—'

'We need to check the pound.' Claire took out her phone.

'I rang them earlier. Both of the Dublin pounds and four animal rescue places.'

Claire was only half listening. It was dark now and she was trying to block out images of Dog getting knocked down by a car or being tied to another trolley by a gang of kids. She started putting her coat back on. 'I'll go and check the supermarket car parks.'

'Now? It's getting kind of late.'

'I'll do it.'

'We'll do it together.' Richard stood up. 'You take Superquinn. I'll take M&S, then we'll meet at Tesco.'

Ray and Willow made a batch of Rice Krispie buns but then they ate most of them and had to make a second batch. Afterwards, Ray dug out a box of stuff from the Smoke Covered Horses days. He upended it on the floor of the living room. Photographs and press clippings in languages he didn't even recognise. Keys to hotel rooms that he'd never returned. Laminates and backstage passes. Labels from bottles of tequila he didn't remember drinking.

'This is what I wanted to show you,' he said as he found the picture of himself with David Bowie. It had been taken at a party in Tokyo eight years ago. David had spent an hour talking to Chip and Ray had run after him with a Polaroid camera as he was leaving. He had his arm slung around Bowie's neck and he was giving the camera the peace sign. Bowie looked, he realised now, politely horrified and he looked very, very drunk.

'Who's that?' Willow asked him.

'That's the other Bowie.'

'No.' She pointed her small finger at the other face. 'Who's he?'

'That's me!' Ray said, puzzled.

'You look different.' She looked from the picture to his face and back down again.

'You mean I look younger?'

Willow thought for a second. 'No. You look sadder.'

Ray helped Willow change into her pyjamas.

'We have to brush my teeth and then I have to pray for all the people I love.' She squeezed paste carefully on to her *Toy Story* toothbrush.

'How do you know?' Ray asked her. 'When you love someone?'

'Your heart goes bump and little stars come out of you.'

'Like in a cartoon?'

'Yes. Except it's not funny.' She looked at the toothbrush. 'This toothpaste smells yellow.'

Ray grabbed the brush from her and sniffed it. Then picked up the toothpaste tube and squinted at it. He held it up to the magnifying mirror. It was Preparation H.

'Willow! Did you put this in your mouth?' She looked scared. 'It's OK. It's just not for teeth, that's all.'

She shook her head. 'What's it for, then?'

Ray dropped the tube into the bin.

'It's for idiots.'

He should have bought Willow an apron, he thought, folding her clothes after she had finally gone to sleep. Her jeans were covered in patches of dried chocolate but she'd be wearing her fancy dress costume tomorrow, so he guessed it didn't matter.

He went over to the bed to turn the lamp off and he stood, with his hand on the switch, looking down at her small, dark head on the pillow. Then he went back into the kitchen and ripped open the Rice Krispie packet and began to scribble down the words of something that he thought might be a song.

Willow's costume was a white ballet tutu with pink tights and a tiara which she insisted on wearing with her tiny trainers. The party was only a few streets away so they decided to walk. Halfway there, she needed to pee, so Ray went into a hairdresser's and asked the girl on reception if they could use their loo.

'Of course!' She smiled at Willow in her coat and tiara. 'Do you want me to take you, Your Majesty?'

'I'm not a real princess,' Willow said, shyly. 'This is just my funsy dress.'

There was a collective 'aaah' from the women at the basins.

Ray waited outside holding Willow's sparkly pink wheelie case and the Tupperware box of Rice Krispie buns; he heard someone calling his name and, when he looked up, Chip Connolly was crossing the road, his small face curled into an angry snarl.

'You stole my fucking song, you cheap shit!' He grabbed Ray's arm. 'For a fucking bagel advert.' And before Ray could say 'sorry', before he could say anything, Chip punched him hard in the face.

Ray's mouth filled with the metallic taste of blood. He slid down the wall and put his head between his knees. He could hear the angry squeak of Chip's trainers as he strode away.

'Oh my God!' The receptionist was standing in the doorway of the salon holding Willow by the hand. 'Are you OK?'

'Yeah.' Ray got unsteadily to his feet. There was a line of shocked faces at the window.

'Come inside,' the receptionist was saying. 'I'll call the police.'

'No!' It was pointless and Willow would miss the party. He took her hand. His own hand, he saw too late, was covered in blood. She looked at him and her bottom lip began to wobble.

'It's just a little nose bleed,' he told her. 'You can still go to the party. We've still got the crispies.' He crouched down beside her. 'It's OK.'

He had to pick her up and carry her in the end. Two taxis

slowed down and took off when they saw the blood on his face but a third stopped.

'I don't want to go to the party now. I want to go home,' Willow whispered. She shrank against the door when he tried to comfort her but she let him carry her up the driveway, bumping the pink suitcase behind him. They had lost the Rice Krispie buns somewhere along the way.

He was expecting to have to explain what happened to his face to Willow's grandmother, but it was Ash who opened the door. 'I thought you were in London,' he stammered.

Her shocked eyes took in the blood on his clothes. 'Ray! What happened. Is Willow hurt?'

'She's fine. It's my blood.' He passed Willow to Ash. Her tutu was splattered with red-brown stains and her pink tights had dark streaks. She was crying, softly.

'It's OK, sweetheart.' Ash wrapped her arms around her. 'It's OK.'

'What's going on?' A man appeared behind her and Ray almost fell over. It was Maurice DeVeau, standing in the hallway of a semi-d in Killiney.

'Daddy!' Willow stretched her arms out to him.

Ash was pale. 'Maurice, can you deal with this?' She carried Willow into the house.

'What happened, man?' Maurice ran a hand through his famous mane of blond hair.

'Guy came out of nowhere and punched me,' Ray said in a shaky voice, 'a guy from my old band, Smoke Covered Horses.'

Maurice DeVeau nodded. Did that mean he knew the band, Ray wondered, or that he understood that someone had punched him?

'You want to come in and get cleaned up?'

Ray did want to go in. He wanted to be with Willow, to make sure that she really was all right. But that might upset her more. 'I'd better head home.'

'OK.'

He put his hand on the door just as Maurice was closing it. 'I'm a huge fan of your work,' he babbled. 'I thought *Only You, Only Me* was an incredible album and—'

'Daddy!' He heard Willow crying in a distant room and he stopped himself.

'You take care, man,' Maurice DeVeau said in his soft Canadian accent, 'and keep it real.'

'You too,' Ray said to the closing door.

23

It was still dark outside when Richard finished getting dressed. He was taking the red-eye to London to present the virals to twenty international brand managers.

'Are you sure you don't want me to cancel?' He sat on the bed.

'No, it's OK.'

'I'll be back tonight. I'm sure Dog will have turned up by then.'

After he was gone, Claire got up and drove around the super-market car parks again. Then walked through the park. There was nobody around. It had rained in the night and the bushes by the path were drenched. She checked behind every one of them in case Dog was sheltering there. He hated the rain.

A few ducks were bobbing on the pond. Claire made herself walk over to the edge of the water and called Dog's name. The swan made a beeline for her, shaking out his tail and turning his head to give her his best profile. He'd be glad, she thought, if Dog never turned up at all.

She did another two circuits of the park and then walked back towards her flat slowly, checking all the gardens on the street and asking all the mothers and kids who were on their way to school if they'd seen Dog. Nobody had.

She spent the morning ringing round the Gardaí stations and the Dublin dog pounds and posting 'lost dog' messages on boards. At about lunchtime, the bell rang. When she opened the door, she thought that Ray was wearing a red tie-dyed T-shirt before she realised that he was covered in blood.

He sat on the side of the bath while she examined the cut on his nose. The bone wasn't broken but the skin was split badly along the bridge.

'Willow was terrified,' Ray was babbling, 'and Ash was furious with me even though it wasn't my fault. I mean, it was my fault. I shouldn't have used Chip's song. But we lost the Rice Krispie buns and Willow couldn't stop crying. And then Maurice DeVeau turned up. Maurice-fucking-de-Veau. It was so weird—'

'Ray!' Claire interrupted him. 'You need go to A & E to get a couple of stitches put in.'

'Just put a plaster on it!'

'It might scar.'

'I don't care.'

She stared at him. Ray freaked out if he got so much as a pimple. 'I'm not sure I believe you but if that's what you want, stop talking and tilt your head back.'

She cleaned the blood off his nose with cotton wool soaked in TCP.

'Shouldn't your girlfriend be doing this?' She pressed on a little pad of cotton wool and taped it into place.

'Izzy is was-sy,' Ray said.

Claire didn't look as smug as he thought she might at this news. In fact, he thought, squinting up at her through the fumes of disinfectant, she looked kind of miserable. 'What's up?'

She wiped her eyes with a piece of cotton wool. 'Dog got out yesterday. A handyman came to fix the pipes and left the gate open. I've looked everywhere. It rained all night and he's so old and he's scared of everything and I'm afraid something's happened to him . . .'

Ray put his hand on her arm. 'Claire, I think Richard let him out.'

She glared at him, put the TCP back into the cabinet and banged the door closed.

'Willow was here yesterday. She saw Richard and Dog in the garden. She said Dog was going for a walk but when I looked out, Richard was still there and—'

'I know what you're doing.' Claire folded her arms. 'You're trying to mess things up between me and Richard so I'll start hanging out with you again.'

'Maybe he didn't let Dog out but he was definitely up to

something. Willow saw him throwing money in the recycling bin and I thought he looked really shifty.'

'Get up!' Claire said quietly. 'And get out.' He had to follow her out into the hall. 'Go!' She unlocked the door that connected her flat to the rest of Ray's house.

'You know I've got good "creepdar",' Ray said. 'I saw through Declan Brady back in the day, and I'm telling you, this guy's a creep. He got rid of those nettles – my nettles, Claire – without my permission. And—'

'You're pathetic!' Claire propelled him through the door and closed it after him. Then she went out to look up and down the laneway just in case Dog had come back. She walked past the bins back up to the kitchen. 'Don't,' she told herself. But she walked over despite herself and lifted the lid on the green one. She moved some squashed food packaging out of the way, her hand touching something slimy. This was exactly what Ray wanted her to do, he was probably watching her right now. She was about to close the lid when she saw something glinting between a pizza box and the pink-tinged styrofoam pad from a packet of mince. Something round and silver that could, to a small girl standing at an upstairs window, have looked just like a coin. It was the worn metal disc from Dog's collar.

Nick had been trying to call Oonagh all day but her phone was switched off. He was standing out in the front garden, trying again, when Brian Cunningham appeared at the wall. 'There are faeces in my borders.'

'I'm sorry. What did you say?'

'Sorry's not good enough!' Mr Cunningham snapped. 'I told your sister that if that animal came into my garden one more time, I'd call the Gardaí.'

'I am calm and relaxed,' Nick told himself, but his self wasn't listening. 'Do you seriously believe that an elderly dog consulted a map and walked four miles, crossing several busy roads just for the pleasure of crapping in your garden?'

Mr Cunningham held up a small plastic bag and dropped it over the wall. 'Yes,' he said. 'I do.'

*

There was a clatter behind him and, when he looked over his shoulder, the old man was making his way down the hall. Somehow, he managed to get as far as the kitchen without his walking aid.

'Christ!' Nick hurried after him. 'What are you doing? You're not supposed to walk without the frame!'

'Dog is in the back garden.' The old man was breathless. 'I saw him from my window.' He hauled himself awkwardly along by the fridge, the cooker then the sink. It hurt, Nick could see that from his face, but he didn't stop and he made it, at surprising speed, to the back door. He pushed it open and a huge grey blur cleared the Cunningham's wall and hurled itself at him. If Nick hadn't been able to pull the old man out of the way, he would have been knocked to the ground. Dog was wet and filthy. His hairy coat was plastered against his long, wiry body. He put his paws up on the sink and stood on his back legs, nibbling the old man's hair and whinnying with delight.

'I thought Claire was looking after him,' the old man panted as Nick eased him into a chair.

'So did I,' Nick said.

Dog lunged at his father again. Nick made a grab for him but he got away and crawled under the table, then he erupted under the old man's chair.

'Dog! You need to calm down!' The old man laughed. Dog did an arthritic circuit of the room and then buried his head in his lap.

Nick could feel his eyes welling up in an allergic reaction. 'He can't stay here. You'll break something else.'

'But he can stay till Claire comes to get him?' The old man looked up at him. 'Can't he?'

Claire stared at Dog in amazement. 'It must be two or three miles.'

Nick sneezed. 'It's four.'

'Bless you!' Claire bent down and smoothed Dog's straggly mutton chop whiskers and tangled her hand in the wet fur at the back of his neck. His tail beat a wild tattoo on the floor of her dad's kitchen and he licked the knee of her jeans thoughtfully.

'You want to know the first thing he did when he got here?'

Nick started to laugh. For a second, Claire saw the ghost of the boy he had been before the accident. She shook her head, not trusting herself to speak.

Nick grinned. 'He jumped over Cunning Ham's wall and crapped in his flower bed.'

The night out in the rain had worn Dog out. He curled up in a tight ball, between the fridge and the cooker, with his head on the draught snake, and he wouldn't come out when Claire turned on the six o'clock news.

She turned the volume up so he could hear it in the kitchen. Anne Doyle's emotionless voice describing the latest Eurozone crisis seemed to soothe him, and by the time the weather came on he was fast asleep.

Claire couldn't believe that Richard had let him out deliberately. There had to be an explanation. When he rang from London she told him that Dog had made his way to her dad's house but she hadn't mentioned that she'd found the disc from his collar in the bin.

'I told you he'd show up, didn't I?' Richard had sounded genuinely delighted.

'Yes,' Claire had said, uncertainly, 'you did.' Maybe she was wrong?

'I'm just going into the meeting now and I'll go straight to Heathrow when it's over. I should be back with you at nine. We'll celebrate!'

Richard kissed Claire and then turned to look at Dog. She watched his eyes widen when he took in the disc that she had re-attached to his collar and the little balloon of hope that had been bobbing around in her chest deflated and sank.

'Well, well. The return of the prodigal dog!' Richard turned away, quickly, and started opening a bottle of champagne he'd taken out of a duty-free bag. 'Not much to celebrate on the viral front, I'm afraid,' he said over his shoulder. 'Europe and America don't want the ads.' She heard the pop and the whisper of the champagne pouring into a glass. 'Which is their mistake.' He turned back to her and held out a glass. She didn't take it.

'How could you do it?' she said flatly.

'What?' A flush began spreading up his neck, past the collar of his white shirt and into his face. 'Come on. You don't even like dogs, Claire, you said so yourself, and this one is ruining our lives. It sheds hair everywhere. It freaks out every time I touch you. I think it ate my bloody Rolex. I was doing us both a favour!'

'In what sick scenario would abandoning an old dog be doing me a favour?' And as she said it, Claire remembered that she had tried to get rid of Dog herself, just a few months ago.

Richard topped up his glass. 'He's the reason you haven't moved in with me.'

Claire grabbed the bottle from him and held it over the sink. The champagne frothed and fizzed around the plughole as she poured it away.

'Hey!' Richard said. 'Steady on! That's a brut!'

Claire whipped around to face him. 'Get out!'

He came over to the sink and put his arms around her. 'Look, I'm sorry. It was just a spur-of-the-moment thing. I opened the kitchen door and it smelled like a lion's den in here. I thought that if I let him go, some kids might find him and take him in.'

'Some kids did find him, twelve years ago!' Claire pulled herself free. 'They tied him to a trolley in a supermarket car park. Please, just go!'

Richard blinked at her. 'You're breaking up with me over a *dog*?' She nodded. 'What am I supposed to tell my family? You're supposed to be coming to Val d'Isère at Easter. Helen was going to ask you to be a bridesmaid at her wedding.'

'Tell them what you did, Richard. They're normal. They'll understand.'

Richard's face darkened. 'What do you know about normal? Your life was a mess till you met me. I fixed up your flat and your computer and put new locks on your doors. I even sorted your bloody plumbing. And I gave you a job, Claire. I put my reputation behind that viral campaign and you screwed it up.'

'*What?*'

'I couldn't see it at the time – I liked you too much – but I realised it as soon as I got into the editing room. You have this look on your face in every shot, like you should be on stage in the

Abbey, instead of getting your hands dirty doing an ad.' He was shouting now. 'So if you want me to go, I'll go! But you'll be sorry. Because I'm the glue that's holding your crappy life together and—'

There was a low throbbing sound, like a car idling, a car with a very large, powerful engine. Dog emerged from around the side of the fridge, his head low, his black lips pulled back to reveal an impressive row of pointy, yellow teeth. If it hadn't been for his ears, one lying flat, the other one sticking straight out and turning up at the end, he would have looked terrifying.

'You don't scare me!' Richard snorted. But he picked up his briefcase and looked at Dog warily.

Dog growled again, and this time, Claire thought, he sounded as if he might mean business. She hooked her fingers around his collar. His fur was still damp from the rain.

'I'd leave, if I were you,' she said to Richard.

He threw his key on the table, opened the back door and slammed it behind him.

Claire couldn't sleep. She felt as if the storm raging outside was inside her. Her head was whirling, replaying the months since she'd met Richard. Finding all the moments when she should have seen this coming. She would have seen it if she hadn't been so desperate to keep the stupid promise she'd made on her birthday. She lay, listening to the clatter of hailstones against her window, wondering whether it was ever really Richard she'd fallen for, or his family. The chance to be part of something she'd never had.

She suddenly remembered the chain he'd given her. The little gold disc that said 'Believe in You.' She got up and took it off. Then she opened the bottom drawer and took out the box of her mother's things. At the bottom, between the bottle of Opium and the hairbrush, she found the locket. She looped it around her neck and fastened it and got back into bed. Then she did what she had done when she was small. She rubbed it between her thumb and forefinger until she fell asleep.

She was woken by a loud thump out in the hall. She froze, then she remembered that Richard had left his key. When she opened the door, Dog was standing there, trembling. There was a deafening roll of thunder and he pasted himself against her legs, his eyes rolling, his ears twitching in terror.

He was too scared to move so Claire hooked her hand around his collar and dragged him over to the bed. She had to haul him up, one stiff leg at a time, and when he lay down, with his long, boney grey back to her, she put her hands over his ears. He smelled of damp dog and leather collar and, strangely, of meringues. Eventually, he gave a huge, shuddering sigh and began to snore.

Nick listened to the wind rattling the old, single-glazed windows and howling through the attic over his head. When Claire was small, she always had one of her nightmares when there was a storm. She'd wake up and Nick would find her asleep outside the old man's door and he'd bring her back to bed and stay with her until she went to sleep again. He wished he could go back to sleep but his mind was wide awake.

A seminar co-ordinator in the UK wanted to discuss a position on their roster of speakers. A women's magazine called *Bliss* wanted to know if he'd be interested in a monthly column on making marriage work. And Oonagh had mailed him a list of potential dates for the two of them to fly to London to sign contracts with Clingfilms.

All the things Nick had daydreamed about a few weeks ago seemed to be falling into his lap, but he didn't want them any more. All he wanted was to turn over in the lumpy bed and find Kelly lying beside him.

Kelly pulled on her robe and went downstairs. The garden looked as if it had been burgled. Litter had blown over the wall. Two patio chairs were lying on their sides on the lawn. A huge plant pot had blown over and cracked and the magnolia, the white one Nick had bought her for her birthday, had snapped in half.

She opened the door. A gust of wind blew her hair straight up in the air and rattled a vase on a shelf on the other side of the room. She forced the door closed again and watched crisp bags, newspapers and chip wrappers whip past the window. Usually, when she couldn't sleep, she went online and logged on to one of her fertility message boards, but she couldn't face them any more.

She filled the kettle and put a camomile tea bag into a cup, then she changed her mind and went into the living room and poured herself a finger of Scotch. She hardly drank at all, not since she was seventeen and her parents had sent her to that awful place. A glass of wine with dinner every few weeks. A flute of champagne at a wedding. She'd stopped completely on her honeymoon. Drinking was a bad idea if you were trying to conceive, that's what all the books said.

She swallowed the whisky in one neat gulp. Every month, for three years and three months, she'd held on to the hope that she might be pregnant. But this month, for the first time, she knew for certain that she wasn't.

Ray had changed the bandage earlier and the cut had started bleeding again. Claire had been right. He should have had it stitched up. It hurt like hell. The wind was howling down the fire escape, playing it like a huge out-of-tune harmonica. He hoped that Willow was asleep. Some kids were scared of storms, though he hadn't been. A good storm had always stopped his parents fighting for some reason. Maybe because it was louder than they were. He felt the old wave of self-pity gathering force out there in the wet, wild night, so he got up, went down to the living room and picked up the weapon he'd always used against it – his guitar. He played the opening chords of 'Asia Sky' and then, without thinking, he shifted into something else. Something new, some-thing good. He remembered the lyrics he'd scribbled on the Rice Krispies box the night Willow stayed over and he knew, before he even searched the bin to find them, that they would fit perfectly.

The storm had finally died down and Nick was drifting back to sleep when the old man started up. Nick flipped the pillow over, squeezed his eyes closed and tried to shut out the moans and groans of pain coming from the surgery below him. Then, when he couldn't take any more, he jumped out of bed, grabbed a T-shirt and went downstairs.

The old man sat up blinking when he switched on the light. 'What is it?' he gasped. 'What's wrong?'

'You're making so much noise I can't sleep.' Nick shook a sleeping tablet into his hand. 'You need one of these.' He popped a painkiller from its blister pack. 'And one of these.'

'I don't need painkillers. I'm fine.'

'Well, I'm not!' Nick snapped. 'This stoical shit about not taking your medication has to stop. It's driving me mad and it's upsetting Claire.'

'I have never done anything to hurt Claire,' the old man said sharply.

'Really? You should have seen her face when she found a couple of vodka bottles in here a few months ago,' Nick said. That woke the old man up. 'I covered for you. Again. But you owe me, Dad.' He held his palm out. 'Take them.'

The old man frowned but he put the tablets in his mouth and washed them down with a gulp of water.

Nick slammed the door and climbed the stairs again. He was back in bed before he realised that he'd called the old man 'Dad'.

24

Ray had been calling Ash for days. She must be screening his calls, he thought. He tried again, this time using his landline, and she picked up straight away. 'Please stop calling me, Ray,' she said when she heard his voice. 'I don't want to talk to you.'

'Is Willow OK?'

'She saw you getting punched in the face. What do you think?'

'I'd like to see her just to—'

'To what? Upset her all over again.'

'I'll call you tomorrow,' he said, 'maybe then—'

'I don't think so.' She hung up.

If he just showed up at the house and knocked on the door, she would have to let him see Willow, wouldn't she? Just for a minute. Long enough to explain that he wasn't hurt and to re-assure her.

There was a row of small shops at the end of Ash's parents' road. A chemist. A dry cleaner. A newsagent. A bell jangled when Ray pushed the door open. The shop was dark and musty and divided into too many narrow aisles with tightly packed shelves. He walked around trying to find something he could get for Willow that would make up for what had happened.

There was a shelf of plastic toy sets in dusty blister packs but they were too cheap and tacky. He looked at the jars of old-fashioned sweets on a shelf behind the counter. Clove rocks. Pineapple cubes. Sour apples. The sweets he used to eat when he was Willow's age.

A stout, middle-aged woman appeared behind the counter. 'What can I do you for?'

Ray pointed at the jars. 'Can I have a . . .' What did they come in, nowadays? Ounces? Pounds? Grammes? '. . . bag of those.'

She lifted down a jar and started weighing sweets out into stainless-steel scales. 'What happened to you?' She blinked at him, curiously, from behind her thick glasses.

'Oh,' he touched the bridge of his nose, 'I fell over . . .' He looked around for inspiration. '. . . a bale of briquettes.'

'No, I mean what *happened* to you? You were Ray Devine, right?'

'Um.' He swallowed. 'Yeah.'

'I used to think you were the hottest thing on two legs.' He saw now that she was far younger than he'd thought. Late thirties maybe. '"Asia Sky" was my wedding song. I can't believe you never wrote another one.'

Ray remembered the night of the storm. 'I think I might have,' he said hotly. 'I mean I did.'

'Really?' Her eyes sparkled behind her glasses. 'Let's hear it, then.'

He shook his head. 'I couldn't—'

'Come on! I was your biggest fan! I went to every gig you did in Dublin. I was right up the front at The Point. I even threw my knickers at you once but they got tangled up in Happy's drumsticks. You owe me!'

Ray had been fantasising about his comeback for nearly four years. He'd imagined it happening in Paris, Berlin or London, not in a musty newsagent's in suburban Dublin. But something came over him. Something he couldn't fight. The raw, messy, eager compulsion to perform. He felt the delicious fight-or-flight cocktail of stage fright seep into his veins, even though there was no stage, just a counter piled with discounted cans of cat food. This was absurd. He picked up a tin, held it, like a microphone, cleared his throat twice and began to sing.

'*She knows the Heineken manoeuvre,*
She had a fraction on her arm,
She suddenly came out of nowhere,
Now she's wearing your heart like a charm.

And little stars come out of you—
You can't believe it but it's true
She takes your old and makes it new
And little stars come out of you.'

'That was . . .' The woman shook her head when he was finished. Ray had a sinking feeling that she was going to tell him
it sounded just like an ad on TV. '. . . even better than "Asia
Sky".'

She slid the bag of sweets across the counter as he reached into
his jacket for his wallet.

'Don't even think about it,' she said. 'These are on me.'

Ray knocked on the door of Ash's parents' house but nobody
answered. He went across the street and sat on a wall under a
cherry tree. After a while, he realised he was hungry, so he started
to eat the sweets.

It was past nine when a car pulled up into the driveway and a
couple in their sixties got out. The man leaned into the back and
lifted Willow out. She was fast asleep with her rabbit backpack
still on. Ray remembered something he'd read once, a line in an
article that said you're not a man until you have carried your
sleeping child from your car into your house.

Now wasn't the time to wake his daughter up to explain that he
was fine. That people fought sometimes but that it wasn't the end
of the world. But there would be a time. He'd make sure of it.

Eilish was back in Dublin for the weekend. She'd promised to
come around and cook dinner for Claire but she was too tired so
she had brought an Indian takeaway instead.

'We're going to have to watch the news, I'm afraid.' Claire
switched on the TV and Dog opened one eye, stared blearily at the
screen then went straight back to sleep.

'Is it all over between Dog and Anne?' Eilish ladled chicken
korma into bowls.

'I don't know. He's not himself and he's off his food.'

Dog had been superglued to Claire ever since the night she'd
broken up with Richard. He followed her from room to room, sat

outside the bathroom door when she went to the loo and slept on her bed every night. He growled in his sleep and his huge paws twitched as if he were chasing something. Claire hoped it was Richard.

'He looks pale,' Eilish dipped her naan bread in her bowl, 'in a canine way.'

'Do you think he's still digesting the Rolex?'

'Long gone. You're not still thinking of giving that bastard a replacement, are you?'

Claire sighed. She'd found a second-hand Submariner for three thousand euros on eBay. If she decided to fix Mossy, too, she'd be broke all over again, but she had morals, even if Richard didn't. 'It's the right thing to do.'

Eilish snorted. 'I can think of righter things to do. Like breaking into his flat and sewing anchovies into his suits! I hope you're not having any regrets about kicking him out?'

Claire shook her head. 'None at all.' Richard had never been right. The signs had been there. The way he always had a shower after they made love. The way he had tried to fix everything. Her locks, her garden, her car, her career. He'd even tried to fix it so that Dog was out of the way so she would move in with him. She missed Richard's family, his lovely mother, his crazy sisters, but she didn't miss him at all.

'Sorry it's such a flying visit.' Eilish hugged Claire at the door. 'I have to be on location in Sneem at seven in the morning. Pete's picking me up at three a.m.'

'You and Pete,' Claire said.

Eilish blushed. 'We're just friends.' She pulled on her fake fur coat. 'With benefits,' she muttered.

'When did this happen?'

'I kissed him at the *Emerald Warriors* wrap party.'

Claire grinned. 'I knew something was going on. Pete is always singing in the background when I call you.'

Eilish put on her gloves. 'It's not a big deal. It's just a shoot thing. You know what they say. "What happens on *Warriors* stays on *Warriors*." Actually, they don't say that but I'm going to enjoy it while it lasts.'

'I can't believe I finally got through to you,' Niamh said. 'I've left about a million messages.'

The only reason Kelly had answered her mobile at all was because she was stuck on the off-ramp at Junction 8 on the M50 and she thought it was her clients ringing to ask why she was so late. 'I'm sorry. I've been meaning to get back to you. I was back in the States for the holidays and it's just been crazy since I got back.'

'We bumped into Nick in the supermarket last weekend. He told us everything.' *Everything?* 'Rory wants me to organise a little dinner, you know, to celebrate.' *A little dinner?* Kelly imagined a tiny meal on a tiny plate. Then it clicked. Niamh wasn't talking about the fact that she'd split up from Nick. She was talking about his Channel 5 job. 'How does Friday week sound?'

'I'm in the car now, Niamh. I'll check my diary and call you back, OK?'

Bath to the Future was in a retail park that had been built at the peak of the property boom but never completed. Kelly parked in the vast empty car park beneath a faded poster of a happy couple cavorting in a hot tub. Her clients, a stressed-looking couple in their thirties, were already inside, bickering by the slipper baths.

The whole place had a grim, abandoned look. Someone had written 'Fintan is a gas pig' in the dust on the mirror of a mocked-up wet room. Kelly led her clients around the massive warehouse, making copious notes, while they scrapped about hidden cisterns and suspended toilets.

'We can't pay a hundred and fifty euros a square metre for the flooring,' the man whispered after fifteen minutes of tense argument about tiles.

'But it's the house we'll live in for ever.' The woman looked as if she might cry.

'Not if we can't pay the mortgage.'

Kelly felt sorry for them. 'You don't have to decide right now. I can get you samples of all the tiles you like and then you can go home, have a glass of wine and talk it over.'

They both looked relieved. She went over to the sales counter, where a man with wispy eyebrows and a goatee was devouring a doughnut.

'I can only give you one sample.' He shifted a lump of doughnut from one side of his mouth to the other.

'You're kidding me, right?'

He took a slurp of coffee from a chipped red mug. 'New rule. People are going around all the showrooms, getting samples then using them to tile their bathrooms.'

'Seriously?' Kelly felt a sharp spasm of pain low on her left side. *No*, she thought. She couldn't get her period now. *Not here*.

The man saw her expression change and sighed. 'Look, if it's that important, I'll do it just this once. You can take as many samples as you need. Just bring them back, OK?'

'Thanks.' She held her breath as she scribbled her name and address on a pink docket. She had to hold on for just one more minute. 'Do you have a toilet?'

'We have eight hundred and seventy-six of them, sweetheart,' he said. 'Take your pick.'

The staff toilet was tiny with boxes of broken tiles in torn cardboard boxes stacked behind the door. The lino was grubby and there was a starburst of cracks in the mirror above the grubby sink.

Kelly leaned against the wall and hugged herself, rocking her body, trying to hold back her tears. She had her period. She'd known it was going to happen this time and she'd thought that knowing it would lessen the heartbreak, but it hadn't.

She couldn't go back out there and put a brave face on in front of her clients. She texted them to say that she had a family emergency and they could pick up their samples at the desk, then she unlocked the door and hurried to the exit, hoping they wouldn't see her.

The boy was about two years old with a fuzzy halo of fair hair. He was wearing a tiny plaid jacket over a pair of denim dungarees with a picture of a yellow JCB on the front. He was standing just outside the automatic glass doors, watching them open and close with a look of wonder.

'Where's your mom?' Kelly squatted down beside him.

He pointed at the vacant car park. There was nobody around.

He put his arms out and she hesitated and then picked him up. He was heavier than he looked and his breath smelled faintly of orange juice.

She jingled her car keys with the silver Tiffany's butterfly charm Nick had given her. The little boy laughed and made a grab for it.

'Let's find your mom. Where did she go? I wonder.'

The boy sucked one wing of the butterfly and frowned, as if he was trying to remember.

Kelly settled his warm weight on to her hip and went back into the warehouse. It was deserted. The couple had disappeared and the cash desk where the man had been drinking his coffee was abandoned.

She went back outside and shaded her eyes. KitchenLand, the warehouse next door, was boarded up and the car park in front of Platinum Furniture was deserted. She picked her way across the littered tarmac to the road and crossed to the other side. Some wide steps led down to a scrubby stretch of grass and, beyond it, to the banks of a murky canal.

The boy jingled her key ring and waved his free hand at some ducks that were bobbing on the water. 'Ugh!'

'Duck!' Kelly said. 'That's right. Clever boy!'

'Ugh!' He pointed again. The downy velvet of his cheek and the cereal smell of his hair made her feel woozy with longing.

She knew she should bring him back to the warehouse. That must be where his mom was. But he just wanted to see the ducks. She went down the steps. There was a scorched circle burned into the grass where a bonfire had been. The boy had started wriggling in her arms but she held on tight and kept going till she got to the canal.

'Duck!' She pointed at the bird that was pecking at a crisp bag.

'Ugh,' the boy said, uncertainly.

Kelly cupped her palm on the warm crown of his head and kissed his forehead. A tear slipped down her face and trickled on to his hand. Then he started to cry too. She bounced him and jiggled him but his wailing only got louder.

'Twinkle, twinkle, little star,' she sang into the dandelion fluff of his hair, 'how I wonder what you are.'

He stopped crying, abruptly, and looked at her.

'You know that song, don't you?' She laughed. 'What comes next, hmmm? Up above the world so high . . .'

The little boy picked up a handful of her hair and examined it shyly. 'Ike-a dimo-din-das-guy,' he sang softly.

Suddenly, Kelly heard voices on the road above them. 'Jason? Jason!'

Panic hit her behind the knees. She really hadn't done anything wrong but that wasn't how it was going to look. She put the boy down on the grass, making sure he was well away from the canal bank, then hurried along the path and hid behind a clump of bushes. Her heart was slamming against the walls of her chest. How could she just have picked him up and taken him like that? Had she lost her mind?

A security guard came running down the steps followed by a crying woman in a red puffa coat.

'Jason!' The woman sank on to her knees and wrapped her arms around the boy. Her eyes were streaming and her face was streaked with wet mascara. 'Don't ever cross the road on your own again!'

Kelly was standing by the Beetle when she remembered her keys. As she turned, she heard the whoosh of the electric doors and saw the security guard hurrying across the car park towards her with his fist clenched. She stood, with her head bent, waiting for him to arrive, already hearing the accusation in her mind. 'Are these yours?' His fist opened and he held out the silver Tiffany's butterfly key ring.

'Oh my gosh, yes!' she said. 'I went for a walk down by the canal and I must have dropped them on the grass.' She took the keys, dropped them, picked them up again then tried to open the door with shaking hands.

'A little boy who got lost found them. It's your lucky day.'

Kelly managed to open the door and sink into the driver's seat of the car before her legs gave way. 'I guess it is.'

Nick lifted the old man's legs one at a time and pushed his feet into a pair of trainers. He had finally agreed to see the physiotherapist. She was going to come every other day for a few weeks to make up for the sessions he had missed.

'The only reason I'm doing this,' he muttered to Nick, 'is so that you can go home, Claire can bring Dog back and I can get back upstairs.'

Nick was only half listening. He had made his mind up to tell Oonagh that he had to pull out of *The Ex-Factor* and whatever happened, he was going to do it. He hadn't taken any more pain-killers since the night of the storm. He couldn't believe that he'd let himself slip into that habit. He felt a twist of shame in his gut. He of all people should have known better.

The physio was in her mid-twenties and South African. She took off her hat and shook out her blonde hair, releasing a breath of the same citrus perfume that Kelly used.

Nick wanted to close his eyes and pretend that she was standing here in the hall with him but he forced himself to speak. 'I was just heading out.'

'You on TV today?' The physiotherapist smiled.

He shook his head. 'Radio.'

'You have a real gift for helping people. That's pretty special, you know.'

Nick felt so ashamed that he had to look away. 'I hope you have a gift for helping people too,' he said. 'Because my father is not looking forward to this. Do you mind letting yourself out?'

'Are you sure it's OK for your father to be on his own?'

He swallowed. 'I'll be dropping back at five to check on him.' If she knew who he was, he didn't want her to know that he was living here.

'I just feel like I've lost him,' the caller said.

Dom smirked. 'Have you looked down the back of the sofa, Mary?'

Nick ignored him. Maybe he couldn't do anything about the mess of his own life but the physio had been right, he did have a gift for helping other people. It was the only thing he had left. 'Don't mind Dom. Go on, Mary.'

'Well, he's just away so much. I'm here with the kids and he's off in Singapore or Koala Lumpur. When he gets back we barely have anything to say to one another any more.'

Dom chortled and clapped his hand over his mouth.

'That's something. Start with that,' Nick said. 'Just say to him, "I feel we have nothing to say to one another." That's the beginning of the conversation. There's an exercise I often use called—'

'Let us know how you get on,' Dom managed to gasp. 'And we'll be back with more problems after this break.' He slipped his headphones off and collapsed on the desk laughing.

Nick glared at him. 'What's so funny?'

'She said "Koala",' Dom snorted. 'Like the bear!'

Tara, the producer, came in and whispered something to Dom, who nodded and shot Nick a sly look. 'Back on air, Doc.' He put his headphones on again.

'Welcome back to "Problem Solved" with our agony uncle, Nick Dillon. We've got Caroline on line two. She's been holding for a while. What do you want to ask Doc Nick, Caroline?'

'Well,' the woman said, 'I'd like to know how he'd deal with a man who is a cheat and a liar.'

Her voice sounded strangely familiar and Nick began to wonder if she'd called in before. 'Are you talking about your husband, Caroline?'

'No,' she said. 'I'm talking about you. You put yourself out there like some kind of guru who can fix other people's marriages, isn't that right?'

Nick stared at Dom. Behind him, in the control room, Tara was glued to the window, watching him with undisguised glee. 'I never said I was a guru—'

'What about your own marriage?' Caroline cut him off. 'If you're so great at sorting out other people's problems, why aren't you living with your wife?'

'I'm not sure I know what you mean,' Nick stammered, but he had placed the voice now. It belonged to Mrs Cunningham.

'I think you do, Nicholas. You've been living in your father's house since before Christmas. We see you every day, sneaking in and out like a thief, hiding your car in the lane. Then we see you on the television, telling the whole country how to make their marriages work. Who do you think you are?'

Nick had to shoulder his way past half a dozen photographers at the gate of his father's house. He held his scarf over his face but he could hear the whirring of camera motor drives as he fumbled with the key and let himself in.

The physiotherapist was just coming out of the old man's room when he opened the front door. She picked up her bag and took her jacket off the coatstand. 'I heard you on the radio,' she frowned. 'Your personal life's your own business but that woman was right – you have no right telling other people how to solve their problems if you can't solve your own.' She opened the front door and closed it behind her.

Nick went upstairs and locked himself in the bathroom. The window was open and, as he leaned over to close it, a bald man poked his head out from the hedge below and took a picture. He leaned on the sink and let the wave of despair break over him. He knew how he was going to look in that picture. Like a guilty man who had just been found out.

25

Malachy MacDaid had once been regarded as one of Ireland's finest actors. He was in his seventies now and had played everyone from Macbeth to Mephistopheles. Claire felt star-struck just sitting across the table from him in the tiny sound booth. 'I suppose that I'm the camp potato,' he said to her in his marvellous voice. 'And you're the sexy strawberry. Do you do a lot of these radio advertisements?'

Claire shook her head. 'It's my first one.'

'It's not the Bard of Avon, my dear, but five hundred euros for an all-station package? That's more than you'd get paid for a week treading the boards on the stage.'

They slipped on their padded headphones. 'OK, let's go for a read,' a voice from the control room said.

'Call me a fussy spud but knobs of butter just don't do it for me,' Malachy lisped. 'So why don't you open my jacket and smother me in Killoran Double Cream?'

Claire attempted a husky Marilyn Monroe whisper. 'I'm a *berry* juicy strawberry. So why don't you tug off my stalk and dip *me* in a bowl of Killoran Double Cream?'

Malachy was right. It wasn't Shakespeare but it was all over in fifteen minutes.

She helped Malachy into his coat then found his scarf for him. When she was picking up her bag she noticed that he'd left his newspaper behind and ran up the steps to the street after him but he was gone. She decided to walk over to the café on the corner of Mespil Road to treat herself to a coffee as she had half an hour left on her parking meter.

She found a free table, curled up in a leather armchair and

opened the paper. Looking out at her, from page eight, was her brother's face. It was one of his publicity shots. His arms were folded and his head slightly tilted back with a smile that was entirely at odds with the headline.

'Relationship Coach Hides Secret Separation from Wife.'

Claire put her coffee down. She had suspected that Nick's marriage was in trouble and here was the proof.

'He is paid hundreds of euros an hour to advise couples on relationship issues. He claims that his simple techniques can save any marriage. But the shocking truth is that TV's Coach on the Couch, Nick Dillon (37), no longer lives with his wife.

'The couple are thought to have separated last year when Dillon left the townhouse he shared with stunning American, Kelly (30) and moved into the Milltown home of his retired father.

'Dillon had just landed a contract to co-present a new UK relationship reality TV show but the shocking revelations about his own personal life may now put him out of the running.'

Claire closed the paper. Poor Nick. He tried so hard to have a perfect life. Kelly was everything to him. Kelly and his work. How would he survive without them both?

Dog rolled over on his rug and groaned when Claire slipped on his lead. He didn't want a walk but if she stayed at home she knew she'd just spend the next hour Googling Nick to see what else had been written about him. Walking was good. Every time she felt angry with Richard, she just put her coat on and got out of the house. Every step she took put another little piece of distance between her and him.

Dog kept lagging behind and she almost had to drag him the last few hundred yards to the park. She sat on a bench inside the gate and he lay down, closed his eyes and put his huge grey head on her foot. 'Is this it?' she asked him, put out. 'Don't you even want to go and wind the swan up?' He lifted his shaggy head and gazed off at the pond wistfully, as if it were Everest and he was a retired explorer who would never make it up there again.

When she got him back home he folded himself up in the corner, put his head on the blue knitted draught snake and went back to sleep again. He hadn't been himself since the day Richard had tried to get rid of him. Did dogs get colds? She put on the kettle, made herself a cup of peppermint tea then sat at the table and opened her laptop to Google 'dog flu' but her fingers had other ideas and typed in 'Nick Dillon marriage break-up' instead.

There were dozens of links. The first one took her to an online edition of an Irish tabloid. The homepage had a shot of Nick pulling a scarf over his face under the headline '*TV Doc Pulls the Wool over His Lies*'. She felt a surge of protective anger. He didn't deserve this.

There was a second picture below it of a woman in her seventies with frosted, blonde hair. Mrs Cunningham. What on earth was *she* doing in a piece about Nick? Claire took a sip of her tea and scrolled down to the second headline.

'*An Alcoholic Mother. A Childhood Marked by Tragedy. A Neighbour Explains Why Life Coach Nick Dillon's Life Is Such a Mess!*'

Claire leaped up, knocking over the cup, splashing scalding-hot tea on to her jeans. 'The *bitch*!' she whispered. The Cunninghams had a long-standing vendetta against her dad but this was going too far. She sat down again and leaned her elbows on the table in the pool of cooling tea. She was so angry that she had to force herself to focus on the words.

'*In the wake of the revelations about his broken marriage, a neighbour in the suburban Dublin estate where Nick Dillon grew up has disclosed details that cast fresh light on his current troubles.*

'*Dillon's mother, Maura, a GP, died in 1983, in a drowning accident. But prior to that, his family life had already been shattered by her struggle with alcoholism.*

'"*Dr Dillon was frequently incoherent and abusive*," *says Caroline Cunningham, whose house overlooks the unkempt garden of Dillon's childhood home. "It was terribly hard on the children, they were both deeply troubled. Especially Nicholas, who was old enough to understand what was going on."*'

Claire couldn't read any more. She picked up her laptop and grabbed her keys. This was slander.

*

Nick was carrying the old man's lunch tray back down to the kitchen when the front door opened. Over Claire's shoulder he could see one of the photographers, the bald guy, pointing his lens.

'Close the door!' he said, quickly.

She slammed it, pulled off her green scarf, opened her satchel and took out her laptop. 'You need to see this.'

Nick shook his head. 'I know what the papers are saying about me.'

Her green eyes were bright with anger. 'I'm sorry about you and Kelly but this isn't just about you any more!' She snapped the laptop open, came over and held it up.

'Seriously,' Nick was still holding the tray. 'I'm in the middle of something.'

'Read it!'

He lifted his eyes and scanned the screen. 'Jesus!' he said, softly. 'Unbelievable.'

'We have to do something!' Claire's freckles were standing out in her pale face, the way they always had when she was sick or upset.

Nick felt his knees begin to give. He put the tray on a pile of old telephone books and sat down heavily on the second step of the stairs. 'What do you want me to do?'

'Get a printed apology from the paper. We can start by going next door and getting that *horrible* woman to admit that she made this all up.'

Nick stared down at the tired carpet between his knees. The brown and fawn pattern had worn away to the cream plastic weave in the middle of the step. 'We can't.'

'Nick, we have to. Please! I know you have your own problems and I'm sorry but we can't let the Cunning Hams get away with this! It's slander. We can go together.'

Nick looked up again. He wanted to put his arms around her, to soften the blow, but he couldn't because he was the one who had to deliver it. 'We can't get her to admit that she made it up,' he said softly, 'because it's true.'

'What?' Her face tightened. Two high spots of colour came into her cheeks.

'Mum had a problem,' he said, carefully. 'She had a lot of problems.'

She backed away from him. Her mouth was trembling, her eyes were filling with tears. He was watching his little sister lose her mother all over again.

'I'm sorry you had to find out like this.'

'I don't . . .' Her voice dropped to a whisper then failed her. 'But . . . but . . . I never saw her drinking,' she said, suddenly certain again.

'You did.' Nick sighed. 'You just didn't know it.'

He remembered Claire's first words. *'The bin is on fire.'* His mother had stupidly emptied an ashtray with a lit cigarette into it and the old man had jumped up from the table, pulled on a mitten and rifled through the bin until he found it. His mother had laughed at him but people died in fires. It happened all the time.

Nick had crept downstairs at night, for months afterwards, just to pour water in on top of the rubbish. He used to hide her lighters and matches. He sometimes hid her keys too, so she wouldn't take Claire out in the car.

Claire looked around the familiar hall trying to find something solid, something that could contradict what Nick had said. 'What about her practice?' she said. 'What about her patients?'

'Most days, nobody came.'

'No!' Claire had to get him to understand. What was wrong with him? 'She was working all the time. Don't you remember? She used to work late every night and at the weekends.'

'She used to lock herself in the surgery.' Nick shook his head. 'But she wasn't working.' He remembered the time the old man had to take the lock off the surgery door because she had passed out in there.

Claire swallowed. 'The bottles we found in the surgery, in the filing cabinet,' she said softly, 'they weren't yours, were they?' A tear ran down her chin and fell on to her collar. Nick took a crumpled tissue out of his pocket and held it out to her, but she shook her head and let her face fall into her hands. So he sat there, on the second to last step of the stairs and listened to the muffled sounds of her crying, waiting for what he knew was coming next.

'What about the day of my birthday?' Claire lifted her head.

Nick shook his head. 'You'll have to ask him.' He pointed at the surgery door. 'Ask your dad.'

He had his head bent over a crossword. He didn't look up but Claire knew, by his face, that he had heard them talking in the hall and knew everything.

'Dad?' she said. 'Is it true?'

He put the cap back on his pen and stared down at the paper for a long time without saying anything. He cleared his throat. 'I wanted to protect you, Claire. I didn't want to destroy the good memories you had of her.'

She crossed the room and stood in front of his chair. 'Had Mum been drinking on the day of the accident?'

'What good is it, going over all this now?' He pressed his lips between his teeth. 'It was nearly twenty-eight years ago.'

'You have to tell me,' she whispered.

He put his hand over his mouth so she had to lean forward to hear him. 'She had an alcohol level of two hundred and ten milligrams in her blood.'

'Tell me what that means.'

He looked up at her, his grey eyes rimmed with red. 'It means "yes".'

A bald man with a camera tried to take Claire's picture through the windscreen of the car. She accelerated out of the driveway so fast that he had to jump out of the way. Loud, gaspy wails escaped through her mouth. She was crying so hard that she could hardly see where she was going. She clipped the kerb as she turned on to the Milltown Road, there was a yelp from the back and a grey blur filled the rear-view mirror. It was Dog. She hadn't wanted to leave him at home on his own. She had forgotten that she had him with her. He was clinging to the seat by his claws but she couldn't slow down. She had to get as far away from the house as possible. If she stopped, the past would catch up with her.

Dog managed to squeeze himself through the gap between the seats and climb into the front. He loomed over her and tried to lick her face, then he curled up in the passenger seat and put his head on her knees. She tangled her fingers in the fur on the back of his neck and drove, only taking her hand away to change gear.

When she got to the end of the road, she didn't know where to turn. Left or right? She remembered how she used to navigate when her mum took her on magical mystery drives. Tears ran down her face and dripped onto Dog's ears and he twitched them away. Claire drove and drove. The suburban streets gave way to the dual carriageway and then she was on the N11 with the witch's-hat peak of the Sugarloaf ahead of her, silhouetted against the fading afternoon sky. She drove on past the turn-off for Ashford and then Rathdrum, and it was only when she saw a sign for the Beehive pub that she finally realised where she was going.

She held her breath as she took the turn and kept holding it as she followed the narrow road between the hedgerows, past tall trees that must have still been saplings when she was a child. She was half hoping that she wouldn't be able to find her way, but there was a sign at the next crossroads. The automatic barrier at the entrance to the car park was closed and she pulled over beside it.

The wind hurled a gritty handful of sand at her face as she opened the door, then it tore at her hair and pulled at the hem of her coat. The shock of being here again stopped her tears but her breath was still coming in broken gasps. She leaned her elbows on Mossy's sagging roof and looked up the track towards the dunes. The sky above them was low with gathering clouds. It was four o'clock on a March afternoon and it was already getting dark. What was she doing here?

She wanted to get back into the bright yellow Yaris. She imagined herself driving away, turning on the radio, going home. But instead she walked around and opened the passenger door. Dog stuck his head out and lifted his nose, sifting the scent of the sea air. One of his ears blew inside out and Claire turned it the right way round again. He licked her cheek then he climbed down stiffly and slipped through the gap at the end of the barrier as if he'd been here a hundred times before.

She watched him for a minute then she stepped on to the track, though her heart was hammering against her ribs as if it was trying to break out. Dog crossed the tarmac car park and disappeared through the gate that led through the dunes.

Claire hurried after him, stopping in the lee of the pebble-dashed wall of the public toilet to catch her breath. She had the same sickening feeling of foreboding that marked the beginning of one of her nightmares. 'Dog!' She wrapped her coat around her and ran to the gate. He was a long way down the sandy path, heading for the sea.

'Dog! Come back!' she yelled, but he disappeared between the dunes and she had to follow him, fighting her instinct to turn around with every step.

Then, through a gap in the dunes, she saw it. The beach where her mum had died. It was as she remembered it except that the sparkling blue sea was almost black today. The long golden strand was grey. The white walls of the ruined bathing hut were covered in layers of graffiti.

In front of the hut, Claire could see the exact spot where her mum had set out their picnic rug. She put her head down and trudged across the sand towards it. Her lungs were burning by the time she finally sat down and hugged her knees to her chest.

Everyone had known. Nick, the Cunninghams, her mother's patients. And Claire had known too, not that her mum was drunk, not that, but that something was wrong. That was why she had been so wretched the day of her birthday. Why she hadn't wanted to go for a drive. Why she had wanted her dad and Nick to be there.

'You're safe now. You can stop crying,' her mum had said when she'd pulled her out of the sea, but Claire hadn't felt safe. She'd been scared ever since they got into the car, that something bad was going to happen. And then it had.

There was a loud crash from the old surgery. When Nick got to the door, the table was lying on its side and the old man was crossing the room, on one crutch.

'None of this would be happening if you hadn't come back,' he said. 'What are you even doing here, Nicholas? When are you going to stop running away?'

Nick stared at him. 'You're talking to me about running away?

The man who's been hiding upstairs for nearly twenty-eight years.'

The old man limped past him into the hall. 'I'm going back up there now.'

'Go right ahead.' Nick picked up the table and set it back on its feet. He listened to the heavy thud of the crutch as his father dragged himself up step by step. Somehow he made it to the top. The bedroom door opened and when Nick heard the familiar sound of it closing, something snapped. He bounded up the stairs and tore it open again. 'This is your solution to everything, isn't it? Do nothing.' Nick never shouted. A part of him, detached, was listening in amazement.

The old man was collapsed on the bed. His face was grey, his forehead clammy with sweat. He had one arm shielding his eyes.

'We could have been killed in a car crash or a fire. I could have lost my eye that day that I fell. Claire could have drowned the day of the accident too. But you did nothing. You knew Claire blamed herself for what happened and you did nothing about that either. You let her think that she had the perfect mother and you made me go along with it.'

'We had to protect her.' The old man's voice was thin. 'She was only a child.'

'I was a child!' Nick yelled. 'I was a child too.'

It was a long time before Claire felt the cold. The damp seeped through her light coat into her jeans and she suddenly realised she was frozen. She remembered Dog. She looked up and down the empty strand. Way off in the gathering dusk, she saw a man and a boy packing away their fishing things. She got up and ran to catch them before they left. 'Have you seen a big, grey dog?' She had to shout to be heard over the wind.

The man pointed out at the ragged black ribbon of sea and there, silhouetted against the black, Claire saw a small grey blur. The boy laughed. 'We thought he was a seal. He's been out there for half an hour, scaring away the fish.'

Claire stood as close as she could to the edge of the surf and yelled his name. Finally, he heard her and he came paddling back and dragged himself out of the water. She grabbed his wet collar and started hauling him back towards the car park, but he was panting hard, and when she stopped to let him catch his breath he lay down on the sand on his side. He was drenched. His eyelashes were crusted with sand and his eyes had a cloudy, opaque look. 'You're an idiot,' Claire put her hand on his ribs, 'do you know that?' She could feel the thunder of his heart far beneath them.

Ten minutes passed, then twenty and Dog wouldn't move. 'Come on,' Claire stood up to encourage him, 'you just have to get to the car.' He tried to haul himself up but his legs went from under him. He looked at her apologetically. It was almost dark now, the wind was driving in from the sea, bringing sheets of steady rain that drilled the sand around them with tiny holes.

She slid her hands under Dog and tried to lift him but he was too heavy. She scanned the beach. They were alone. She pulled her phone out. It was almost out of battery. Eilish's number rang out. Nick's phone was switched off. She rang directory enquiries and asked for the number of the vet in Wicklow Town. The woman who answered said the vet would see Dog if Claire brought him in.

'I can't bring him in, that's the problem!'

'Try your own vet,' the woman said. 'If it's an emergency, maybe someone will come out for him.'

There was only a sliver of charge left when she got the number of Barnhill Veterinary Practice.

'Hello?' It was Shane.

'I've got an emergency.' Claire had to raise her voice above the wind. 'My dog has collapsed.'

'I'm just closing up here but the Veterinary Hospital is open all night. I'll give you the number.'

'It's Claire Dillon from *The Spaniard*. I'm in Brittas Bay in Wicklow. Dog collapsed on the beach and I can't get him back to the car.'

There was a long pause. 'You're going to have to get someone else to help you because—'

'I can't,' Claire said. 'My battery's nearly gone and—' Her phone went dead.

*

Claire took off her coat and spread it over Dog. Her jeans were soaked through now. She couldn't stay here till the morning if Shane didn't come, but she just couldn't leave Dog here on the beach either. She lay down beside him and squeezed in under the coat. She had finally come back to the place she'd been running away from all her life and now she couldn't leave.

Just when she had given up, Claire saw the yellow beam of a torch moving along the beach.

'How long has he been like this?' The hood of Shane's yellow rain jacket hid his face but she didn't have to see his eyes to tell he was angry.

'Since about an hour before I called you. He was swimming. I don't know how long he was in the water. I was distracted.'

He shook his head in disbelief, then lifted the coat and opened one of Dog's eyelids.

'He hasn't been well for a few days. He was out in the rain all night last week.' Claire's teeth were chattering. 'And he might have eaten a watch.'

Shane opened his bag and took out a stethoscope. 'Hold his mouth closed so I can listen to his heart.'

Claire put her hands around Dog's muzzle. He looked up at her through half-closed eyes and the tip of his tail twitched as if he wanted to wag it.

Shane put the stethoscope away and took out a thermometer. 'He's got a temperature,' he said after a minute, 'and he's very dehydrated. I'm going to need to put him on a drip and run some blood tests in the morning, so I'll have to bring him back to the surgery.' He shouldered his jacket off. 'You'd better have this.'

'It's okay—'

'Just put it on!'

She draped it over her shoulders. It was heavy and it smelled of him. She recognised the scent – a blend of antiseptic hand-wash and pencil shavings. She picked up his bag, he picked up Dog, and they made their way back through the driving rain to the car park.

The Land Rover was parked crookedly beside her car. 'Can you get my keys?' Shane looked over his shoulder. 'They're in the pocket of my jacket.' Claire found them and opened the back door of the Land Rover. Shane laid Dog down carefully on the back seat and covered him with a blanket.

'Come into the surgery at about half twelve tomorrow. I'll have the results of the blood tests back by then.' He closed the door. His jumper was soaked through and his hair was plastered to his head. It was too dark to see his eyes.

'You'd better take this.' She handed him back his jacket. 'Thank you for coming out.'

He opened the driver's door then slammed it shut and she stood watching his tail-lights until they disappeared and she was left standing in the dark.

Claire stood under the scalding water for as long as she could bear it but she was still frozen. She waited for the banshee wail of the pipes to begin but Richard's handyman had fixed them. The flat was eerily silent. She cleared a patch in the condensation and looked in the mirror. Water ran from her locket, down between her collarbones. Before the accident, the oval frames inside used to hold two tiny black and white pictures. One of Claire as a baby, one of Nick, but her mother's body had been in the sea for three days before it was found. Salt water had leaked into the locket. Their faces had disappeared, the way the image of her mother, the picture that she had always carried in her heart was disappearing now.

26

She had drowned when she was thirty-three but she had been gone long before that. Locked in her surgery, lost in a fog, leaving the old man to look after them. The part Nick hadn't understood was, she was a *doctor*. Why couldn't she make herself better?

The day of the accident, she hadn't turned up to bring him home from school. 'Would you like a lift, Nicholas?' Mrs Coyle rolled down the driver's window. Peter Coyle watched Nick warily from the back seat. They had been friends in fourth class but hadn't spoken since Christmas.

'No thanks,' Nick lied. 'My mum will be here any minute.'

'Are you sure?' Mrs Coyle shaded her eyes and looked doubtfully up and down the empty road.

Nick stared down at a piece of chewing gum that was stuck to the path. 'She said she might be a bit late today.'

Mrs Coyle started the engine. 'Well, if you're certain.'

He stayed exactly where he was outside the school gates until the red Fiat Panda had turned the corner at the top of the road, then he began the long walk home.

Mrs Coyle had brought him home to her house in December because she'd been picking Peter up from violin practice and she'd seen Nick waiting outside the school gate in the rain. She rang his mother but she was out. It was evening before she arrived to pick him up. Nick and Peter were on the landing playing with Peter's Transformers when she rang the doorbell.

'Is it Sean or Simon?' they heard her saying to Peter's dad when he opened the door. 'You look more like a Simon. I think it's the beard. It's kind of biblical.'

'It's Steve.' Mr Coyle sounded embarrassed. 'Come in, Maura.'

Mrs Coyle brought her into the kitchen and tried to make her drink some coffee. Nick and Peter could hear the row as it broke out.

'Why don't you let Steve drive you both home?' Mrs Coyle kept saying. 'He can walk back. He doesn't mind.'

'His name is Simon,' his mother said, 'and I'm fine to drive. So you can give me back my keys!'

'I don't think I—'

'Oh, please,' his mother said, wearily. 'Just give me the fucking KEYS!'

Peter looked at Nick with a mix of horror and admiration, but he pretended not to see. He stood up and went downstairs.

'The prodigal son!' His mother gave him a hug and kissed the top of his head. Beyond the sweet smell of Juicy Fruit and the minty smell of smoke, he could smell the vodka. A sweet, oily, sly smell that gave him a pain in his stomach.

Mr and Mrs Coyle stood at the front door and watched them getting into the Citroën.

'Bye, Simon!' his mother said. 'Tell Garfunkel I said hello!' She began to sing 'The Sound of Silence'. 'Did you have fun?' she turned to Nick.

He shrugged. 'It was OK.'

'Ok-ey smok-ey!' She pushed the dashboard cigarette lighter. He was supposed to open the glove compartment and take a cigarette out of the green and white packet and light it. He loved pressing the white tip against the red element. The crackle as threads of tobacco caught fire. The first thin plume of grey smoke. But, this time, he didn't move, and after a minute, she leaned over and took out the pack herself.

The car swerved into the middle of the road as she bent her head to light the cigarette and the spaghetti hoops and toast Nick had for tea came back up into the back of his mouth and he thought he might be sick.

She blew a wobbly smoke ring. 'You've got to stop caring what people think about you otherwise you'll always feel the way you do right now.'

Nick leaned as far away from her as he could, pushing himself against the passenger door until the handle of the window was digging into his chest. He pressed his face against the glass, watching the mist of his breath fogging it up and then clearing, and he wished that she were dead.

The day of the accident, Nick had gone the long way home so he didn't have to pass Peter Coyle's house. He didn't want Mrs Coyle to know that his mother had forgotten to pick him up again. He worried, all the way, about Claire. Why hadn't she been at school today? It was her birthday, she'd been looking forward to it.

The house was locked and his mother's car wasn't in the drive. He climbed over the wooden gate at the side of the house. Claire's school bag was on the grass beside two deckchairs. A line of ants was marching up the leg of the table past a half-full ashtray to a plate of chocolate biscuits, and then marching down the other leg carrying crumbs.

There were two glasses on the table. One was half full of milk. The other had a lipstick mark and the remains of something brown and sticky at the bottom. He took off his own heavy school bag, sat under the chestnut tree and took out the birthday card his dad had bought for him to give to Claire.

It had a picture of a dog on it and the words 'Yappy Birthday!' Claire's present was going to be a dog. Nick felt fizzy with excitement thinking about it. It would be his dog too. Claire was nice about sharing.

He tried to read his school books to pass the time but they were too boring. After a while he felt thirsty. He took the milky glass to the tap by the back door and filled it. The water was warm and rusty but he drank it anyway, then he brushed a few ants off the chocolate biscuits and ate them too. After a while he realised he needed the toilet. He held on until it hurt so much that he had to go, then he peed at the end of the garden by the hedge. He saw Mrs Cunningham watching him from her window and he pretended he was looking for a bird's nest until she had gone away.

He sat down under the tree again and then he must have fallen asleep. When he opened his eyes it was dark and someone was shaking him. There were pins and needles in his legs. 'Nicholas?' It was a Garda in a uniform with a hat. 'You'd better come inside.'

Every light in the house was on. There were two more Gardaí standing in the kitchen beside the fridge. Nick wondered if the house had been burgled, and then he saw his father's face and he knew that it was worse than that.

People kept arriving with plates of food. People who had never come to the house before. Neighbours, two teachers from school, his swimming coach's wife. They milled around drinking tea and whispering, but his father couldn't speak to anyone who tried to talk to him. Mr Lennon from the newsagent's shook Nick's hand and two women who worked in the library hugged him. The smell of their perfume made him feel sick.

Claire was in her pyjamas. She was passed around the women like a parcel, her eyes round, her face pale from exhaustion. When she was put down for a moment, Nick took her hand and brought her into the living room then closed the door and turned the key.

He helped her to do a jigsaw – a cartoon horse jumping over a pile of flowerpots.

'You know the puppy I was supposed to get for my birthday? I don't want him any more!' She was trying to fit a piece of saddle into the sky.

'It's OK,' he said. 'I don't think he's coming now.'

After the jigsaw was finished, they sat on the corduroy sofa watching a quiz programme with the sound turned down, and Claire fell asleep on Nick's shoulder while he stared at the multiple-choice answers, trying to guess the questions.

a) John McEnroe
b) Jack Nicklaus
c) Rod Laver
d) Bjorn Borg

He hadn't really meant it when he wanted his mother to die. He wished that she would walk through the door now but he was old enough to know that wasn't going to happen. Claire's hair was still damp and it had gone crazy, the way it did when it got wet. He covered her with a woollen poncho that someone had left on the sofa. She could have drowned, he thought. It could have been her instead of his mother, or it could have been both of them.

*

Claire had been awake for most of the night. She woke up groggy and late with barely enough time to make it to Shane's surgery by half twelve.

The receptionist sent her through to the exam room. It was empty but after a moment Shane brought Dog in. He looked bedraggled but more like himself again. When he saw her he gave an excited little whinny and came over and stuck his long snout under her arm, then leaned against her until she had to steady herself against the table. Shane's dark eyes widened in surprise.

'I kept him,' Claire rubbed Dog's ears, 'it's a long story.' She was suddenly aware of how awful she must look. She hadn't dried her hair last night, her eyes were puffy. She was wearing a pair of dog-walking jeans and the old Smoke Covered Horses T-shirt she sometimes slept in. But Dog was OK, that was all that mattered.

'Listen.' Shane folded his arms. His tan had faded. The white ring mark on his left hand had disappeared. 'I need to be straight with you. Dog's not well, Claire.'

'But he looks fine.'

'His white blood cell count is five times what it should be and his spleen is inflamed.'

Claire dug her hands into the wiry fur at the back of Dog's neck. 'He just got drenched last week and then again last night.'

'I think he has lymphocytic leukaemia.'

'*Leukaemia?*' Claire stared at him.

'I'm sorry. I could do a definitive test but that would mean extracting bone marrow and I don't want to put him through that. I'm pretty sure about this diagnosis, I've seen it before.'

She swallowed. 'What's the treatment?'

'Chemotherapy. Blood transfusions.'

'Well, you can do that, can't you?'

'It's expensive and invasive and—'

'I can pay for it.' If she didn't get Richard a new watch or get Mossy fixed, she could.

'Look,' Shane said, softly, 'Dog's at least fourteen years old, maybe more. It's a very aggressive therapy and there's only a thirty per cent chance it'll work. The best thing you can do is let him go.'

Claire stared at him. 'You mean he's going to *die?*'

'Not today. I think he's got another couple of weeks or so. I can give him some steroids but the best thing you can do is take him home and make him comfortable until he's ready to go.'

'No! I can't.' She bent her head. 'I'm sorry.'

'Right.' She felt him looking at her but she couldn't meet his eyes. 'Well, we can let him go now, if that's easier. I'll just get his file.' He turned away to face the computer and sat down. There was a volley of barking from the next room where the cages were and Dog shrank back against Claire's legs.

'It's OK,' she whispered. 'You don't have to go back there.' She thought she had cried out every millilitre of water in her but now a new tear streaked down her face and plopped on to one of Dog's ears. He twitched it and gave her an offended look.

'Wait!' she said to Shane. 'I'll take him home.'

Nick made an omelette and carried it on a tray upstairs. The old man was already dressed, leaning on his crutch, when he opened the bedroom door. 'Can you help me back downstairs?'

Nick blinked at him in disbelief. 'I don't get it. All you've ever wanted to do since the moment you came home from the hospital is get back up here and now you want to go back down again?'

'This is where you're sleeping,' the old man mumbled. 'I don't want you having to carry everything up and down.'

'Fine!' Nick said through gritted teeth. 'Whatever.' They were both out of breath by the time they got down to the surgery.

'Wait!' The old man put his hand on Nick's arm as he turned to go back upstairs for the tray. 'I want . . .'

'What?' Nick was so exhausted that the thought of having to climb the stairs again was almost unbearable.

The old man's face crumpled, as if he was having a spasm of pain. His fingers plucked at Nick's sleeve, pinching the fabric and letting it go. 'I want to say that I'm sorry.'

Nick and his therapist had role-played this scene at least a dozen times over the years. Nick had listed all the good reasons why he couldn't, wouldn't, forgive the old man. But what was the point in saying them now? What good would they do?

Instead, he covered the old man's hand with his own, just for a moment, then he straightened up. 'We've got to put the past in the past,' he said, automatically. 'We can't change it. All we can do is move forward.' Then he went upstairs to get the tray before the omelette got cold.

All the photographers were gone except one, the bald man in a sheepskin jacket. Every time Nick looked out, he was huddled under the fuchsia, looking frozen. Nick was starting to feel sorry for him. He made a mug of Nescafé, put a few of his father's Jaffa Cakes on a plate and opened the front door a crack.

'Put the camera down,' he called, 'and I'll bring you out a coffee.'

The photographer lowered the camera. 'Any comment on the news?'

'What news?'

'We had a tip-off that you and Oonagh Clancy are out of the running for *The Ex-Factor*.'

Poor Oonagh, Nick thought tiredly. 'No comment.' He handed over the cup and the plate.

'Jaffa Cakes!' The photographer picked one up. 'I loved that ad! Full moon.' He took a bite. 'Half-moon.' He took another bite, then popped the last little crescent of biscuit into his mouth. 'Total eclipse!'

Nick went back inside and closed the door. He had no diary to check. No coaching sessions booked. The producer of the OO show had fired him by email. '*Sorry, Nick. Not my decision. Bitchard and Rudie strike again.*' Classy.

Tara from Fish had left a short gleeful message to say that his contract had been 'terminated'. There were a couple of messages from journalists wanting to interview him to get 'his side of the story'. But there was only one person he wanted to talk to and there was no point in calling her.

Kelly turned over and a plate slid off the bed on to the floor. It wasn't important, she thought, curling up in the dark beneath the duvet, because any minute now the phone would ring.

Somebody must have seen her, carrying the little boy across the road. Someone driving by or at an upstairs window of the bathroom showroom or in the estate on the other side of the canal.

And if they hadn't, then she must have been caught on a CCTV camera out on the street and leaving the showroom. Someone would review the footage and they'd see her crossing the road with the little boy in her arms. They'd trace her car and come and find her.

So it didn't matter that she hadn't left the house in days or answered the phone, or checked her emails. Or that a bowl of half-eaten pasta was upturned on the green silk Laura Ashley rug on the bedroom floor. Because any minute now, someone would hammer on the door and she'd have to explain what she'd done.

She hugged her knees to her chest. It was Nick's fault. She couldn't have a child of her own. That was why she had done it. If he hadn't walked out on her, it never would have happened.

Ray was supposed to be working on a jingle for a Malaysian brand of dog food. Sounds Familiar wanted a 'Walk on the Wild Side' soundalike with woofs instead of words. But, instead, he'd spent the morning tweaking 'Little Stars'. Every time he played it, he thought that the woman in the shop might just be right. He'd written a song. He'd written a good one. And now, he thought, putting his guitar down, he'd better leave it alone, before he screwed it up.

He made himself a pot of coffee and went online. The papers still had the knives out for Claire's brother and a couple of them had now picked up on the story about her mother. Ray had had some pretty nasty stuff written about him during the Horses split. The fact that the tabloids could eat your life up and spit it out wasn't news to him, but it had to be news to Claire. He wished he could help her but she'd made it pretty clear she didn't want his help when he'd told her about that creepy boyfriend of hers.

His phone rang and he picked it up, hoping it might be her, but it was Ash. 'Are you at home? I was going to drop in.'

'Have you got Willow? How long can she stay?'

'It's just me. I want to have a quick chat.'

Ray didn't like the sound of this. 'When will you get here?'

The doorbell rang. 'I'm here now.'

*

'D'you want coffee? I just made a pot.'

'No.' Ash was standing at the window, looking nervous, with her hands in the pockets of her brown leather jacket.

'That's Willow's spot.' Ray smiled. 'That's where she stands to spy on the neighbours. She'd make a great private detective.'

Ash stared down at the bare patch of earth where the nettles had been. 'I'm taking her back to live in London.'

Ray blinked at her. 'Why?'

'It's not working out here. Living with my parents is a nightmare.'

'You can move in here for a while!' Why hadn't he thought of this before? 'I've got a spare bedroom and loads of free time. I can bring Willow to school and pick her up and—'

'It's not about childcare, Ray. Maurice and I are going to give it another try.'

'I thought that was all over now.'

'So did I.' She sighed. 'But he came to Dublin to try to persuade me to go back. I knew if I saw him with Willow I'd cave in so I left her with you. Then you brought her back in that terrible state and she just wanted to hold on to him all evening. He's her dad. I have to give it another try. I owe it to her.'

Ray felt his chest tighten. 'I'm her dad.'

'Ray, Maurice has been around for her since she was a few months old.'

'Really?' Ray said sharply. 'How can someone be around when they're touring for ten months of the year?'

'That's all changing. He's leaving In Your Dreams. He's a good man. You should be glad that Willow has someone like that in her life!'

Ray held the cooling cup of coffee in his hands. 'Someone who's put half of Colombia's GDP up his nose?'

'He went into rehab when we met. He doesn't even drink nowadays. And, sorry, but you can't talk, you got into a punch-up in broad daylight when you were supposed to be looking after your daughter.'

Ray swallowed. 'When are you leaving?'

'A week, maybe two.'

'I need to see Willow before you go.'

'I'm not sure that would be a good idea. It'll just upset her more. But we'll be back in Dublin from time to time.'

Ray put his coffee down. A dark wave of it sloshed over the rim of the cup on to the table. 'So that's it? You keep Willow a secret from me for six years. You use me as a babysitter. And now that you've patched things up with your boyfriend, you want me out of the way again?'

'It's not about *you*. It's about what's best for *her*. Being a parent isn't just about going to bloody petting zoos and playing word games. She misses London, she misses Maurice. Don't you want her to be happy? Because that's what being a dad means, Ray. That's what it's all about.'

Pete had given Eilish the day off so she'd driven up to Dublin, bringing chicken soup for Dog that he didn't eat and a bottle of wine that sat untouched on the table. She made peppermint tea, instead, and sat beside Claire on the yellow velvet sofa, patting her back and passing her tissues.

'Your poor mum.' She pressed her lips together. 'She must have been so lonely.'

'I know.' Claire was tearing a tissue into tiny shreds. 'I thought her life was perfect. Now all I can think is how lonely and unhappy she must have been. Why didn't she get help?'

'It was different back then.' Eilish shook her head. 'There was still such a stigma about being an alcoholic and she was a woman and a doctor. That would have made it so much harder.'

Dog was lying with his head under the sofa. Claire tucked her bare feet beneath him. He let out a huge shuddering sigh. 'I thought I knew her, but I didn't.'

'Of course you did.'

'Not really.' Everything Claire remembered was changed through the lens of what she knew now. 'I think I was beginning to realise that something was wrong but I didn't understand what it was.' She put her hands over her face. 'I was awful to her the day she died. She kept trying to find ways to make me happy because it was my birthday and I was . . .' She pressed her knuckles hard against her mouth until her teeth bit into the inside of her lip. 'She went back into the sea because I wouldn't

305

stop crying. She was trying to get my swimming ring. That's why she drowned. It was my fault.'

Dog turned around three times, trampling the duvet, then lay down with his long, bony back to Claire. Up close, his long, shaggy coat was every shade of grey, from charcoal to smoke, to slate, to silver.

He whimpered as he settled himself and she slipped an arm around him and held on to one his heavy paws. She did it to soothe him but it comforted her. She stroked the rough pads with the little tufts of fur between them.

The last thing she remembered before she went to sleep was what Eilish had said. She had put her hands on Claire's shoulders and pulled her close until they were eye to eye, waiting patiently until Claire had finally looked back at her. 'It wasn't anyone's fault. It was an accident.'

27

'Call me when you think he's ready to go,' Shane had said.

'How will I know?' Claire asked him.

'You'll know.'

That first week, she still drove Dog to the park. She would help him out of the car and they would get as far as the bench near the gate, then he'd have to have a lie-down and, after a while, he'd get up and she'd drive him home again. But at the start of the second week, when she put on her coat, he didn't even lift his head up so she put his lead away in a drawer, at the back, where neither of them had to look at it.

The first week, she could still get him to eat. Half a smoked mackerel. A few slices of salami. A bowl of yogurt. But his appetite gradually dwindled away to nothing. She was supposed to hide his steroid tablets in a spoonful of peanut butter or a lump of pâté but he just sniffed the spoon and put his head down on his paws, so she had to wedge his jaws open with one hand while she pushed the tiny white pills down his tongue and into his throat. He looked slightly alarmed, but also impressed, as if this was a trick he'd taught her. Afterwards, he licked her hand to thank her. How had she ever been scared of him? she wondered.

He spent most of the day lying on the rug in the living room with his head on one of her winter boots or his favourite draught snake. She had told her agent that she was going away for a couple of weeks so she could stay with Dog. She sat on the sofa with her bare feet tucked under him, losing her mother again.

She unpacked her memories one by one and turned each one over in her mind, in the light of what she knew now, and let the truth float up to the surface.

The night her mum had woken her and they had sat for hours in the garden in the snow. That sickening clench in her stomach on magical mystery drives. The evening she'd crept downstairs and seen her mum dancing in her slip in the living room, with her arms draped around her dad's neck. The silence when Claire pressed the disc of the old stethoscope to the door of the surgery and listened.

'You mustn't disturb your mum when she's busy,' her dad had said.

Claire had built her own life around the certainty that her mum was perfect, then she had hated herself for failing to measure up. And nine months ago, on her birthday, she had given herself one last year to be like someone who had never existed.

She tipped her box of mementoes on to the sofa. The empty perfume bottle and the dried-up stump of lipstick. The yellowing lace dress, the single Aran mitten with a scorch mark on the palm, the hairbrush with the few copper hairs still caught in the bristles. She pulled the worn rubber band off the stack of photographs and let them fall through her fingers on to the floor. They pooled around Dog on the rug. She picked one up, then another, searching them for some sign of what she knew now. But the woman in the photographs looked as carefree as she always had. She was still keeping her secrets. Claire felt a rush of anger which broke and dissolved into a flood of protective love for this beautiful, flawed stranger who she could never know.

Claire stared into the chill cabinet for a long time and then she called Eilish. 'How do you know when a chicken is really good?'

'It has a halo and a saintly smile on its beak?'

'I'm serious. I need to find a good one. Dog hasn't eaten anything for nearly three days.'

'Maybe you should just get him a fresh cod from the chipper. Dogs love fish.'

'I think that's cats.'

'Roast cat. He'd eat that.' Eilish was on constant mood-lightening duty. 'You catch one. I'll cook it.'

'Please!' Claire said. 'I'm freezing here.'

'Just go for the one with the plumpest thighs.'

Claire was deliberating between two when she heard a familiar voice.

'Saoirse, what a lovely name. Are the poussins free range?'

She turned around and there was Richard, with his back to her, talking to a girl in a Superquinn uniform.

'These ones are.' Saoirse handed him a pair of pathetically small chickens in a styrofoam packet. As he reached out to take them, his cuff rode up and Claire saw his wrist.

'Your Rolex!' she gasped.

Richard turned, surprised. 'I bought another one,' he said, hastily, as he tried to pull his cuff down. 'In Weir's.'

'They didn't have any in Weir's!'

His face began to flush.

Claire took a step forward. 'You pretended Dog had eaten it so I'd feel bad and get rid of him, didn't you?'

'Calm down.' Richard held up the poussin packet, like a shield. A tiny trickle of blood escaped from the plastic and splashed onto his sleeve.

'You bastard!' Claire reached into the cabinet, grabbed the nearest chicken and hurled it at him hard. It hit him in the stomach with a wet thud then landed with a crack on his foot. It was an extra-large chicken with very plump thighs.

Richard yelped and fell back against a picnic display. Packets of paper cups and plates and straws rained down around him.

'Are you OK?' Saoirse asked.

'No!' Claire said. 'He's a liar and a control freak and he tried to kill my dog.'

The assistant looked horrified.

'If my toe is broken, you'll pay for it, Claire!' Richard had slipped off his moccasin to massage his foot.

'I'm sorry,' Saoirse whispered to Claire. 'I'm afraid you'll have to pay for that as well or take it with you.' They looked at the chicken, lying on the tiled floor, then at Richard, who was limping away, with one shoe on and one shoe off, and then they both began to laugh.

'Any word from Claire?' the old man asked. Nick shook his head. He'd been expecting her calls but they hadn't come. He wished he had the energy to call her himself, to try to help her through all this, but he could barely get himself through the day.

'Are you going out?'

Nick hadn't been planning to. Every time he left the house, someone had a go at him. He understood why everyone was angry. Why the girl at the checkout in Tesco had called him a fraud and why the man who was digging a hole in Baggot Street had climbed out of it just to shout at him and why a nice old lady in a Mercedes had rolled down her window at a red light and flipped him the bird. But understanding didn't make it any easier to deal with. 'Do you need something, Dad?'

'I was wondering if you were going to the shops. I thought, you could just call in on Claire to see if she's OK.'

'I think she just needs some time. She has a lot to process.' Nick picked up the tray. *Process*, he thought sadly, was too clinical a word to describe what went on in the big, messy engine of a person's heart.

'I need the prescription for these painkillers filled again.'

Great, Nick thought. That would give the woman in the pharmacy another chance to glare at him. 'Okay.'

'You might pick up a couple of lamb chops,' his father said. 'And some potatoes.'

Chops and potatoes? Nick raised an eyebrow; that was adventurous. His father hadn't eaten anything except omelettes and Jaffa Cakes for twenty-seven years. 'Anything else?'

The old man stared at the floor. 'I told her I'd take you and Claire away from her if she didn't stop but I couldn't do it. I thought it would kill her if I did that. It was my fault that she got so bad.'

'It wasn't anyone's fault.' Nick sighed. 'It's a disease.'

'What about what I did afterwards?' the old man said, quietly. 'What about leaving you and Claire to look after yourselves? Is cowardice a disease too?'

Nick dumped the dishes into the sink and ran the hot water over the empty plates. This morning the old man had asked for bacon and sausages and he'd just eaten the Tesco lasagne that Nick had been planning to have for lunch. He'd have to make himself an omelette, he thought. He couldn't face the supermarket again.

His phone rang and he retrieved it with a soapy hand. 'Nick, I need to talk to you.' Oonagh's voice took him by surprise. It was her professional television voice. 'Tork tu yo' instead of 'tawk-ta-ya'. This was the first time she'd called since the papers had revealed that his marriage was in trouble.

'Oonagh, I've left a dozen messages for you. I just wanted to say how sorry—'

She cut across him. 'Can we meet for coffee in an hour?'

'I'm not sure meeting is such a great idea. I'm still getting a lot of flak when I go out in public.'

'Three o'clock? Pasta Tosca?' There it was again, Oonagh's fake TV twang. 'Posta Tosca?'

Nick had shot down her dream job. He supposed that he owed her a chance to rip him apart.

Oonagh was sitting under the awning outside the restaurant. She was wearing a skin-tight red dress and no coat, even though it was a chilly afternoon. Nick guessed she must be going someplace afterwards.

'You don't want to put up with the abuse we're going to get if we stay out here,' he said. 'We'd better go inside.'

She frowned but she got up and followed him and he found a table at the back. He went to the counter and ordered coffees from an Italian waitress who seemed blissfully unaware that she was serving Ireland's most hated man.

'So, "no skeletons" and "happily married".' Oonagh shook a sachet of sugar. 'That's what you told Curtis.'

'I know. And I lied. I want to apologise to you again, for everything.'

'It doesn't matter.' She was sitting up very straight the way she did when she was on-screen.

'It does. I completely undermined the credibility of the OO show and it's my fault that you won't get to present *The Ex-Factor*. You were really straight with me about the problems you were having in your marriage but I didn't have the decency to tell you I was having problems in mine.'

'Nobody's perfect.' She fluttered her eyelashes and gave him a dazzling smile.

Nick was confused. He had been expecting tears and fireworks. 'You're being really kind about this. Way kinder than I deserve.'

'Well . . .' She stood up. She hadn't even touched her coffee. 'Thanks for meeting me. I have to go.' She stood up and glanced around as if she was looking for someone.

They'd only been here for five minutes but it was pretty big of her to have met him at all, Nick thought. He put some change on the table and they walked out into the street.

'Thanks,' he said, 'for being so incredibly understanding about *The Ex-Factor*. Do you know what you're going to do? Do you have a Plan B?'

She put her hands on his shoulders and looked up at him with a dreamy expression, then she kissed him hard on the mouth. She pulled away. 'I am the queen of Plan B, Nick. You take care now.' She hurried away, surprisingly quickly, in her towering red heels.

Nick wiped a smear of lipgloss off his mouth with the back of his hand and stared after her. 'What,' he thought, 'was that all about?'

'Howya, boss!' a bald man in a sheepskin jacket said, stepping into the street to pass Nick. He looked familiar but Nick couldn't place him. He nodded then turned away quickly in case the man decided to have a go.

Nobody was going to come and question Kelly about taking the little boy. The security guard had been right. It had been her lucky day.

The bedroom looked like a squat. The duvet cover was stained. There was a puddle of pasta sauce on the pale green rug. The baby clothes she had unpacked at Christmas were strewn around the floor. Things were even worse downstairs. She hadn't loaded the dishwasher or done a wash for weeks. She was going to have to tackle it.

She pulled off the wrinkled cotton nightdress she'd been living in and ran a shower. She soaped herself, washed and conditioned her hair and shaved her legs. She put on clean grey sweats then went back into the bedroom, sat on the padded blue velvet stool and plugged in her hairdryer. Then she sat there staring at her pale face in the mirror. What was the point of drying her hair and putting on make-up and cleaning the house? Who was she doing it for? She didn't care about any of it and Nick wasn't here.

She went downstairs with her hair still wet and took the last carton of home-made courgette soup out of the freezer. It was labelled and dated in her own neat handwriting. There was even a little 'v' for vegetarian. Every time she had cooked for herself and Nick, she had made extra to freeze. She'd been living on these meals for weeks now. Eating risotto for breakfast and Thai curries at three in the morning.

While the soup was warming she collected a pile of unopened post from where it was lying in the hall and dumped it on the kitchen table. She pulled out an envelope and tore it open. It was a Christmas card. She stared at the photograph of Rory and Niamh on the front. Linh stood between them, beaming, waving a sparkler like a wand. 'Merry Xmas!' it said, 'from our family to yours!' She stuffed it quickly back into the envelope and tossed it away.

She opened her laptop and stared at the dozens of emails in her inbox, then composed an 'out of office' reply and shut it again. She sat at the table eating the soup while she listened to her phone messages. Most of them were from clients, a few were from Niamh, there were at least a dozen from Nick. She skipped through them without listening. The last message was from Pauline, the woman whose garden she'd fallen in. That day felt like a hundred years ago now.

'Hello, Kelly. I'm not hassling you about the estimate for the extension or anything. We probably can't afford it anyway! I was just worried about you that day when you were here. Hope the Clomid is doing its job and not driving you too crazy. Call if ever you want to talk or even scream. I understand what you're going through.'

Kelly's hand hovered over the call-back button. Then she imagined what Pauline would think if she had seen her crossing the road with the little boy. She pushed her bowl away, went upstairs and got back into bed.

28

Dog couldn't stand up. Claire tucked a towel under his hind-quarters and hoisted him up on to his feet and they made their way, slowly, out into the garden. He stood blinking in the watery sunshine, for a moment, sniffing the air, and then his back knees folded beneath him. He looked up at her, confused. His pupils were tiny black blurs in the hazy yellow irises of his eyes.

'This is good,' she said, 'let's just stay out here for a while.'

She went back inside for a rug and some cushions. She thought that maybe after he'd had a rest he'd be strong enough to get up again, but after an hour he was still there. She lay down beside him, face to face. His mouth was slack, his nose was dry and the fur on his face was clumped and dull.

'Good Dog,' she whispered to him. He frowned and his eyes half opened then closed again.

She rubbed his back and stared up through the metal matrix of the fire escape trying to find shapes in the clouds, trying not to feel the cold concrete pressing against her back through the rug. But after an hour, all the clouds merged into one and Dog still hadn't moved and she knew what she had to do next.

Dog's ears pricked up. They turned, like satellite dishes, tracking her dad's voice as he limped into Claire's garden, leaning on Nick's arm. By the time he got to the bottom step, Dog had managed to haul himself to his feet. He led them all, unsteadily, into the house then collapsed, exhausted, just inside the door.

Her dad lowered himself into a chair. 'How are you, Claire?' He was looking straight at her, something he never did.

'I'm OK.' She had been angry with him for not telling her about her mum but the anger had burned itself out. She couldn't bear to watch him saying goodbye to Dog. She made an excuse and went into the living room and sat on the sofa. After a minute, Nick followed her in.

He sat in the armchair opposite her and tented his fingers. 'Are you OK?'

'I don't know.'

'I knew you blamed yourself for what happened. I should have told you years ago.'

'We haven't really seen each other for years, though, have we?'

Nick's face was drawn and there were dark shadows under his eyes. It must have been hard for him, she thought, to keep that secret for so long.

'Can I ask you something?'

He nodded. 'You can ask me anything.'

'Why did she start drinking?'

His shoulders lifted and then dropped. 'She always had highs and lows but, after you were born, they got really bad. Sometimes I think it might have been post-natal depression. But honestly, I don't know.'

The draught snake used to have a little red leather forked tongue, but Dog had nibbled it off. Claire picked at a loose thread of blue wool. 'If you knew it wasn't my fault,' she said quietly, 'then why did you hate me?'

'I never hated you.' Nick remembered the first time he'd held his little sister. The way the back of her neck smelled like a sea-shell. The way she used to hold his hand so tightly when they went into a dark cinema. That school picture he'd kept of her on his desk in Washington. Claire had been the one good thing about his childhood, before the accident and after.

'But you had to look after me,' she was saying. 'You had no proper childhood.'

'*The children of alcoholics. Always a child, never a child,*' Nick's therapist used to say. Claire hadn't grown up at all and he had grown up too fast. 'It helped me, having you to look after,' he said.

'What was she really like?'

The intensity in her green eyes made him want to look away but

315

he didn't. His throat tightened as he tried to find the truth. 'She was clever and funny and she didn't give a damn what other people thought. She could be hard and sarcastic, but I think,' he paused and then continued, 'it was because she was angry with herself. Underneath it, she was shy and even kind of vulnerable. And she was really, really beautiful.' He looked down at his hands and then he looked up at his sister. He swallowed. 'At her best, she was a lot like you.'

The receptionist at Barnhill told Claire that Shane would be there as soon as he could. He arrived too quickly, carrying a small black bag. Dog was still lying on the floor by the door. He hadn't even moved when Nick and her dad left. Shane knelt beside him and Claire turned away and looked at her own blurry reflection in the glass door. She had that feeling again, as if her heart was stuck in her throat. 'Do you have to put him down now?' Her voice sounded thin. 'I think he's going to die anyway.'

Shane sighed. 'It might take a few days. Nature isn't always kind. I think he's ready to go now. But why don't I make us a coffee and you can think about it?'

He pulled his jumper off and tossed it on the sofa. Claire stared out at the garden and listened to him moving around behind her, opening and closing cupboards, filling the kettle. He seemed to know, without being told, where everything was. After a minute she heard him putting two mugs on the table so she went over and sat down opposite him.

She wrapped her hands around her cup and looked over at Dog. 'What will happen?'

'I'll give him an injection of phenobarbital. He'll fall asleep and then his heart will stop. He won't feel anything, I promise. I've let animals go hundreds of times.' Claire remembered the piece of paper he'd given her the day he had dropped Dog back. 'This one's on your conscience,' he'd said. Now it would be.

'Dog didn't eat that watch,' she said, stalling for time. 'My ex-boyfriend just pretended he did so I'd get rid of him.'

'*Ex*-boyfriend? That plan backfired, then.'

Claire almost smiled. Richard had tried to get rid of Dog, but in the end, Dog had got rid of him.

Dog shuddered and let out a mixture of an exhausted sigh and a whimper. She stood up and nodded at Shane. 'Just give me a second.'

Shane looked surprised when Claire opened the door so that Dog could hear the news from the TV in the living room. 'Listen to that,' she knelt beside him. 'Can you hear? It's Anne Doyle.' Dog's eyelids parted slightly. 'I'm sorry,' she whispered. She lifted his head carefully on to her lap. Shane was filling a syringe with bright pink liquid that looked too cheerful to be lethal.

'Why don't you talk to him,' he said, 'while I'm doing this.'

Claire remembered standing in the garden, with her dad, listening to him talking to the fuchsia and the lilac and the sweet peas. 'How do you know what you're supposed to say to them?' she'd asked him, and he'd smiled. 'You just say whatever comes into your head, they'll understand.'

She leaned down so her hair fell over Dog's face. She thanked him for keeping her dad company for so many years. She told him that his barking had probably saved his life when he'd fallen off the ladder. And how proud she was that he'd stood up to Richard and how much she was going to miss him. She saw the life going out of him, a dying spark behind his opaque marmalade eyes, but she kept whispering to him even after it was gone.

Shane carried Dog out to the Land Rover wrapped in his rug and laid him carefully in the back.

'Where will you take him?' Claire wrapped her arms around herself.

'Back to the surgery. I can arrange to have him cremated, if that's what you'd like?'

Claire made herself nod. 'Can I come with you? I just don't want to . . .' She didn't want to say 'leave him yet'. It sounded stupid. Shane looked at her for a long moment. 'Of course.'

Neither of them spoke on the journey. Claire sat beside him holding Dog's worn leather collar.

When Shane opened the boot, she gave one of Dog's limp paws a last squeeze, pressing her fingers against the pads, one by one.

317

But she had to look away while Shane carried his body into the surgery.

'I should get a taxi,' she said when he came out.

'I've got to go somewhere but I'll drive you home first. I think I left my jumper in your kitchen.'

They didn't talk on the journey back either. Shane followed her back into the house and she found his jumper on the arm of the sofa and handed it to him.

'Anne Doyle.' He shook his head. 'That's pretty unusual.'

She nodded. 'He's a pretty unusual dog. I mean *was*.' She sat on the battered sofa and stared down at the collar in her hands. It was beginning to sink in now.

'I saw the inside of your fridge,' Shane said. 'Is there anything you didn't try to get Dog to eat?'

'Roast cat,' Claire croaked.

'That's a relief. I'd have to report you to the ISPCA for that.' He sat down beside her on the sofa and then after a long time he said, 'The beach where I came to pick him up? Was that where your mother drowned?' Claire nodded. He looked away. 'I go back to Laragh sometimes. That's where my brother, Finn, died. Though,' he rubbed his chin hard with the flat of his hand, 'I don't think it really matters much where someone dies. It's all the moments before that count.'

His face was turned away; all Claire could see was the side of his head and the tip of an ear through his brown hair. He was sitting incredibly still but she thought, from the way he was breathing, his chest rising and falling deeply, that he might be crying. She put her hand on his knee.

He didn't turn around but, after a minute, he slipped his arm around her shoulder and they sat there, like that, for a long time, still without saying anything, as it grew dark in the basement flat.

Claire was lying on the sofa, her head at an awkward angle on Shane's chest. The kitchen was in darkness except for a quivering rectangle of moonlight that pooled on the floor by the door.

'Oh my God, I'm so sorry.' She sat up. 'You said you had to be somewhere. I didn't mean to keep you here all night.'

'It's OK. You fell asleep. I didn't want to leave you.' She could feel his breath on her cheek but his face was in shadow.

'I should go.'

Neither of them moved. Claire was suddenly very conscious of every centimetre of space between her lips and his. She couldn't tell whether she was moving towards Shane or whether he was moving towards her but the distance between them was shrinking and then they were kissing. It was a long, deep kiss and it sent a current through Claire that connected every part of her, from the roots of her hair to the soles of her feet. Shane bit her lip and she felt her nipples harden beneath her thin T-shirt and she knew from the way his breath changed that he felt it too. She slid back down on to the sofa and he fell down with her. His mouth moved from her lips to her neck.

'I can't do this,' he mumbled, into her hair, but he didn't let go. She could feel his body pressing against her. He kissed her ears then swooped from her hairline to the tip of her shoulder and her head fell back over the arm of the sofa. Through the warped glass pane of the door, she saw a sky full of upside down stars.

Then Shane pulled her to her feet and peeled off his jumper, he yanked her T-shirt over her head and they stumbled glued at the lips and the hips through her kitchen and staggered up the steps to the dark hall. He lifted her up and pushed her against the door that led up to Ray's flat, but she managed to drag herself away, breathing hard and they both tottered into her bedroom. Then they were falling on to the bed and Shane was pulling off the rest of his clothes and she was telling him through gritted teeth to hurry. She had wanted this ever since she'd seen him across the courtyard on her first day on *The Spaniard*. Eight months was a long time to wait; she couldn't wait a second longer.

Claire lay perfectly still, savouring the weight and the heat of Shane's body beside her. Then, finally, she turned her head on the pillow and looked at him. Up close, his face seemed to contain every colour. There were tiny pixels of mauve and violet in the dip above his upper lip. The dark shadow of his stubble had flecks of yellow and crimson. There were speckles of copper and silver in his heavy eyebrows. Her head was telling her that the most beautiful man in the world couldn't possibly be in her bed but her heart was telling her that he was. He opened his eyes and smiled at her but there was a wariness in that smile which dropped into the spreading pool of her happiness like a heavy stone. She shivered. He tucked a strand of hair behind her ear. 'Your hair used to be curly. You changed it.'

'It's changing back.' The twelve-week blow-dry was wearing off. She could feel the curls and the kinks beginning to return.

'Listen,' he said, and she nodded though she already knew she wouldn't want to hear what he was going to say. She wanted to push herself into him and pull him into her so they didn't have to get up and face reality. The empty rug in the kitchen and the hollow in her heart where the memories of her mother used to be.

'Last night,' Shane reached under the covers and threaded his fingers through hers, 'was incredible,' he squeezed her hand, 'but I wasn't . . .' he rubbed his thumb along her palm to her wrist and back again, and again, 'I didn't expect this to happen. The thing is, I was on my way to meet my wife. We just started seeing one another again. Trying to figure out if we can try to work things out.' He sighed. 'I don't know that we can but right now it's—'

'Complicated?' She smiled, sadly.

'Open ended. I should have explained, I'm sorry.' He turned to look at her.

'Don't be,' she said, and she meant it because if he had stopped to explain everything then last night wouldn't have happened.

After he was gone, Claire pulled her clothes off again and got back into the bed. The pillow still smelled faintly of Shane. She buried her face in it and fell deeply asleep again.

The nightmares always began differently. In this one, Claire was floating out to sea, perched on a plank of wood. She was a few yards away from the shore, trying to paddle back in, but the current was taking her away from the shallow water that danced with sequins of light, out towards the grey line of the horizon. Then the plank was gone and she was in the water, the tremendous weight of it closing over her head. She tried to fight her way back up but her body was heavy and the force of the water was too strong. Then, just as she was about to give up, she felt an arm around her neck dragging her upwards. Her face broke the surface and she gasped for air. She was on her back and someone was swimming behind her, pulling her in to the shore away from danger. When it was shallow enough to stand, Claire found her feet and turned around. The woman had long wet red hair and green eyes. Her eyelashes were spiky with water. For a moment, Claire thought it was her mum, then the woman smiled and she saw the tiny gap between her top front teeth and she realised she was looking at herself.

29

There was nothing left in the freezer except the turkey that Kelly had frozen at Thanksgiving. She wasn't hungry but she had to eat something because if she didn't she might damage her body and that would be a waste of the Clomid she'd taken. Her precious second to last cycle. So she pulled her lank hair into a ponytail, found her purse and drove to the petrol station. She filled a basket with pasta, eggs, butter and milk. The guy at the till slipped one of the tabloids into her bag.

'It's free if you spend ten euros.' He pointed at a sign. 'Something for nothing. Sure, you can't argue with that.'

She made herself scrambled eggs and stood at the window while she ate. She hadn't cleared up after the storm. Litter was still caught in the branches of the tree, the magnolia was lying on its side with its roots exposed and shards of the broken pot were scattered on the patio. The kitchen looked even worse. The bin was overflowing. Dirty plates were piled up in the sink. A full washing basket was standing by the washing machine, the clothes that wouldn't fit in heaped on the floor beside it.

Nick wouldn't recognise the house if he saw it. For a moment, she let herself imagine the sound of his key in the lock. If he walked in right now, she would bring it all out into the open. Tell him what she'd done at the bath showroom, show him the baby clothes in the bedroom, explain what had happened when she was seventeen. Then he would understand why having a baby wasn't a choice for her but a necessity.

She finished her toast and flipped open the paper. Today was day fifteen. She'd been carefully keeping count of the days of her cycle but she'd lost track of the actual date and when she saw it

322

she realised that it was Nick's birthday. She piled her dish and her cup on top of the paper and carried them to the sink, pushing the other birthdays out of her mind. The year she'd surprised him with a weekend in 10 Fitch in Auburn. The year she'd taken him to dinner at Casa La Femme on Charles Street. The year they got married, when they'd spent the whole day in a single bed in a B&B on Inish Mor. As she tried to stuff the paper into the overflowing bin, a magazine called *Hot Gossip* slid out on to the floor. Jennifer Aniston was smirking on the cover. Below her was a smaller photograph of Nick kissing Oonagh Clancy.

'*OO's That Girl?*' the caption read, and beneath it, in smaller type: '*Chat Show Blonde Caught in Steamy Clinch with Couples Coach*'.

Kelly stared at the picture. Now she knew why Nick had been so half hearted about having a baby, why he'd been so desperate to get the Channel 5 job. He had been screwing Oonagh Clancy all the time. She forced the magazine deep into the bin. He isn't going to walk in the door today or ever, she told herself, he doesn't want you, he wants Oonagh Clancy, a woman who already has three kids and won't want to have any more.

She went upstairs calmly and ran the shower. It was day fifteen. It was time to stop waiting for her husband to come back and take things into her own hands.

Nick watched a familiar figure with frosted blonde hair retreat down the driveway. There was a magazine lying on the carpet in front of the letterbox. As he bent to pick it up, he froze. The picture had to be a fake, didn't it? But even as he bent down he recognised the window of Pasta Tosca and the tight red dress that Oonagh was wearing. He ripped through the glossy pages until he found the article.

'*The Hunky Doctor Who I Turned to for Help Nearly Cost Me My Marriage!*'

There was another photograph of Oonagh in a leopard-skin dress holding a baby.

'*"The animal attraction between Nick Dillon (36) and me was sizzling from day one," admits curvaceous TV star Oonagh Clancy (35).*'

' "On-screen, Nick and I were helping couples to have happier marriages, but off-screen, I was struggling to save my own. In desperation, I turned to him and begged him to help me to salvage my relationship with my husband. But soon our secret coaching sessions were tearing both our marriages apart. Owen and I were sharing the same house but we were living separate lives while Nick split up from his gorgeous wife."

'The chat show star is too coy to reveal the steamy details of her fling with the cheating couples coach. "All I can say is that I knew it had to stop before I lost my husband and my family. It almost killed Owen to hear the truth but he has taken me back with open arms and we have renewed our love for one another." The celebrity couple also hope to renew their contract for their popular TV show, OO in the Afternoon, in September.'

The magazine slipped through Nick's hands. He remembered the bald guy he'd seen that day they met in Pasta Tosca. It was the photographer who used to lurk out in the garden. He was Oonagh's Plan B. She had set him up and sold the story to a tabloid to salvage her career. He pulled out his phone. Kelly's number went straight to voicemail.

'Listen,' he said. 'I know you don't read the tabloids but in case you see something about me and Oonagh Clancy, I want you to know that none of it is true.'

The flat was all wrong without Dog. Claire kept expecting to hear his claws on the floorboards in the hall or to see him lurking at the kitchen door, his shaggy head low, the tip of his long tail swinging slowly as if he was keeping time to a jazz track that only he could hear. His water bowl was still half full and there was something squashed in at the back of his favourite spot by the fridge. She knelt down and pulled it out. It was one of the brown leather gloves she had given Richard for Christmas. There were tiny puncture holes all along the thumb and that made her smile. 'Good Dog,' she whispered.

The doorbell rang and she hurried down the path in her bare feet to answer it, hoping it was Shane, but Eilish was standing in the laneway. 'I thought you were still in Kerry.' Claire let her in.

'We wrapped a day early and I have good news.' She followed

Claire into the house and put a stack of Tupperware boxes on the table. 'Seventy per cent chocolate brownies with white chocolate chips. I know! Dogs aren't supposed to eat chocolate but, at this stage, I thought they couldn't do him any real harm.'

Claire shook her head. 'I'm sure he would have loved them but—'

Eilish's eyes went from the empty rug under the table to the empty collar on the mantelpiece. 'Oh,' she said.

Claire swallowed hard and turned to fill the kettle. 'I had to call Shane to come and put him to sleep.'

Eilish came over and put her arms around her. 'That's awful. You should have called me after he'd left.'

'He didn't.'

Eilish took a step back and her eyes widened. 'And you . . . ?'

Claire nodded.

'And it was . . .'

Claire nodded again.

'I know people are always falling into bed at funerals but I didn't realise it happened with dogs.' Eilish stared at Claire. 'But that's good, right? You really like Shane . . .'

'Yes. But no, it isn't good. He's just started seeing his wife again. They're trying to make things work.'

Eilish sighed, opened the lid of a Tupperware box, took out two brownies and handed one to Claire. 'Here!' she said. 'Everything is always a bit better after you've eaten.'

Claire broke off a corner. 'You said you had good news?'

'You'd better sit down,' Eilish looked rueful. Claire slid into one of the folding chairs. 'Pete's asked me to be his partner.'

'Business partner?' Claire stared at her. 'Or?'

'Both! It was the shoes that made me do it, Claire, the "love" shoes I bought in Deja Vus. They were supposed to work on you and Richard but they worked on me and Pete! All that "liebe" and "zamilowanie" went to my head.'

Claire grinned. 'I always knew he had a thing for you! "Nigella Lawson's younger, sexier sister"!' Her phone rang. 'I have to take this,' she said. 'Dad.'

He didn't say anything for a long time after she told him about Dog, then he cleared his throat. 'He would have been gone months ago if it wasn't for you.' There was another long-drawn-out silence then he said, 'Nicholas is in a bad way. There's a horrible thing in one of the papers saying he was carrying on with that Clancy woman.'

'What?' Claire didn't believe this for a second. Nick would never do that to Kelly.

'And it's his birthday today.'

Claire had completely forgotten. The twenty-fifth of March. Nick was thirty-eight.

'I thought,' her dad began, nervously, 'that maybe we'd have a little party to take his mind off things.'

'A party?!?' Claire wondered if Dog's death had unhinged him completely.

'Nothing fancy. Just some wine and nibbles. You can bring someone.' Her father never nibbled anything except omelettes and biscuits and this was the first time that he'd shown any interest in her personal life.

'I don't have a someone to bring.'

'I'm someone,' Eilish hissed. 'You can bring me.'

'Dad, are you sure this is a good idea?' Claire said, carefully. 'We're not really,' she thought of all the unmarked birthdays over the years, 'party people.'

'I know, but Nicholas is upset. You've just been through a terrible shock finding out about your mother. We've lost Dog. I think we all need a bit of cheering up.'

It was the desperation in his voice that did it. 'OK.'

'Would you see if you can get Kelly to come?'

'I'll try.' Claire stared at Eilish after he'd hung up. 'Is there something in these brownies or did my dad just ask me to come to a party for my brother?'

'Seventy-five per cent Valrhona and my body weight in butter. Do I have time to go home and change? I'd invite Pete but he's gone up to Belfast to check out a new van.'

'Eilish, my family doesn't do parties. We barely do conversations. Don't even think about coming.'

Ray had called Ash every day for nearly two weeks until she had finally given in and agreed to bring Willow over the afternoon before she took her back to London. 'No big scenes,' she warned him. 'I want this to be a normal day.'

When they arrived, Willow wouldn't look at Ray's face. He squatted down until they were eye to eye. 'You see this tiny little cut?' He pointed at the scar on the bridge of his nose. 'This is where all that blood came from that day you got scared.'

Willow hung on to Ash's hand and leaned over to peer at it. 'It's not a very big hole. Does it hurt?'

'Not any more.'

She nodded. 'Why did that man hit you?'

'I stole something belonging to him,' Ray said.

'Stealing is wrong.' Willow started to take off her rabbit backpack. 'Can we watch a DVD?'

Ten minutes into *Shrek*, she scooted across the sofa to look at the scar again, then she put her arms around him and gave him a hug. He pretended he had something in his eye. 'I'll just go and get it out,' he said hoarsely.

'Pull yourself together,' he hissed at himself in the bathroom mirror. 'Take off that stupid beanie.' He had to go out there and act as if everything was normal even though it wasn't. Ash was right. He had to do what was right for Willow. He couldn't just rock up every couple of months and expect that to work. She already had a dad. She didn't need him at the edges of her life complicating things.

As he opened the door he heard her laughing at the DVD. A high, sweet ripple of sound that set him off again. He closed the door and called Claire.

'I'm sorry. I know we're not really speaking but this is an emergency. I'm stuck in the bathroom.'

'Call a locksmith.'

'It's me that's the problem. Ash is taking Willow back to London tomorrow. I only have her for a few more hours and I didn't realise it would be this hard. I don't want her to know I'm upset. Can I bring her down to see Dog just to distract her till I get hold of myself?'

'He's gone.'

'Back to your dad's?'

'I had to have him put him down the day before yesterday.'

'No! I liked him. I thought he looked a bit like Keith Richards.'

'Speaking of Richards,' Claire sighed. 'Your creepdar turned out to be fairly accurate. Richard let Dog out on purpose. He was trying to get rid of him. We broke up.'

'I'm sorry.'

'You did me a favour.'

'Anytime.'

Claire remembered her mother's anniversary, last year, when Ray had dropped everything to spend the day with her. 'If you're really stuck, you and Willow can come to a party in my dad's house.'

'A *party* at your *dad's*? Are we playing oxymorons? Because if we are, I give up, you win.'

The curtains were drawn and nobody answered the door so Claire wrote a note on a petrol receipt in eye pencil. She was posting it through the letterbox when she saw a shadow in the hall.

'Kelly!' She peered in through the sandblasted glass. 'Are you in there?'

Her sister-in-law opened the door reluctantly. She was wearing a dressing gown and a lot of make-up. She looked terrible. The floor behind her was littered with junk mail and there was an open carton of milk on the gilt hall table beside a dead orchid.

'Claire. What a surprise.'

'I was wondering if you knew what day it is?'

'It's Thursday,' Kelly folded her arms, 'right?'

'It's Nick's birthday.'

'And?' What was Nick's sister doing on her doorstep? They barely knew one another.

Claire fiddled with her locket. 'Look, I know you and Nick have been having a rough time and I don't know what's been going on—'

'Well, if you want to catch up, you should pick up a copy of *Hot Gossip*, it's got all the juicy details.'

'Nick wouldn't have an affair. I've known him all my—'

'How's that? You've seen him, what, a dozen times in the last twenty years?'

Claire flushed. 'He cares about you more than he's ever cared about anyone.'

Kelly nodded. 'Right! Did he send you here to tell me that?'

'My dad sent me. He's having a party for Nick this afternoon. He wanted to invite you.'

'I'm busy today. Why don't you invite Oonagh Clancy instead?' Kelly started to close the door. 'I hear she's always ready to party.'

30

'Surprise!' a little dark-haired girl Nick had never seen called when he opened the door. The living room was full of people. Nick looked at them, baffled. There was Ray Devine, whom he loathed. The physiotherapist, who loathed him. His dad, his sister, a woman in a purple, sparkly dress and the little girl who, for some reason, was holding Devine's hand. What had happened?

'Make a wish!' The woman in the purple dress shoved a plate of brownies with a half-dozen flaming candles under his nose. Nick wished that they'd all just disappear so he could pull down the blind and watch TV, which is how he'd been planning to spend his birthday.

'What the hell were you thinking?' he asked, when he finally managed to corner Claire by the window.

'I'm as surprised as you are. This was Dad's idea.'

They looked over at the old man, who was talking to the woman in the purple dress. He was making such an effort to seem relaxed and at ease that it was almost painful to watch.

'He saw all that stuff about you and Oonagh Clancy in the paper,' Claire whispered. 'He wanted to help.'

'Well, he's helped to make this the worst birthday ever,' Nick said miserably.

'Oh,' Claire raised an eyebrow, 'I wouldn't compete with me in the worst birthday stakes if I were you.'

'Sorry!' Nick winced.

'Listen.' She tugged at her locket. His mother used to do that too, when she was nervous, zip it back and forth on the gold chain. 'I'm not going to say "Happy Birthday", because I know it isn't. But you'll get through it, Nick. Look what you've already survived.'

Ray sat down in his old spot on the brown corduroy sofa and listened to Willow talking to the South African girl, who was Claire's dad's physio.

'I like your rabbit,' the physio was saying. 'What's his name?'

'Bowie.'

'Like the knife?' The girl had no idea who David Bowie was, Ray realised.

'Like the man,' Willow said. 'David Bowie. Ray's friend.'

'Who's Ray?'

Willow pointed at him. 'He used to be a singer,' Ray heard her whisper, 'but now he has inferiority cornflakes.'

'What?'

'My mummy says they're what you get when you're not famous any more.'

'Hello, Raymond.' Ray flinched. Eilish always enjoyed calling him by his full name, just to wind him up. 'And who is this beautiful creature?'

'This is Willow and she'd like a brownie.'

Eilish slid one on to a plate. Willow took a polite bite. 'It tastes too dark,' she whispered to Ray.

Claire's dad cleared his throat. 'Would she like a Jaffa Cake instead? I've got some in the kitchen.' Eilish, slightly offended, went off to get them.

'Oh!' Willow elbowed Ray in the knee. 'We nearly forgot the *present*!' She'd insisted on buying one. The six-year-old's birthday party etiquette was very clear. You couldn't arrive at a party without a gift. Ray dug around in his jacket pocket and handed it over.

'You have to come with me,' Willow said, 'in case I'm too shy.'

Claire's brother was sitting in the armchair by the window staring miserably at a cake slice as if he was thinking of ending it all. All that jaunty, American 'have a nice day' bounce was gone out of him. He looked almost human, Ray thought.

331

Willow tapped his arm and handed him the small package. 'Happy Birthday!' she said, then scurried back to Ray's side.

'Thank you.' Nick looked flustered.

'You're supposed to open it,' she prompted.

This wasn't as easy as it sounded. Old Beaky Lennon in the shop had lent Willow a roll of Sellotape and she'd used most of it. Nick managed to tear a hole in the paper and pulled the key ring out through it.

It had a big yellow plastic disc with 'Dad' printed on it. Ray had tried to explain to Willow that Claire's brother wasn't a dad but yellow was her favourite colour so she'd insisted on buying it anyway.

Nick looked up at the loathsome Devine to see if this was some kind of cruel joke but he had turned away and the little dark-haired girl was beaming at him.

'This is awesome!' He took out his own key chain and used the point of the cake knife to slide his keys off then slotted them on to the new ring. The office key, the car key, the key to his dad's place. The last key was the one to his house, the key to his old life with Kelly. He stared at it.

'You put them all on,' the little girl explained, 'so they don't get lost.'

'I might not need this one.'

'You have to put it on, just in case.' She looked around. 'Is this your party?' He nodded. 'Are you going to have a man who makes balloon animals or a piñata?'

Nick tried to think of something to say but he hadn't had much contact with children since Claire. He picked up a Jaffa Cake. 'Full moon!' He took a bite, 'Half-moon.' He popped the rest into his mouth.

'I know what comes next!' the little girl laughed. 'Totally clips.'

When Nick went into the kitchen to get a glass of water, the woman in the purple dress was washing out Tupperware boxes at the sink. She extended a soapy hand. 'I'm Eilish.' She handed him a tea towel. 'Don't tell Claire but I think you're brilliant on the telly.'

'Not any more.' Nick began to dry one of the boxes.

'Why's that?'

'You don't buy the papers?'

'I do.' Eilish lifted her hand out of the soapy water, made a circle with her thumb and forefinger and blew a bubble. 'I just don't buy the bullshit that's printed in them. Can I ask you something?'

He sighed, 'No, "I did not have sex with that woman".'

'I was going to ask you why you're letting the media tear you to pieces? Why don't you fight back?'

'I don't do confrontation.'

Eilish shook her head. 'Did nobody ever tell you that if you don't get pissed off you get pissed on?'

Ray looked around the room. 'A party at your dad's. Jesus! What's next? Are my parents going to waltz in, hug me and tell me that they always loved me?'

'I wish they would,' Claire said. She was avoiding his eyes.

'How do you feel?'

Claire could still feel the sharp ache she got in her chest when the light went out of Dog's eyes. The flare of electricity that had run through her body when Shane kissed her. And the clarity that had filled her head when she had woken from her dream. A few months ago, she would have told Ray about all of this but now she just smiled. 'How do I feel? Through a series of nerve endings at the tips of my fingers.' That was what he always used to say, when they were young.

Ray tossed a peanut into the air and caught it in his mouth. 'Have you seen Willow working the room?' He grinned. 'She's charming the pants off everyone.'

'And you're not doing the same to Miss Cape Town?'

Ray tossed another peanut and missed it. 'Too young.'

Claire gave him a sceptical look.

'She doesn't even know who David Bowie is. You were always on at me to go out with women of my own age. Maybe you were right.'

Claire retrieved the peanut from under the TV. 'I don't know whether I'm more amazed by the fact that you're considering seeing women the same age as you or that you're considering seeing the same woman more than once.'

'Listen, Claire.' Suddenly Ray felt as awkward as he'd been the first time he was here on that rainy afternoon nearly twenty years ago. 'I know you probably need more time-stroke-space, but if you ever want to hang-out-stroke-go-for-a-road-trip-stroke-have-a-Perfect-Day any time just come upstairs.'

'Thanks, but I'm probably going to find my own place now that Dog is gone.'

He shook his head. 'You don't have to do that.'

'But I want to.'

'Don't rush anything. Let's talk about it. I've got to go now. I promised I'd have Willow back to Ash by six. Hey, I've got a new one for you. It's too carnivorous for Willow. "Every time you go away",' he sang, ' "you take a piece of meat with you".'

'Ha ha!'

'Always so stingy with the "ha's".' Ray sighed. 'But I'm going to let you off because you invited us to a party.' He tried to catch her eye. 'Thank you. I couldn't have done this without you.'

He watched Claire chatting to Willow while she helped her into her coat and put Bowie into her backpack. She was good with kids, he thought. She was a natural.

'I was expecting the Addams Family.' Eilish was washing the plates. 'I got the Brady Bunch. I'm confused.'

Claire opened the back door and tossed some nuts on to the grass for the birds.

'It just goes to show that parking machines are on to something when they say that "Change is possible". Look at your family. Look at me and Pete.' Eilish turned to look at Claire over her shoulder. 'Sorry I won't be coming back to acting, Claire. I hope you're not too upset.'

A year ago, Claire would have been devastated. But now the idea of being out there on her own didn't faze her at all. Her job on *The Spaniard* was over but she'd just keep going to auditions until she got something else. It would work out. She smiled at Eilish. 'You'll be doing something you love with someone you love. I'm delighted.'

Eilish pulled the last plate out of the sink. 'Ladies and gentlemen, I'd like to present this prestigious award to Claire Dillon for her outstanding performance in,' she did a quick calculation, *'Nine and Half Months*!'

Claire took the dripping plate. 'I don't know about that but I'll always treasure this.'

'I'm serious.' Eilish leaned over and touched her cheek with a soapy finger. 'If Holly turns out to be half the woman you are, I'll be the happiest mother in the world.'

'What about the "wold"?' Claire began to dry the plate.

'That too.'

Claire offered her dad her arm.

'I'm fine,' he said. She watched him limping slowly down the hall. He wasn't fine, not yet, but he was determined to get better. She could see it in his eyes.

'That was a good thing you did for Nick, Dad,' she said, when he'd lowered himself into his chair in the surgery.

'I kept looking at that little girl of Ray's and thinking how small you were when Maura died.' He put his hand on her arm lightly. 'She would have been so proud of you.'

Claire's friend had left one of her Tupperware boxes on the worktop. When Nick opened the cupboard under the sink to tidy it away, the little plastic anatomical doll fell out.

He picked it up and shook the organs out into his palm, the way his mother used to. He'd judged her because her life had been out of control but that was unfair. He thought of the weeks he'd lost when he moved back into this house in the fog of the old man's painkillers. He was more like his mother than he realised. Not just because he had fallen apart when things got bad but because they'd both tried, in different ways, to heal other people and neither of them had been able to heal themselves.

He fitted the tiny plastic organs back into the doll one by one. The burgundy liver, the plum-coloured kidneys, the brown appendix. The pink heart with its yellow valves and blue arteries slotted in last, with a soft click.

*

335

'Nothing much going on this month, I'm afraid,' the technician's voice was sympathetic. Kelly stared up at the ceiling instead of at the ultrasound screen. There was a missing tile above her and she could see a tangle of tubes and pipes in the crawl space. Under the surface, everything was a mess, she thought, tiredly. So much energy went into hiding it.

The technician gave the wand one last swoop. 'Wait! There is one follicle here.' She clicked on it. 'Seventeen millimetres. It's a little small,' she smiled, 'but I've known it to happen!'

Ray tucked the CD into Willow's rabbit backpack.

'What's that?' She tried to see over her shoulder.

'It's a song I wrote for you. But I promise I won't get inferiority cornflakes if you don't like it.'

She nodded.

'OK.'

He put his finger on the bell and waited one last moment before he rang it. Ash answered the door immediately. 'Hey,' she said to Willow. 'Did you have a good time?'

'We watched *Shrek* and we went to a party. Do we have Jaffa Cakes?'

'Ask Grandma.' Willow started to run down the hall. 'Hey! Aren't you going to say goodbye to Ray?'

She walked back. 'Bye, Ray.' He bent down and she gave him a quick hug. Her face was cold and she smelled of crayons, chocolate and fabric softener. Ray had to force himself to open his arms and let her go. The ears on her rabbit backpack bounced as she ran down the hall again and then she was gone.

'Don't be a stranger,' Ash said. 'You can come and see us in London any time.'

'I will,' Ray lied, then he put his hands in his pockets and walked away.

'Gorgeous dress! Special occasion?' the girl with peroxide hair shouted over the roar of the hairdryer.

'My husband's birthday.' Kelly stared down at the magazine in her lap.

The girl blasted her fringe with hot air. 'Get him something nice?'

'I have no idea what he wants.'

'Talk to me about it,' the hairdresser said. 'Men are impossible, aren't they?'

Kelly asked the barman for a Tequila Sunrise. That was her drink back in the day. She'd tell her mom she was studying over at Jennifer's. They'd get high in Jennifer's brother's bedroom and then they'd all pile into his car and drive across the border to Canada to go to a club.

When the cocktail came, she took the umbrella out and sucked up a half-inch of it through the bendy straw. Her precious follicle would have to take its chances with alcohol tonight; she knew the risks but she couldn't do this without a little Dutch courage.

A tall, blond guy in a suit a few stools along was checking her out. Way too young, she thought, then stopped herself. What did that matter? He could be a hundred years old. All that counted were his genes.

Colm didn't smoke or take drugs. He'd never been arrested. He played squash. He'd done science at college, so he had to have some smarts, but he was very slow on the uptake.

Kelly had been flirting with him for four and a half cocktails now and he still couldn't take the hint. He was droning on about the gap year he'd spent travelling in Asia. 'Indonesia's incredible. You ever been?'

She shook her head and sneaked a look at her watch. Quarter after ten. She crossed her legs provocatively and pretended to be entranced while he told a long story about a monkey in Ubud who'd stolen his sunglasses.

'Hey, I think I've got a picture on my iPhone!' He started scrolling though his library.

'Colm.' She put her hand on his arm. 'Can we just get out of here?'

He looked as if he'd just won the Euromillions lottery then lost his ticket. 'Thing is I don't really have a place. I kinda live with my folks in Stillorgan.'

'What?' Kelly stared at him in disbelief. She couldn't take him back to her house. It was a mess, and anyway, she didn't want him to know anything about her. A hotel room? The back of her car? No, she just wanted rid of Colm, now. She was going to have to find some other guy and start all over again. She grabbed her jacket and stood up. 'I'm sorry,' she said. 'Got to go. Nice meeting you.'

Ray tossed back another shot of tequila but he still felt shockingly sober. Time to bring in the big guns. He tried to catch the barman's eye to order a Long Island Iced Tea. If he went home sober, he'd spend the whole night thinking about Willow, so he wasn't leaving Rococo until he was completely pissed.

'Well, look who it is!' A woman with long, caramel hair slid on to the stool beside him. She was wearing a tiny black dress and very high heels. 'Want to buy me a drink?' It was Emma Lacey.

Ray snorted. 'What do you think?'

She sighed. 'Come on, Ray, give me a break. I've had a hard day.'

'Harder than mine?' Ray remembered Willow's cold cheek against his, the sound of her footsteps in the hallway.

'I was almost trampled to death by a stampeding horse today.' Emma waved imperiously at the barman. 'Beat that.'

'Lady Kathryn is the best thing about *The Spaniard*.' Emma stabbed at the ice in the bottom of her empty glass with her straw. 'I was heavy-pencilled for the next two series. All I did was sneak off to London for *one* little audition and they fired me. They had an emergency script meeting and wrote me out, just like that! Then my fiancé, my *ex*-fiancé, Declan, you remember him?' Ray nodded. 'He told me it was my own fault. Another drink?'

Ray stood up. 'I don't think so.'

He was on his way to the door when he passed a couple having a fight. A young, red-faced guy in a suit. A very pretty, dark-haired woman in an off-the-shoulder cream dress. It was Claire's sister-in-law.

'Please! I have to go!' she was saying.

338

'You've been all over me all evening.' The guy was holding her arm. 'You don't just walk away like that. It's not cool.'

Ray stepped between them. 'Kelly, where've you been?'

She blinked at him, confused and, Ray saw, completely drunk. 'Sorry, man,' he said smoothly. 'Was my wife hitting on you? We had a row. Sorry!' He took Kelly's arm and pulled a fifty out of his pocket. 'Will this cover your bar bill?'

The guy squinted at him. 'Hey, aren't you—?' he began.

'Taking her home.' Ray put his arm around Kelly and steered her through the crowd to the door.

'Well, well,' Kelly said when they were outside. 'Ray Devine. I wouldn't have pegged you for a hero.'

'I wouldn't have pegged you for a cradle snatcher so we're even.' Ray whistled and a taxi pulled over.

'Good New York whistle! I'm impressed.'

'And completely hammered.' Ray opened the door of the taxi. 'Time to go home.'

Ray Devine was rummaging around in her kitchen. *Not if he was the last man in the world.* Even though her mind was muddled with cocktails, Kelly remembered thinking this exact thought when he had come here for lunch with Claire. But she only had one viable follicle and he had great genes. He was ridiculously good looking with all that messy dark hair and those cheekbones and that big mouth that lead singers in bands always seemed to have. He reminded her of . . . but she stopped herself. She wasn't going there. That would just make her too sad. She found a compact in her bag, put on some lipgloss, pulled off her jacket and arranged herself on the sofa. She left her shoes on. He was probably the kind of guy who liked that kind of thing.

'Your kitchen could use a clean.' Ray came in with two glasses.

'Oh, I can think of way more fun things to do,' she gave him what she hoped was a wicked smile, 'than clean a kitchen.'

He came over, sat down beside her and half-filled two glasses with Scotch. 'I'm not sure you should have this.' Ray had thought about making her a sandwich but all he had found in her fridge was a couple of eggs and a frozen turkey.

'Why don't I put on some music?' Kelly teetered over to the

stereo and nearly tripped over a pile of plates on the floor. Just looking at her was making Ray feel sober again. He finished his Scotch and picked up her glass. She'd had way too much already. She was prodding at an iPod in the dock. The sound of whale song filled the room. 'Oops!' She giggled. There was more prodding and Feist came on.

'Want to dance?' She held out her hand.

She really was very pretty and Ray really was very miserable. If he hadn't seen Claire's pain-in-the-arse brother, Nick, considering suicide by cake slice a few hours ago, he would have been tempted. He shook his head.

'OK.' Kelly began to fumble with the little bow at the back of her dress. 'Let's cut to the chase.'

'You're supposed to be a man slut,' Kelly grumbled after Ray had managed to manoeuvre her on to the bed but refused to touch her. 'You're supposed to sleep with everyone, irregardless. Oh, I said "irregardless". I'm turning into an Irish person. I'll be saying "pacifically" instead of "specifically" next, "antidote" instead of "anecdote".' Ray pulled off her shoes, tossed them on the floor and covered her with the duvet.

'Come to bed.' She made a grab for him but he moved out of her reach. 'You've got to be kidding me. You're turning me down?'

Ray nodded. 'Apparently.'

'I know why you won't sleep with me!' She sat up, suddenly.

Ray was glad she was still just about in her dress. 'You're in love with Nick's sister.'

'Don't be ridiculous.'

Kelly fumbled for a hair tie on the cluttered bedside table and twisted her long hair into a topknot. 'OK,' she said, 'if you could be with anyone, anywhere, where would you be right now?'

'On stage in the Ruby Room in Bangkok,' Ray said, in a flash. But that was a lie. He would be sitting beside Claire Dillon on her lumpy sofa eating cereal and bickering over whose turn it was to have the remote control.

There was something weird about the bedroom, Kelly thought, when she woke up. The baby clothes that had been strewn around

340

the floor since Christmas had been put away, the bags neatly lined up in the corner. Her bedside table had been cleared. Plates and cups were gone from the dressing table. Someone had tidied it all while she was asleep. She put her hands over her face. Ray Devine!

Her heart jumped into her parched throat. Had something happened? She half-remembered him putting her to bed. She was pretty sure he still had all his clothes on at that point and she was still mostly dressed except for her shoes.

She crawled out of bed and went downstairs. The kitchen was gleaming. The dishes and glasses were all neatly stacked in the open dresser. The floor had been hoovered. The laundry basket was empty. He must have run the machine two or three times.

She slid into a chair and stared at the wall. She had spent weeks choosing just the right shade of grey paint but last night she'd gone out to find a random stranger to father a child. When that hadn't worked out, she had tried to sleep with Ray Devine, a man she despised. But now she couldn't even despise him any more because he'd turned her down, put her to bed and cleaned her house.

Kelly yanked open the drawer where she kept her medicines. She pulled out the last blister pack of Clomid and punched the tablets out on to the worktop one by one then ground them up with the back of a spoon, scooped the powder into her palm, and tossed it into the sink.

The doorbell woke Claire. She grabbed a sweatshirt, unlocked the kitchen door and hurried, barefoot, down the garden path. She knew it couldn't be Shane but her heart still fell when she opened the door and saw Ray slouched against the wall in the laneway.

'Is Willow gone?'

He nodded. 'Seven o'clock flight to London. I've been up all night.'

'Doing what?'

'Walking around, thinking.' This wasn't true but it sounded a hell of a lot better than 'I've been fighting off your horny sister-in-law and cleaning her house'. 'I need a coffee. Can I come in?'

Claire gave a little shrug. 'OK.'

Ray took his jacket off and sat on one of the folding chairs.

Claire was wearing a long sweatshirt and her hair was pulled over one shoulder in a coppery tangle. Foreigners always thought that everyone in Ireland had red hair, but it was actually pretty unusual. It took two people with two copies of a recessive gene on chromosome 16 to make a redhead as beautiful as Claire. When she turned away to fill the kettle, he realised, with a jolt, that he would know her back anywhere. The left shoulder a fraction of an inch higher than the right. The triangle of freckles between her shoulder blades.

He knew now what had made him write 'Asia Sky'. He cleared his throat. 'Hey, you want to know something funny?'

'I'm not exactly full of "ha's", Ray.' Claire spooned coffee into a glass cafetière then poured in boiling water.

He tried to keep his voice light. 'I've only written two decent songs in my life. One was for Willow and the other one was for you.'

Claire held up the cafetière. 'Damn! There's a crack in this.'

'Claire, I need . . .' His throat closed over a lump of emotion before he could finish.

'I know. It's on the way.' She was still peering at the cafetière.

'I need to tell you something. I didn't realise until Kelly said it, but it's true.'

'Kelly?' She looked up at him suspiciously. 'When were you talking to Kelly?'

'I found her in a bar, really drunk, so I took her home and . . .'

'What?' She was frowning at him now.

'Nothing.' He stood up. 'Why?' He crossed the small kitchen. 'Would you be jealous?'

'Jealous?' Claire's green eyes widened.

'Shh!' He put his hands lightly on her shoulders. Then he leaned down and kissed her.

The cafetière hit the floor and smashed. Scalding coffee splashed up over Ray's jeans. He jumped away as Claire stepped out of his reach.

'Did you hear that?' Ray was smiling. He couldn't help himself. 'That was the sound of you and me breaking the One Kiss Clause. We have to try being a couple now for a year. That was the deal.'

Claire was looking at him as if he'd lost his mind.

He took a step towards her, heard the crackle of broken glass under his shoe and stopped. 'I love you,' he said quietly. 'I think that I always have. I just didn't know it till last night.'

'Ray. You're just upset about Willow.' Claire slipped past him and grabbed his jacket. 'Go and get some sleep.'

'I know this is sudden but when you think about it—'

'I don't want to think about it.'

'You love me too, Claire.'

'No.' She shook her head. 'I don't. I love someone else.'

'Richard?' Ray felt a jab of doubt, like a stitch, in his side. 'I thought you said he was gone?'

'He is. And now I need you to go. Please.'

Ray's heart was sinking like a stone. He'd thought it all through while he was cleaning Kelly's house. They could gut the house, turn it into one big living space. And they could have a child. They could make what neither of them had ever had – a real family.

'Look,' he tried to find her eyes, 'I know this is a shock, on top of finding out the truth about your mother—'

Claire froze. 'You knew about Mum,' she said softly, 'didn't you?'

He nodded. Even seven years after the accident, when his parents moved into Hawthorn Drive, the neighbours were still talking about 'poor Maura Dillon'.

'You never told me.'

'I didn't think it would do any good.' He tried to take her hand but she pushed him away.

'I've changed my mind,' she said. 'You can stay.' Relief washed over him. Then he saw her face. 'I'll go.'

'Go where? You live here.'

She shook her head. 'Not any more.'

Ray listened as Claire banged around in her bedroom then watched her bump her wheelie suitcase past him and up the stone steps into the garden.

After she'd closed the door, he made himself a cup of instant coffee, folded up a pizza flyer and tucked it under the leg of the wonky table, then sat down and stared around the kitchen. There was a tiny smear of blood on the lino where Claire must have stepped on a shard of broken glass.

He'd thought about telling her that day, after the Leaving Cert, when they got drunk on tequila and she told him about the accident. And every year, on her birthday, he thought about telling her again. Maybe this year, he thought, she'll be ready for the truth. But how could he tell her? Claire had built her whole life around the idea that her mother was perfect and it was so precious that he couldn't bear to take it away from her.

31

'Kelly, I love everything about it!' Pauline looked up from the CAD drawing on the computer screen and then around her shabby kitchen.

'That's a little play stove,' Kelly pointed out, 'for the boys. It slides in beneath the breakfast bar.'

'Wow!' Pauline nibbled her lip. 'I just don't see how you can do all this for seven and a half grand. That's our absolute limit.'

'It's tight but it can be done.' Kelly opened up a spreadsheet.

She'd stayed at her desk all day after Ray had left, working through her hangover on mood boards and plans, then she'd gotten on the phone and pulled in every favour she could to bring the renovation in for a third of cost price.

The kitchen was an ex-display model from a German show-room that was closing down. The tiles were from an extension that had been planned and then cancelled. Kelly was getting them free, along with the windows, as long as she collected them herself. The builder was knocking down the wall and putting in the window for a fraction of his daily fee because he had a crush on her. The carpenter was doing the shelves and the wooden floors as a trade-off for a bathroom revamp.

'I don't see a fee here for you?' Pauline was scanning the column of figures.

'I get a percentage as a kickback from the contractors,' Kelly lied. 'It doesn't show up in the budget.'

'You are an absolute life-saver.' We were planning to have moved to a bigger place by now but we're in so much negative equity that I think the only way we'll ever get out of here is in a box! What about you? How's the Clomid going?'

Kelly closed her laptop. 'I've put that on hold for the moment.'

'You'll get pregnant,' Pauline smiled, 'when the time is right. It'll work out.'

Kelly bent her head. 'I was pregnant before,' she said quietly, 'when I was seventeen.'

She and Jennifer had both had a crush on the same guy. The lead singer of a Vancouver band. They crossed the border to see them every time they played. One night, when they were going crazy at the front, he had pulled Kelly up on stage and they'd gone back to his hotel. And six weeks later, her period still hadn't come.

'What happened?' Pauline asked softly.

'He never even knew. It was just a one-night thing. And I wanted to keep the baby. I wanted it so badly but I was in my senior year and my parents said it would ruin my life so I had a termination and they sent me to a detox place in Denver. And they were right. It did ruin my life.'

Kelly remembered the small bare room she had shared with a Goth girl whose name she had forgotten. The acres of snow outside the window. The group meetings where everyone was supposed to talk about their problems, but all she could talk about was how angry she was with her mom and dad for forcing her to have a termination.

'I got rid of my baby,' she said quietly. 'I think that damaged me in some way and now I'll never have another chance.'

Pauline pulled a tissue out of her sleeve and she took it. 'I'm sorry. I didn't mean to fall apart. I've never told anyone about this. Not even my husband.'

'You'll have another chance,' Pauline said kindly. 'And if you don't, you'll make one. You'll get IVF or an egg donation or you'll adopt. You'll find a way.'

'Paging Doctor Fraud!' the girl behind the counter said.

'Sorry?' Nick was trying to find the laundry ticket in his wallet.

She folded her arms across her chest. 'You're that bastard who tried to break up the Clancys' marriage. We don't want your business.'

'You already have it. I dropped my laundry in here last week.'

A man in the queue behind Nick snapped a picture with his phone.

'You're barred,' the girl said. 'Next?'

Nick was getting into his car when he heard footsteps behind him. He turned around. A woman in her thirties with limp blonde hair was hurrying after him. 'What do you want to say?' he sighed. 'Come on, let's get it over with.'

'Thank you,' she smiled.

'What?'

'It's me, Roisin, I met you last summer at a salsa class, remember?'

'I didn't mean to snap at you like that. You must think I'm very rude.'

'You're a bloody saint for putting up with that abuse,' she said. 'It meant a lot to me when you gave me your card. I told my husband that I'd had an affair. I was honest with him, like you said.'

'And?'

'Things were very rocky for a while but we're getting there. Can I give *you* some advice?'

Nick nodded, trying not to wince. Here it came.

'If you really did have an affair with Oonagh Clancy, be honest with your wife about it.'

'I didn't.'

'Then tell her that.'

Nick hit a speed bump fast on the Rathmines Road, his CD ejected and Dom Daly's laugh burst into the car.

'Just had an email from a guy in a launderette in Blackrock. Apparently, Doc Nick has just been barred from the premises. Seems like it really is a bad idea to air your dirty laundry in public.'

Nick pulled into the car park of an abandoned office block. He punched the number of Fish FM on his phone and asked to be put through to Tara. 'I want to talk to Dom!' he demanded.

'Are you sure?' Tara sounded amused. 'Some guy just texted in a picture of you. You look kind of crazed.'

'Whatever you're doing,' Dom said, 'drop it because we have

the dodgy doc himself live on the line. Hello, Doc Nick. What have you got to confess to the people of Ireland?'

'Firstly, Dom,' Nick said, 'I'm not a doctor. I never said I was. That was something that started on the OO show. I should have cleared it up at the time. I was stupid not to.'

'Let's talk about what happened behind the scenes at the OO show!' Dom began.

'Secondly,' Nick cut across him, 'I did not try to break up the Clancys' marriage.'

'So what were you doing snogging her on the street?'

'That was a set-up. A trap arranged between Oonagh and a photographer called Brian Coakley.'

'Well, why is Oonagh saying—'

'You'll have to ask her about that. Thirdly . . .' Nick was on shakier ground now and he knew it. His anger had burned away, taking the adrenalin with it. *Do one thing that scares you every day*. 'I'd like to apologise to you, Dom, and to all your listeners. I'm sorry if I misled anyone.'

'We don't want your "sorries!"' Dom chuckled. 'We all want to know why you told so many porky pies about your own marriage.'

Nick stared out at the half-built office block. Buttercups were blooming among the nettles in the cracks in the tarmac outside the marble and glass foyer. He remembered his mother holding a buttercup under his chin to see if he liked butter.

'My wife wanted a baby and I . . .' He sighed. '. . . went along with it, but I was scared.'

'If you ever stop feeling scared,' Dom snorted, 'come around to my place and change my six-year-old's sheets three times in one night.'

'I used to do that for my sister when she was that age.'

'Your younger sister? You looked after her when your mother died, right? Is that what put you off having kids?' Dom was sharp.

Nick frowned. This was a good question. 'I felt overwhelmed by it. I wanted to make everything OK for her but I couldn't. That was hard. I think the reason I didn't want to have a baby was that I was afraid that if Kelly got pregnant,' Nick said, 'she'd change.'

'I wish my missus would change,' Dom snorted. 'She's been

living in a tracksuit since the kids arrived. Not exactly an aphrodisiac, the trackie.'

'You need to tell your wife how much you love seeing her in flattering clothes. There's a great exercise called Complimentition that—'

'What about your wife, Nick?' Dom interrupted. 'What do you want to tell *her*?'

'Are you coaching me?'

'Yeah, I think I might be.'

'It doesn't really matter what I want to tell her. She won't talk to me.'

'Maybe she's listening now?'

Kelly was trying to compose an email to Nick. She needed to get it all down. From the night Maurice DeVeau had pulled her out of the audience in Rogers Arena in Vancouver to the first day of their honeymoon when she'd thrown away her contraceptive pills, to the night she'd nearly slept with Ray Devine. She was on her fifth attempt when the text came though.

'*Turn on Fish FM now! Niamh x.*'

'*. . . I want you to know that I didn't have an affair,*' Nick was saying. '*There's never been anyone else. Not from the moment I saw you. I love you and if you'll let me come back, I'll do whatever it takes—*'

'*Stop!*' Dom Daly sniffed. '*Enough! If you're listening, Mrs Nick, I'm not surprised you want to have his babies. I think I might have them myself.*'

'Thanks.' Claire opened the front door just as Nick was lifting his key on the yellow key ring.

'For what?'

'Telling the entire country that I used to wet the bed live on air.'

'Sorry about that.' Nick ran a shaking hand over his hair. 'I was disinhibited.'

'We all heard you. Me, Dad, Kelly—'

'Kelly?'

'She's been trying to call you.'

Nick pulled his phone out. There were five missed calls.

The physiotherapist wheeled her bike into the driveway and took off her helmet. 'You walked the walk!' she smiled at Nick. 'About bloody time. Are you coming or going?'

'He's going,' Claire said.

'I am?'

She nodded. 'You're going home.'

'Who's going to look after Dad?'

'I'll stay. I need somewhere to live for a while.'

She watched him reversing, too fast, out on to the road, feeling, for the first time, like an older sister instead of a younger one.

Mrs Cunningham looked over her wall. 'That's dangerous driving, you know. I've a good mind to report that to the Gardaí.'

'Oh get a life, you nosy cow!' Claire snapped.

'Claire Dillon.' Mrs Cunningham pursed her thin lips. 'You sound just like your mother!'

'Thank you,' Claire grinned, then she closed the door.

There were thousands of euros' worth of recording equipment in Ray's living room but, for some reason, he could write better downstairs in Claire's tiny kitchen. And since his heart had been trampled into what felt like several million pieces, he'd been writing songs non-stop.

He was sitting on the lumpy sofa with his acoustic guitar in his lap and his notebook open when the doorbell rang.

There was a tall bloke with curly brown hair standing in the lane. He was holding a green cardboard tube with a photograph of trees on it.

'Sorry.' Ray began to close the door, hurriedly. 'I don't want to buy it.'

The guy frowned. 'What?'

Ray nodded at the tube. 'The calendar? The poster of the rainforest? Whatever you've got there.'

'I'm looking for Claire.'

'She's not here.' Ray took a proper look at him. Wasn't he that guy Claire had been talking to outside Johnny Foxes the day he'd found out about Willow?

'Can you give her this?' The guy handed over the tube. 'And a message from me. Hang on.' He pulled a piece of paper out of his pocket, rested it against his leg and scribbled something. Then he folded it up and handed it to Ray.

'What's in here?' Ray shook the cardboard tube.

'It's ashes.'

Ray was confused. 'You know Ash?'

The guy folded his arms. 'The ashes from Claire's dog.'

Ray held the tube at arm's length. 'Are you serious?'

'Yeah.' The guy squared his shoulders and looked at him in a loaded way. 'I am.'

Ray wondered if he was going to be punched again. He half wanted it to happen. A bit of physical pain would be a nice little holiday from the state of permanent misery he'd been in since he'd lost Willow and Claire. But the guy just turned away and got into a rusty old Land Rover and drove away. When he was gone, Ray unfolded the note and read it.

'Things aren't complicated any more. I'd love to see you again. Call me, S. PS: This is Dog's number. You already have mine.'

Ray turned the piece of paper over. There was a number on the back. 'Five hundred and sixty-eight.'

What did that mean? A snatch of song came into his head. He took the lid off the tube, stuffed the note inside so it didn't get lost and hurried back into the house before he forgot it.

32

'What are we going to do with you?' Claire's dad patted the lid of the long green tube. Dog's ashes had been on the table in the flat when she went back to pack up her things. Shane must have dropped them over. She'd retrieved them and they'd now been sitting on her dad's mantelpiece for weeks.

'Maybe I'll get a nice Dicentra and put Dog's ashes under it when we plant it. We could drive to the garden centre, some time, when you're not busy.'

'I'm not busy now.' Claire closed her book and acted as if going to a garden centre was the kind of thing her dad did every day, and not something he'd last done in 1982. 'I'll just go and start the car.'

Mossy was back on the road again, moss free, rust free, with a reconditioned gearbox, a new floorpan and wipers on the outside that worked. Claire's head had told her she was crazy, that she should hold on to her money for a deposit for a flat and the first few months' rent, but her heart had told her that she wasn't ready to let her mum's car go just yet. Something would come up.

The day after she paid the mechanic, it had. Lorcan had called to say that she had been cast in the second series of *The Spaniard*. For some reason, the producers had decided to kill off Emma Lacey's character, Lady Kathryn, and come up with a new storyline involving the shepherdess and the Earl. The shoot was starting in July and Claire would be needed for twenty full days. She wondered if Shane would be on the set. Every time she thought about him, she felt dizzy with longing. She guessed that things had worked out with his wife and she knew she should be glad for him, so she tried to be.

The Dicentra had long stems of feathery leaves and spires of small, heart-shaped, pink flowers. All her dad's old tools had fallen apart so Claire had bought him some new ones. The trowel she used to dig the hole still had the label attached with a little plastic thread.

'Is that deep enough?' She shaded her eyes to look up at him.

'Plenty deep.' He took the lid off the green tube. 'There's a note in here. I don't have my glasses.'

Claire was shaking the Dicentra roots free from the plastic pot. 'It's probably just the invoice from the cremation company. I'll take care of that, Dad.'

He tucked the note into the empty plant pot, sighed and shook the tube over the hole. Claire watched the fine grey powder and grit falling and thought of Dog's tangle of coat-hangery legs, his warm yellow eyes, the way the front half of him turned a corner before the back half, the weight of his huge paws. It seemed impossible that all that life could be reduced to a little pile of grey powder and grit. She put the plant into the hole and piled the soil back in, pressing it down with her hands. Then she rested her hand on the earth, as if she was giving Dog one last pat. 'I hope he's up in dog heaven,' her voice was hoarse, 'watching Anne Doyle reading the news.'

'The funny thing is,' her dad leaned on his stick, 'I think he just used the news as an excuse to get me out of my room a couple of times a day. It did me good, you know, not to be in there all the time.' He handed her the cardboard tube and the plant pot. 'All those years, I thought I had rescued Dog. Now I think that he rescued me.'

Claire stood at the sink, watching her dad talking to the Dicentra. She'd decided to stay and look after him until the end of May. By then, he should be able to look after himself. She rinsed the little crumbs of dirt off her fingers and dried her hands then picked up the tube and the empty plant pot and dropped them into the bin. Just as the lid was closing, she saw the note.

Shane didn't answer his mobile. 'He's gone out for lunch,' the receptionist said when Claire rang the surgery.

'Do you know where?'

'I can't really say.'

'He left me a message to call him,' Claire's heart was hammering, 'but he's not picking up.'

'Well,' the receptionist sounded reluctant to disclose any information, 'he had his running gear on. He might have gone for a jog in Blackrock Park but I couldn't really say for certain.'

There were a few joggers doing circuits of the park but they were too far away for Claire to see properly. She was heading for the track when the dog raced past her. He was black and white and he was wearing a jaunty red bandana. The pond was covered in algae and he must have thought it was a continuation of the grass. When he tried to run across it, his paws pedalled in the air for a moment, then he fell through it and disappeared. Claire held her breath and watched the water. After a moment, she saw him bobbing back up again with a long trail of pondweed draped over one eye.

The swan saw him too. He shot across the pond, hissing so loudly that Claire could hear him thirty feet away. The dog paddled to the bank and tried to haul himself out but the sides were too steep. He paddled back out towards the swan.

Claire ran to the edge of the pond. 'Here boy!' Claire shouted, but he saw the swan bearing down on him and started to swim in panicky little circles trying to get away.

'Get. Your. Dog. Away. From. That. Swan!' Claire turned and saw the shouty old man hobbling towards her, waving his stick. When she turned back, the swan had reached the dog. She heard its beak snapping like castanets as it pecked him. He went under again and came back up again, choking.

Before she knew what she was doing, Claire had kicked off her shoes. She grabbed the stick from the astonished old man, sat down on the grass and swung her legs into the pond. It was shockingly cold. She took a breath and slid in. The water closed around her knees and then her thighs, her hips, her waist and her chest. She felt the soft mud oozing between her toes.

'I can't swim,' she whispered, though there was nobody to hear except the old man, who stamped off to find the park keeper. She held on to the bank with one hand and waved the stick. 'Leave him alone!' she shouted. The swan was fifteen feet away, circling the floundering dog. It whipped out its long neck and the dog let out a yelp.

Claire's heart was hammering as she let go of the bank and her chattering teeth were keeping time. The water was up to her shoulders now. The smell of it turned her stomach. She edged out into the pond, step by shaking step.

The swan flapped his wings and rose up in the water when he saw her, but she managed to hook the walking stick around the dog's bandana. As she turned for the bank again, she caught her foot on something sharp and plunged, face first under the water. Her eyes closed. She felt the air escaping from her mouth when she gasped. She staggered and fell farther, her free hand clawing at nothing. Then she felt something above her, churning through the water. The dog.

Claire grabbed hold of him and managed to pull herself up. The bank was only a few feet away. She held on to the dog's bandana and made one last lunge. She hauled herself out then pulled the dripping dog out behind her. He shook himself happily then galloped off towards the bandstand without a backward glance.

Claire kneeled on the grass and spat out a mouthful of dank pond water. Her hair was plastered to her head, her arms and hands covered in green slime.

'That was pretty impressive,' a voice said, 'for someone who's scared of water and dogs.' Shane was standing over her in shorts and a T-shirt. There was a sheen of sweat on his forehead. He held out his hand and Claire wiped her hand on the grass then let him help her up. Filthy water was streaming from her hair. She smelled appalling. 'I was looking for you!' she gasped.

'I was looking for some crazy woman who was supposedly attacking a swan.' His brown eyes were amused. 'Someone just called the surgery to report it.'

'I found your note.' Claire put her hand into the pocket of her shirt to pull it out but it had dissolved into mushy pulp.

Shane frowned. 'Just now? I asked your friend to give it to you two weeks ago.'

The shouty old man was heading towards them with the park warden. 'That's her,' Claire could hear him saying. 'She stole my stick, then attacked the swan!'

Shane pulled a piece of pondweed out of Claire's hair. 'I thought you didn't want to see me.'

'I wanted to so badly.'

There was a smile at the corners of his mouth. 'Here I am.'

'Hold on to that woman!' the shouty old man bellowed at Shane. 'Don't let her go!'

Shane put his hands on Claire's wet shoulders, his smile turning, slowly, into a grin. 'Sounds like good advice to me.'

The taxi was stuck at the lights in Blackrock. 'This bloody city,' the driver sighed, 'does my head in.'

'Mine too.' Ray was glad to be leaving it.

'Off to London.' The driver looked in the rear-view mirror. 'Business or pleasure?'

'I've got family there.' Ray had rented a small house in Notting Hill, a five-minute walk from where Ash and Maurice DeVeau lived. He had a couple of songs that he might show to Paul Fisher but there was no hurry with that. Finding a way to be part of Willow's life was more important.

'She misses you,' Ash had said on the phone, yesterday. 'She keeps telling everyone that her other dad is best friends with David Bowie.'

The driver nodded at the park below the road. 'Bit nippy for a dip, even with all your clothes on.'

Ray turned and saw a woman standing by the pond in dripping clothes talking to a jogger. He was too far away to see her properly. She looked like Claire but it couldn't be Claire, he told himself, as the lights changed and the taxi pulled away again. Claire was terrified of water.

A year ago, Kelly thought, the Dillons had looked like strangers waiting in line at the bank; now they looked like a family.

Claire was standing between Nick and Tom, her hair a coppery blur beneath Nick's dark umbrella.

Nick looked over his shoulder and she smiled at him. A tiny feather of fear fluttered down her spine as she thought how close they'd come to losing one another. Things weren't going to be easy, Nick was struggling to find work. It might take years before they could afford IVF. But they had one another. That was all that mattered. They'd work the rest out.

'Well,' Claire's dad put a bunch of Dicentra on the grave and straightened up, 'I'm just going to see if I can find Phil Lynott's marker.' He made his way slowly along the row of headstones, leaning on his stick, the wind tearing at his raincoat and blowing his grey hair around his head.

'He isn't even buried here,' Nick said. 'He's in the graveyard in Sutton.'

They stood, side by side on the wet grass, huddled under the umbrella, looking down at the slim, white marble headstone. Claire pulled her coat around her and read the faded silver inscription on the white marble.

'Tread carefully, for you tread on my dreams.'

Twelve months ago, on her thirty-third birthday, Claire had dreamed of changing her life, getting her career back on track, and mending her broken heart. She could never have imagined back then how much real change the year would bring.

Or how much better she would come to know her father, her brother, her mother, herself.

It had been a wet day, just like this, Nick remembered. Summer rain, slanting in sideways. The sun coming out, now and then, glancing off the cellophane bouquets on the other graves. The smell of turned soil.

Someone had given them a white rose each. Claire's had a tiny thorn on the stem so he had swapped with her. At the end, after the coffin had been lowered into the grave, he dropped his rose in on top of the shiny lid and squeezed Claire's hand. 'You have to drop your flower in now.'

But she wouldn't. He tried to unpeel her fingers from the stem one by one, but she held on tight. 'I want to keep it for Mum,' she whispered.

He turned to look at his sister now. She was holding a bunch of garden flowers in her hand. Long green stems with tiny, pink, heart-shaped flowers. She bent down and held on to them for a long while and then she let them go.

Epilogue

The woman looked out at Claire from a dazzling summer's afternoon. Her coppery hair was pulled back into an untidy bun. A few wet tendrils had escaped and stuck to her neck, below her ears. She wore a dark green swimsuit with lighter green straps and her pale shoulders were jewelled with tiny beads of water. Behind her, there was a wonky triangle of light blue sky and a little scrap of darker blue sea. She was grinning at the camera, shading her face with one hand, her dark green eyes sparkling with excitement. She looked so happy that it was hard, looking at her, not to feel happy too.

It was Claire's favourite photograph of herself. The one Shane had taken on her thirty-fifth birthday, the day he had started teaching her how to swim.

BIRTH NOTICES

DILLON Kelly and Nick are over the moon to announce the birth of their daughter Maura Claire on 12 June 2012. She is welcomed with much love by her parents and their families in Dublin and Seattle.

From Wikipedia
'Little Stars'
Label – Tarantula

'Little Stars' is a pop song written by Irish singer-songwriter Ray Devine and performed by Canadian singer Maurice DeVeau on DeVeau's debut solo album *Chromosome 16*. It was the first of many collaborations between the pair and topped the charts, in the UK, Canada, Australia and Japan.

Thank You

Thank you to generous fellow writers Marian Keyes, Kate Kerrigan and Cathy Kelly for all their help and encouragement.

To my old friend Wendy Williams and my new friend Bernice Barrington for reading early drafts.

To my wonderful brother Bernard and my dear friend Susan McNulty for dotting all the 't's and crossing all the 'i's. (You can see why I need their help!)

To my lovely sister Frances McClelland for giving my first book to every single person she knows.

To my brilliant agent, Jonathan Lloyd. To my patient and insightful editor Kate Mills. And to everyone at Orion, especially Susan Lamb, Juliet Ewers and Jemima Forrester.

To everyone who helped with research. Eamonn Moore, Ailish Connolly, Nick Kelly, Sarah Francis, Dara McClatchie, Barry Grace, Gemma Reeves, Fiona Kerrigan, Eithne Hand, Noel Storey, Doug Lee and, of course, Haggis.

And to my husband, Neil Cubley, who is everywhere in this book and in my heart.

For reading every single draft. For his advice and his edits and his brilliant suggestions.

For cheering me up and talking me down and taking me out. For having faith in me. For making me laugh every single day. And for coming down that hill in Skyros, eleven years ago this week, to find me.